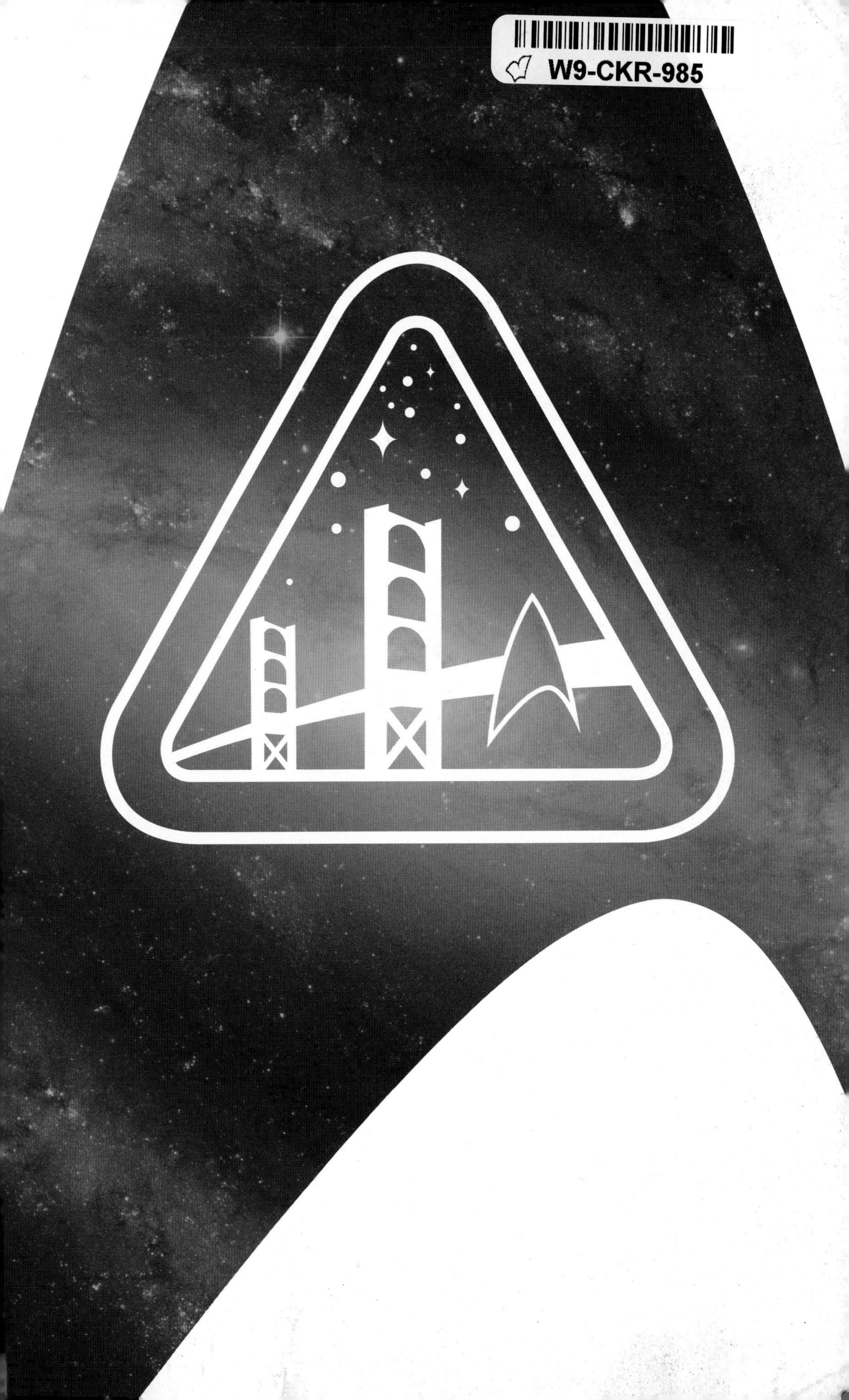

IDW

Facebook: **facebook.com/idwpublishing**
Twitter: **@idwpublishing**
YouTube: **youtube.com/idwpublishing**
Tumblr: **tumblr.idwpublishing.com**
Instagram: **instagram.com/idwpublishing**

COVER ART BY
DEREK CHARM

BACK COVER ART BY
DAVID MALAN

COLLECTION EDITS BY
JUSTIN EISINGER
AND ALONZO SIMON

COLLECTION DESIGN BY
JEFF POWELL

PUBLISHER
TED ADAMS

ISBN: 978-1-63140-663-8   19 18 17 16   1 2 3 4

Originally published as STAR TREK: STARFLEET ACADEMY issues #1–5.

Ted Adams, CEO & Publisher
Greg Goldstein, President & COO
Robbie Robbins, EVP/Sr. Graphic Artist
Chris Ryall, Chief Creative Officer/Editor-in-Chief
Matthew Ruzicka, CPA, Chief Financial Officer
Dirk Wood, VP of Marketing
Lorelei Bunjes, VP of Digital Services
Jeff Webber, VP of Digital and Subsidiary Rights
Jerry Bennington, VP of New Product Development

Special thanks to Risa Kessler and John Van Citters of
CBS C   mer Products fo   their invaluable assist

STAR TREK
STARFLEET ACADEMY

WRITTEN BY
MIKE JOHNSON AND **RYAN PARROTT**

ART BY
DEREK CHARM

LETTERS BY
NEIL UYETAKE (#1–4)
AND **ANDWORLD DESIGN** (#5)

SERIES EDITS BY
SARAH GAYDOS

STAR TREK CREATED BY GENE RODDENBERRY

ART BY **DEREK CHARM**

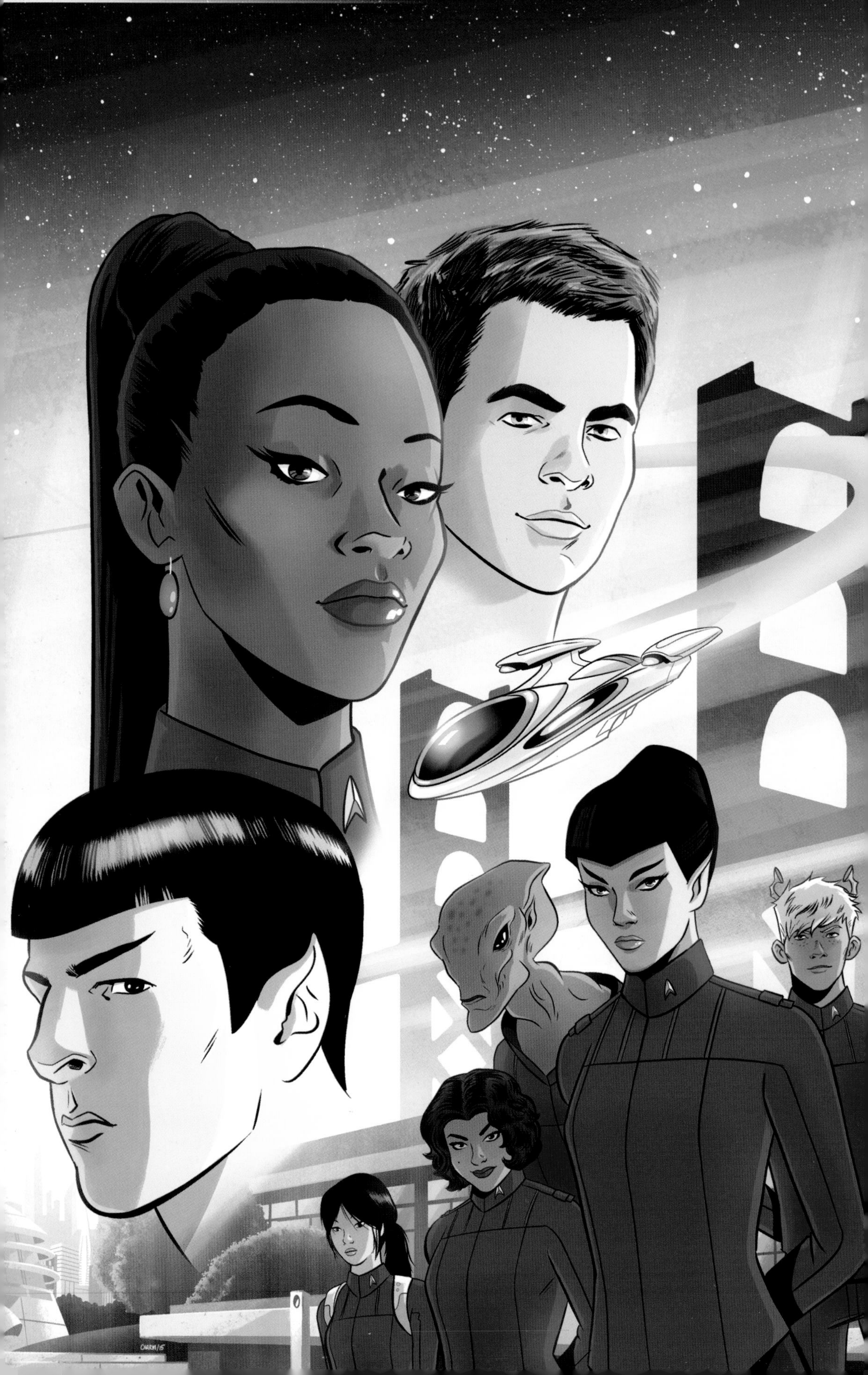

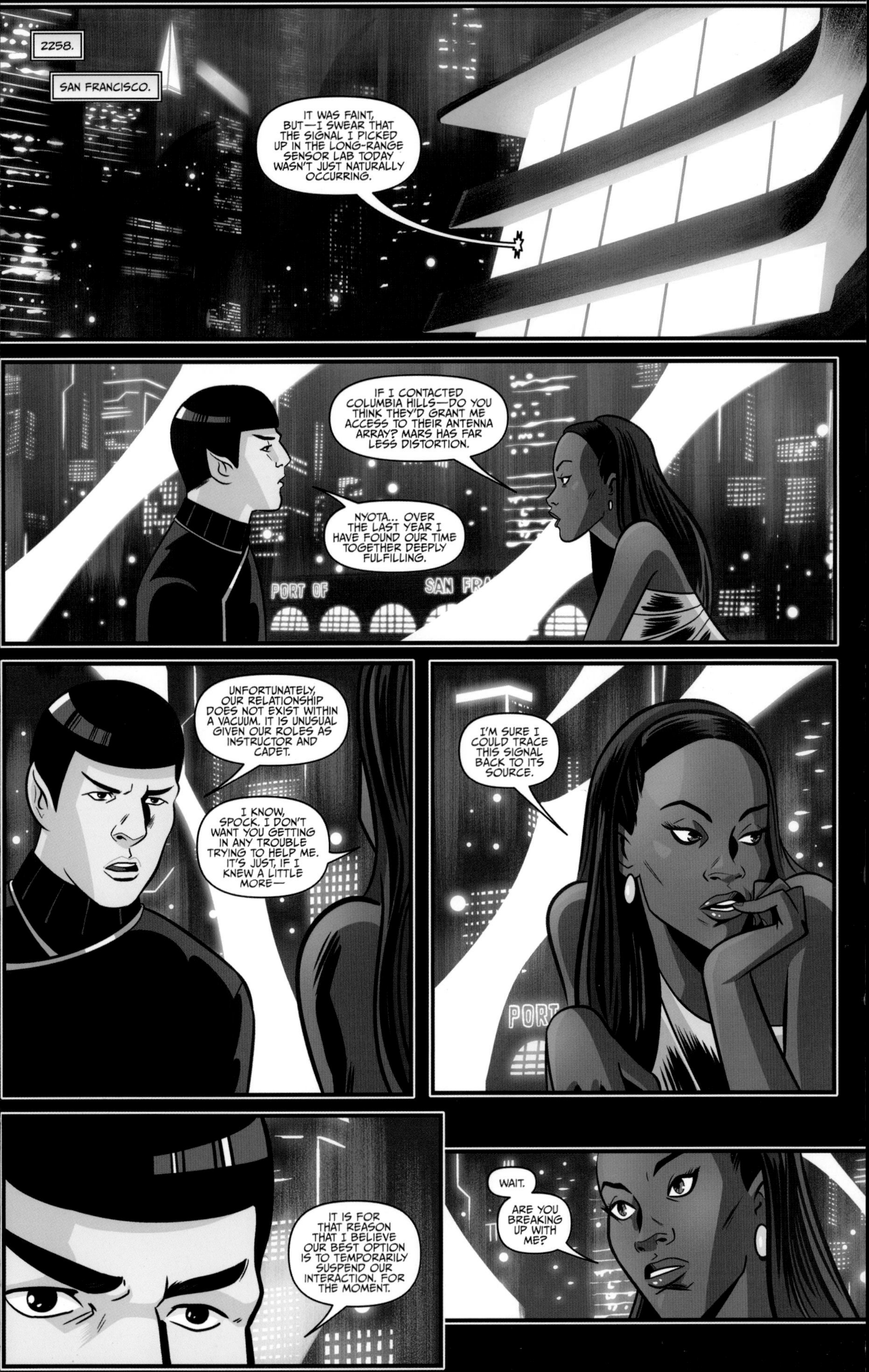
2258.
SAN FRANCISCO.
IT WAS FAINT, BUT—I SWEAR THAT THE SIGNAL I PICKED UP IN THE LONG-RANGE SENSOR LAB TODAY WASN'T JUST NATURALLY OCCURRING.
IF I CONTACTED COLUMBIA HILLS—DO YOU THINK THEY'D GRANT ME ACCESS TO THEIR ANTENNA ARRAY? MARS HAS FAR LESS DISTORTION.
NYOTA... OVER THE LAST YEAR I HAVE FOUND OUR TIME TOGETHER DEEPLY FULFILLING.
PORT OF
SAN FR
UNFORTUNATELY, OUR RELATIONSHIP DOES NOT EXIST WITHIN A VACUUM. IT IS UNUSUAL GIVEN OUR ROLES AS INSTRUCTOR AND CADET.
I KNOW, SPOCK. I DON'T WANT YOU GETTING IN ANY TROUBLE TRYING TO HELP ME. IT'S JUST, IF I KNEW A LITTLE MORE—
I'M SURE I COULD TRACE THIS SIGNAL BACK TO ITS SOURCE.
PORT
IT IS FOR THAT REASON THAT I BELIEVE OUR BEST OPTION IS TO TEMPORARILY SUSPEND OUR INTERACTION. FOR THE MOMENT.
WAIT.
ARE YOU BREAKING UP WITH ME?

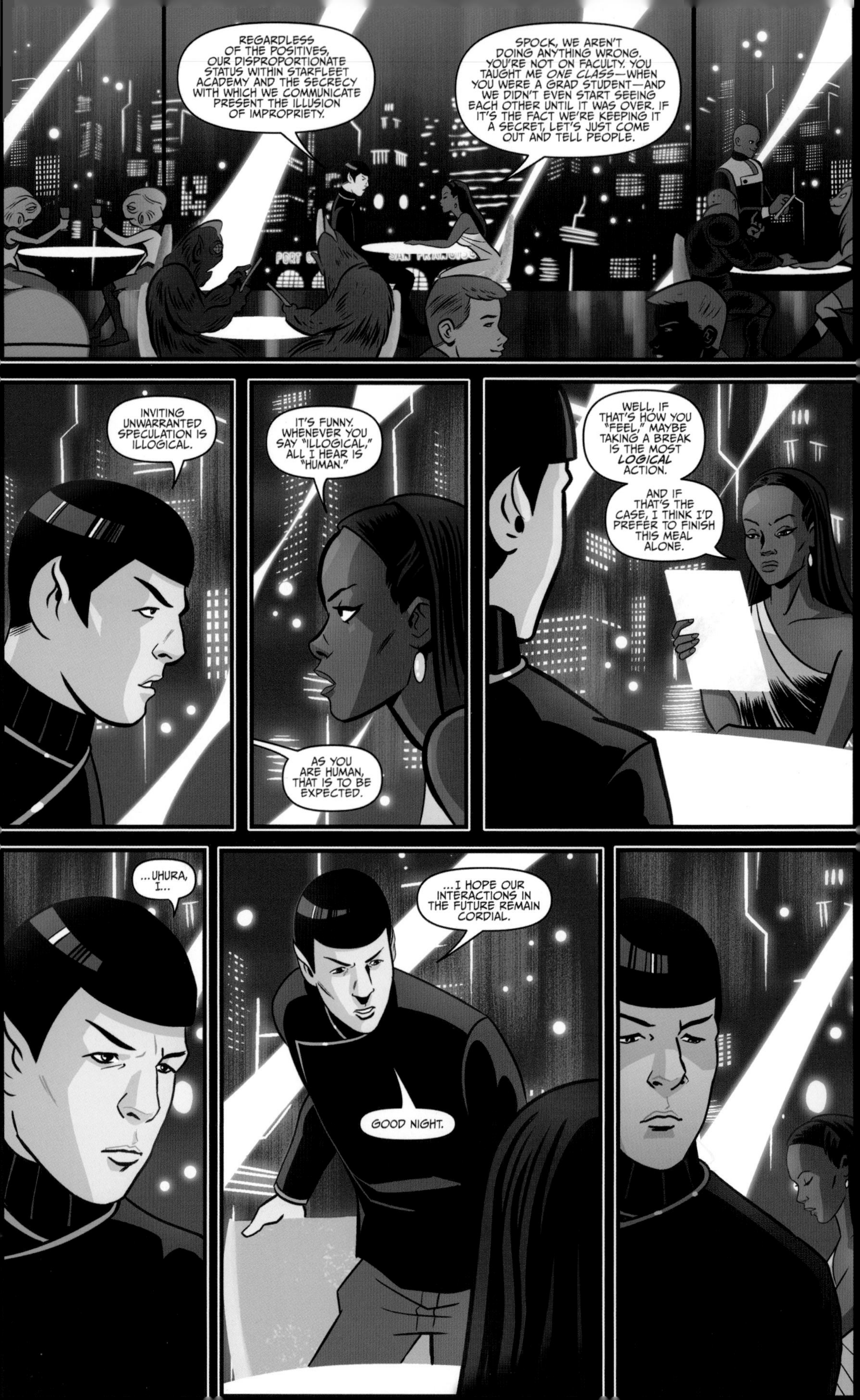
REGARDLESS OF THE POSITIVES, OUR DISPROPORTIONATE STATUS WITHIN STARFLEET ACADEMY AND THE SECRECY WITH WHICH WE COMMUNICATE PRESENT THE ILLUSION OF IMPROPRIETY.
SPOCK, WE AREN'T DOING ANYTHING WRONG. YOU'RE NOT ON FACULTY. YOU TAUGHT ME *ONE CLASS*—WHEN YOU WERE A GRAD STUDENT—AND WE DIDN'T EVEN START SEEING EACH OTHER UNTIL IT WAS OVER. IF IT'S THE FACT WE'RE KEEPING IT A SECRET, LET'S JUST COME OUT AND TELL PEOPLE.
INVITING UNWARRANTED SPECULATION IS ILLOGICAL.
IT'S FUNNY. WHENEVER YOU SAY "ILLOGICAL," ALL I HEAR IS "HUMAN."
AS YOU ARE HUMAN, THAT IS TO BE EXPECTED.
WELL, IF THAT'S HOW YOU "FEEL," MAYBE TAKING A BREAK IS THE MOST ***LOGICAL*** ACTION.
AND IF THAT'S THE CASE, I THINK I'D PREFER TO FINISH THIS MEAL ALONE.
...UHURA, I...
...I HOPE OUR INTERACTIONS IN THE FUTURE REMAIN CORDIAL.
GOOD NIGHT.

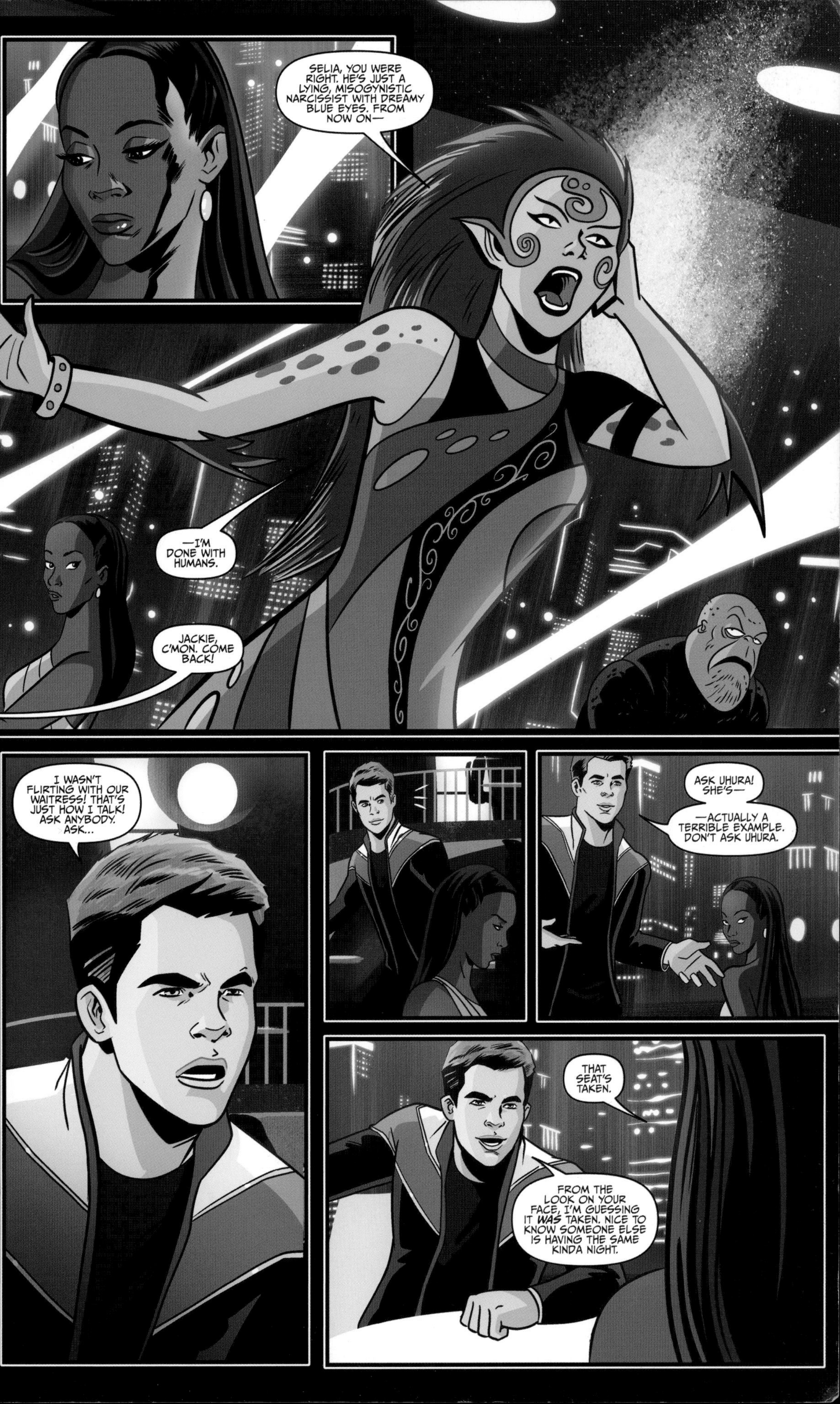
SELIA, YOU WERE RIGHT. HE'S JUST A LYING, MISOGYNISTIC NARCISSIST WITH DREAMY BLUE EYES. FROM NOW ON—
—I'M DONE WITH HUMANS.
JACKIE, C'MON. COME BACK!
I WASN'T FLIRTING WITH OUR WAITRESS! THAT'S JUST HOW I TALK! ASK ANYBODY. ASK...
ASK UHURA! SHE'S—
—ACTUALLY A TERRIBLE EXAMPLE. DON'T ASK UHURA.
THAT SEAT'S TAKEN.
FROM THE LOOK ON YOUR FACE, I'M GUESSING IT *WAS* TAKEN. NICE TO KNOW SOMEONE ELSE IS HAVING THE SAME KINDA NIGHT.

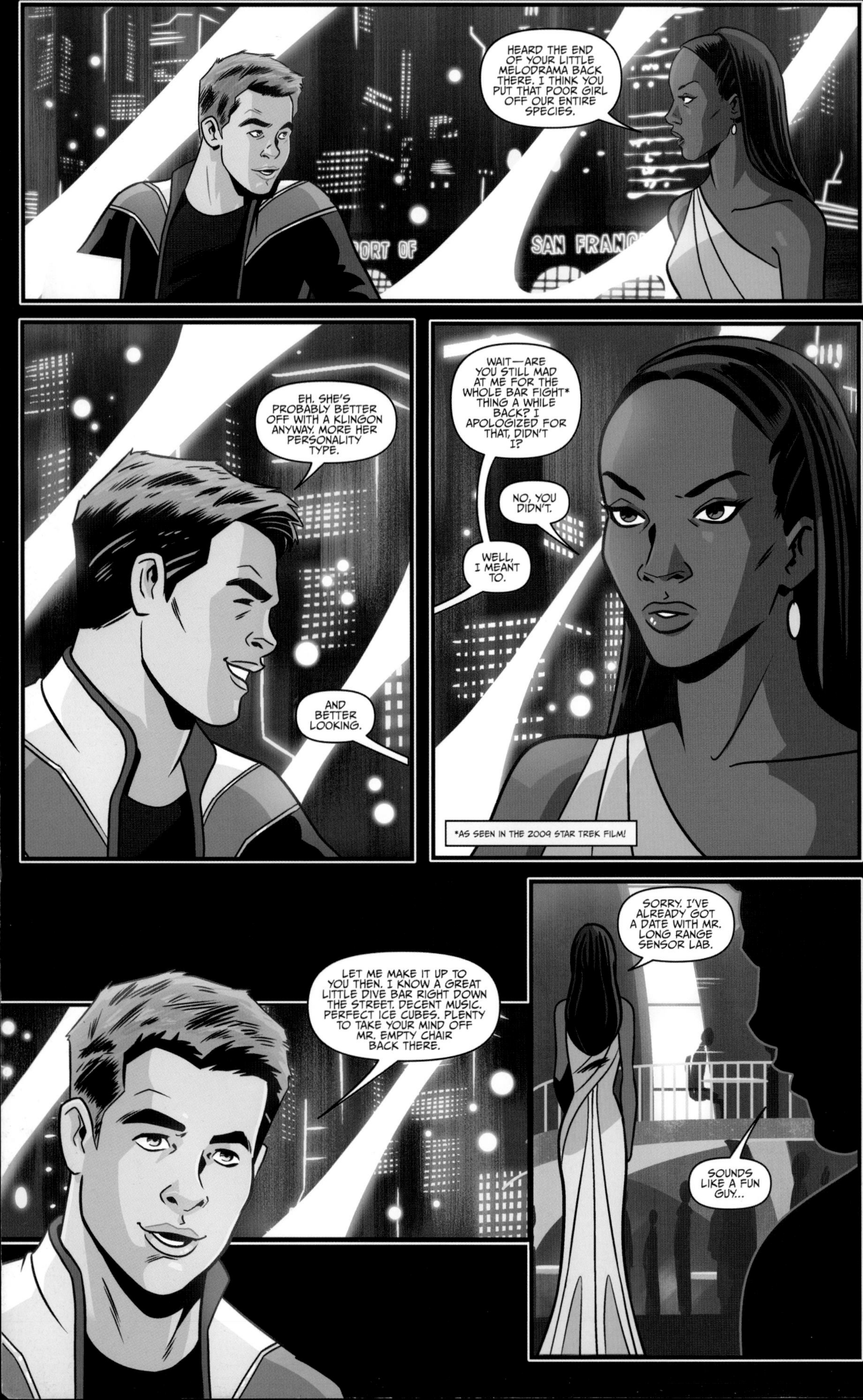
HEARD THE END OF YOUR LITTLE MELODRAMA BACK THERE. I THINK YOU PUT THAT POOR GIRL OFF OUR ENTIRE SPECIES.
ORT OF
SAN FRANC
EH. SHE'S PROBABLY BETTER OFF WITH A KLINGON ANYWAY. MORE HER PERSONALITY TYPE.
AND BETTER LOOKING.
WAIT—ARE YOU STILL MAD AT ME FOR THE WHOLE BAR FIGHT* THING A WHILE BACK? I APOLOGIZED FOR THAT, DIDN'T I?
NO, YOU DIDN'T.
WELL, I MEANT TO.
*AS SEEN IN THE 2009 STAR TREK FILM!
LET ME MAKE IT UP TO YOU THEN. I KNOW A GREAT LITTLE DIVE BAR RIGHT DOWN THE STREET. DECENT MUSIC. PERFECT ICE CUBES. PLENTY TO TAKE YOUR MIND OFF MR. EMPTY CHAIR BACK THERE.
SORRY. I'VE ALREADY GOT A DATE WITH MR. LONG RANGE SENSOR LAB.
SOUNDS LIKE A FUN GUY...

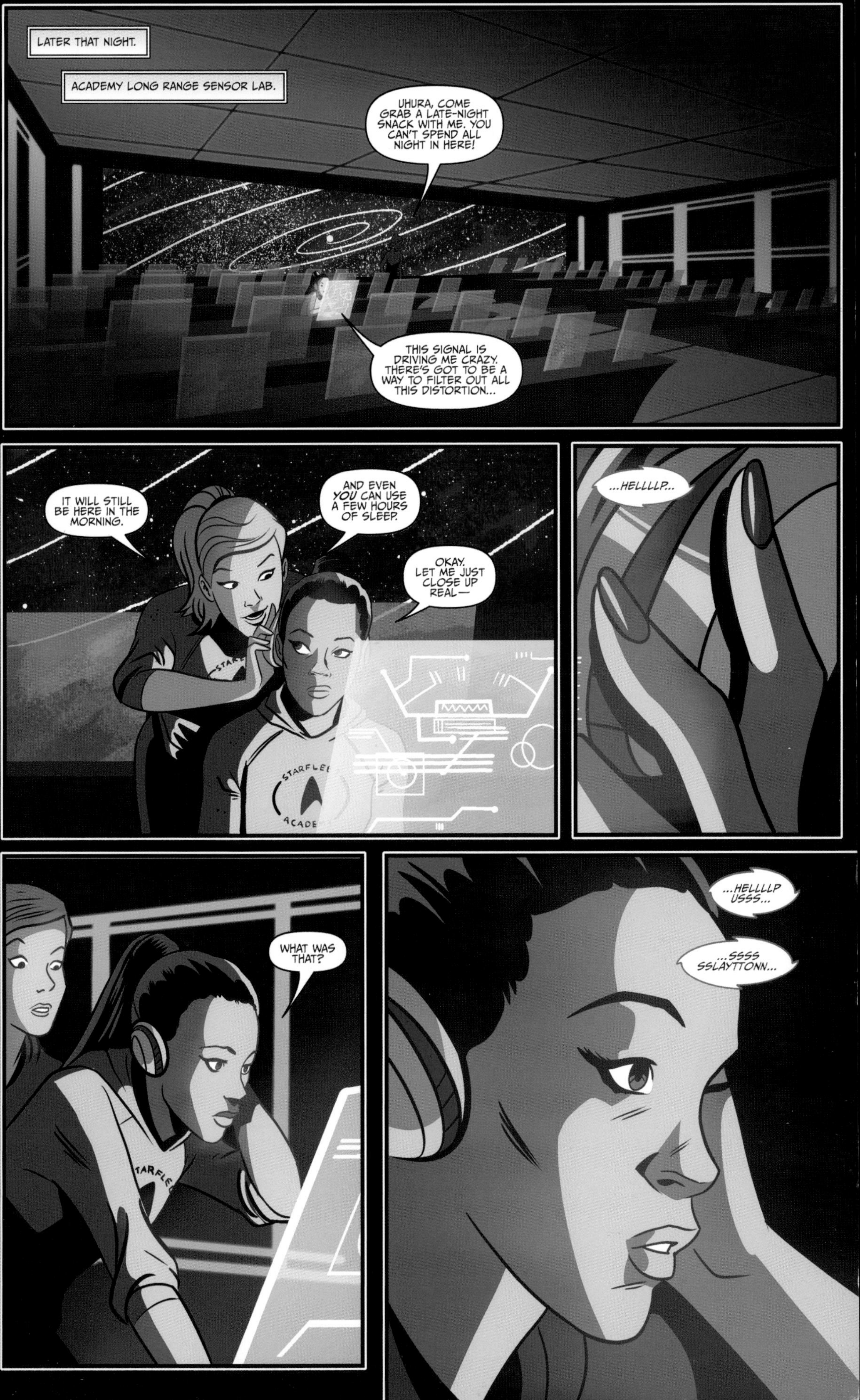
LATER THAT NIGHT.
ACADEMY LONG RANGE SENSOR LAB.
UHURA, COME GRAB A LATE-NIGHT SNACK WITH ME. YOU CAN'T SPEND ALL NIGHT IN HERE!
THIS SIGNAL IS DRIVING ME CRAZY. THERE'S GOT TO BE A WAY TO FILTER OUT ALL THIS DISTORTION...
IT WILL STILL BE HERE IN THE MORNING.
AND EVEN YOU CAN USE A FEW HOURS OF SLEEP.
OKAY. LET ME JUST CLOSE UP REAL—
STARFLEET ACADEMY
...HELLLLP...
WHAT WAS THAT?
...HELLLLP USSS...
...SSSS SSLAYTTONN...

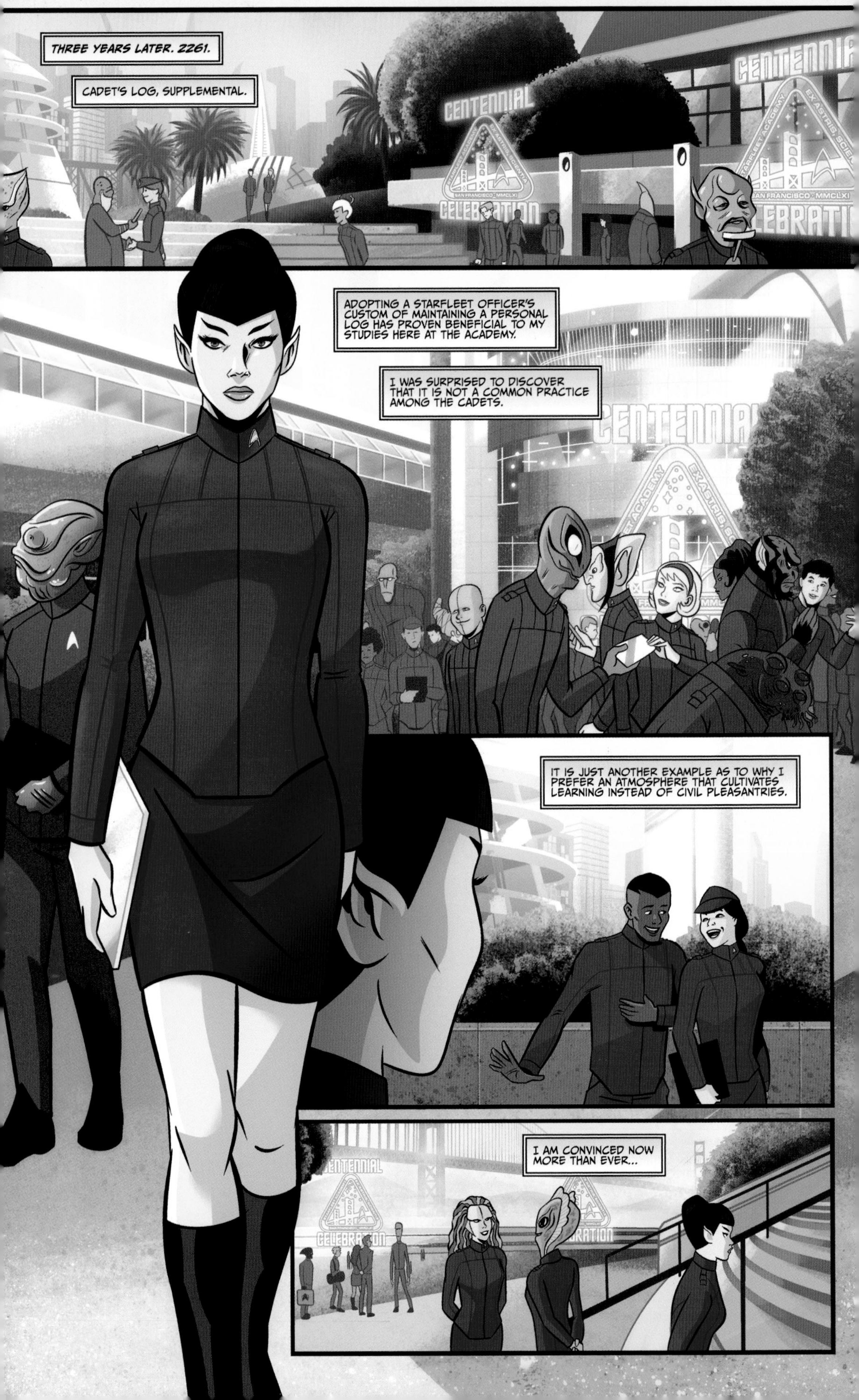
THREE YEARS LATER. 2261.
CADET'S LOG, SUPPLEMENTAL.
CENTENNIAL
CELEBRATION
ADOPTING A STARFLEET OFFICER'S CUSTOM OF MAINTAINING A PERSONAL LOG HAS PROVEN BENEFICIAL TO MY STUDIES HERE AT THE ACADEMY.
I WAS SURPRISED TO DISCOVER THAT IT IS NOT A COMMON PRACTICE AMONG THE CADETS.
CENTENNIAL
IT IS JUST ANOTHER EXAMPLE AS TO WHY I PREFER AN ATMOSPHERE THAT CULTIVATES LEARNING INSTEAD OF CIVIL PLEASANTRIES.
I AM CONVINCED NOW MORE THAN EVER...
CENTENNIAL
CELEBRATION

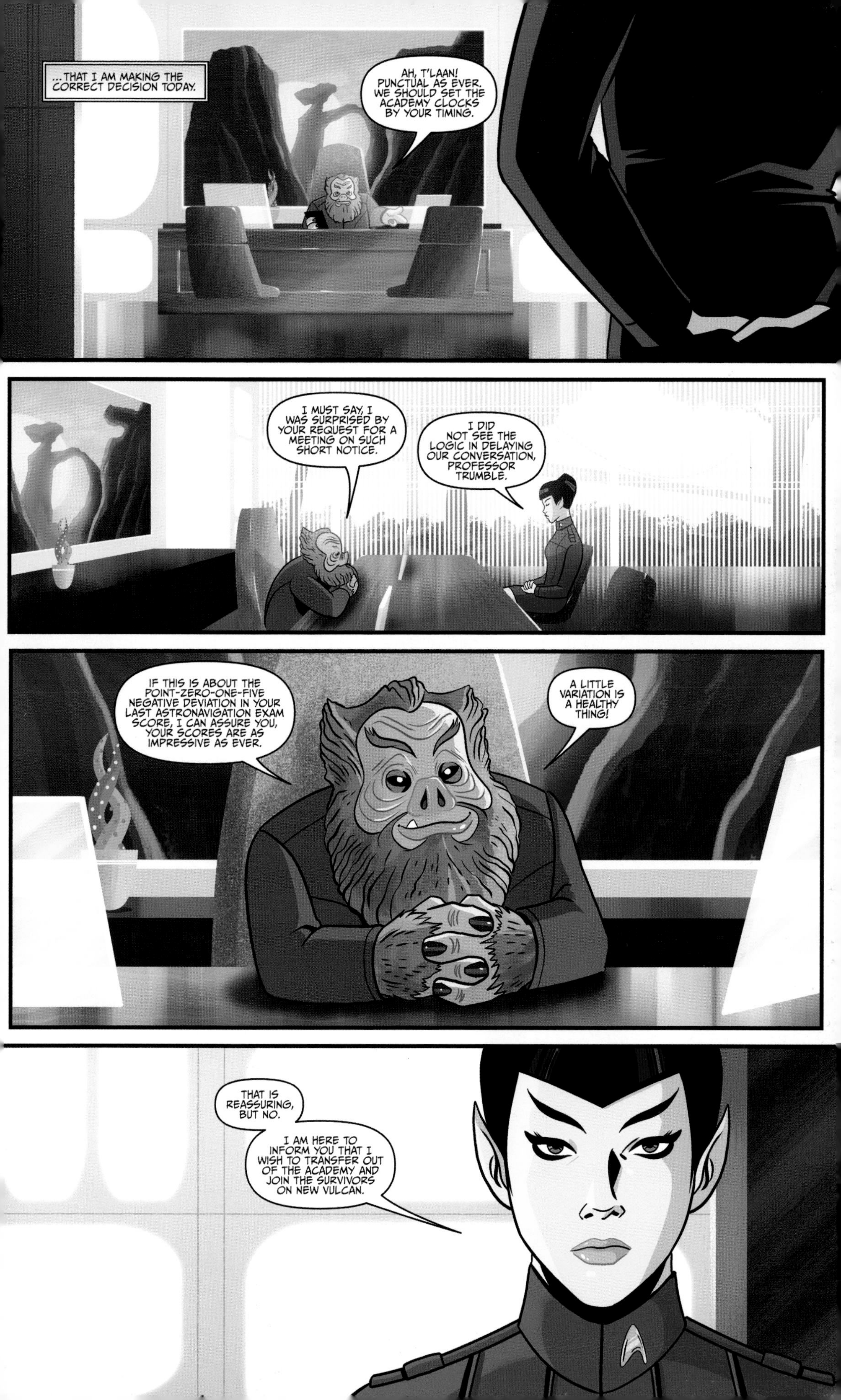

...THAT I AM MAKING THE CORRECT DECISION TODAY.
AH, T'LAAN! PUNCTUAL AS EVER. WE SHOULD SET THE ACADEMY CLOCKS BY YOUR TIMING.
I MUST SAY, I WAS SURPRISED BY YOUR REQUEST FOR A MEETING ON SUCH SHORT NOTICE.
I DID NOT SEE THE LOGIC IN DELAYING OUR CONVERSATION, PROFESSOR TRUMBLE.
IF THIS IS ABOUT THE POINT-ZERO-ONE-FIVE NEGATIVE DEVIATION IN YOUR LAST ASTRONAVIGATION EXAM SCORE, I CAN ASSURE YOU, YOUR SCORES ARE AS IMPRESSIVE AS EVER.
A LITTLE VARIATION IS A HEALTHY THING!
THAT IS REASSURING, BUT NO.
I AM HERE TO INFORM YOU THAT I WISH TO TRANSFER OUT OF THE ACADEMY AND JOIN THE SURVIVORS ON NEW VULCAN.

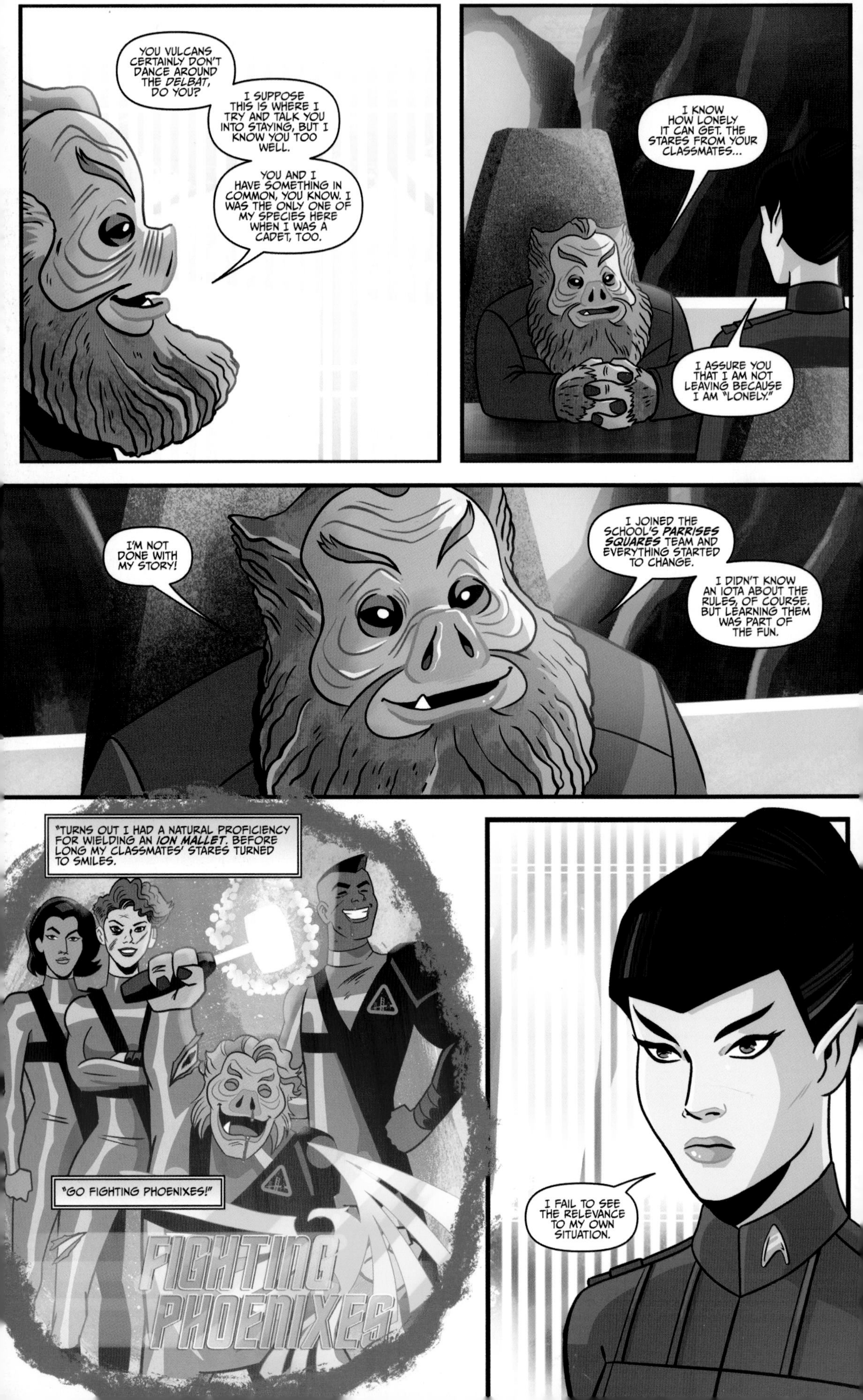

YOU VULCANS CERTAINLY DON'T DANCE AROUND THE *DELBAT*, DO YOU?
I SUPPOSE THIS IS WHERE I TRY AND TALK YOU INTO STAYING, BUT I KNOW YOU TOO WELL.
YOU AND I HAVE SOMETHING IN COMMON, YOU KNOW. I WAS THE ONLY ONE OF MY SPECIES HERE WHEN I WAS A CADET, TOO.
I KNOW HOW LONELY IT CAN GET. THE STARES FROM YOUR CLASSMATES...
I ASSURE YOU THAT I AM NOT LEAVING BECAUSE I AM "LONELY."
I'M NOT DONE WITH MY STORY!
I JOINED THE SCHOOL'S ***PARRISES SQUARES*** TEAM AND EVERYTHING STARTED TO CHANGE.
I DIDN'T KNOW AN IOTA ABOUT THE RULES, OF COURSE. BUT LEARNING THEM WAS PART OF THE FUN.
"TURNS OUT I HAD A NATURAL PROFICIENCY FOR WIELDING AN *ION MALLET*. BEFORE LONG MY CLASSMATES' STARES TURNED TO SMILES.
"GO FIGHTING PHOENIXES!"
FIGHTING PHOENIXES!
I FAIL TO SEE THE RELEVANCE TO MY OWN SITUATION.

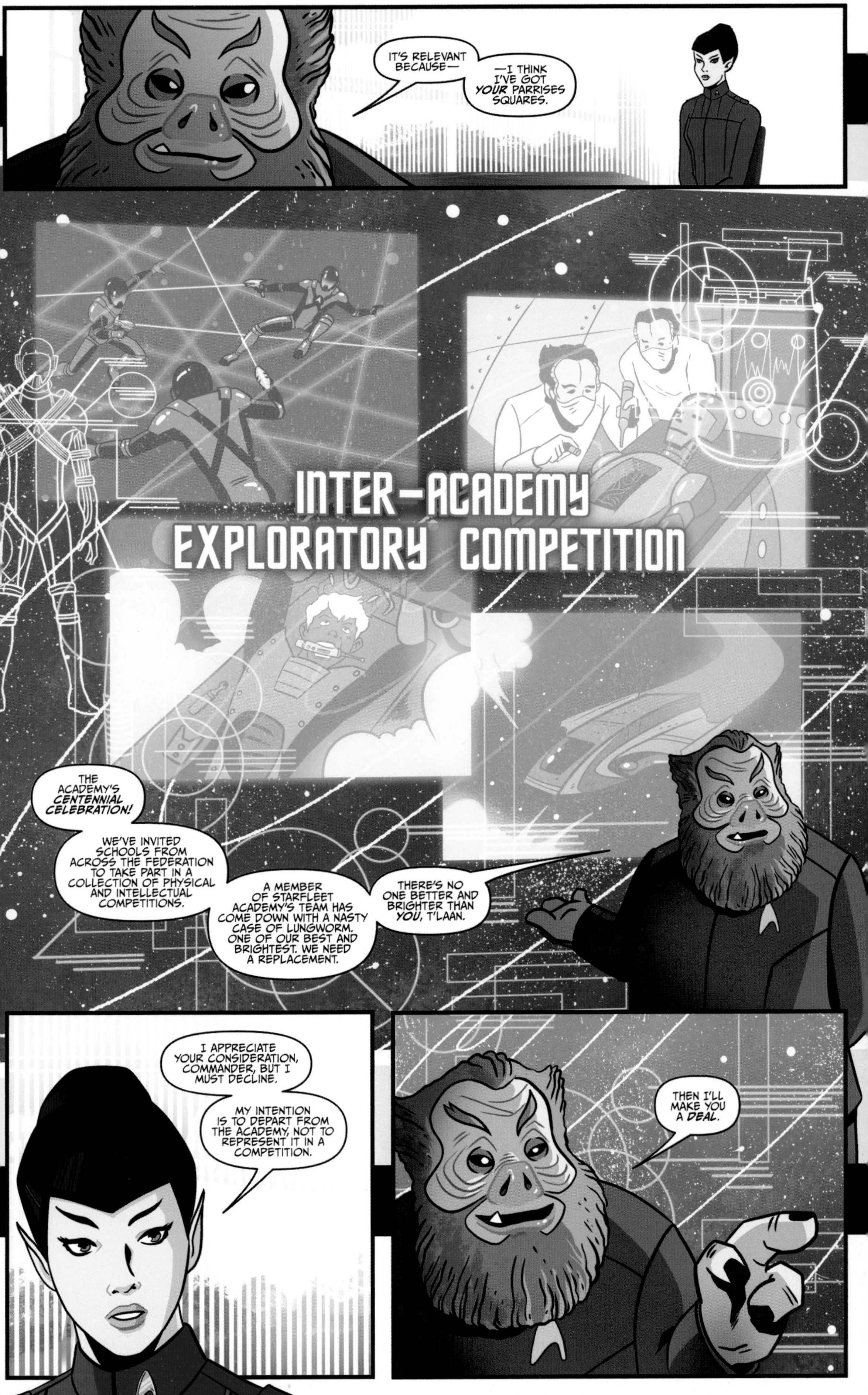
IT'S RELEVANT BECAUSE—
—I THINK I'VE GOT YOUR PARRISES SQUARES.
INTER-ACADEMY EXPLORATORY COMPETITION
THE ACADEMY'S CENTENNIAL CELEBRATION!
WE'VE INVITED SCHOOLS FROM ACROSS THE FEDERATION TO TAKE PART IN A COLLECTION OF PHYSICAL AND INTELLECTUAL COMPETITIONS.
A MEMBER OF STARFLEET ACADEMY'S TEAM HAS COME DOWN WITH A NASTY CASE OF LUNGWORM. ONE OF OUR BEST AND BRIGHTEST. WE NEED A REPLACEMENT.
THERE'S NO ONE BETTER AND BRIGHTER THAN YOU, T'LAAN.
I APPRECIATE YOUR CONSIDERATION, COMMANDER, BUT I MUST DECLINE.
MY INTENTION IS TO DEPART FROM THE ACADEMY, NOT TO REPRESENT IT IN A COMPETITION.
THEN I'LL MAKE YOU A DEAL.

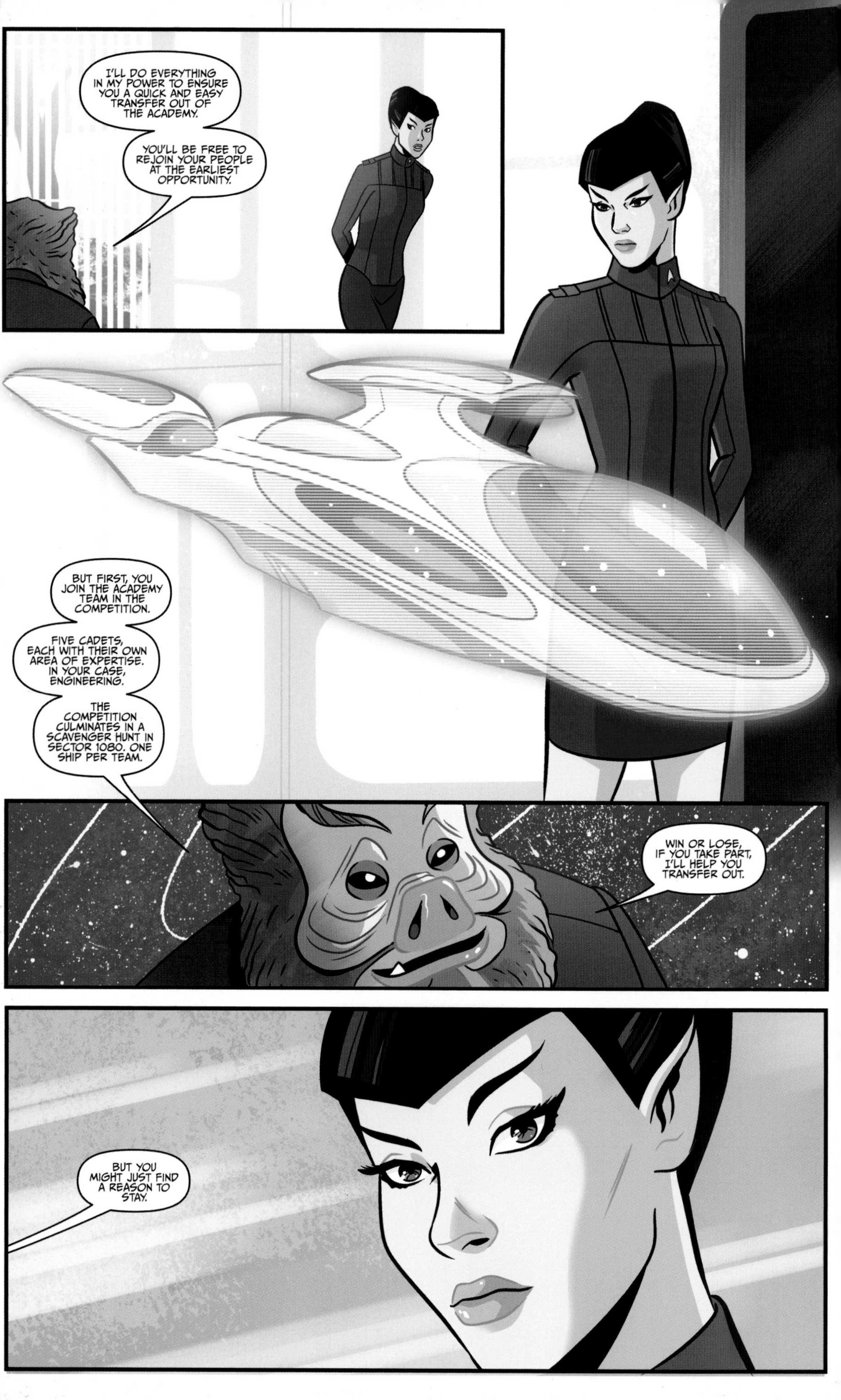

I'LL DO EVERYTHING IN MY POWER TO ENSURE YOU A QUICK AND EASY TRANSFER OUT OF THE ACADEMY.
YOU'LL BE FREE TO REJOIN YOUR PEOPLE AT THE EARLIEST OPPORTUNITY.
BUT FIRST, YOU JOIN THE ACADEMY TEAM IN THE COMPETITION.
FIVE CADETS, EACH WITH THEIR OWN AREA OF EXPERTISE. IN YOUR CASE, ENGINEERING.
THE COMPETITION CULMINATES IN A SCAVENGER HUNT IN SECTOR 1080. ONE SHIP PER TEAM.
WIN OR LOSE, IF YOU TAKE PART, I'LL HELP YOU TRANSFER OUT.
BUT YOU MIGHT JUST FIND A REASON TO STAY.

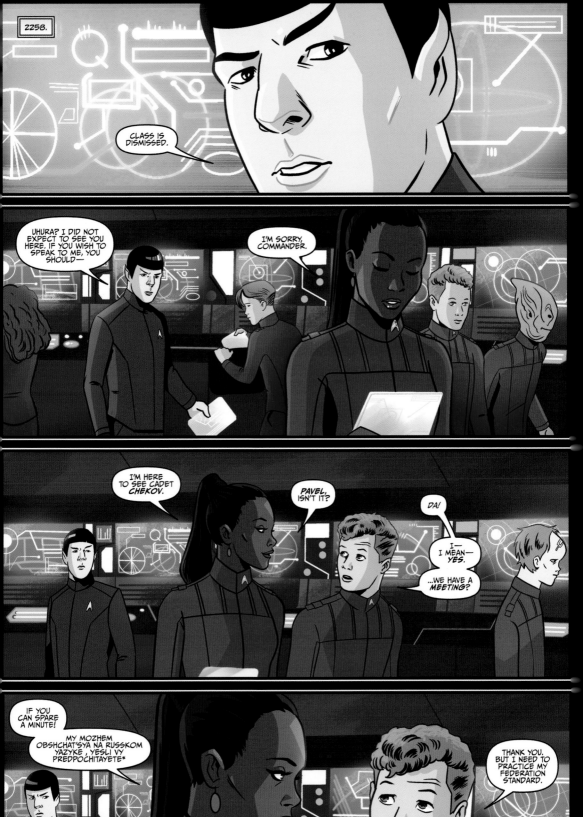

2258.

CLASS IS DISMISSED.

UHURA? I DID NOT EXPECT TO SEE YOU HERE. IF YOU WISH TO SPEAK TO ME, YOU SHOULD—

I'M SORRY, COMMANDER.

I'M HERE TO SEE CADET CHEKOV.

PAVEL, ISN'T IT?

DA! I— I MEAN— YES. ...WE HAVE A MEETING?

IF YOU CAN SPARE A MINUTE!

MY MOZHEM OBSHCHAT'SYA NA RUSSKOM YAZYKE , YESLI VY PREDPOCHITAYETE*

THANK YOU. BUT I NEED TO PRACTICE MY FEDERATION STANDARD.

*WE CAN CONVERSE IN RUSSIAN IF YOU PREFER.

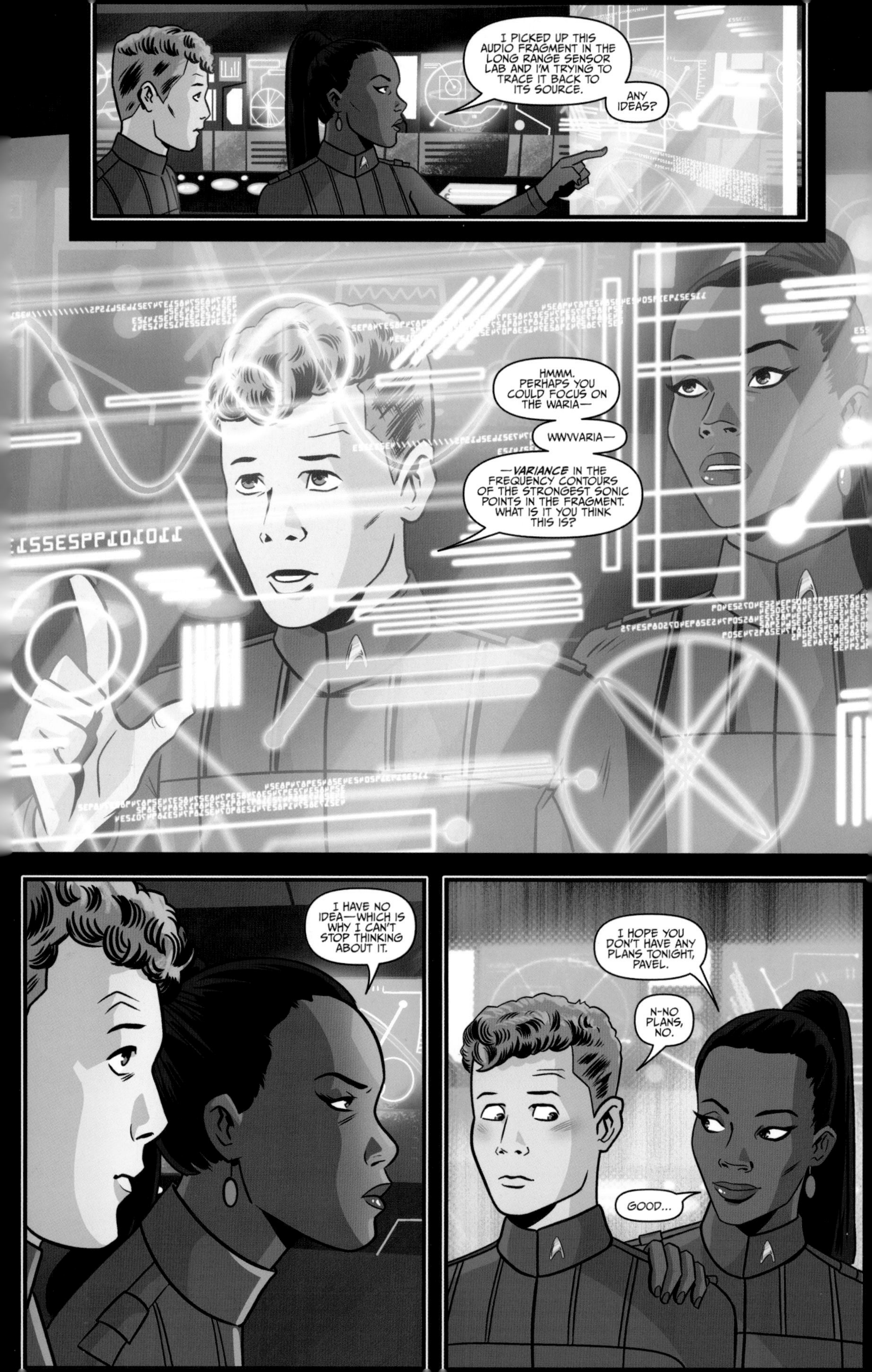

I PICKED UP THIS AUDIO FRAGMENT IN THE LONG RANGE SENSOR LAB AND I'M TRYING TO TRACE IT BACK TO ITS SOURCE.
ANY IDEAS?
HMMM. PERHAPS YOU COULD FOCUS ON THE WARIA—
WWVVARIA—
—VARIANCE IN THE FREQUENCY CONTOURS OF THE STRONGEST SONIC POINTS IN THE FRAGMENT. WHAT IS IT YOU THINK THIS IS?
I HAVE NO IDEA—WHICH IS WHY I CAN'T STOP THINKING ABOUT IT.
I HOPE YOU DON'T HAVE ANY PLANS TONIGHT, PAVEL.
N-NO PLANS, NO.
GOOD...

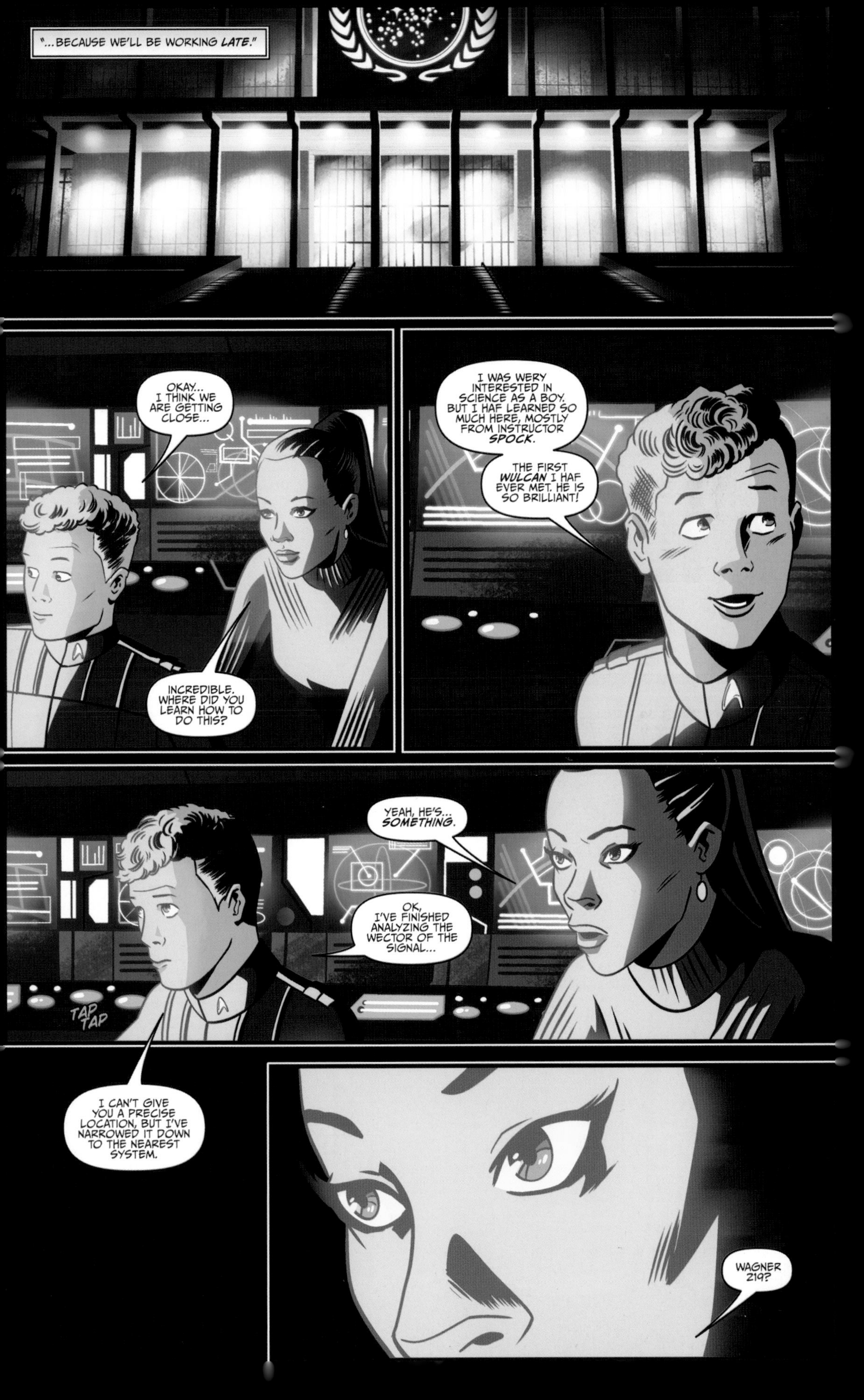
"...BECAUSE WE'LL BE WORKING *LATE*."
OKAY... I THINK WE ARE GETTING CLOSE...
INCREDIBLE. WHERE DID YOU LEARN HOW TO DO THIS?
I WAS WERY INTERESTED IN SCIENCE AS A BOY. BUT I HAF LEARNED SO MUCH HERE, MOSTLY FROM INSTRUCTOR *SPOCK*.
THE FIRST *WULCAN* I HAF EVER MET. HE IS SO BRILLIANT!
YEAH, HE'S... *SOMETHING*.
OK, I'VE FINISHED ANALYZING THE WECTOR OF THE SIGNAL...
TAP TAP
I CAN'T GIVE YOU A PRECISE LOCATION, BUT I'VE NARROWED IT DOWN TO THE NEAREST SYSTEM.
WAGNER 219?

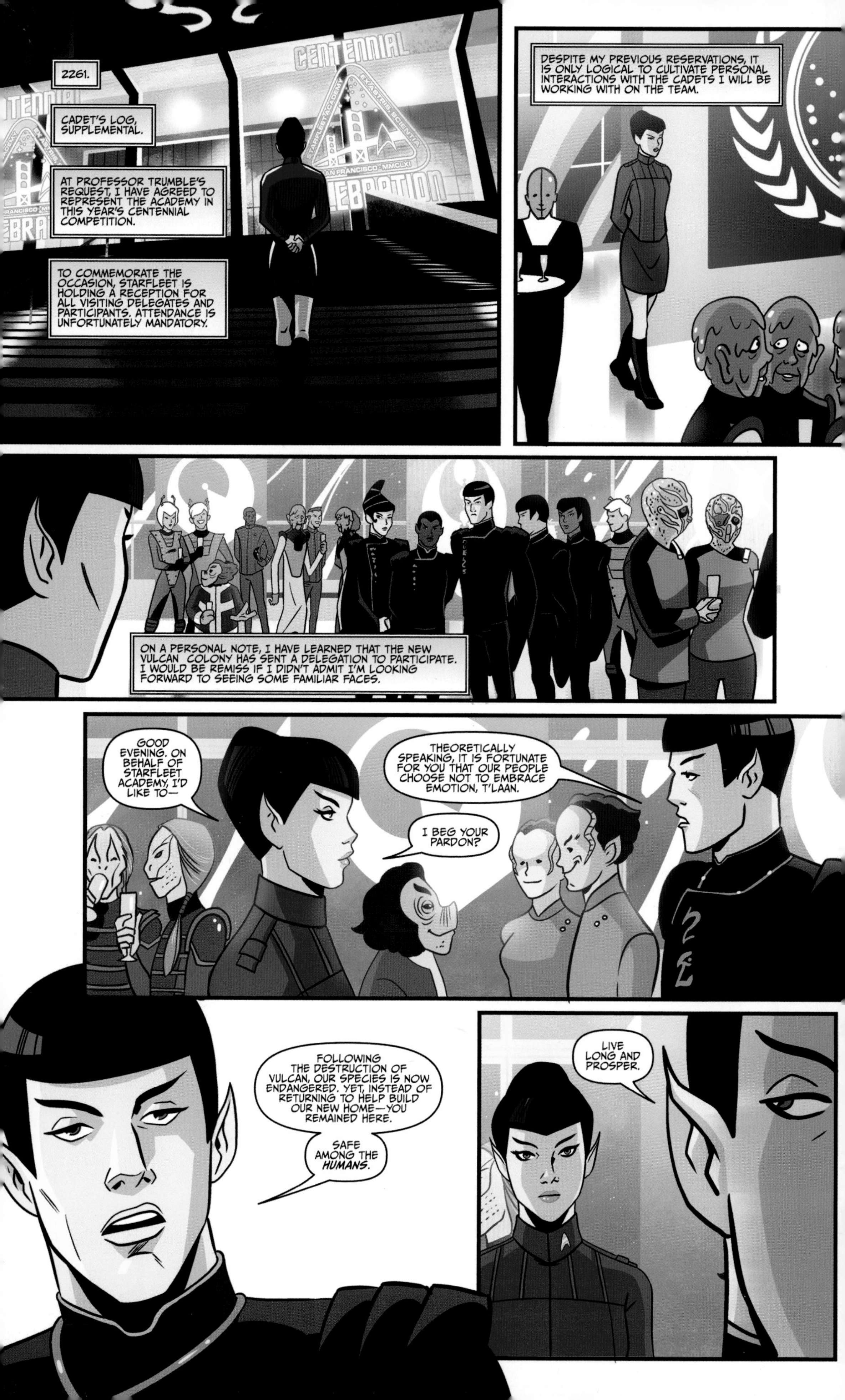
CENTENNIAL
STARFLEET ACADEMY · EX ASTRIS, SCIENTIA
SAN FRANCISCO · MMCLXI
CELEBRATION
2261.
CADET'S LOG, SUPPLEMENTAL.
AT PROFESSOR TRUMBLE'S REQUEST, I HAVE AGREED TO REPRESENT THE ACADEMY IN THIS YEAR'S CENTENNIAL COMPETITION.
TO COMMEMORATE THE OCCASION, STARFLEET IS HOLDING A RECEPTION FOR ALL VISITING DELEGATES AND PARTICIPANTS. ATTENDANCE IS UNFORTUNATELY MANDATORY.
DESPITE MY PREVIOUS RESERVATIONS, IT IS ONLY LOGICAL TO CULTIVATE PERSONAL INTERACTIONS WITH THE CADETS I WILL BE WORKING WITH ON THE TEAM.
ON A PERSONAL NOTE, I HAVE LEARNED THAT THE NEW VULCAN COLONY HAS SENT A DELEGATION TO PARTICIPATE. I WOULD BE REMISS IF I DIDN'T ADMIT I'M LOOKING FORWARD TO SEEING SOME FAMILIAR FACES.
GOOD EVENING. ON BEHALF OF STARFLEET ACADEMY, I'D LIKE TO—
THEORETICALLY SPEAKING, IT IS FORTUNATE FOR YOU THAT OUR PEOPLE CHOOSE NOT TO EMBRACE EMOTION, T'LAAN.
I BEG YOUR PARDON?
FOLLOWING THE DESTRUCTION OF VULCAN, OUR SPECIES IS NOW ENDANGERED. YET, INSTEAD OF RETURNING TO HELP BUILD OUR NEW HOME—YOU REMAINED HERE.
SAFE AMONG THE *HUMANS*.
LIVE LONG AND PROSPER.

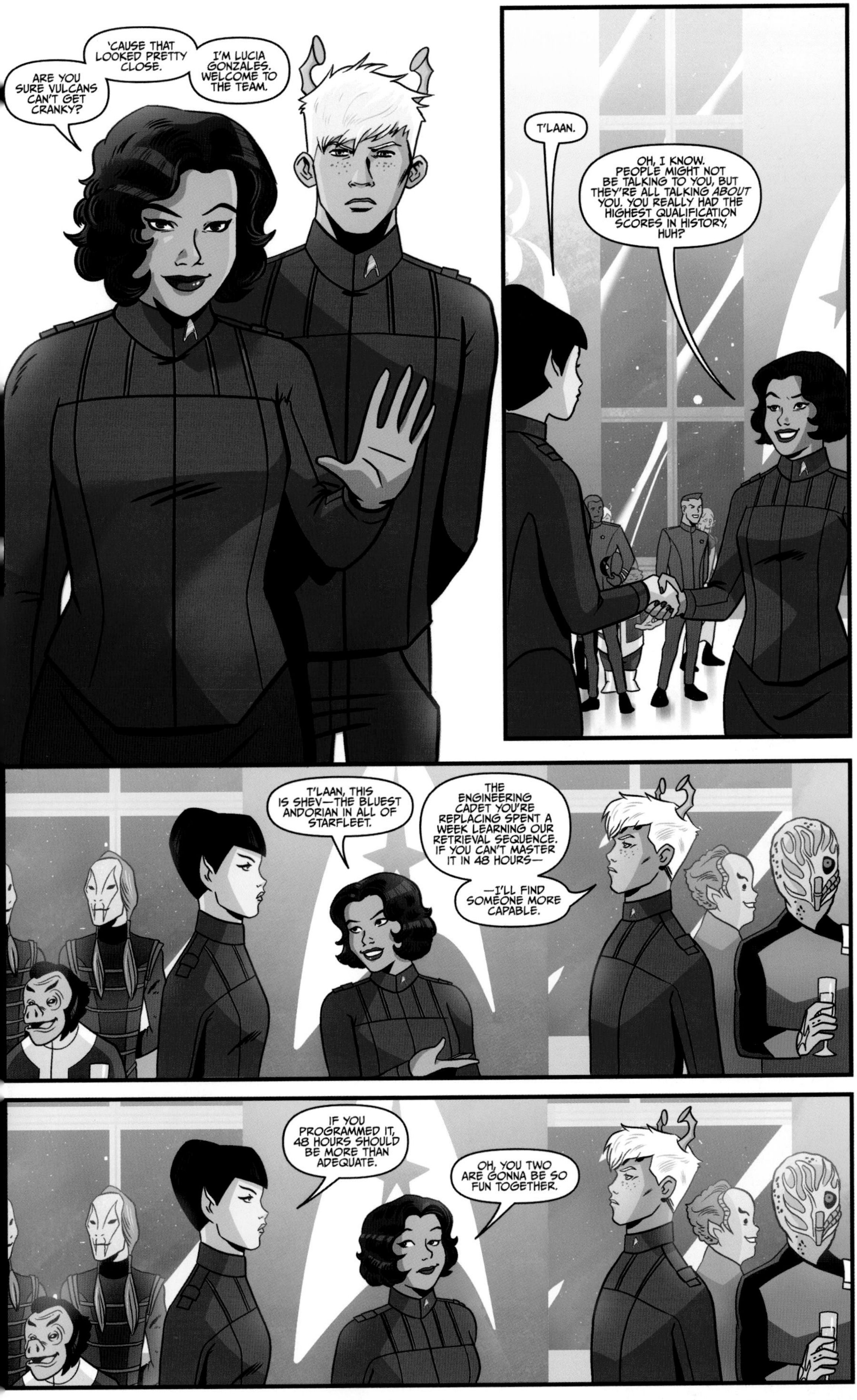

ARE YOU SURE VULCANS CAN'T GET CRANKY?
'CAUSE THAT LOOKED PRETTY CLOSE.
I'M LUCIA GONZALES. WELCOME TO THE TEAM.
T'LAAN.
OH, I KNOW. PEOPLE MIGHT NOT BE TALKING TO YOU, BUT THEY'RE ALL TALKING *ABOUT* YOU. YOU REALLY HAD THE HIGHEST QUALIFICATION SCORES IN HISTORY, HUH?
T'LAAN, THIS IS SHEV—THE BLUEST ANDORIAN IN ALL OF STARFLEET.
THE ENGINEERING CADET YOU'RE REPLACING SPENT A WEEK LEARNING OUR RETRIEVAL SEQUENCE. IF YOU CAN'T MASTER IT IN 48 HOURS—
—I'LL FIND SOMEONE MORE CAPABLE.
IF YOU PROGRAMMED IT, 48 HOURS SHOULD BE MORE THAN ADEQUATE.
OH, YOU TWO ARE GONNA BE SO FUN TOGETHER.

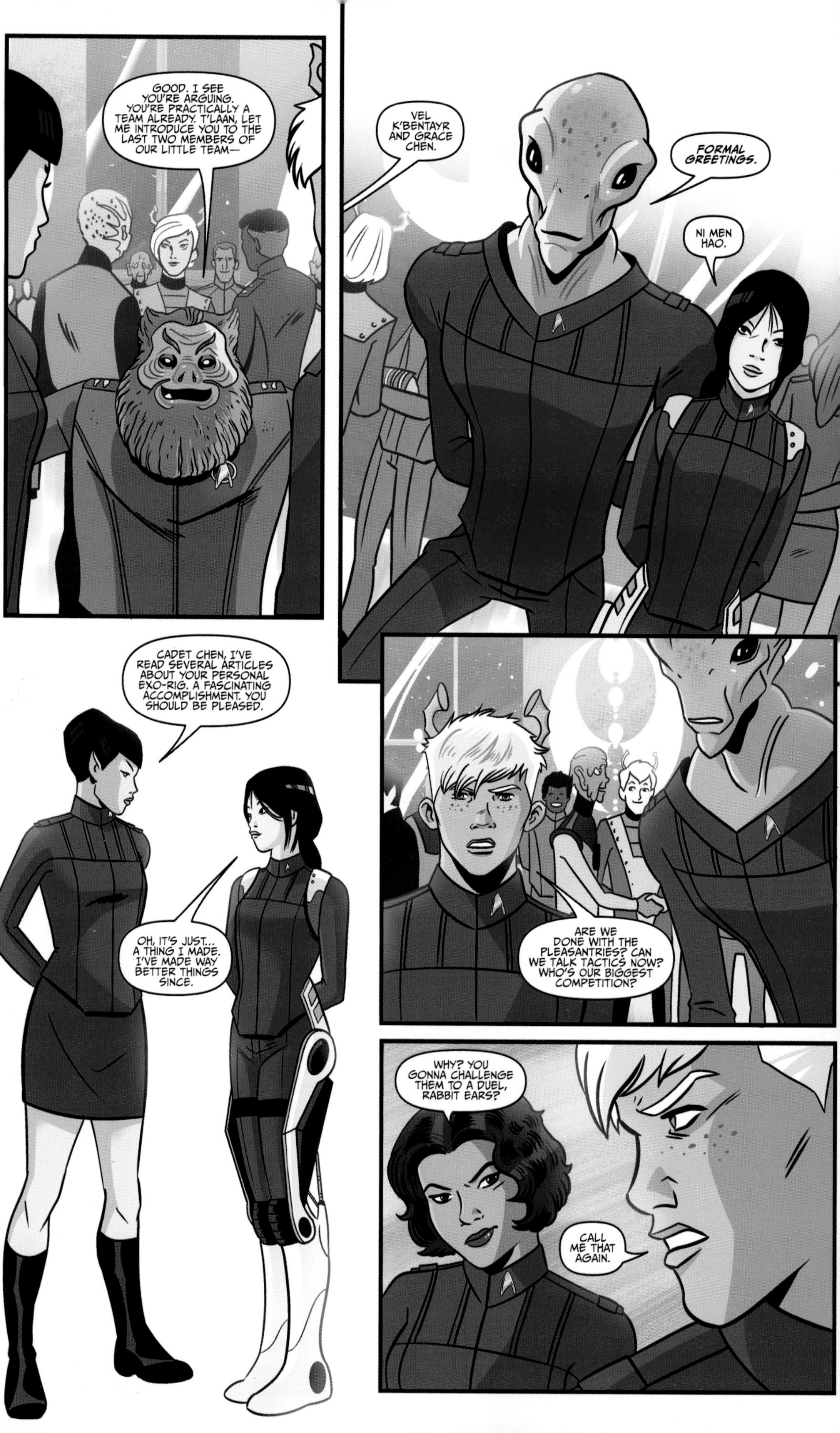
GOOD. I SEE YOU'RE ARGUING. YOU'RE PRACTICALLY A TEAM ALREADY. T'LAAN, LET ME INTRODUCE YOU TO THE LAST TWO MEMBERS OF OUR LITTLE TEAM—
VEL K'BENTAYR AND GRACE CHEN.
FORMAL GREETINGS.
NI MEN HAO.
CADET CHEN, I'VE READ SEVERAL ARTICLES ABOUT YOUR PERSONAL EXO-RIG. A FASCINATING ACCOMPLISHMENT. YOU SHOULD BE PLEASED.
OH, IT'S JUST... A THING I MADE. I'VE MADE WAY BETTER THINGS SINCE.
ARE WE DONE WITH THE PLEASANTRIES? CAN WE TALK TACTICS NOW? WHO'S OUR BIGGEST COMPETITION?
WHY? YOU GONNA CHALLENGE THEM TO A DUEL, RABBIT EARS?
CALL ME THAT AGAIN.

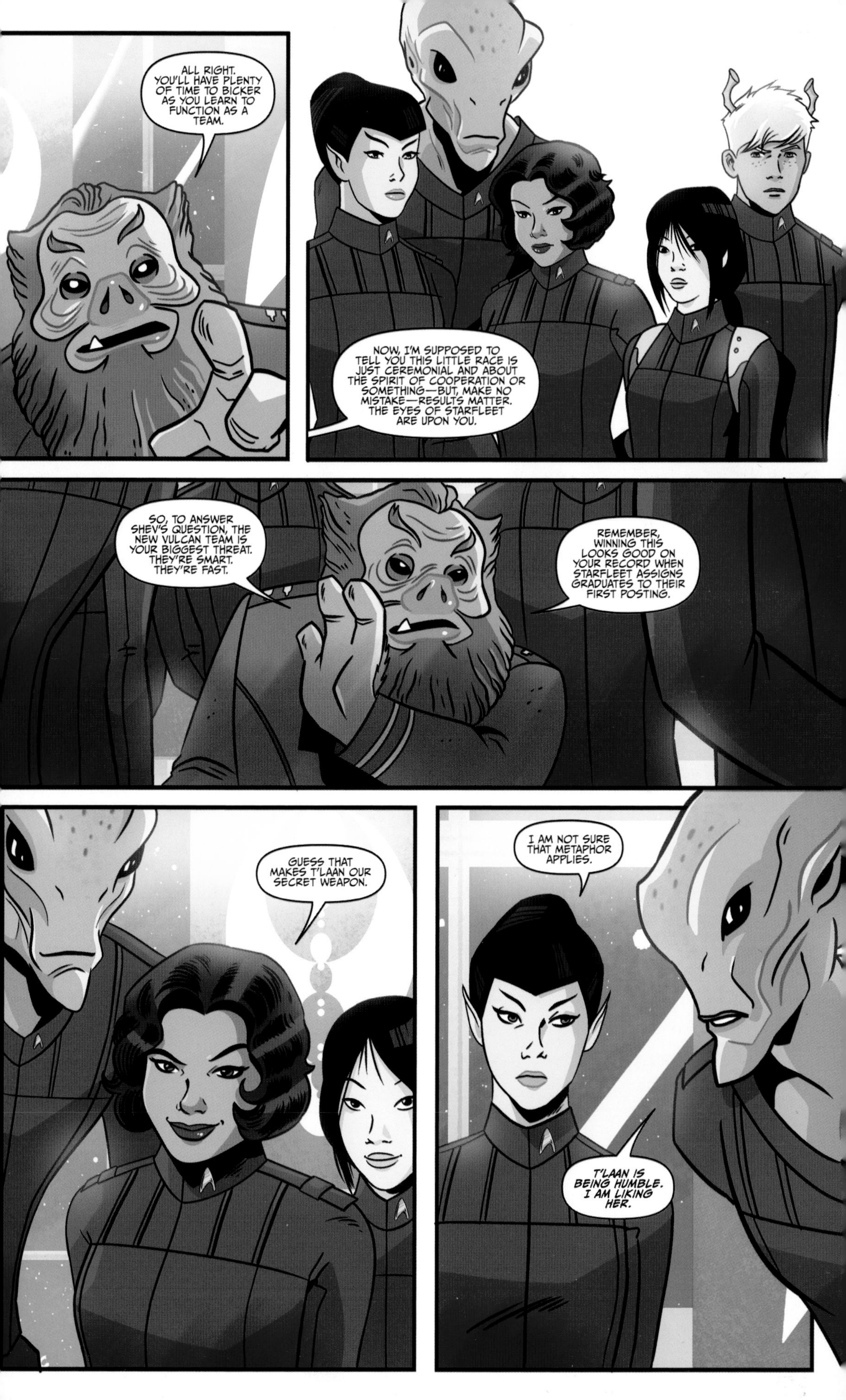
ALL RIGHT. YOU'LL HAVE PLENTY OF TIME TO BICKER AS YOU LEARN TO FUNCTION AS A TEAM.
NOW, I'M SUPPOSED TO TELL YOU THIS LITTLE RACE IS JUST CEREMONIAL AND ABOUT THE SPIRIT OF COOPERATION OR SOMETHING—BUT, MAKE NO MISTAKE—RESULTS MATTER. THE EYES OF STARFLEET ARE UPON YOU.
SO, TO ANSWER SHEV'S QUESTION, THE NEW VULCAN TEAM IS YOUR BIGGEST THREAT. THEY'RE SMART. THEY'RE FAST.
REMEMBER, WINNING THIS LOOKS GOOD ON YOUR RECORD WHEN STARFLEET ASSIGNS GRADUATES TO THEIR FIRST POSTING.
GUESS THAT MAKES T'LAAN OUR SECRET WEAPON.
I AM NOT SURE THAT METAPHOR APPLIES.
T'LAAN IS BEING HUMBLE. I AM LIKING HER.

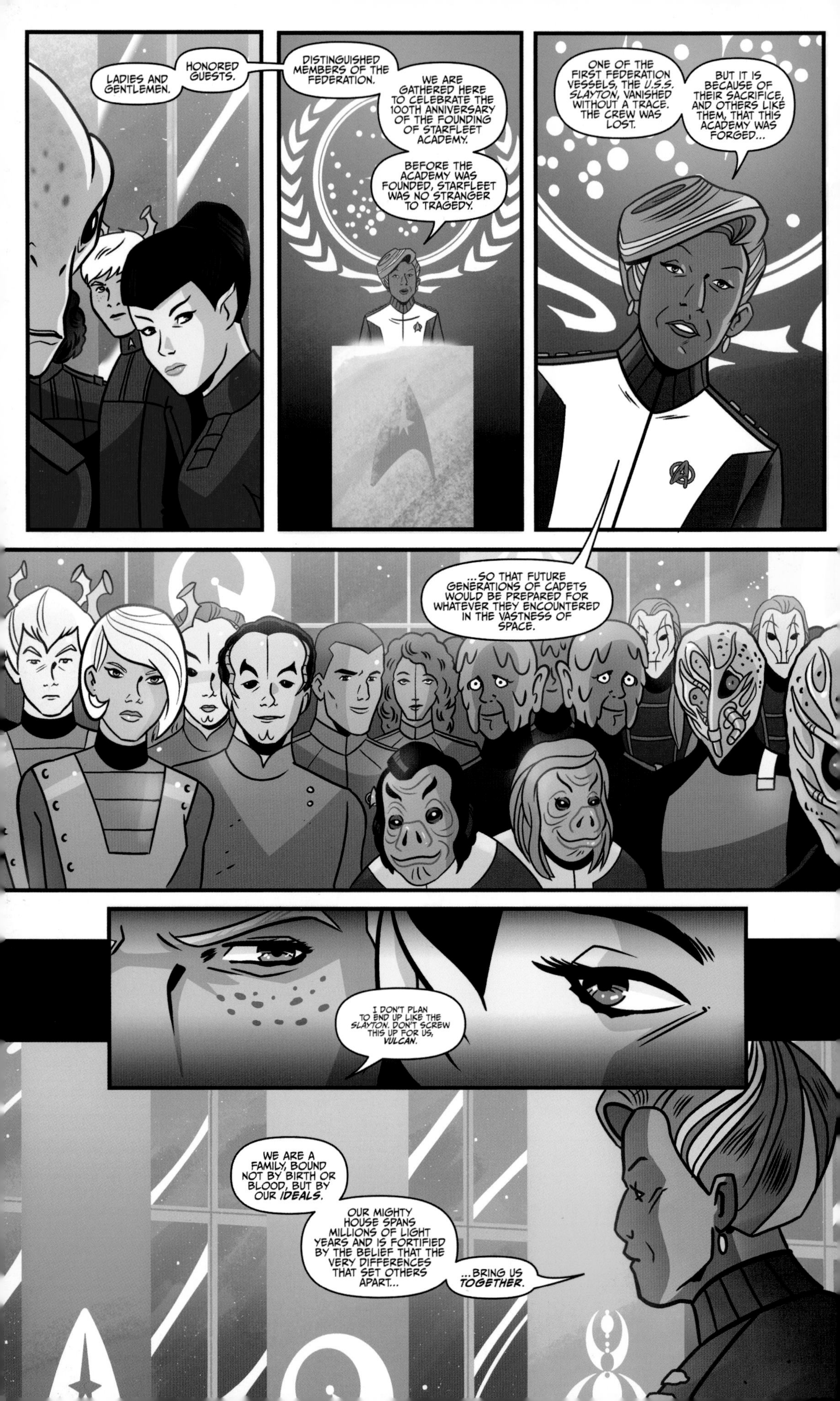
LADIES AND GENTLEMEN.
HONORED GUESTS.
DISTINGUISHED MEMBERS OF THE FEDERATION.
WE ARE GATHERED HERE TO CELEBRATE THE 100TH ANNIVERSARY OF THE FOUNDING OF STARFLEET ACADEMY.
BEFORE THE ACADEMY WAS FOUNDED, STARFLEET WAS NO STRANGER TO TRAGEDY.
ONE OF THE FIRST FEDERATION VESSELS, THE U.S.S. SLAYTON, VANISHED WITHOUT A TRACE. THE CREW WAS LOST.
BUT IT IS BECAUSE OF THEIR SACRIFICE, AND OTHERS LIKE THEM, THAT THIS ACADEMY WAS FORGED...
...SO THAT FUTURE GENERATIONS OF CADETS WOULD BE PREPARED FOR WHATEVER THEY ENCOUNTERED IN THE VASTNESS OF SPACE.
I DON'T PLAN TO END UP LIKE THE SLAYTON. DON'T SCREW THIS UP FOR US, VULCAN.
WE ARE A FAMILY, BOUND NOT BY BIRTH OR BLOOD, BUT BY OUR IDEALS.
OUR MIGHTY HOUSE SPANS MILLIONS OF LIGHT YEARS AND IS FORTIFIED BY THE BELIEF THAT THE VERY DIFFERENCES THAT SET OTHERS APART...
...BRING US TOGETHER.

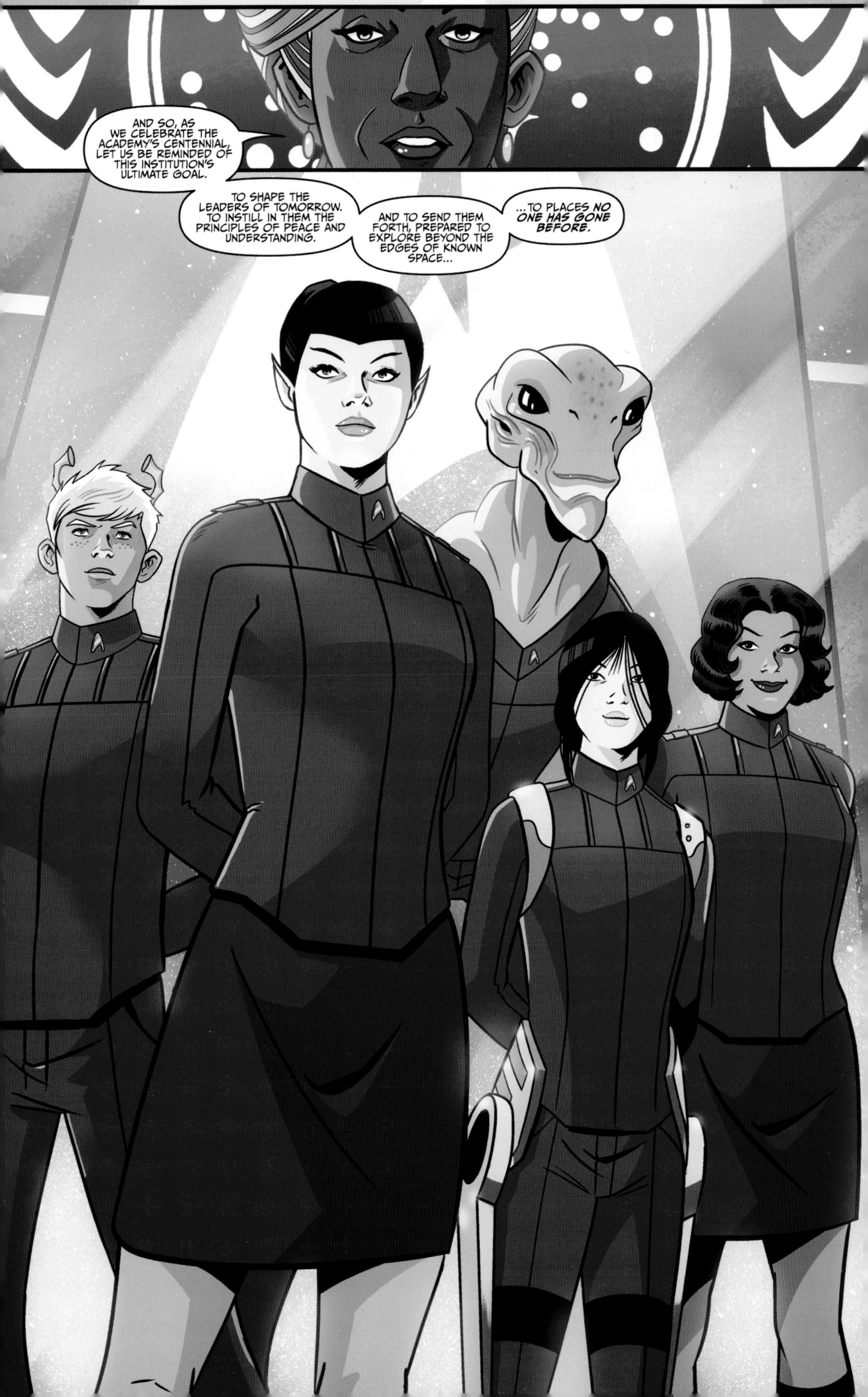
AND SO, AS WE CELEBRATE THE ACADEMY'S CENTENNIAL, LET US BE REMINDED OF THIS INSTITUTION'S ULTIMATE GOAL.
TO SHAPE THE LEADERS OF TOMORROW. TO INSTILL IN THEM THE PRINCIPLES OF PEACE AND UNDERSTANDING.
AND TO SEND THEM FORTH, PREPARED TO EXPLORE BEYOND THE EDGES OF KNOWN SPACE...
...TO PLACES NO ONE HAS GONE BEFORE.

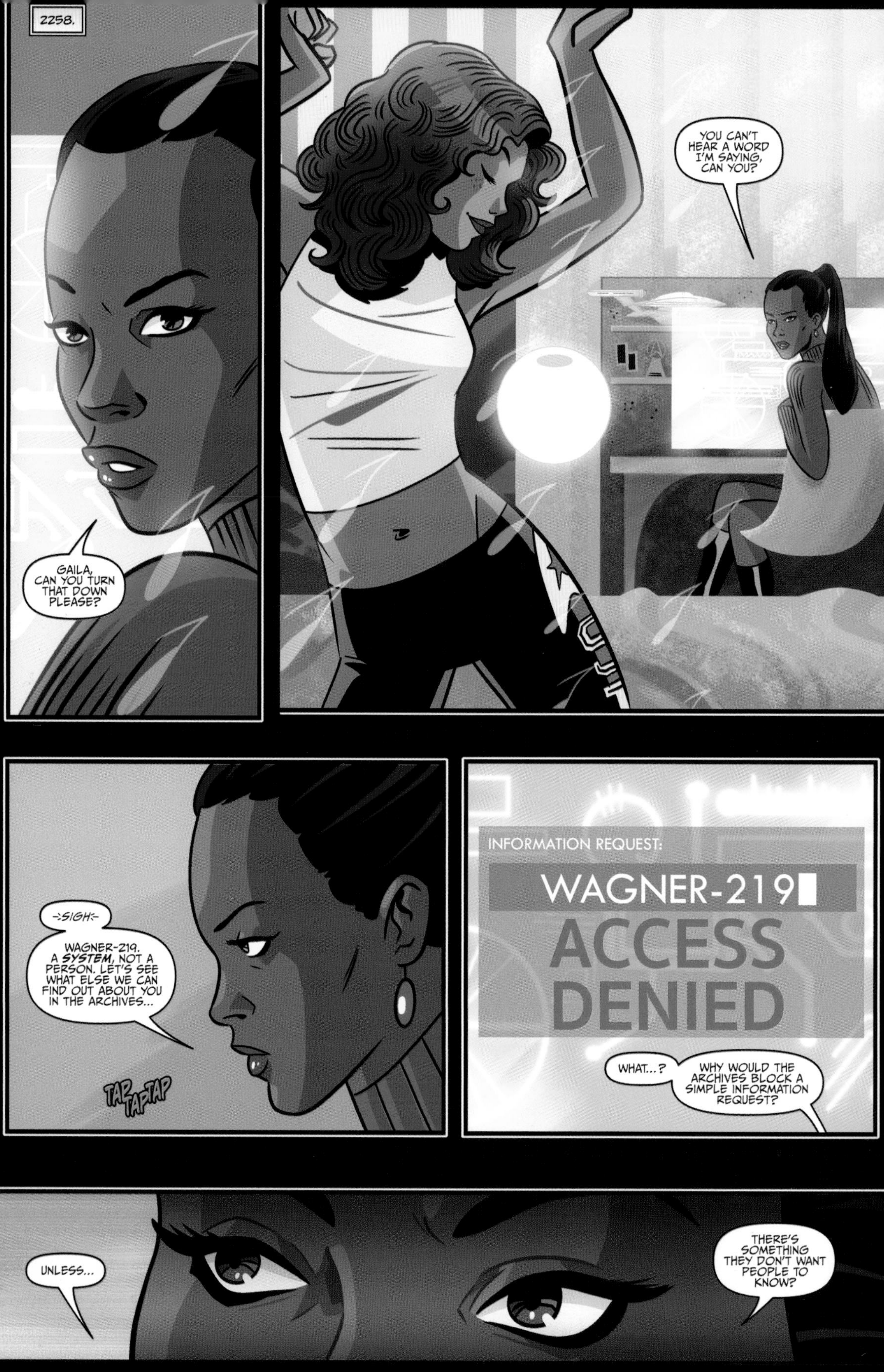
2258.
YOU CAN'T HEAR A WORD I'M SAYING, CAN YOU?
GAILA, CAN YOU TURN THAT DOWN PLEASE?
-SIGH-
WAGNER-219. A SYSTEM, NOT A PERSON. LET'S SEE WHAT ELSE WE CAN FIND OUT ABOUT YOU IN THE ARCHIVES...
TAP TAPTAP
INFORMATION REQUEST:
WAGNER-219
ACCESS DENIED
WHAT...?
WHY WOULD THE ARCHIVES BLOCK A SIMPLE INFORMATION REQUEST?
UNLESS...
THERE'S SOMETHING THEY DON'T WANT PEOPLE TO KNOW?

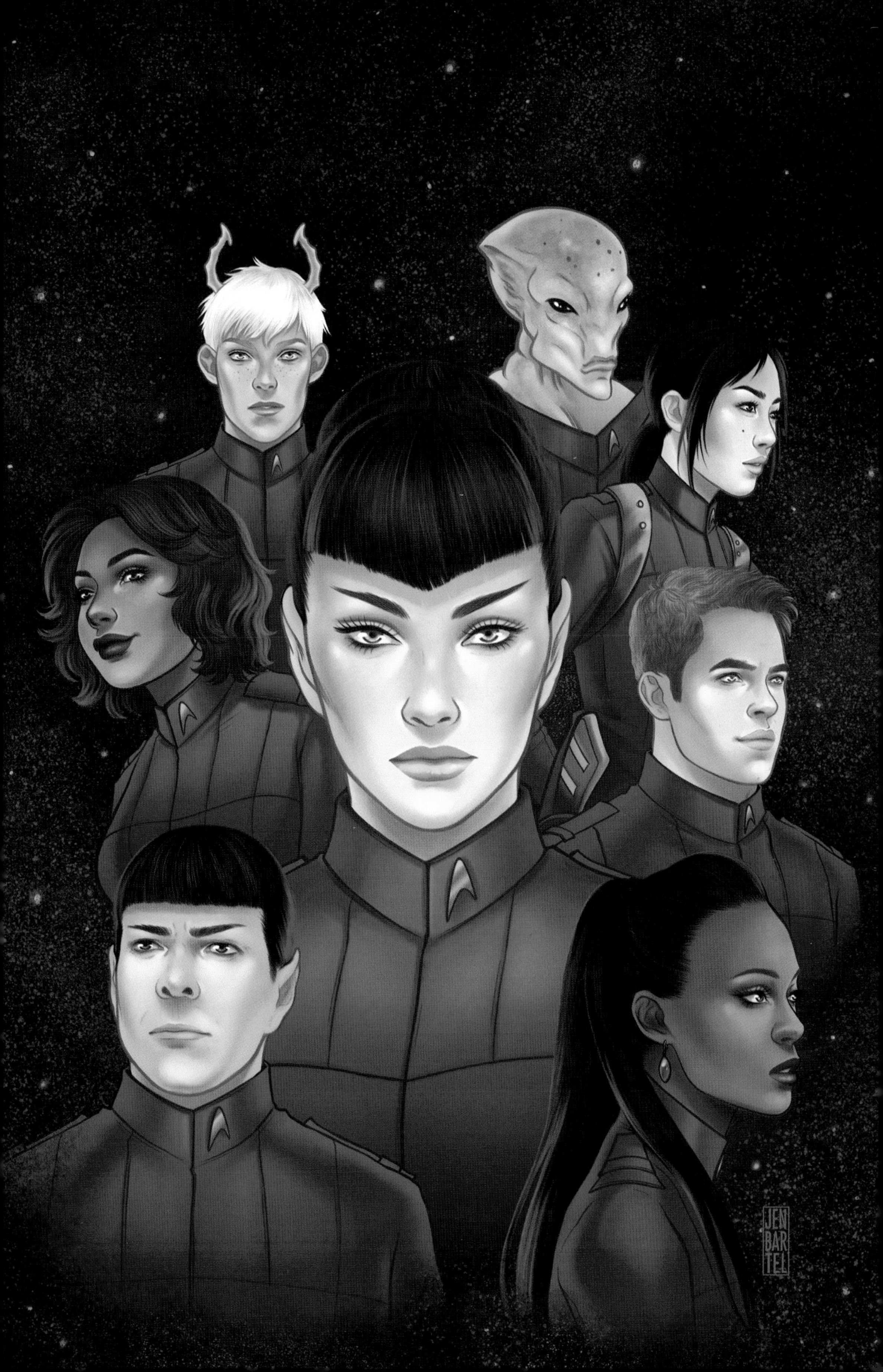
JEN
BAR
TEL

ART BY **DEREK CHARM**

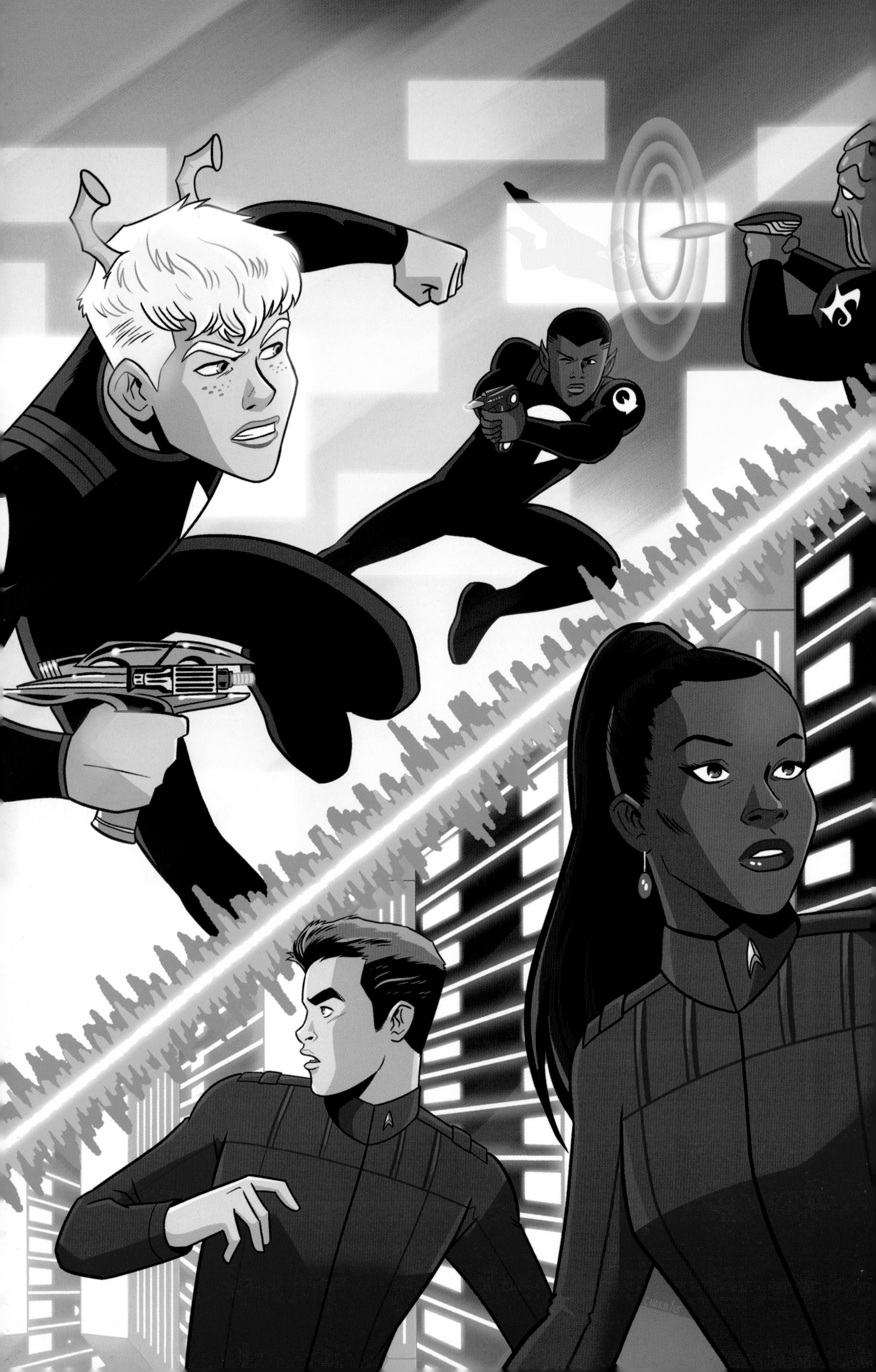

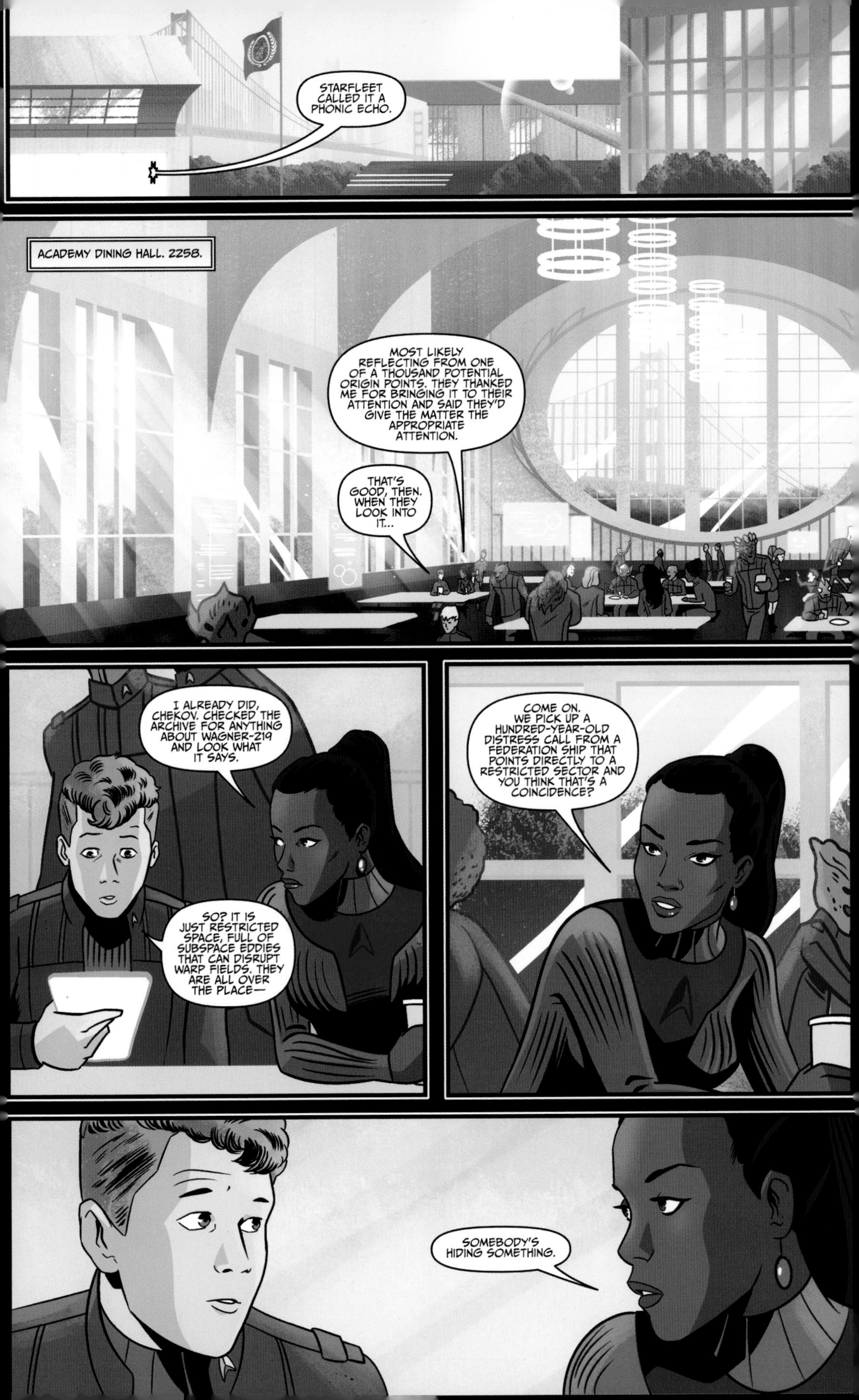
STARFLEET CALLED IT A PHONIC ECHO.
ACADEMY DINING HALL. 2258.
MOST LIKELY REFLECTING FROM ONE OF A THOUSAND POTENTIAL ORIGIN POINTS. THEY THANKED ME FOR BRINGING IT TO THEIR ATTENTION AND SAID THEY'D GIVE THE MATTER THE APPROPRIATE ATTENTION.
THAT'S GOOD, THEN. WHEN THEY LOOK INTO IT...
I ALREADY DID, CHEKOV. CHECKED THE ARCHIVE FOR ANYTHING ABOUT WAGNER-219 AND LOOK WHAT IT SAYS.
SO? IT IS JUST RESTRICTED SPACE, FULL OF SUBSPACE EDDIES THAT CAN DISRUPT WARP FIELDS. THEY ARE ALL OVER THE PLACE—
COME ON. WE PICK UP A HUNDRED-YEAR-OLD DISTRESS CALL FROM A FEDERATION SHIP THAT POINTS DIRECTLY TO A RESTRICTED SECTOR AND YOU THINK THAT'S A COINCIDENCE?
SOMEBODY'S HIDING SOMETHING.

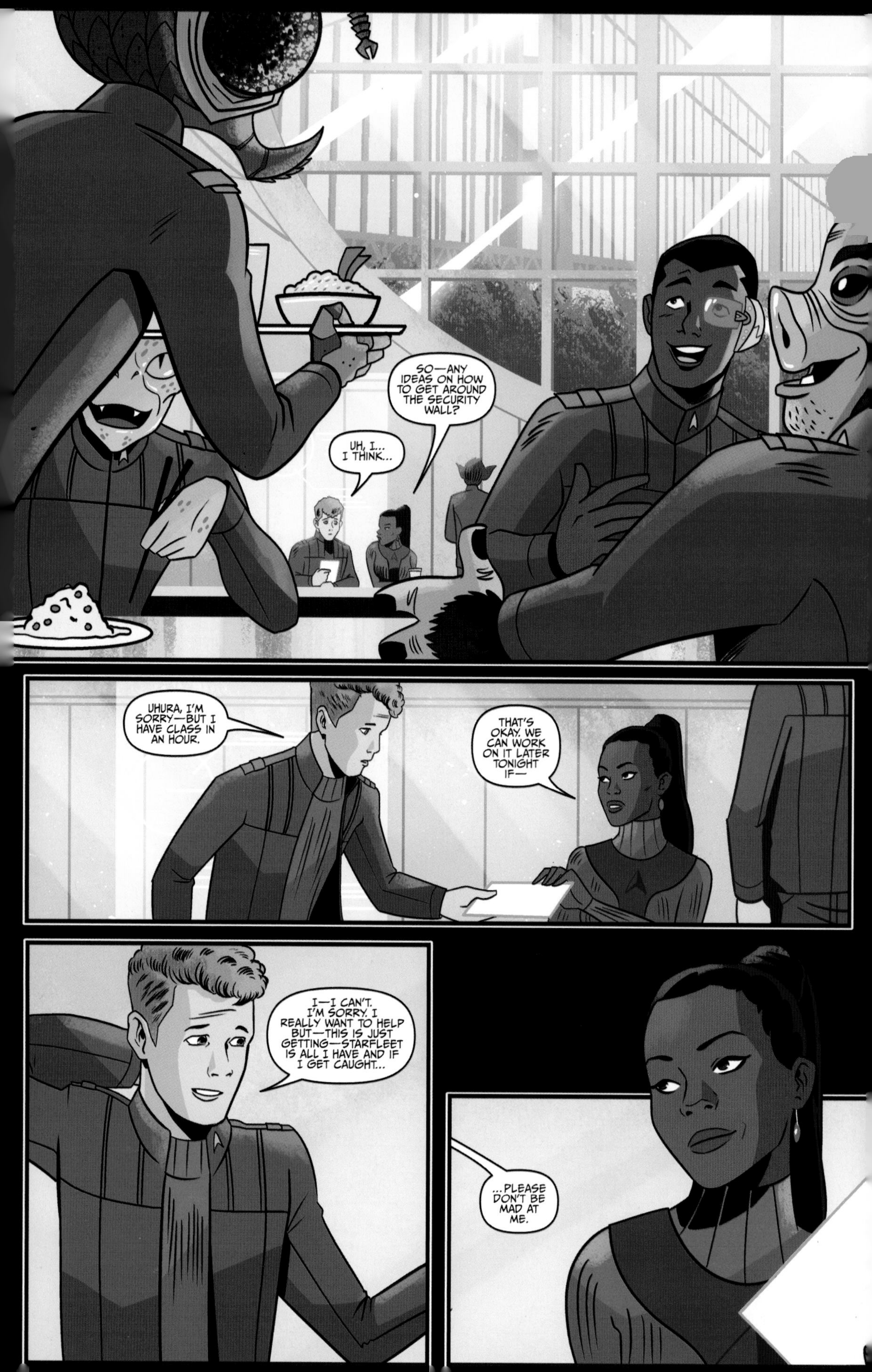
SO—ANY IDEAS ON HOW TO GET AROUND THE SECURITY WALL?
UH, I... I THINK...
UHURA, I'M SORRY—BUT I HAVE CLASS IN AN HOUR.
THAT'S OKAY. WE CAN WORK ON IT LATER TONIGHT IF—
I—I CAN'T. I'M SORRY. I REALLY WANT TO HELP BUT—THIS IS JUST GETTING—STARFLEET IS ALL I HAVE AND IF I GET CAUGHT...
...PLEASE DON'T BE MAD AT ME.

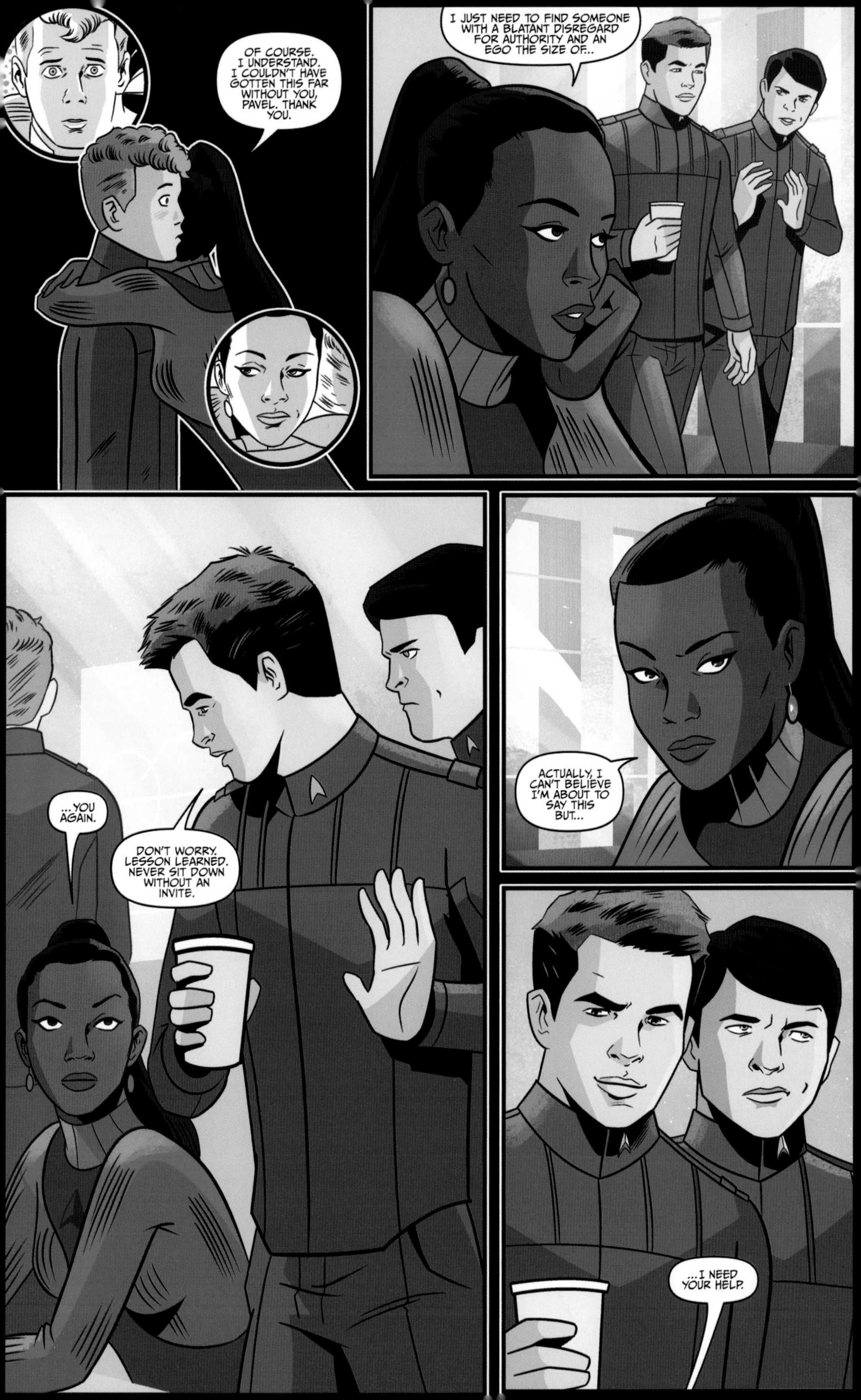

OF COURSE. I UNDERSTAND. I COULDN'T HAVE GOTTEN THIS FAR WITHOUT YOU, PAVEL. THANK YOU.
I JUST NEED TO FIND SOMEONE WITH A BLATANT DISREGARD FOR AUTHORITY AND AN EGO THE SIZE OF...
...YOU AGAIN.
DON'T WORRY. LESSON LEARNED. NEVER SIT DOWN WITHOUT AN INVITE.
ACTUALLY, I CAN'T BELIEVE I'M ABOUT TO SAY THIS BUT...
...I NEED YOUR HELP.

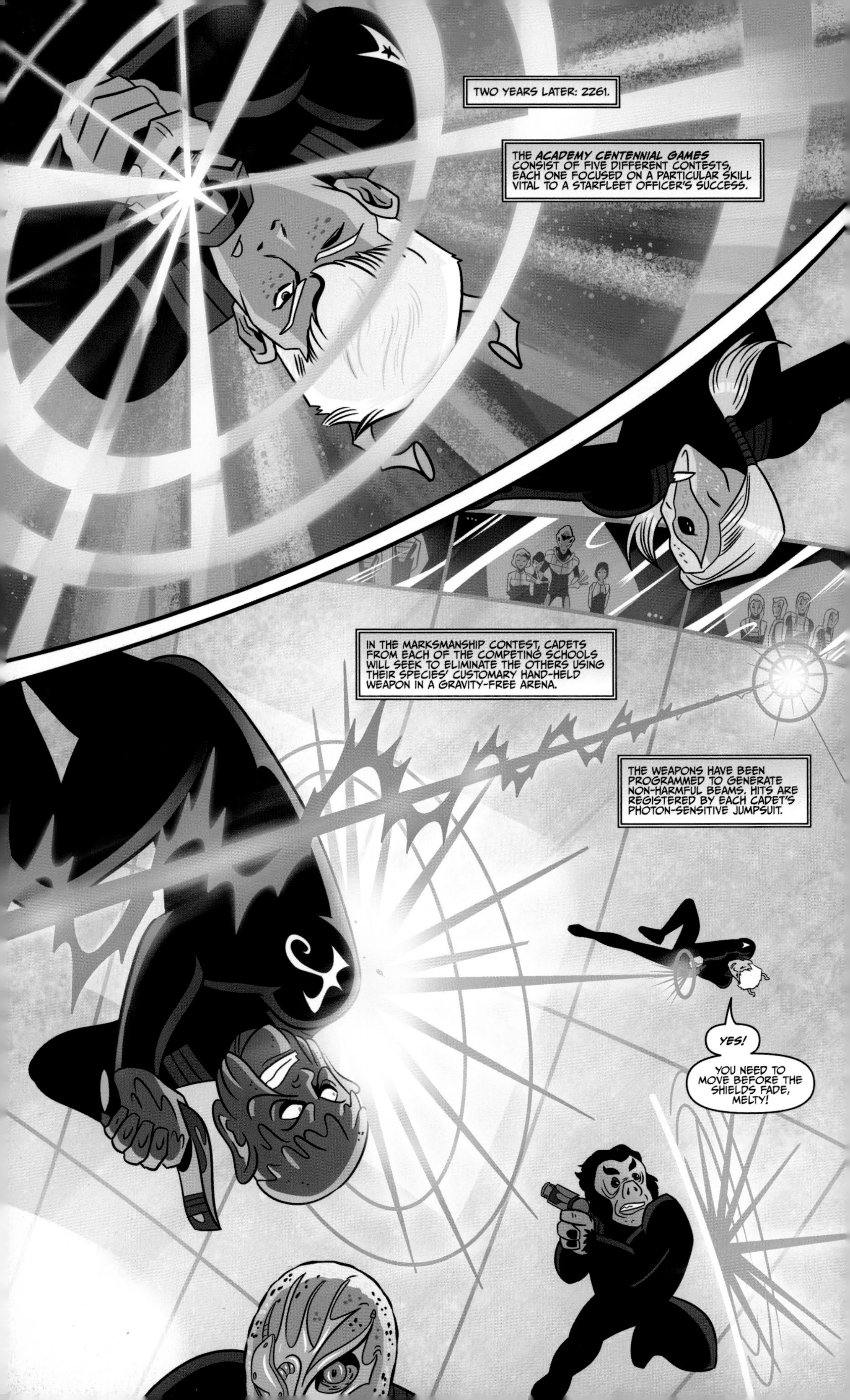
TWO YEARS LATER: 2261.
THE ACADEMY CENTENNIAL GAMES CONSIST OF FIVE DIFFERENT CONTESTS, EACH ONE FOCUSED ON A PARTICULAR SKILL VITAL TO A STARFLEET OFFICER'S SUCCESS.
IN THE MARKSMANSHIP CONTEST, CADETS FROM EACH OF THE COMPETING SCHOOLS WILL SEEK TO ELIMINATE THE OTHERS USING THEIR SPECIES' CUSTOMARY HAND-HELD WEAPON IN A GRAVITY-FREE ARENA.
THE WEAPONS HAVE BEEN PROGRAMMED TO GENERATE NON-HARMFUL BEAMS. HITS ARE REGISTERED BY EACH CADET'S PHOTON-SENSITIVE JUMPSUIT.
YES!
YOU NEED TO MOVE BEFORE THE SHIELDS FADE, MELTY!

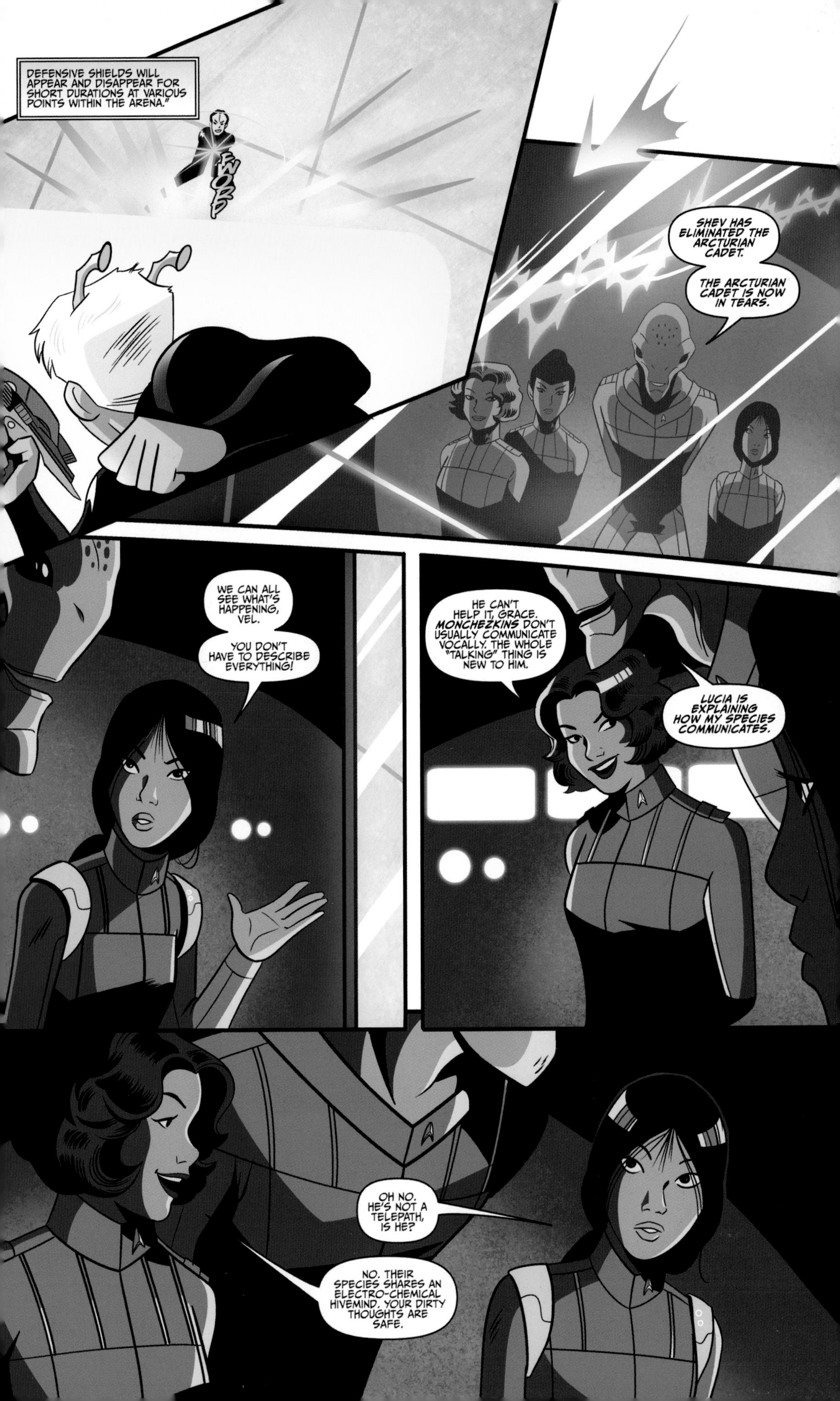
DEFENSIVE SHIELDS WILL APPEAR AND DISAPPEAR FOR SHORT DURATIONS AT VARIOUS POINTS WITHIN THE ARENA."
FWORP
SHEV HAS ELIMINATED THE ARCTURIAN CADET.
THE ARCTURIAN CADET IS NOW IN TEARS.
WE CAN ALL SEE WHAT'S HAPPENING, VEL.
YOU DON'T HAVE TO DESCRIBE EVERYTHING!
HE CAN'T HELP IT, GRACE. MONCHEZKINS DON'T USUALLY COMMUNICATE VOCALLY. THE WHOLE "TALKING" THING IS NEW TO HIM.
LUCIA IS EXPLAINING HOW MY SPECIES COMMUNICATES.
OH NO. HE'S NOT A TELEPATH, IS HE?
NO. THEIR SPECIES SHARES AN ELECTRO-CHEMICAL HIVEMIND. YOUR DIRTY THOUGHTS ARE SAFE.

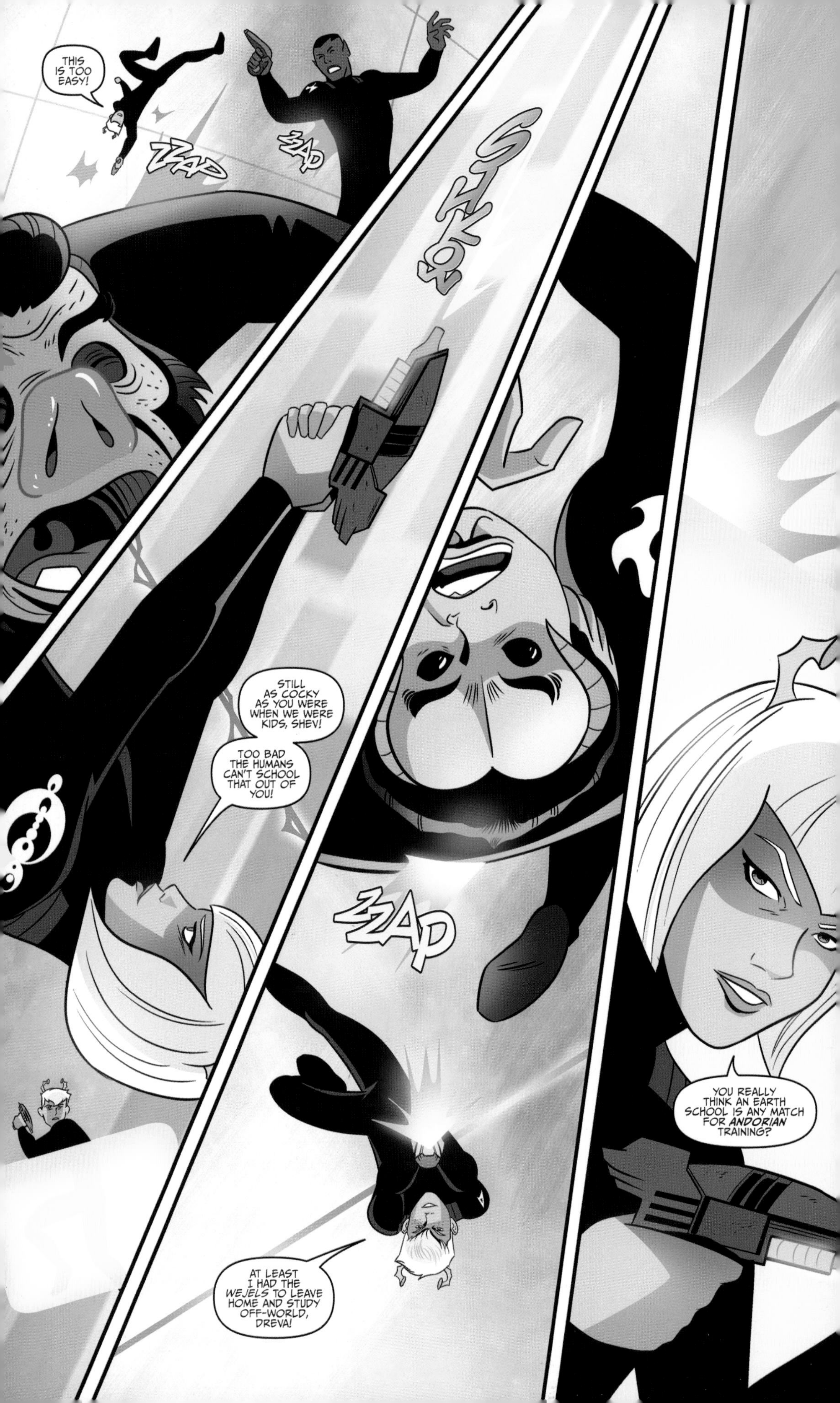
THIS IS TOO EASY!
ZZAP
ZZAP
SHHKOW
STILL AS COCKY AS YOU WERE WHEN WE WERE KIDS, SHEV!
TOO BAD THE HUMANS CAN'T SCHOOL THAT OUT OF YOU!
ZZAP
YOU REALLY THINK AN EARTH SCHOOL IS ANY MATCH FOR ANDORIAN TRAINING?
AT LEAST I HAD THE WEJELS TO LEAVE HOME AND STUDY OFF-WORLD, DREVA!

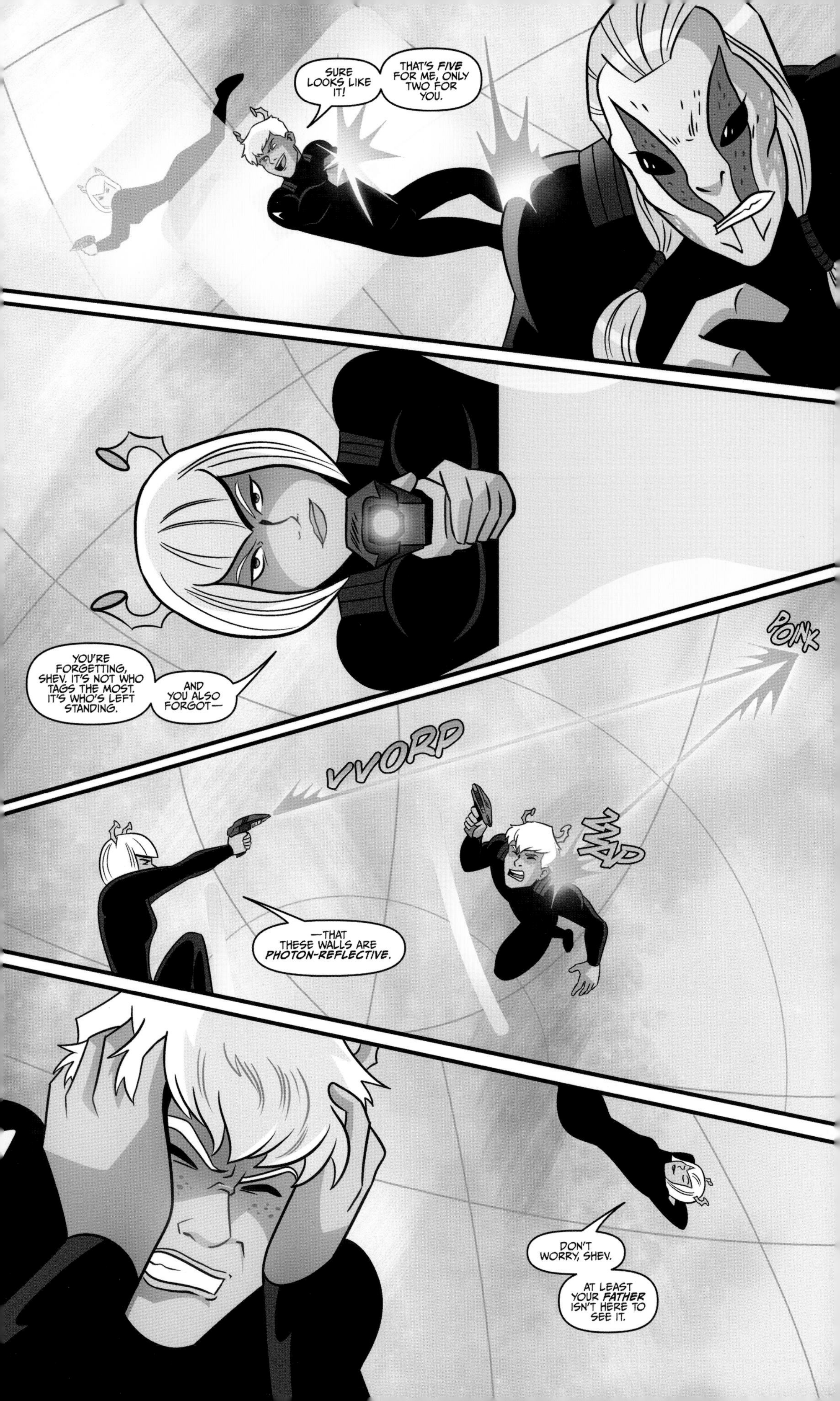
SURE LOOKS LIKE IT!
THAT'S *FIVE* FOR ME, ONLY TWO FOR YOU.
YOU'RE FORGETTING, SHEV. IT'S NOT WHO TAGS THE MOST. IT'S WHO'S LEFT STANDING.
AND YOU ALSO FORGOT—
POINK
VVORP
—THAT THESE WALLS ARE *PHOTON-REFLECTIVE*.
DON'T WORRY, SHEV.
AT LEAST YOUR *FATHER* ISN'T HERE TO SEE IT.

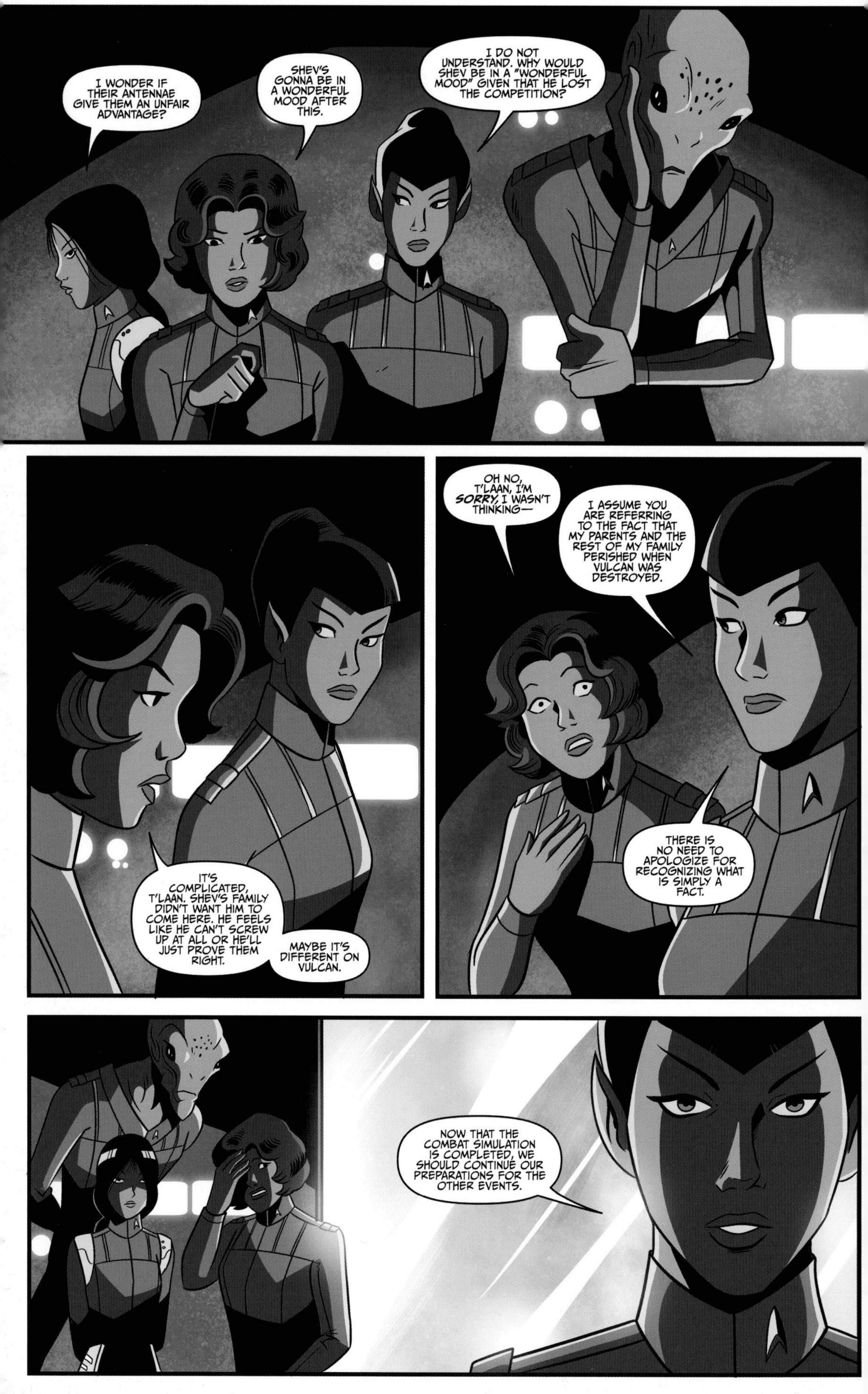
I WONDER IF THEIR ANTENNAE GIVE THEM AN UNFAIR ADVANTAGE?
SHEV'S GONNA BE IN A WONDERFUL MOOD AFTER THIS.
I DO NOT UNDERSTAND. WHY WOULD SHEV BE IN A "WONDERFUL MOOD" GIVEN THAT HE LOST THE COMPETITION?
IT'S COMPLICATED, T'LAAN. SHEV'S FAMILY DIDN'T WANT HIM TO COME HERE. HE FEELS LIKE HE CAN'T SCREW UP AT ALL OR HE'LL JUST PROVE THEM RIGHT.
MAYBE IT'S DIFFERENT ON VULCAN.
OH NO, T'LAAN, I'M SORRY, I WASN'T THINKING—
I ASSUME YOU ARE REFERRING TO THE FACT THAT MY PARENTS AND THE REST OF MY FAMILY PERISHED WHEN VULCAN WAS DESTROYED.
THERE IS NO NEED TO APOLOGIZE FOR RECOGNIZING WHAT IS SIMPLY A FACT.
NOW THAT THE COMBAT SIMULATION IS COMPLETED, WE SHOULD CONTINUE OUR PREPARATIONS FOR THE OTHER EVENTS.

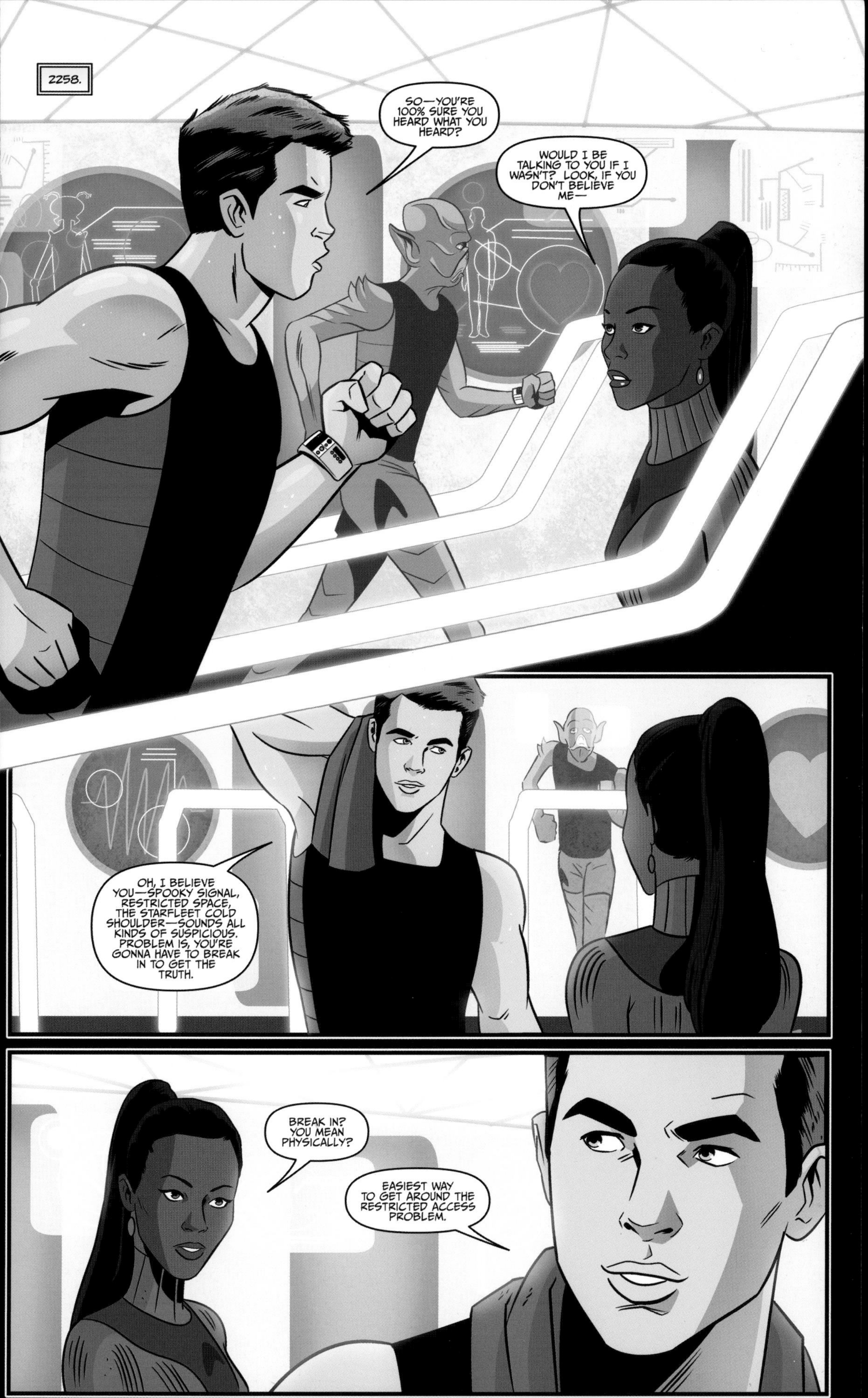
2258.
SO—YOU'RE 100% SURE YOU HEARD WHAT YOU HEARD?
WOULD I BE TALKING TO YOU IF I WASN'T? LOOK, IF YOU DON'T BELIEVE ME—
OH, I BELIEVE YOU—SPOOKY SIGNAL, RESTRICTED SPACE, THE STARFLEET COLD SHOULDER—SOUNDS ALL KINDS OF SUSPICIOUS. PROBLEM IS, YOU'RE GONNA HAVE TO BREAK IN TO GET THE TRUTH.
BREAK IN? YOU MEAN PHYSICALLY?
EASIEST WAY TO GET AROUND THE RESTRICTED ACCESS PROBLEM.

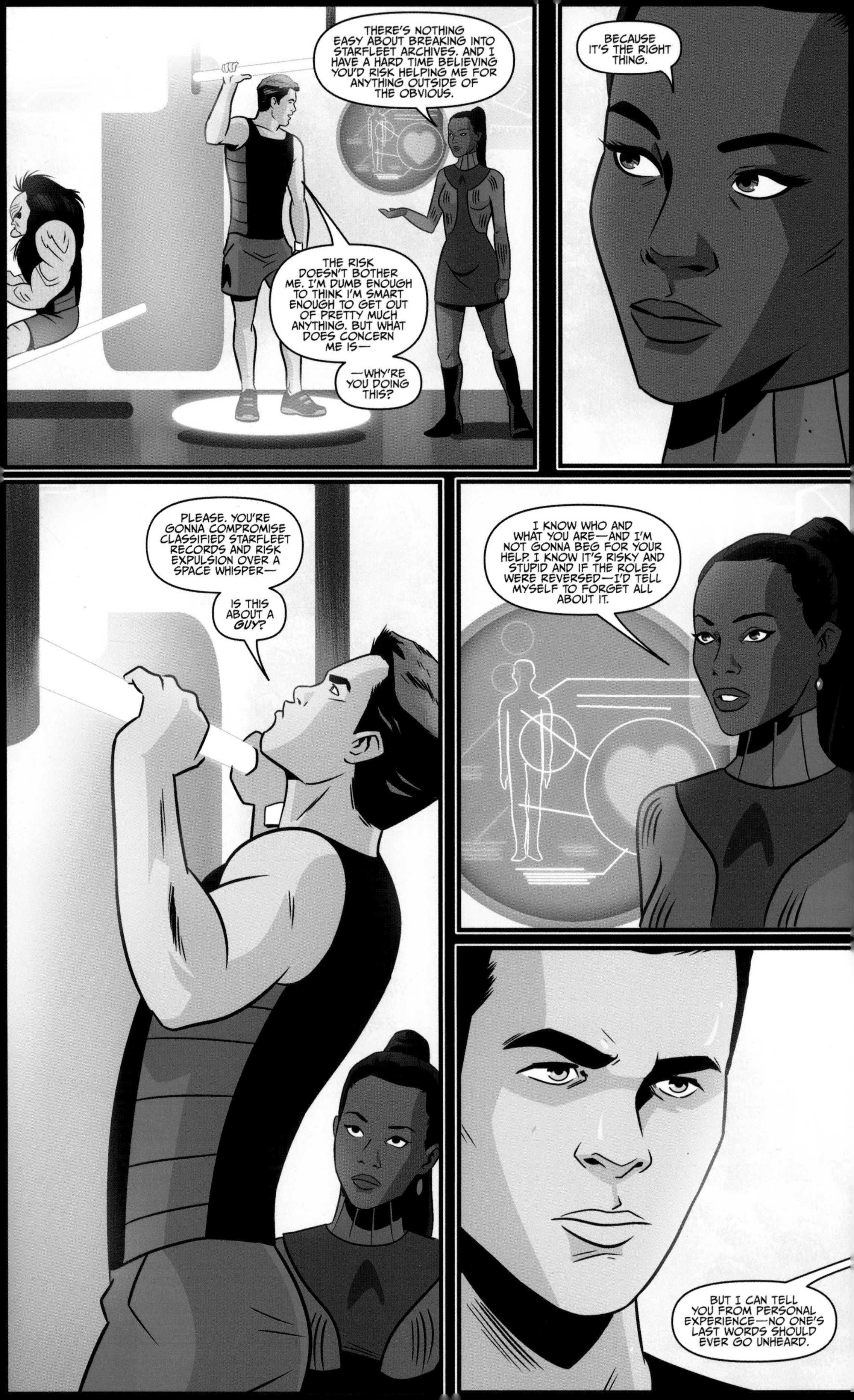
THERE'S NOTHING EASY ABOUT BREAKING INTO STARFLEET ARCHIVES. AND I HAVE A HARD TIME BELIEVING YOU'D RISK HELPING ME FOR ANYTHING OUTSIDE OF THE OBVIOUS.
THE RISK DOESN'T BOTHER ME. I'M DUMB ENOUGH TO THINK I'M SMART ENOUGH TO GET OUT OF PRETTY MUCH ANYTHING. BUT WHAT DOES CONCERN ME IS—
—WHY'RE YOU DOING THIS?
BECAUSE IT'S THE RIGHT THING.
PLEASE. YOU'RE GONNA COMPROMISE CLASSIFIED STARFLEET RECORDS AND RISK EXPULSION OVER A SPACE WHISPER—
IS THIS ABOUT A *GUY*?
I KNOW WHO AND WHAT YOU ARE—AND I'M NOT GONNA BEG FOR YOUR HELP. I KNOW IT'S RISKY AND STUPID AND IF THE ROLES WERE REVERSED—I'D TELL MYSELF TO FORGET ALL ABOUT IT.
BUT I CAN TELL YOU FROM PERSONAL EXPERIENCE—NO ONE'S LAST WORDS SHOULD EVER GO UNHEARD.

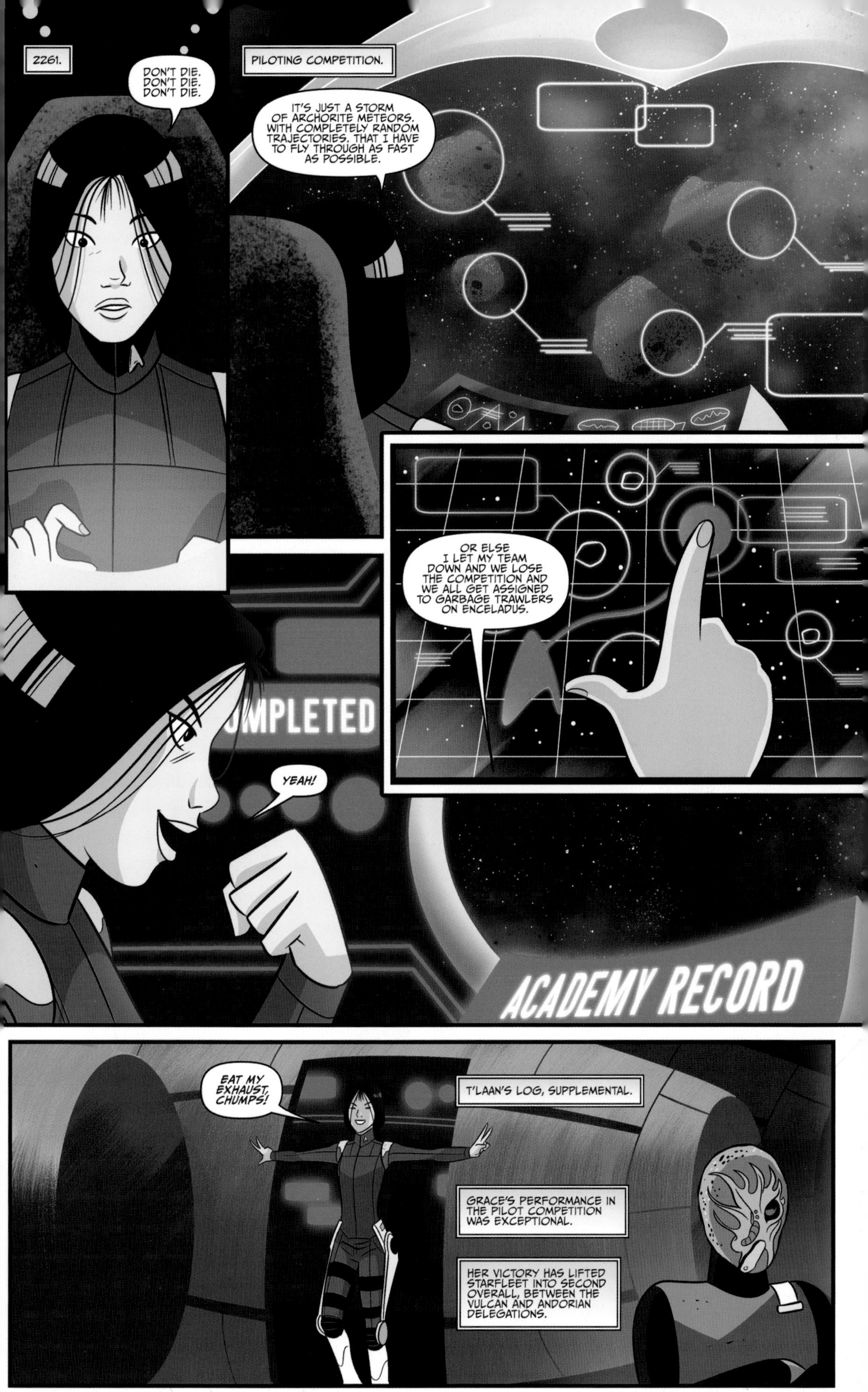
2261.
DON'T DIE. DON'T DIE. DON'T DIE.
PILOTING COMPETITION.
IT'S JUST A STORM OF ARCHORITE METEORS. WITH COMPLETELY RANDOM TRAJECTORIES. THAT I HAVE TO FLY THROUGH AS FAST AS POSSIBLE.
OR ELSE I LET MY TEAM DOWN AND WE LOSE THE COMPETITION AND WE ALL GET ASSIGNED TO GARBAGE TRAWLERS ON ENCELADUS.
UMPLETED
YEAH!
ACADEMY RECORD
EAT MY EXHAUST, CHUMPS!
T'LAAN'S LOG, SUPPLEMENTAL.
GRACE'S PERFORMANCE IN THE PILOT COMPETITION WAS EXCEPTIONAL.
HER VICTORY HAS LIFTED STARFLEET INTO SECOND OVERALL, BETWEEN THE VULCAN AND ANDORIAN DELEGATIONS.

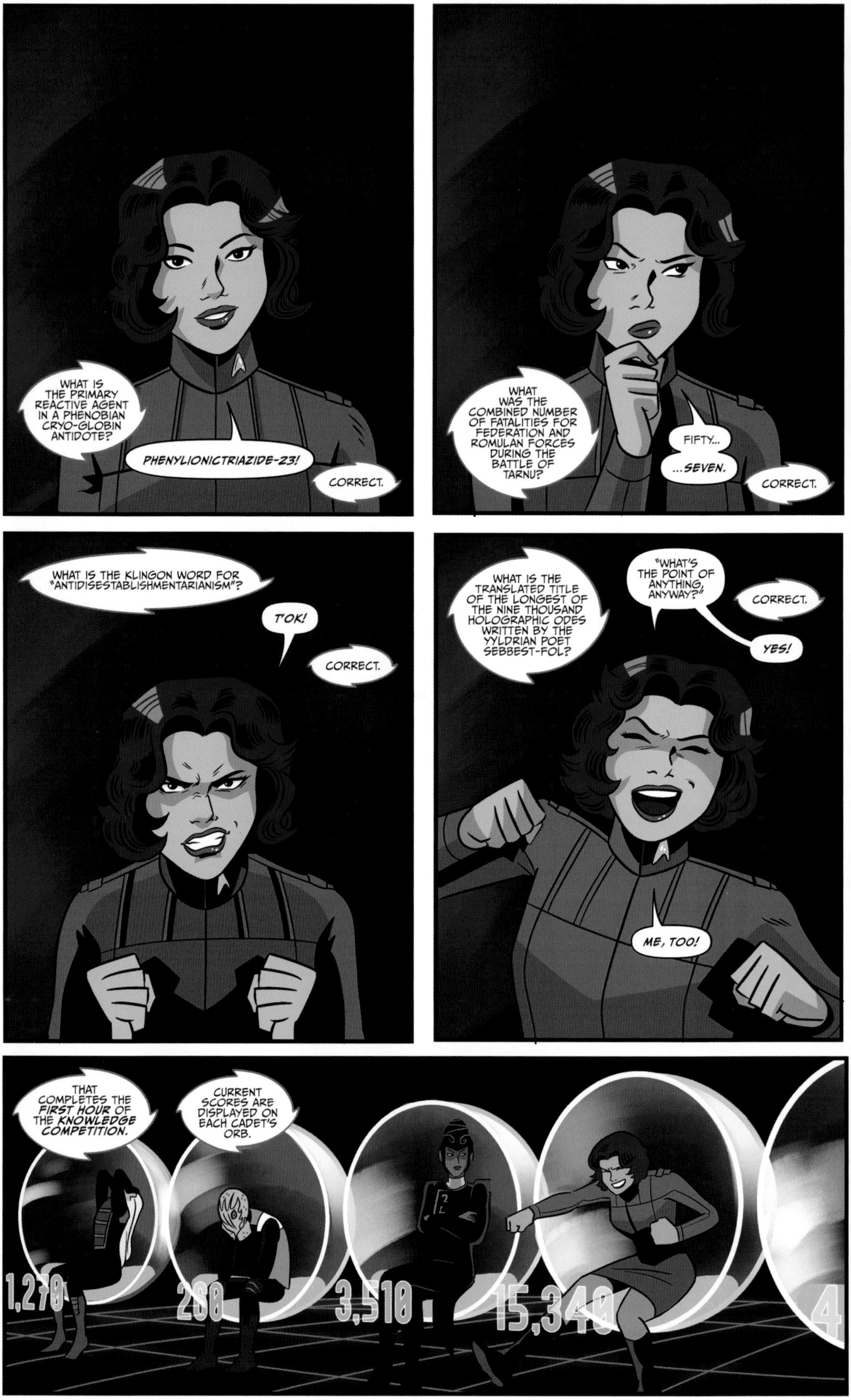
WHAT IS THE PRIMARY REACTIVE AGENT IN A PHENOBIAN CRYO-GLOBIN ANTIDOTE?
PHENYLIONICTRIAZIDE-23!
CORRECT.
WHAT WAS THE COMBINED NUMBER OF FATALITIES FOR FEDERATION AND ROMULAN FORCES DURING THE BATTLE OF TARNU?
FIFTY...
...SEVEN.
CORRECT.
WHAT IS THE KLINGON WORD FOR "ANTIDISESTABLISHMENTARIANISM"?
T'OK!
CORRECT.
WHAT IS THE TRANSLATED TITLE OF THE LONGEST OF THE NINE THOUSAND HOLOGRAPHIC ODES WRITTEN BY THE YYLDRIAN POET SEBBEST-FOL?
"WHAT'S THE POINT OF ANYTHING, ANYWAY?"
CORRECT.
YES!
ME, TOO!
THAT COMPLETES THE FIRST HOUR OF THE KNOWLEDGE COMPETITION.
CURRENT SCORES ARE DISPLAYED ON EACH CADET'S ORB.
1,270
260
3,510
15,340
4

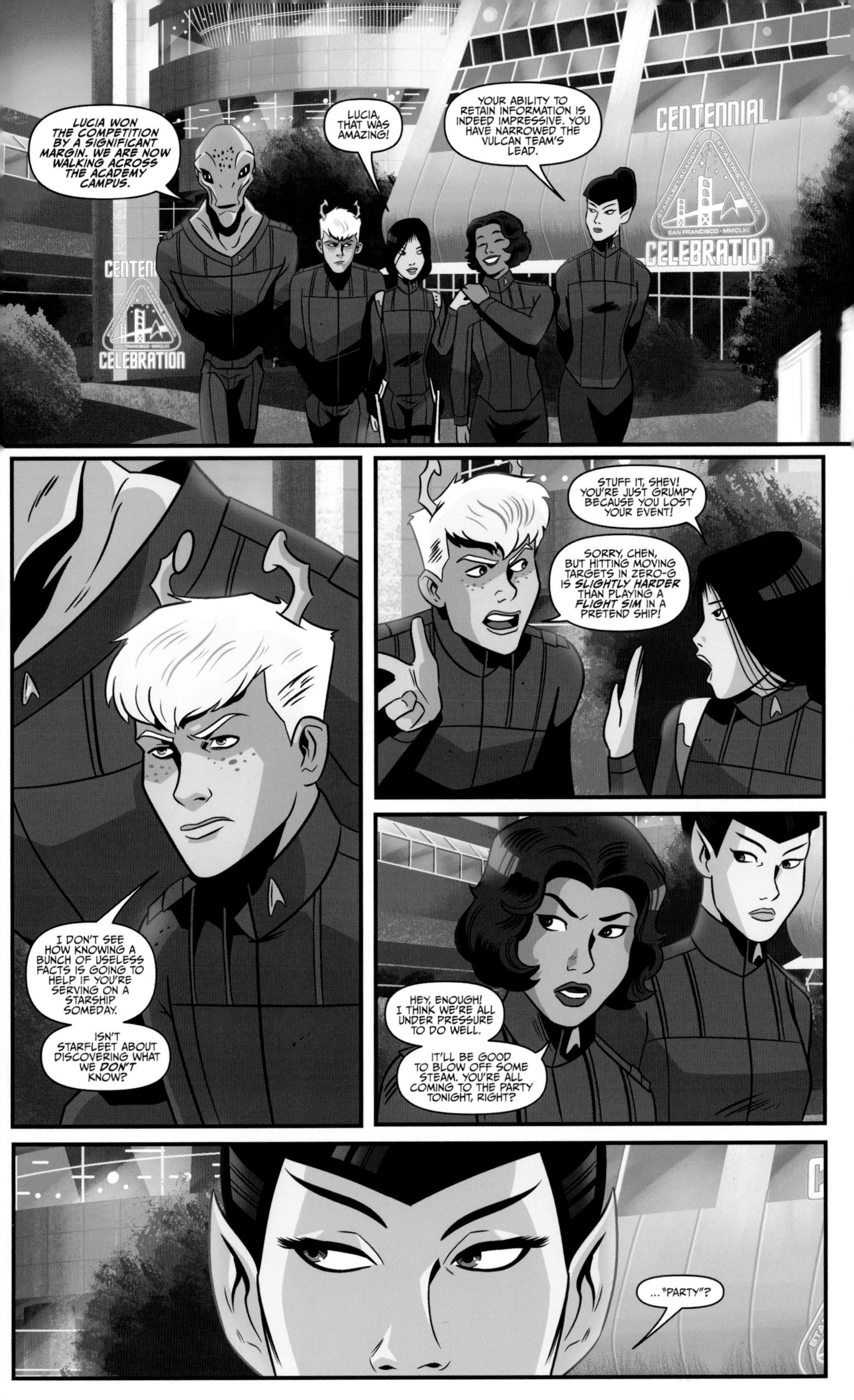
LUCIA WON THE COMPETITION BY A SIGNIFICANT MARGIN. WE ARE NOW WALKING ACROSS THE ACADEMY CAMPUS.
LUCIA, THAT WAS AMAZING!
YOUR ABILITY TO RETAIN INFORMATION IS INDEED IMPRESSIVE. YOU HAVE NARROWED THE VULCAN TEAM'S LEAD.
CENTENNIAL
STARFLEET ACADEMY
EX ASTRIS, SCIENTIA
SAN FRANCISCO · MMCLXI
CELEBRATION
CENTENNIAL
CELEBRATION
I DON'T SEE HOW KNOWING A BUNCH OF USELESS FACTS IS GOING TO HELP IF YOU'RE SERVING ON A STARSHIP SOMEDAY.
ISN'T STARFLEET ABOUT DISCOVERING WHAT WE *DON'T* KNOW?
STUFF IT, SHEV! YOU'RE JUST GRUMPY BECAUSE YOU LOST YOUR EVENT!
SORRY, CHEN, BUT HITTING MOVING TARGETS IN ZERO-G IS ***SLIGHTLY HARDER*** THAN PLAYING A ***FLIGHT SIM*** IN A PRETEND SHIP!
HEY, ENOUGH! I THINK WE'RE ALL UNDER PRESSURE TO DO WELL.
IT'LL BE GOOD TO BLOW OFF SOME STEAM. YOU'RE ALL COMING TO THE PARTY TONIGHT, RIGHT?
..."PARTY"?

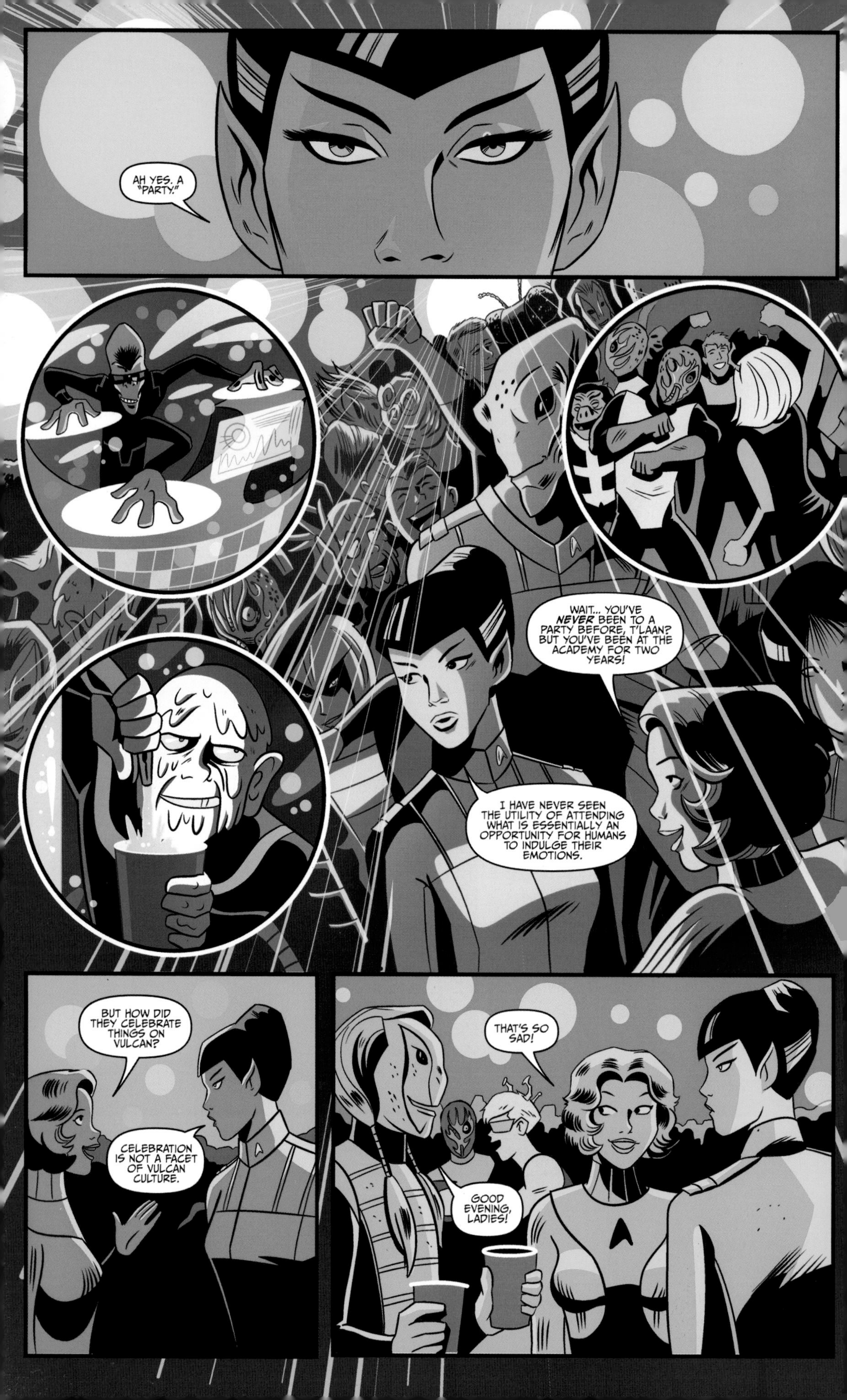
AH YES. A "PARTY."
WAIT... YOU'VE NEVER BEEN TO A PARTY BEFORE, T'LAAN? BUT YOU'VE BEEN AT THE ACADEMY FOR TWO YEARS!
I HAVE NEVER SEEN THE UTILITY OF ATTENDING WHAT IS ESSENTIALLY AN OPPORTUNITY FOR HUMANS TO INDULGE THEIR EMOTIONS.
BUT HOW DID THEY CELEBRATE THINGS ON VULCAN?
CELEBRATION IS NOT A FACET OF VULCAN CULTURE.
THAT'S SO SAD!
GOOD EVENING, LADIES!

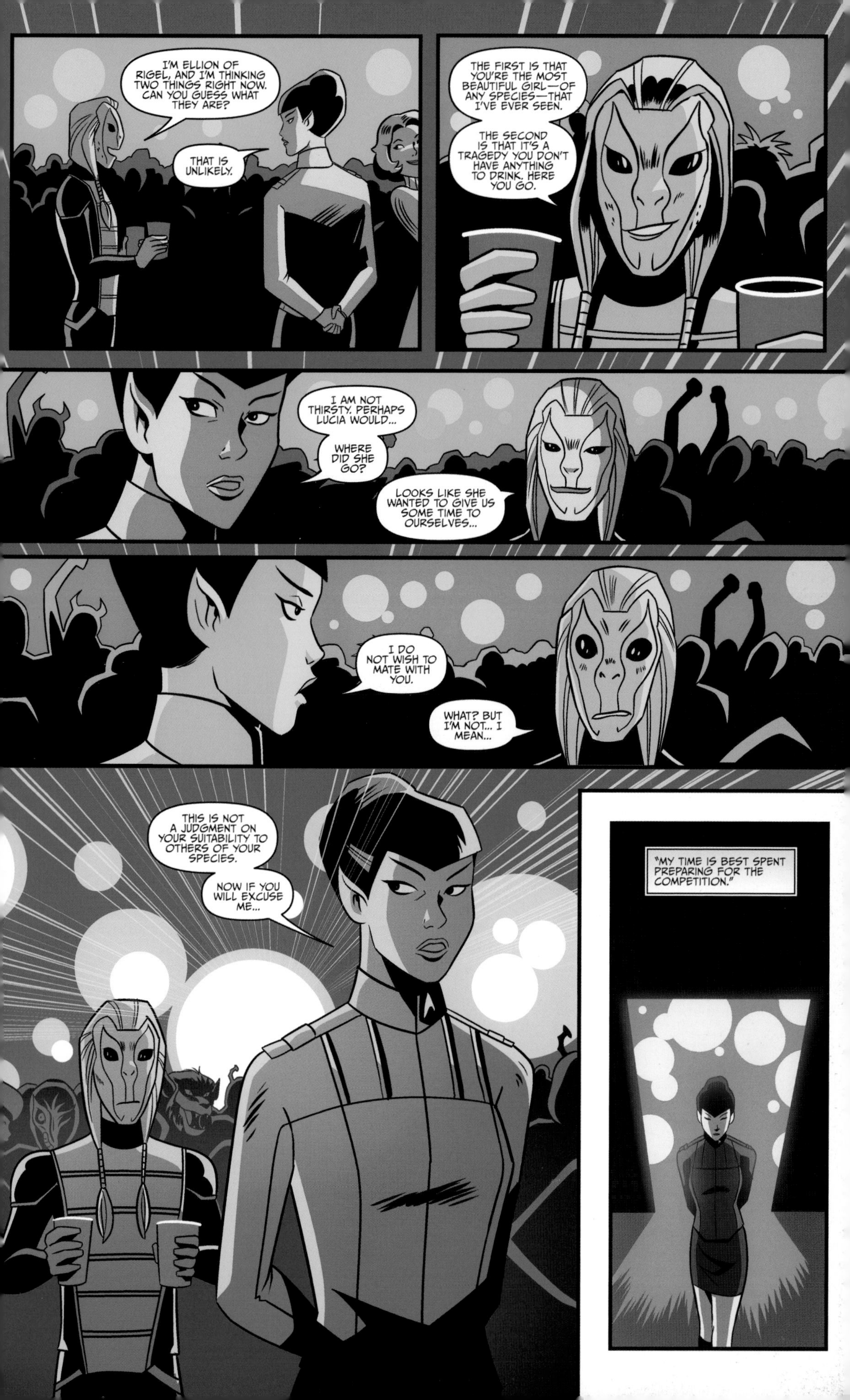
I'M ELLION OF RIGEL, AND I'M THINKING TWO THINGS RIGHT NOW. CAN YOU GUESS WHAT THEY ARE?
THAT IS UNLIKELY.
THE FIRST IS THAT YOU'RE THE MOST BEAUTIFUL GIRL—OF ANY SPECIES—THAT I'VE EVER SEEN.
THE SECOND IS THAT IT'S A TRAGEDY YOU DON'T HAVE ANYTHING TO DRINK. HERE YOU GO.
I AM NOT THIRSTY. PERHAPS LUCIA WOULD...
WHERE DID SHE GO?
LOOKS LIKE SHE WANTED TO GIVE US SOME TIME TO OURSELVES...
I DO NOT WISH TO MATE WITH YOU.
WHAT? BUT I'M NOT... I MEAN...
THIS IS NOT A JUDGMENT ON YOUR SUITABILITY TO OTHERS OF YOUR SPECIES.
NOW IF YOU WILL EXCUSE ME...
"MY TIME IS BEST SPENT PREPARING FOR THE COMPETITION."

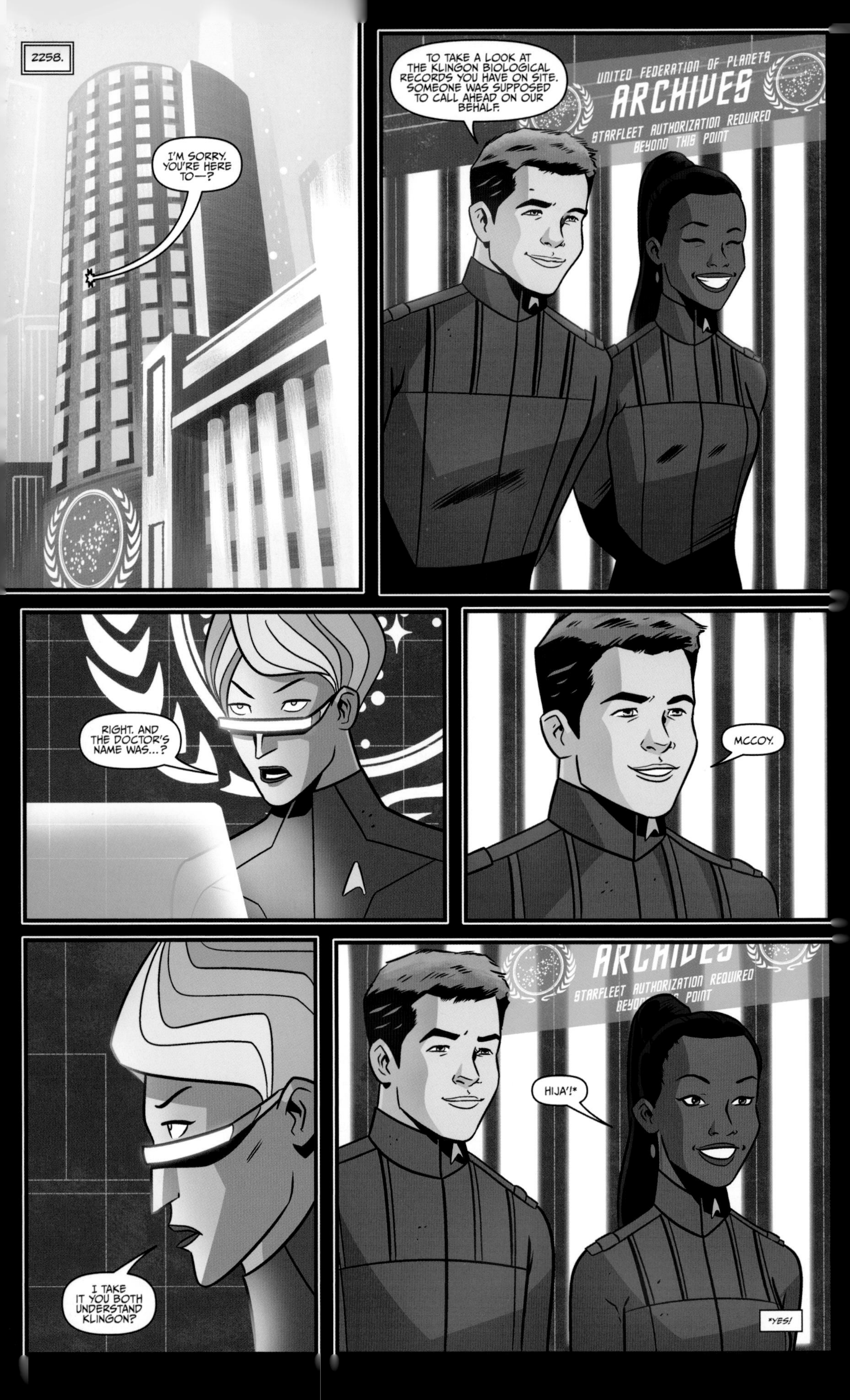
2258.
I'M SORRY. YOU'RE HERE TO—?
TO TAKE A LOOK AT THE KLINGON BIOLOGICAL RECORDS YOU HAVE ON SITE. SOMEONE WAS SUPPOSED TO CALL AHEAD ON OUR BEHALF.
UNITED FEDERATION OF PLANETS
ARCHIVES
STARFLEET AUTHORIZATION REQUIRED BEYOND THIS POINT
RIGHT. AND THE DOCTOR'S NAME WAS...?
MCCOY.
I TAKE IT YOU BOTH UNDERSTAND KLINGON?
ARCHIVES
STARFLEET AUTHORIZATION REQUIRED
HIJA'!*
*YES!

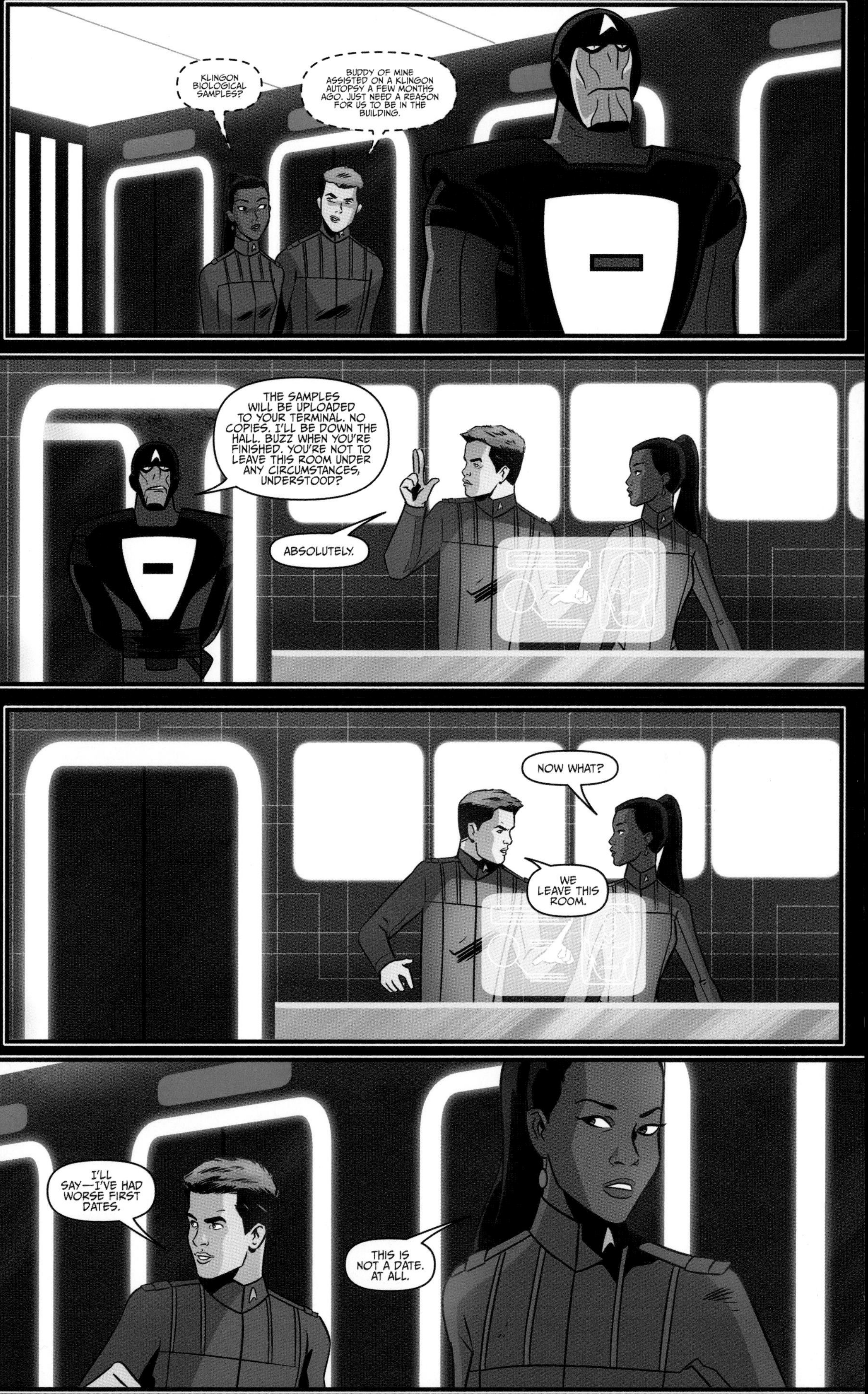
KLINGON BIOLOGICAL SAMPLES?
BUDDY OF MINE ASSISTED ON A KLINGON AUTOPSY A FEW MONTHS AGO. JUST NEED A REASON FOR US TO BE IN THE BUILDING.
THE SAMPLES WILL BE UPLOADED TO YOUR TERMINAL. NO COPIES. I'LL BE DOWN THE HALL. BUZZ WHEN YOU'RE FINISHED. YOU'RE NOT TO LEAVE THIS ROOM UNDER ANY CIRCUMSTANCES, UNDERSTOOD?
ABSOLUTELY.
NOW WHAT?
WE LEAVE THIS ROOM.
I'LL SAY—I'VE HAD WORSE FIRST DATES.
THIS IS NOT A DATE. AT ALL.

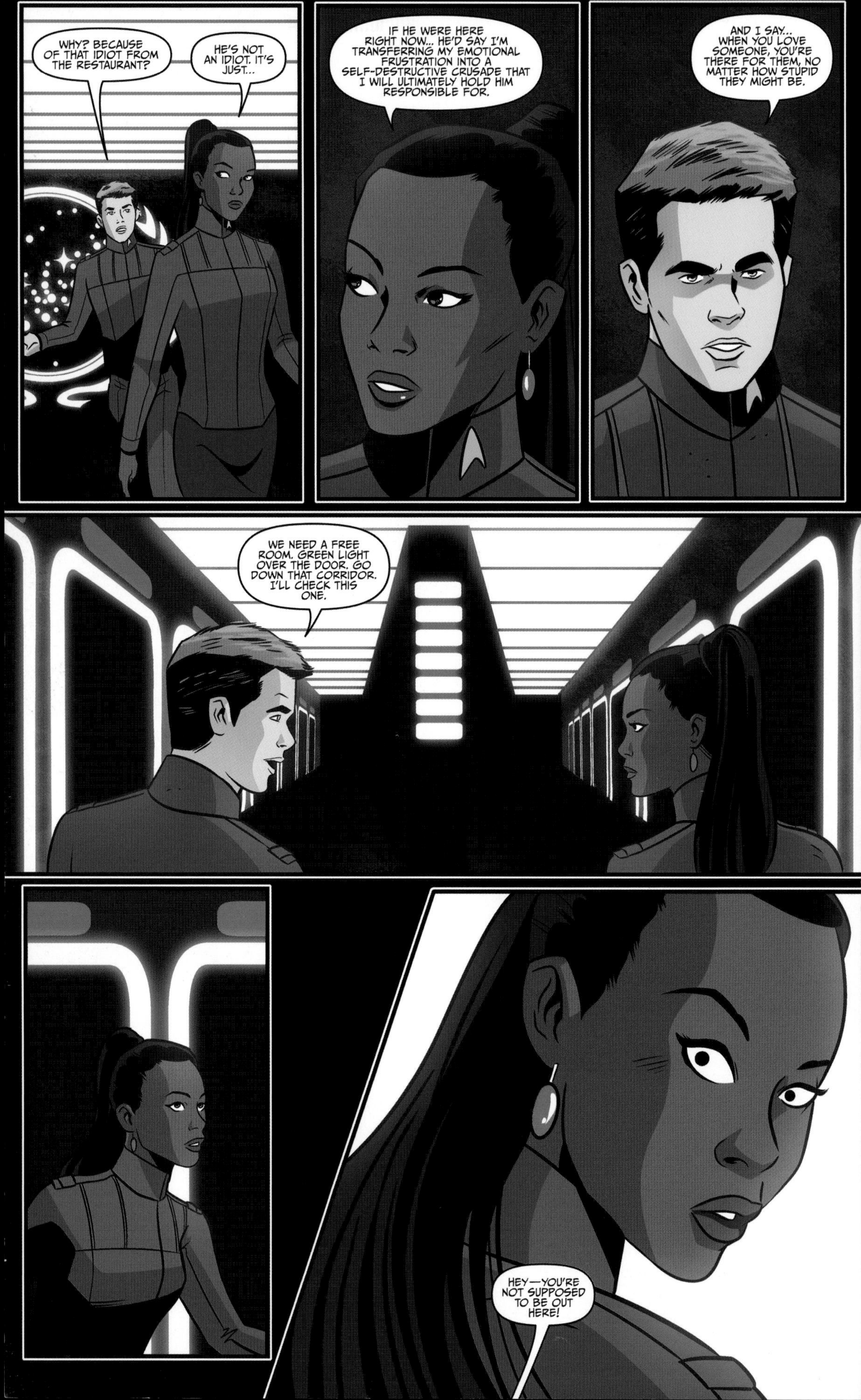
WHY? BECAUSE OF THAT IDIOT FROM THE RESTAURANT?
HE'S NOT AN IDIOT. IT'S JUST...
IF HE WERE HERE RIGHT NOW... HE'D SAY I'M TRANSFERRING MY EMOTIONAL FRUSTRATION INTO A SELF-DESTRUCTIVE CRUSADE THAT I WILL ULTIMATELY HOLD HIM RESPONSIBLE FOR.
AND I SAY... WHEN YOU LOVE SOMEONE, YOU'RE THERE FOR THEM, NO MATTER HOW STUPID THEY MIGHT BE.
WE NEED A FREE ROOM. GREEN LIGHT OVER THE DOOR. GO DOWN THAT CORRIDOR. I'LL CHECK THIS ONE.
HEY—YOU'RE NOT SUPPOSED TO BE OUT HERE!

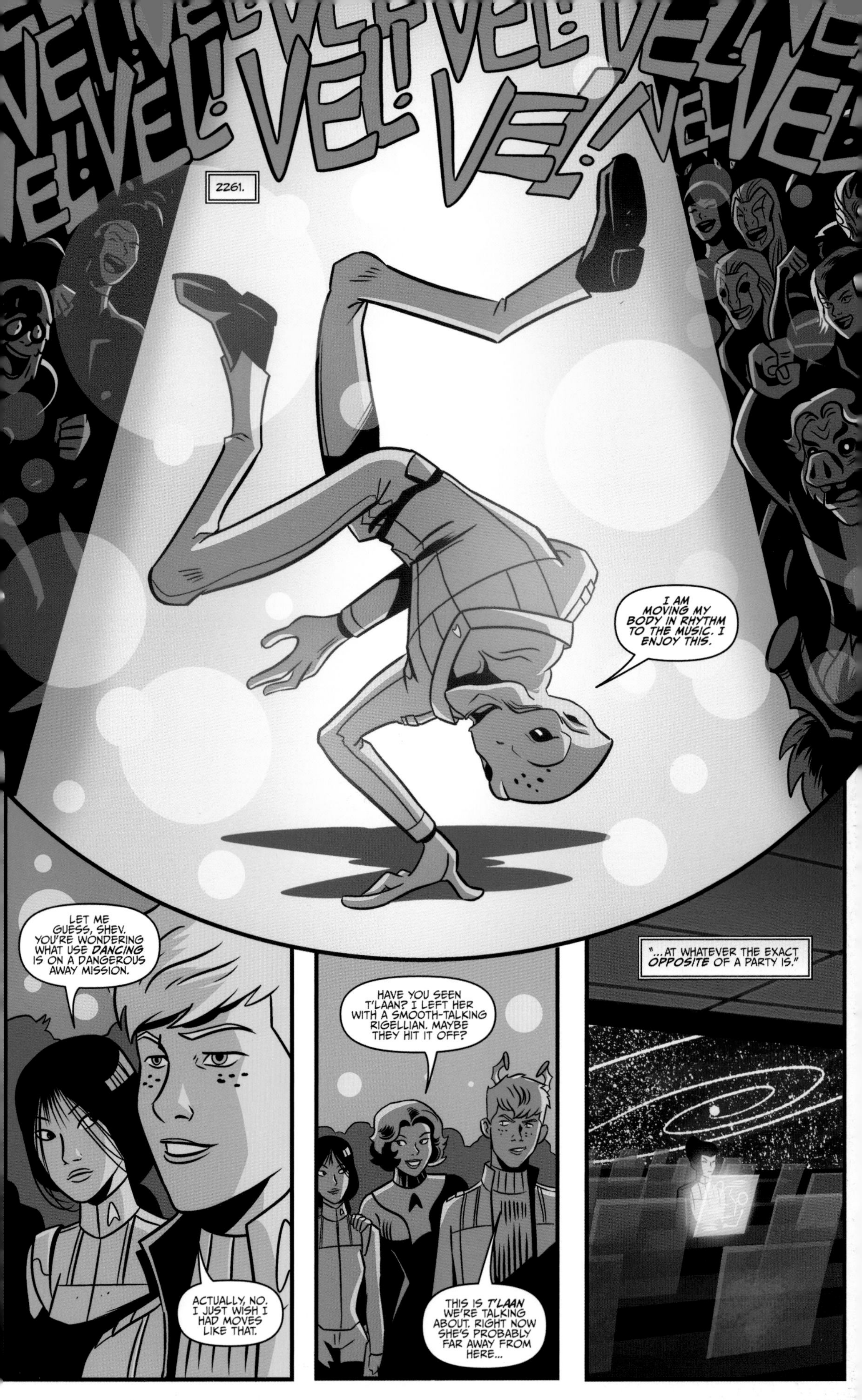
VEL! VEL! VEL! VEL!
VEL!
2261.
I AM MOVING MY BODY IN RHYTHM TO THE MUSIC. I ENJOY THIS.
LET ME GUESS, SHEV. YOU'RE WONDERING WHAT USE DANCING IS ON A DANGEROUS AWAY MISSION.
ACTUALLY, NO. I JUST WISH I HAD MOVES LIKE THAT.
HAVE YOU SEEN T'LAAN? I LEFT HER WITH A SMOOTH-TALKING RIGELLIAN. MAYBE THEY HIT IT OFF?
THIS IS T'LAAN WE'RE TALKING ABOUT. RIGHT NOW SHE'S PROBABLY FAR AWAY FROM HERE...
"...AT WHATEVER THE EXACT OPPOSITE OF A PARTY IS."

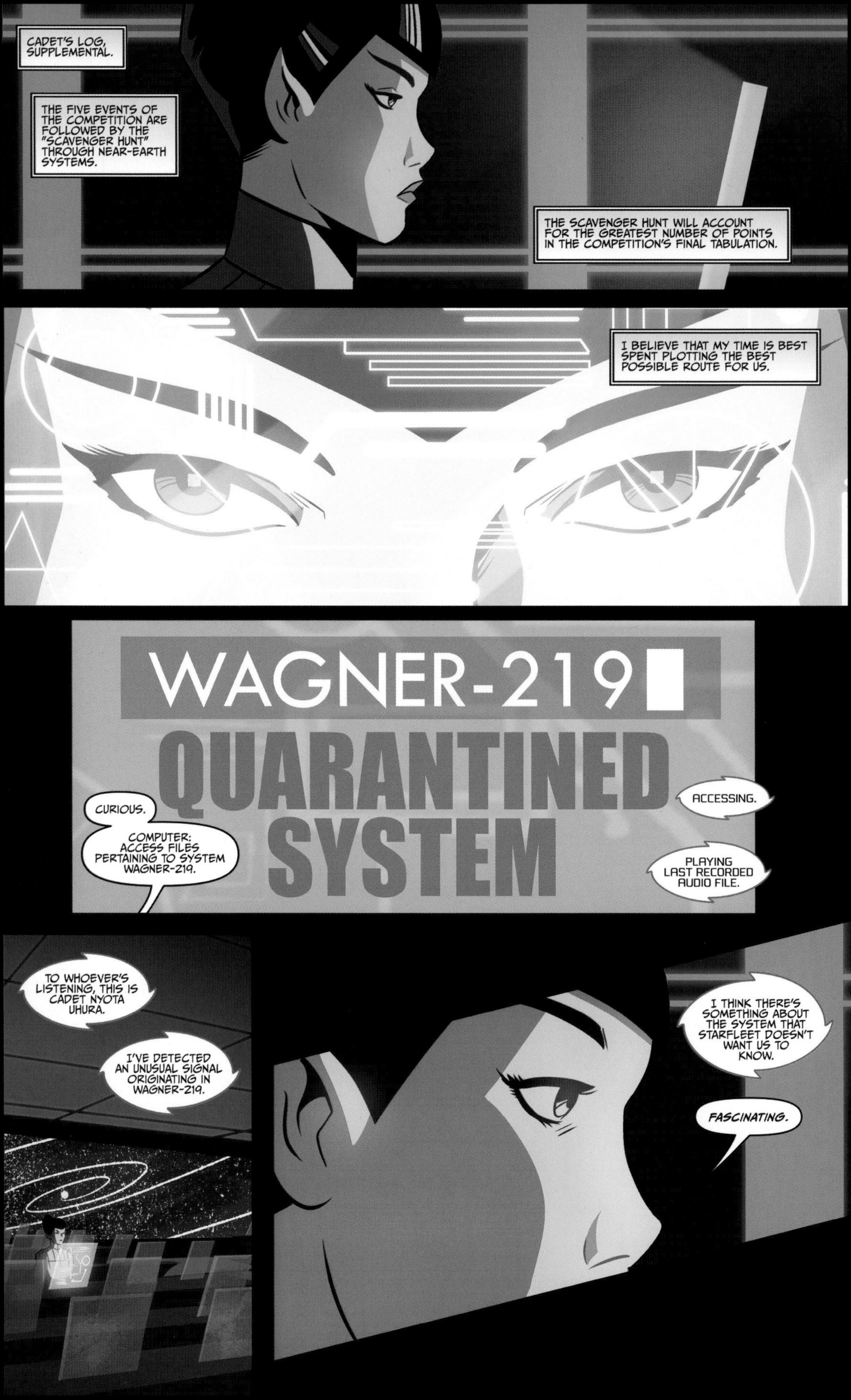

CADET'S LOG, SUPPLEMENTAL.
THE FIVE EVENTS OF THE COMPETITION ARE FOLLOWED BY THE "SCAVENGER HUNT" THROUGH NEAR-EARTH SYSTEMS.
THE SCAVENGER HUNT WILL ACCOUNT FOR THE GREATEST NUMBER OF POINTS IN THE COMPETITION'S FINAL TABULATION.
I BELIEVE THAT MY TIME IS BEST SPENT PLOTTING THE BEST POSSIBLE ROUTE FOR US.
WAGNER-219
QUARANTINED SYSTEM
CURIOUS.
COMPUTER: ACCESS FILES PERTAINING TO SYSTEM WAGNER-219.
ACCESSING.
PLAYING LAST RECORDED AUDIO FILE.
TO WHOEVER'S LISTENING, THIS IS CADET NYOTA UHURA.
I'VE DETECTED AN UNUSUAL SIGNAL ORIGINATING IN WAGNER-219.
I THINK THERE'S SOMETHING ABOUT THE SYSTEM THAT STARFLEET DOESN'T WANT US TO KNOW.
FASCINATING.

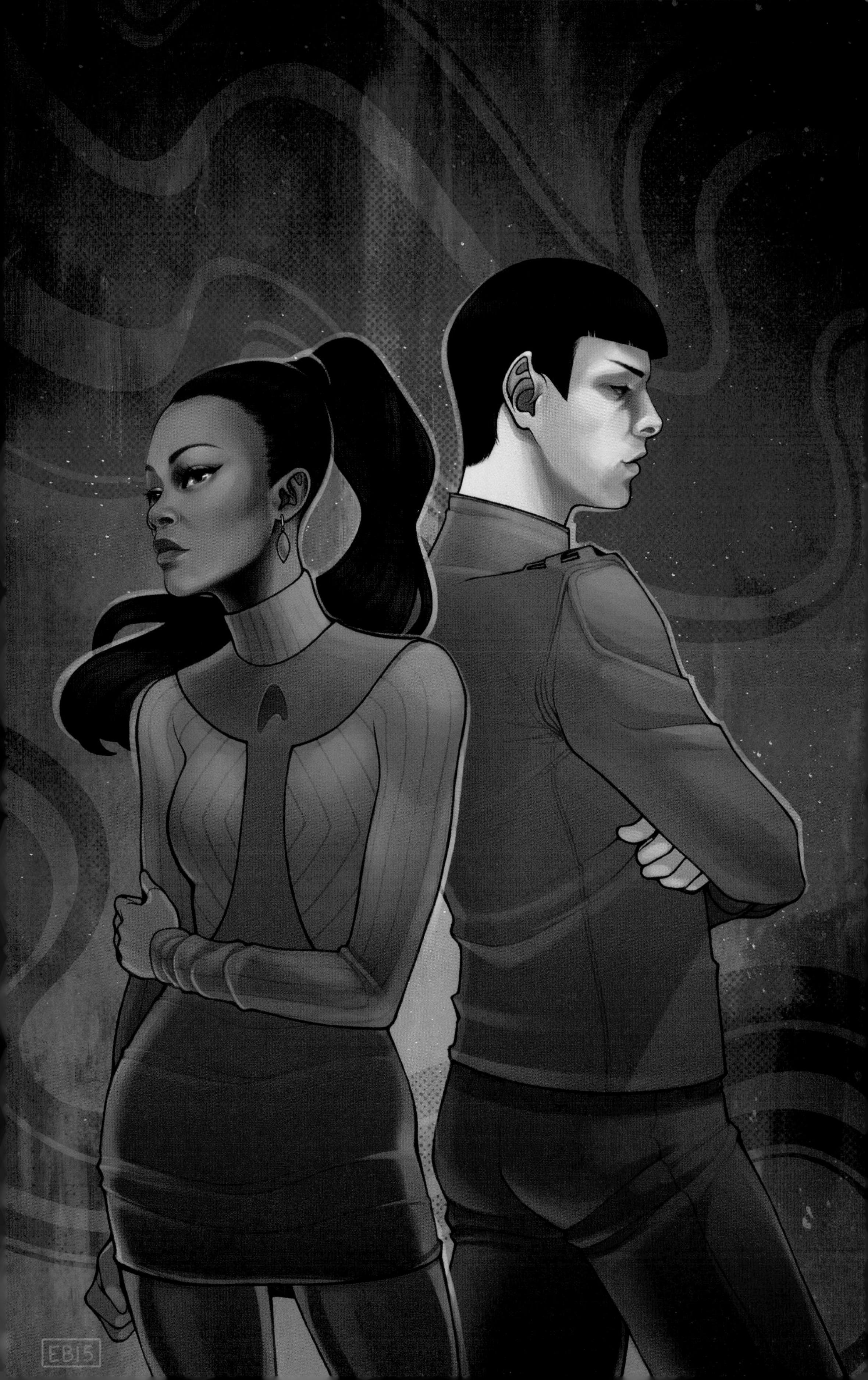
EB15

ART BY **DEREK CHARM**

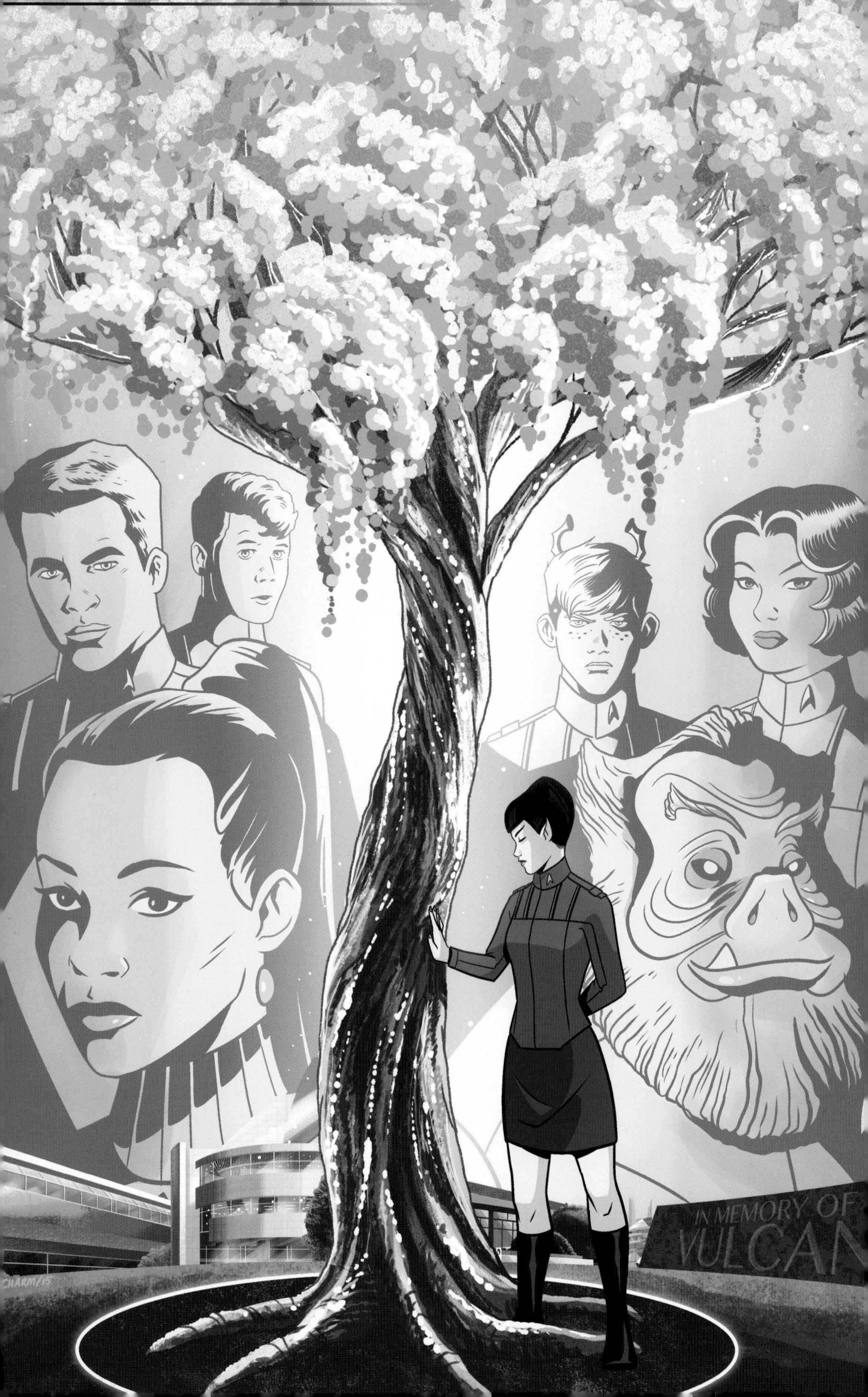

CHARM/15
IN MEMORY OF

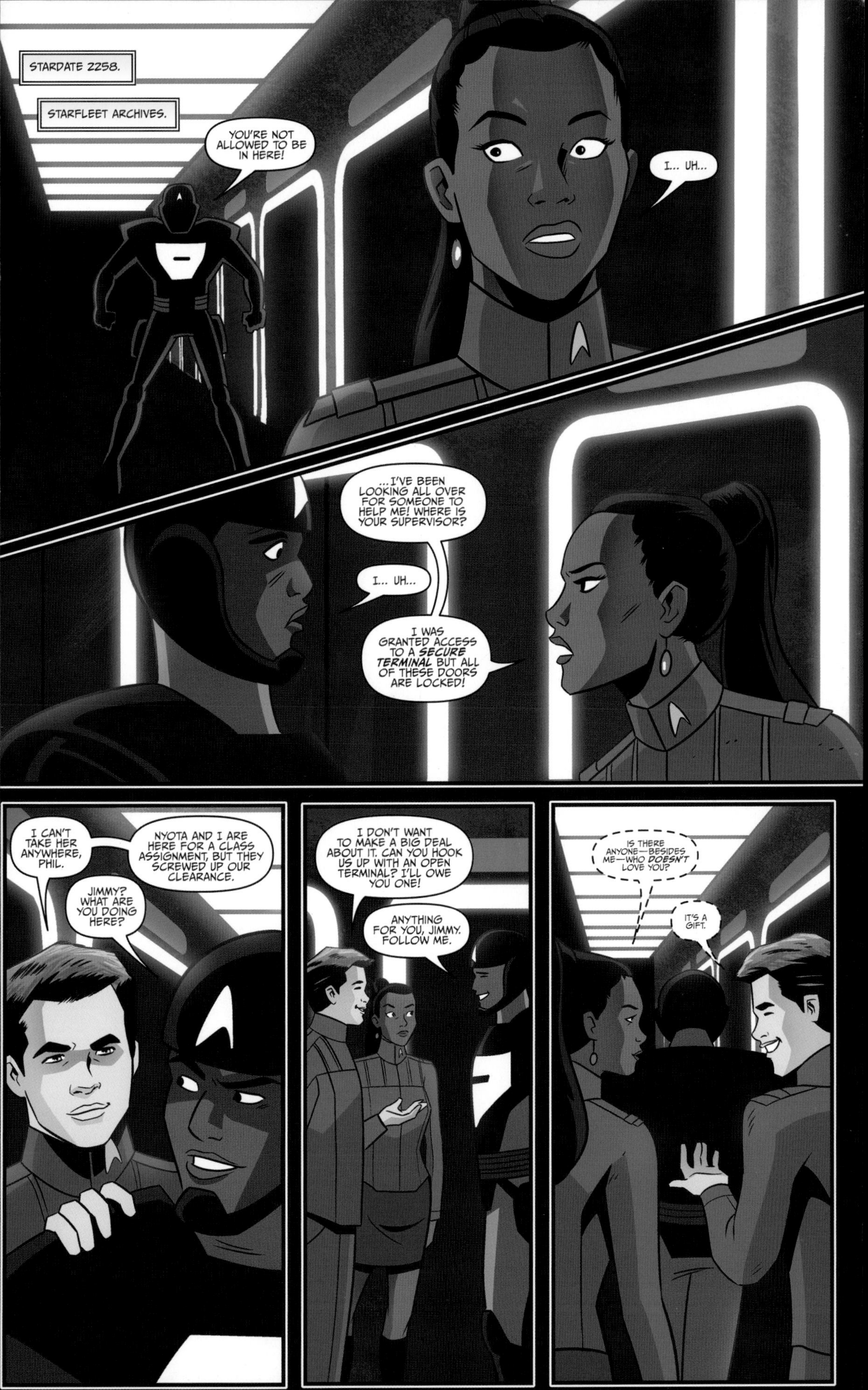
STARDATE 2258.
STARFLEET ARCHIVES.
YOU'RE NOT ALLOWED TO BE IN HERE!
I... UH...
...I'VE BEEN LOOKING ALL OVER FOR SOMEONE TO HELP ME! WHERE IS YOUR SUPERVISOR?
I... UH...
I WAS GRANTED ACCESS TO A SECURE TERMINAL BUT ALL OF THESE DOORS ARE LOCKED!
I CAN'T TAKE HER ANYWHERE, PHIL.
NYOTA AND I ARE HERE FOR A CLASS ASSIGNMENT, BUT THEY SCREWED UP OUR CLEARANCE.
JIMMY? WHAT ARE YOU DOING HERE?
I DON'T WANT TO MAKE A BIG DEAL ABOUT IT. CAN YOU HOOK US UP WITH AN OPEN TERMINAL? I'LL OWE YOU ONE!
ANYTHING FOR YOU, JIMMY. FOLLOW ME.
IS THERE ANYONE—BESIDES ME—WHO DOESN'T LOVE YOU?
IT'S A GIFT.

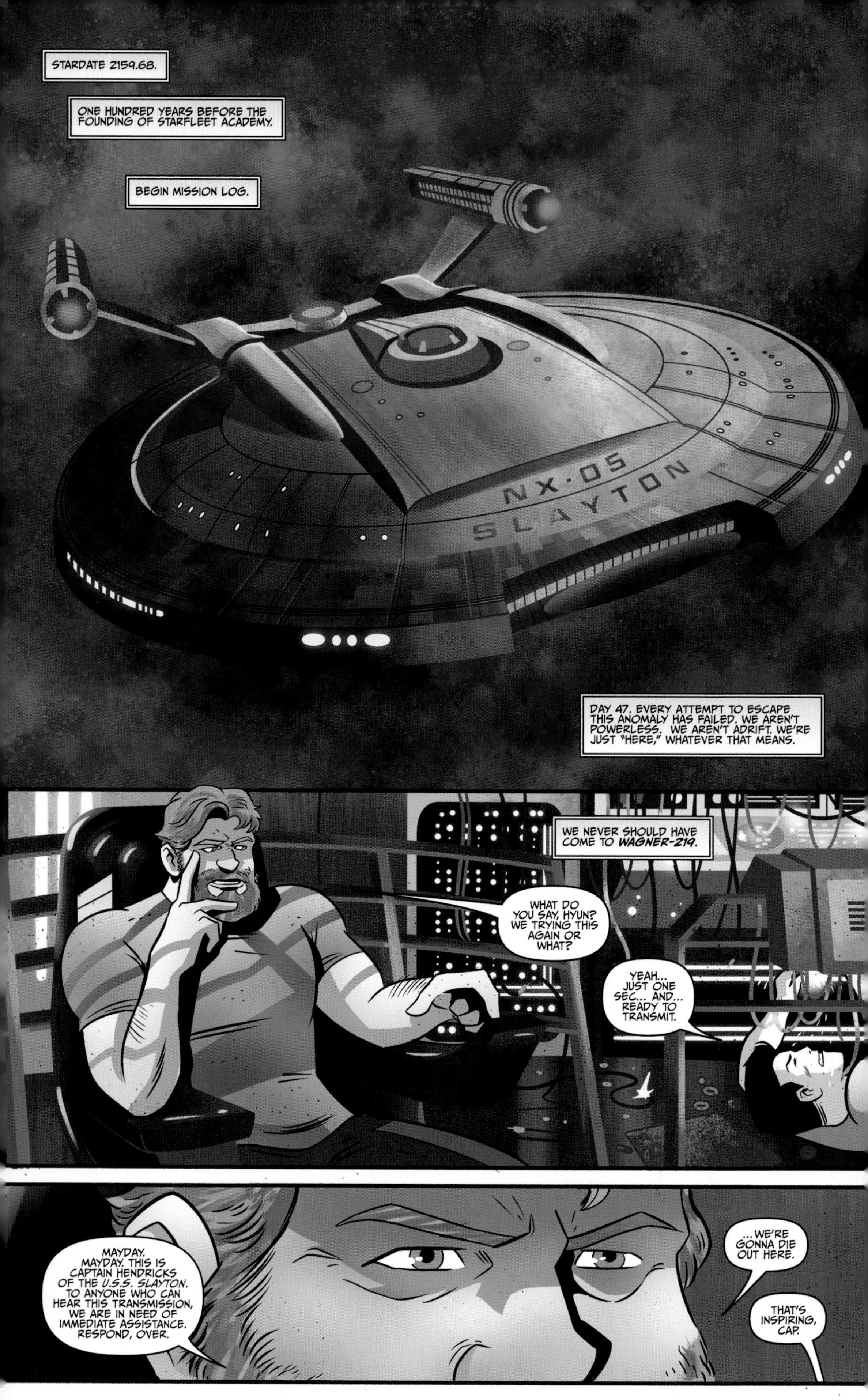
STARDATE 2159.68.
ONE HUNDRED YEARS BEFORE THE FOUNDING OF STARFLEET ACADEMY.
BEGIN MISSION LOG.
NX-05 SLAYTON
DAY 47. EVERY ATTEMPT TO ESCAPE THIS ANOMALY HAS FAILED. WE AREN'T POWERLESS. WE AREN'T ADRIFT. WE'RE JUST "HERE," WHATEVER THAT MEANS.
WE NEVER SHOULD HAVE COME TO WAGNER-219.
WHAT DO YOU SAY, HYUN? WE TRYING THIS AGAIN OR WHAT?
YEAH... JUST ONE SEC... AND... READY TO TRANSMIT.
MAYDAY. MAYDAY. THIS IS CAPTAIN HENDRICKS OF THE U.S.S. SLAYTON. TO ANYONE WHO CAN HEAR THIS TRANSMISSION, WE ARE IN NEED OF IMMEDIATE ASSISTANCE. RESPOND, OVER.
...WE'RE GONNA DIE OUT HERE.
THAT'S INSPIRING, CAP.

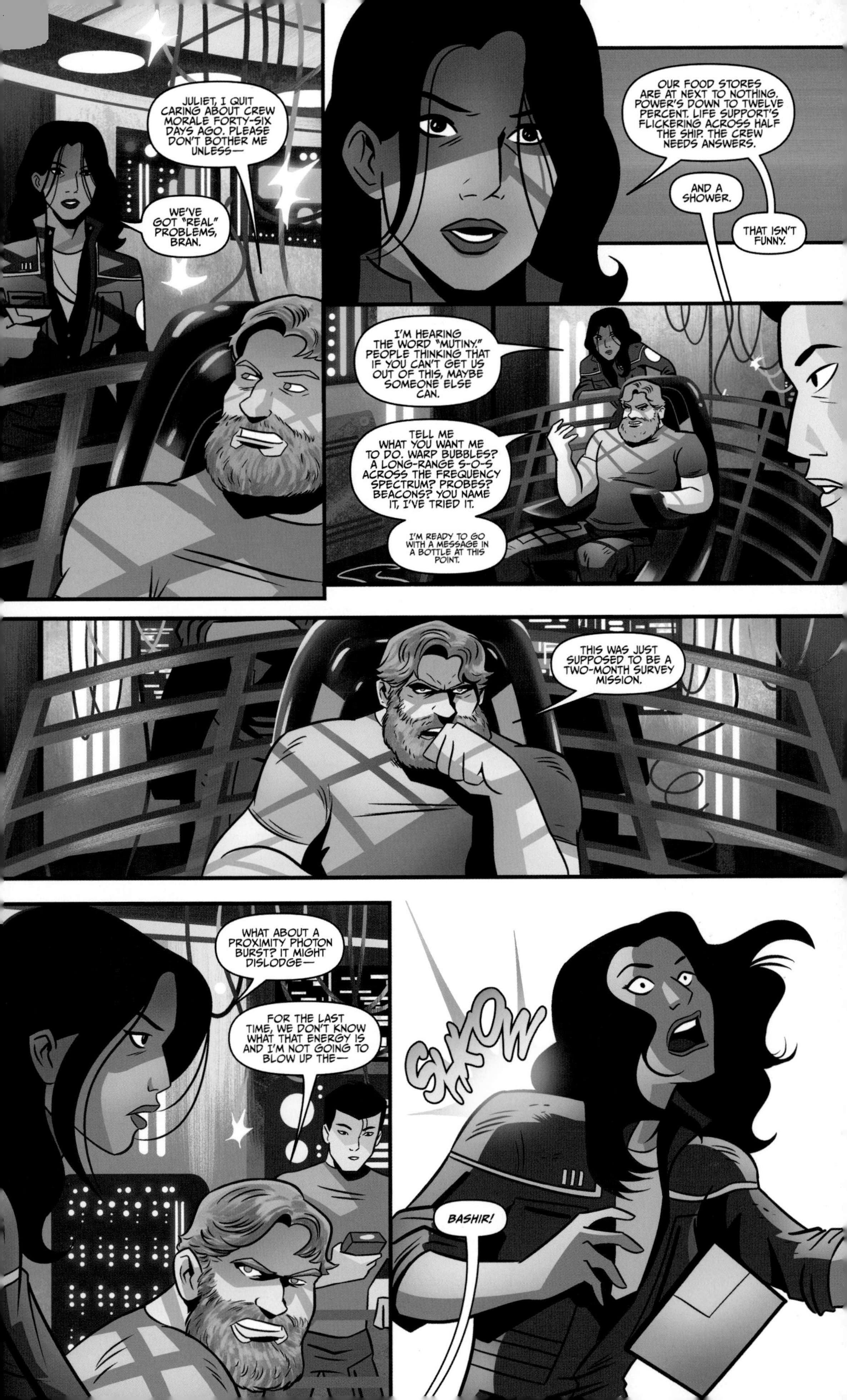
JULIET, I QUIT CARING ABOUT CREW MORALE FORTY-SIX DAYS AGO. PLEASE DON'T BOTHER ME UNLESS—
WE'VE GOT "REAL" PROBLEMS, BRAN.
OUR FOOD STORES ARE AT NEXT TO NOTHING. POWER'S DOWN TO TWELVE PERCENT. LIFE SUPPORT'S FLICKERING ACROSS HALF THE SHIP. THE CREW NEEDS ANSWERS.
AND A SHOWER.
THAT ISN'T FUNNY.
I'M HEARING THE WORD "MUTINY." PEOPLE THINKING THAT IF YOU CAN'T GET US OUT OF THIS, MAYBE SOMEONE ELSE CAN.
TELL ME WHAT YOU WANT ME TO DO. WARP BUBBLES? A LONG-RANGE S-O-S ACROSS THE FREQUENCY SPECTRUM? PROBES? BEACONS? YOU NAME IT, I'VE TRIED IT.
I'M READY TO GO WITH A MESSAGE IN A BOTTLE AT THIS POINT.
THIS WAS JUST SUPPOSED TO BE A TWO-MONTH SURVEY MISSION.
WHAT ABOUT A PROXIMITY PHOTON BURST? IT MIGHT DISLODGE—
FOR THE LAST TIME, WE DON'T KNOW WHAT THAT ENERGY IS AND I'M NOT GOING TO BLOW UP THE—
SKKOW
BASHIR!

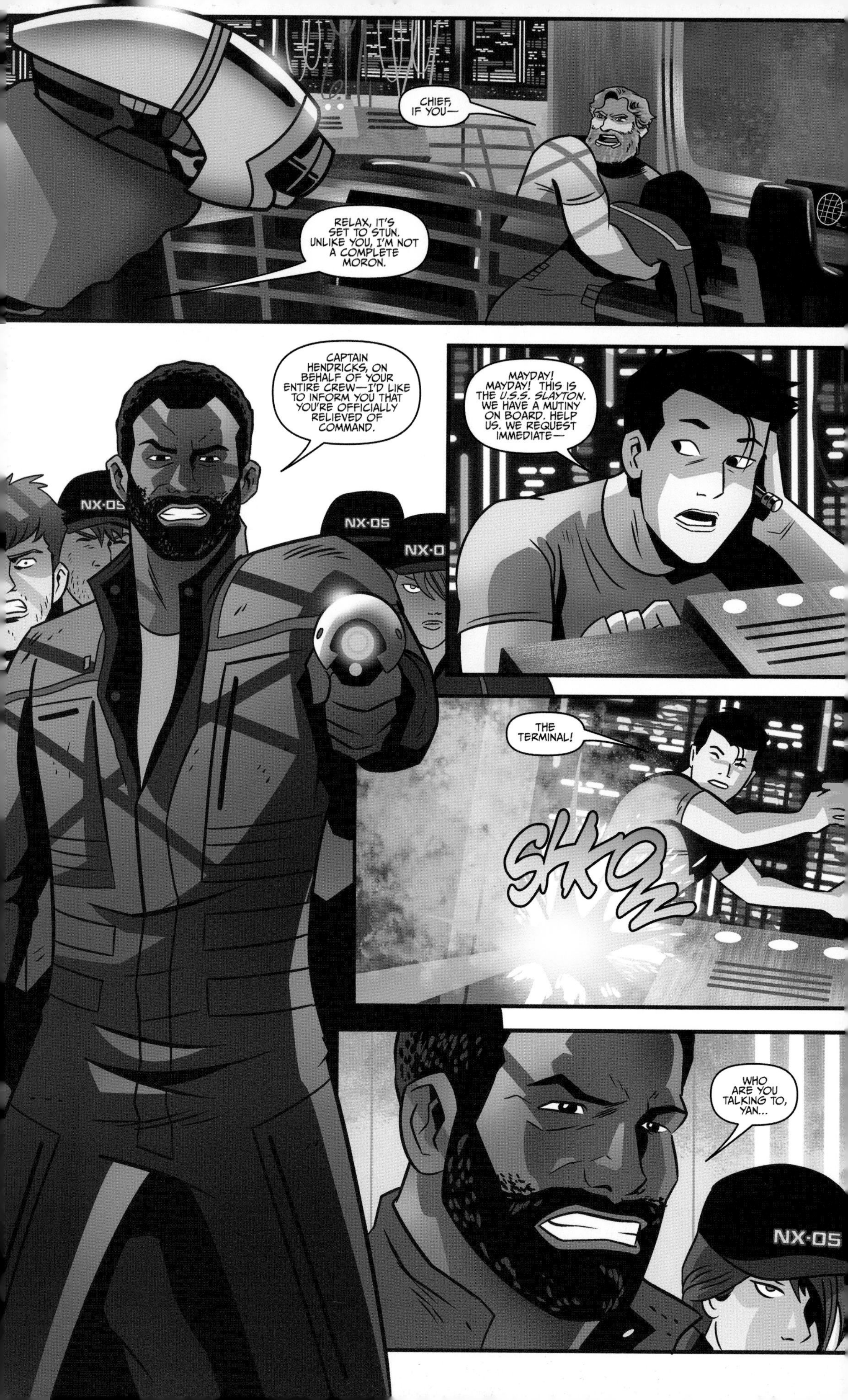
CHIEF, IF YOU—
RELAX, IT'S SET TO STUN. UNLIKE YOU, I'M NOT A COMPLETE MORON.
CAPTAIN HENDRICKS, ON BEHALF OF YOUR ENTIRE CREW—I'D LIKE TO INFORM YOU THAT YOU'RE OFFICIALLY RELIEVED OF COMMAND.
NX-05
NX-05
MAYDAY! MAYDAY! THIS IS THE U.S.S. SLAYTON. WE HAVE A MUTINY ON BOARD. HELP US. WE REQUEST IMMEDIATE—
THE TERMINAL!
SHKOW
WHO ARE YOU TALKING TO, YAN...
NX-05

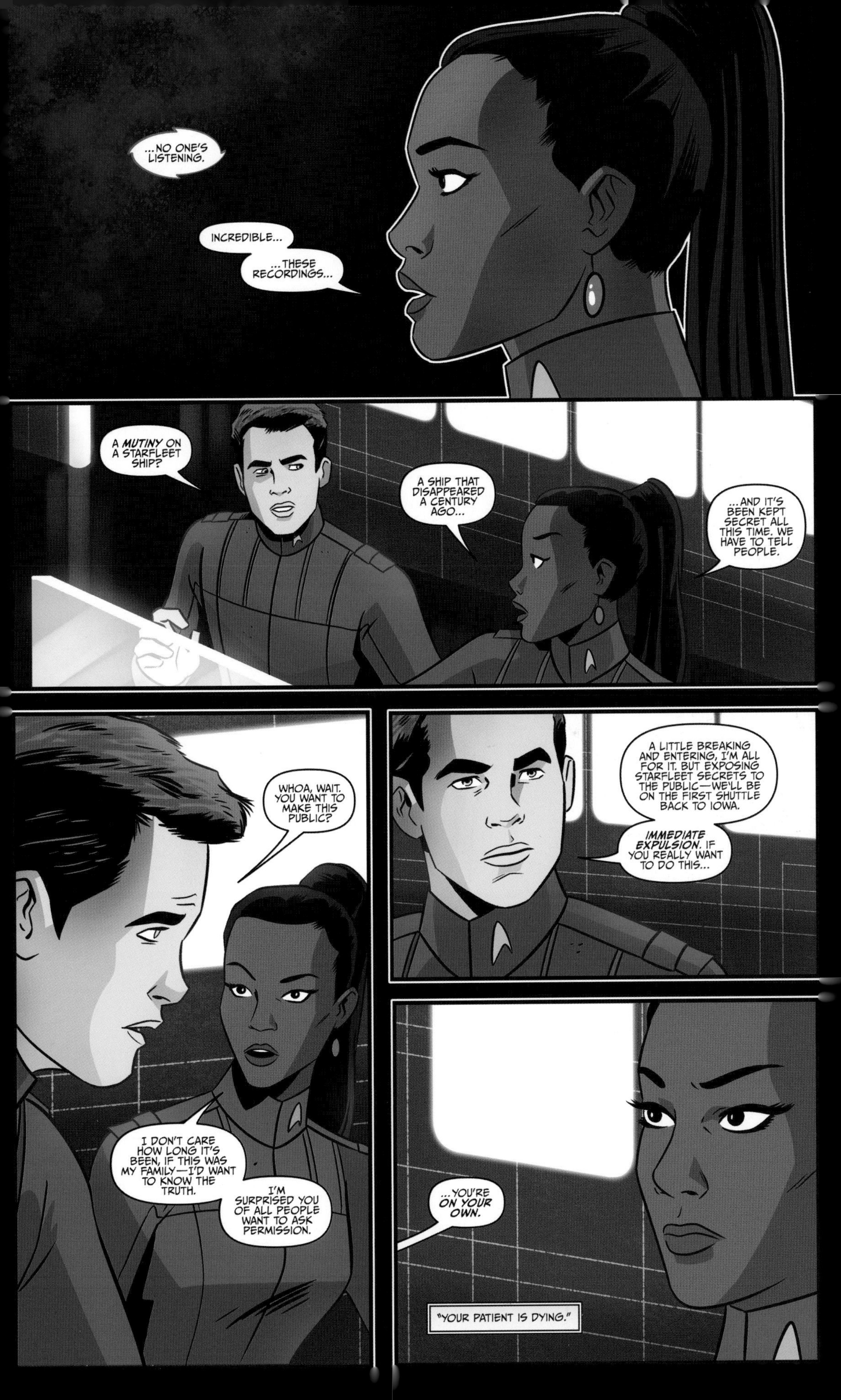

...NO ONE'S LISTENING.
INCREDIBLE...
...THESE RECORDINGS...
A MUTINY ON A STARFLEET SHIP?
A SHIP THAT DISAPPEARED A CENTURY AGO...
...AND IT'S BEEN KEPT SECRET ALL THIS TIME. WE HAVE TO TELL PEOPLE.
WHOA, WAIT. YOU WANT TO MAKE THIS PUBLIC?
I DON'T CARE HOW LONG IT'S BEEN, IF THIS WAS MY FAMILY—I'D WANT TO KNOW THE TRUTH.
I'M SURPRISED YOU OF ALL PEOPLE WANT TO ASK PERMISSION.
A LITTLE BREAKING AND ENTERING, I'M ALL FOR IT. BUT EXPOSING STARFLEET SECRETS TO THE PUBLIC—WE'LL BE ON THE FIRST SHUTTLE BACK TO IOWA.
IMMEDIATE EXPULSION. IF YOU REALLY WANT TO DO THIS...
...YOU'RE ON YOUR OWN.
"YOUR PATIENT IS DYING."

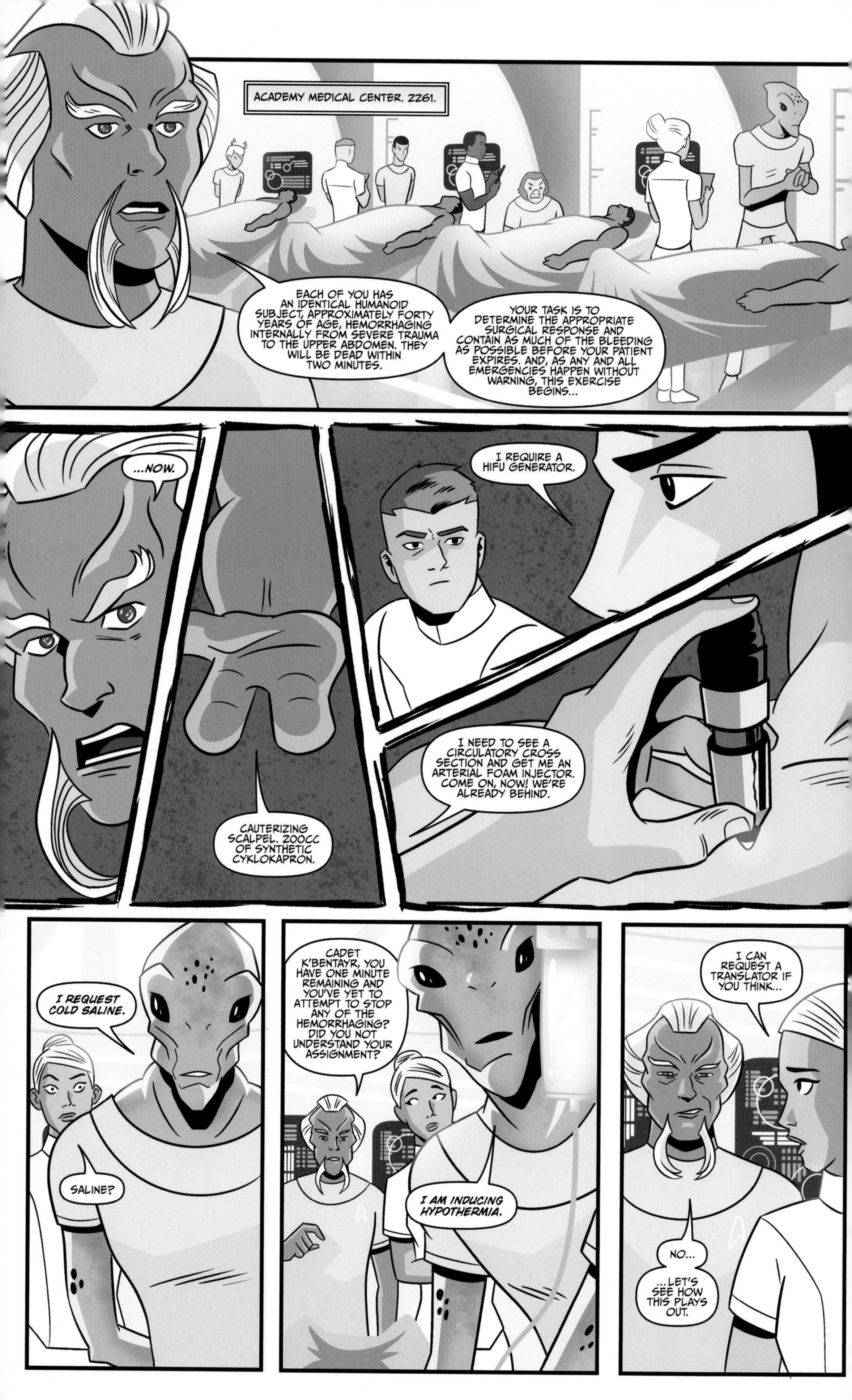
ACADEMY MEDICAL CENTER. 2261.
EACH OF YOU HAS AN IDENTICAL HUMANOID SUBJECT, APPROXIMATELY FORTY YEARS OF AGE, HEMORRHAGING INTERNALLY FROM SEVERE TRAUMA TO THE UPPER ABDOMEN. THEY WILL BE DEAD WITHIN TWO MINUTES.
YOUR TASK IS TO DETERMINE THE APPROPRIATE SURGICAL RESPONSE AND CONTAIN AS MUCH OF THE BLEEDING AS POSSIBLE BEFORE YOUR PATIENT EXPIRES. AND, AS ANY AND ALL EMERGENCIES HAPPEN WITHOUT WARNING, THIS EXERCISE BEGINS...
...NOW.
CAUTERIZING SCALPEL. 200CC OF SYNTHETIC CYKLOKAPRON.
I REQUIRE A HIFU GENERATOR.
I NEED TO SEE A CIRCULATORY CROSS SECTION AND GET ME AN ARTERIAL FOAM INJECTOR. COME ON, NOW! WE'RE ALREADY BEHIND.
I REQUEST COLD SALINE.
SALINE?
CADET K'BENTAYR, YOU HAVE ONE MINUTE REMAINING AND YOU'VE YET TO ATTEMPT TO STOP ANY OF THE HEMORRHAGING? DID YOU NOT UNDERSTAND YOUR ASSIGNMENT?
I AM INDUCING HYPOTHERMIA.
I CAN REQUEST A TRANSLATOR IF YOU THINK...
NO...
...LET'S SEE HOW THIS PLAYS OUT.

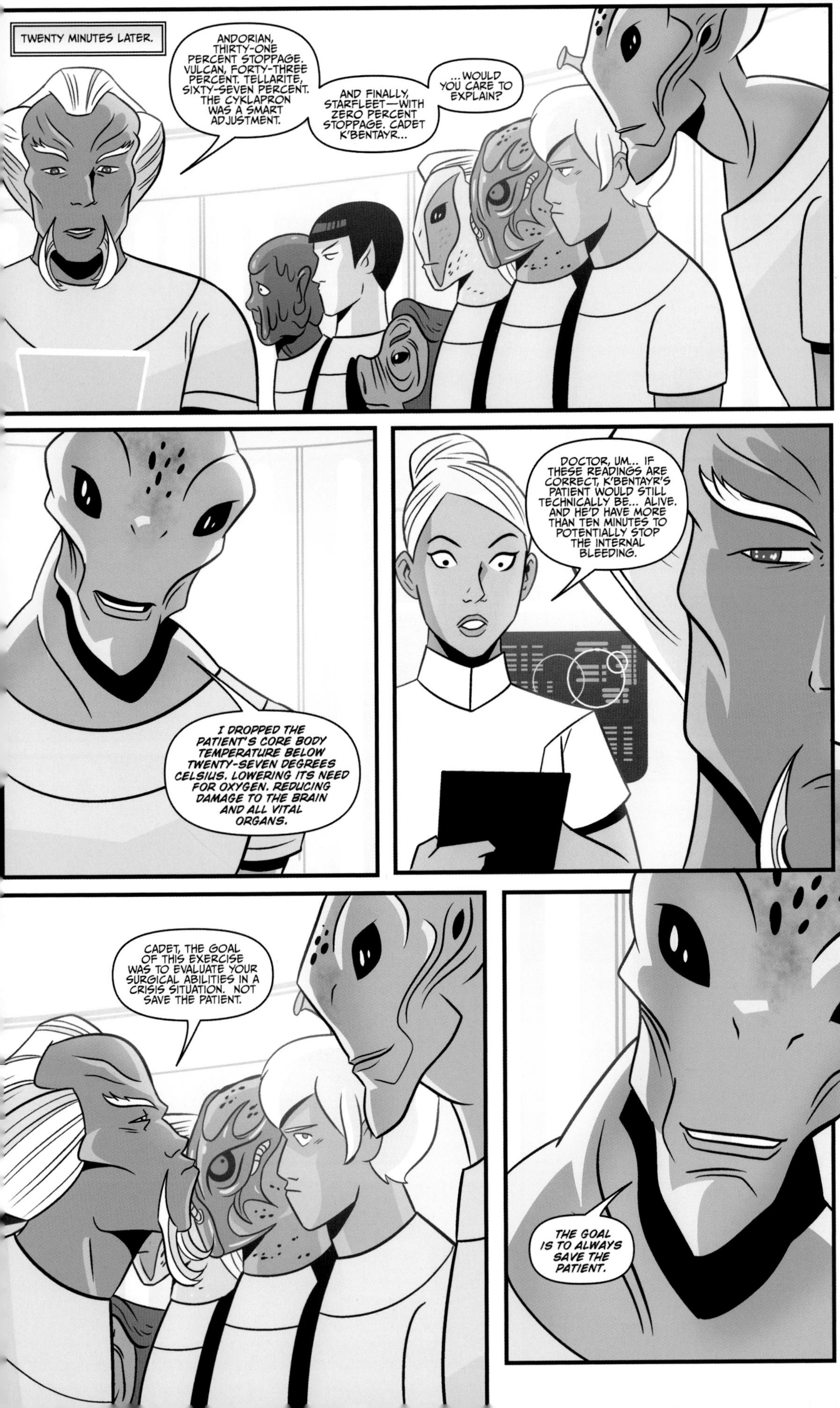
TWENTY MINUTES LATER.
ANDORIAN, THIRTY-ONE PERCENT STOPPAGE. VULCAN, FORTY-THREE PERCENT. TELLARITE, SIXTY-SEVEN PERCENT. THE CYKLAPRON WAS A SMART ADJUSTMENT.
AND FINALLY, STARFLEET—WITH ZERO PERCENT STOPPAGE. CADET K'BENTAYR...
...WOULD YOU CARE TO EXPLAIN?
I DROPPED THE PATIENT'S CORE BODY TEMPERATURE BELOW TWENTY-SEVEN DEGREES CELSIUS. LOWERING ITS NEED FOR OXYGEN. REDUCING DAMAGE TO THE BRAIN AND ALL VITAL ORGANS.
DOCTOR, UM... IF THESE READINGS ARE CORRECT, K'BENTAYR'S PATIENT WOULD STILL TECHNICALLY BE... ALIVE. AND HE'D HAVE MORE THAN TEN MINUTES TO POTENTIALLY STOP THE INTERNAL BLEEDING.
CADET, THE GOAL OF THIS EXERCISE WAS TO EVALUATE YOUR SURGICAL ABILITIES IN A CRISIS SITUATION. NOT SAVE THE PATIENT.
THE GOAL IS TO ALWAYS SAVE THE PATIENT.

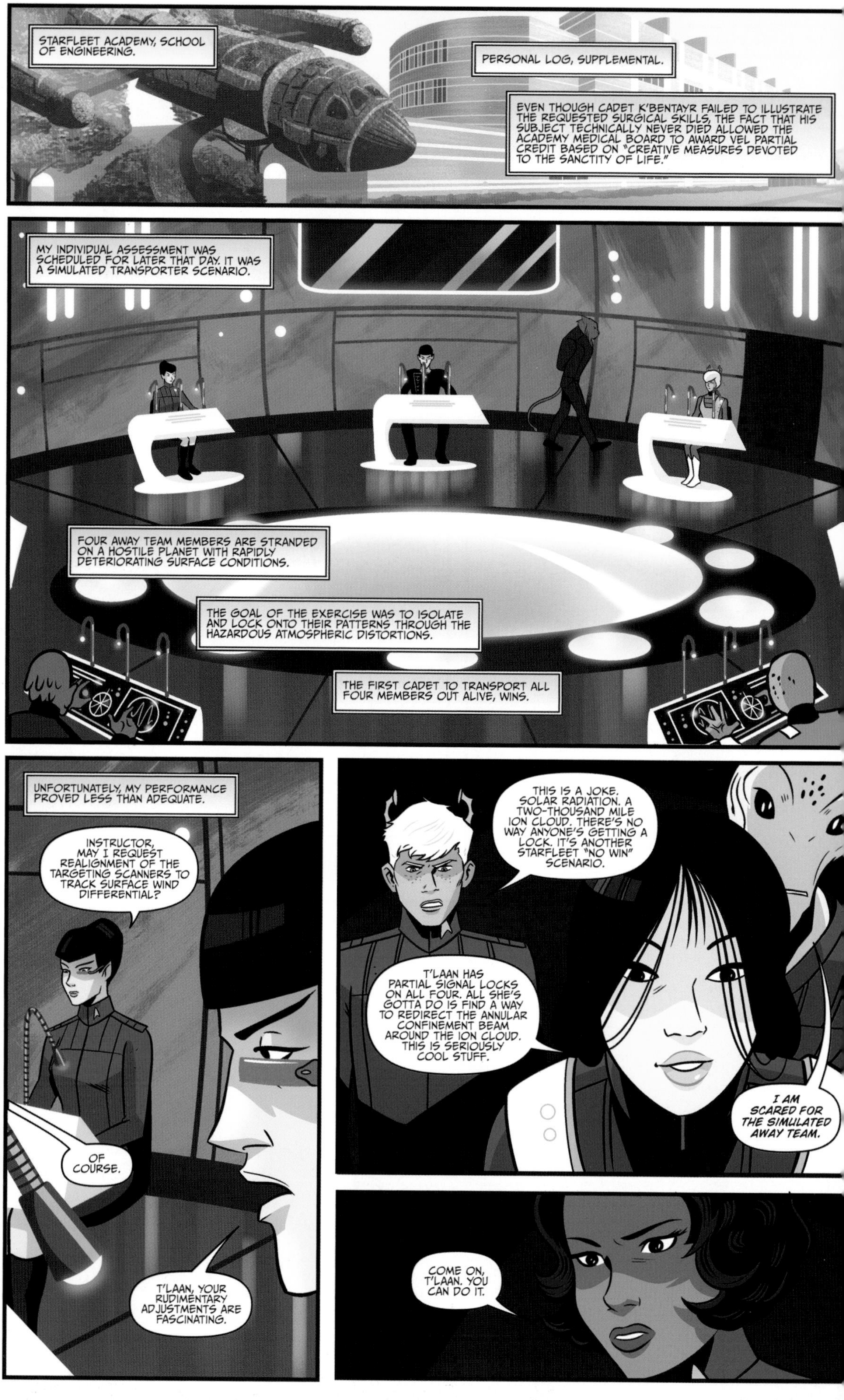
STARFLEET ACADEMY, SCHOOL OF ENGINEERING.
PERSONAL LOG, SUPPLEMENTAL.
EVEN THOUGH CADET K'BENTAYR FAILED TO ILLUSTRATE THE REQUESTED SURGICAL SKILLS, THE FACT THAT HIS SUBJECT TECHNICALLY NEVER DIED ALLOWED THE ACADEMY MEDICAL BOARD TO AWARD VEL PARTIAL CREDIT BASED ON "CREATIVE MEASURES DEVOTED TO THE SANCTITY OF LIFE."
MY INDIVIDUAL ASSESSMENT WAS SCHEDULED FOR LATER THAT DAY. IT WAS A SIMULATED TRANSPORTER SCENARIO.
FOUR AWAY TEAM MEMBERS ARE STRANDED ON A HOSTILE PLANET WITH RAPIDLY DETERIORATING SURFACE CONDITIONS.
THE GOAL OF THE EXERCISE WAS TO ISOLATE AND LOCK ONTO THEIR PATTERNS THROUGH THE HAZARDOUS ATMOSPHERIC DISTORTIONS.
THE FIRST CADET TO TRANSPORT ALL FOUR MEMBERS OUT ALIVE, WINS.
UNFORTUNATELY, MY PERFORMANCE PROVED LESS THAN ADEQUATE.
INSTRUCTOR, MAY I REQUEST REALIGNMENT OF THE TARGETING SCANNERS TO TRACK SURFACE WIND DIFFERENTIAL?
OF COURSE.
T'LAAN, YOUR RUDIMENTARY ADJUSTMENTS ARE FASCINATING.
THIS IS A JOKE. SOLAR RADIATION. A TWO-THOUSAND MILE ION CLOUD. THERE'S NO WAY ANYONE'S GETTING A LOCK. IT'S ANOTHER STARFLEET "NO WIN" SCENARIO.
T'LAAN HAS PARTIAL SIGNAL LOCKS ON ALL FOUR. ALL SHE'S GOTTA DO IS FIND A WAY TO REDIRECT THE ANNULAR CONFINEMENT BEAM AROUND THE ION CLOUD. THIS IS SERIOUSLY COOL STUFF.
I AM SCARED FOR THE SIMULATED AWAY TEAM.
COME ON, T'LAAN. YOU CAN DO IT.

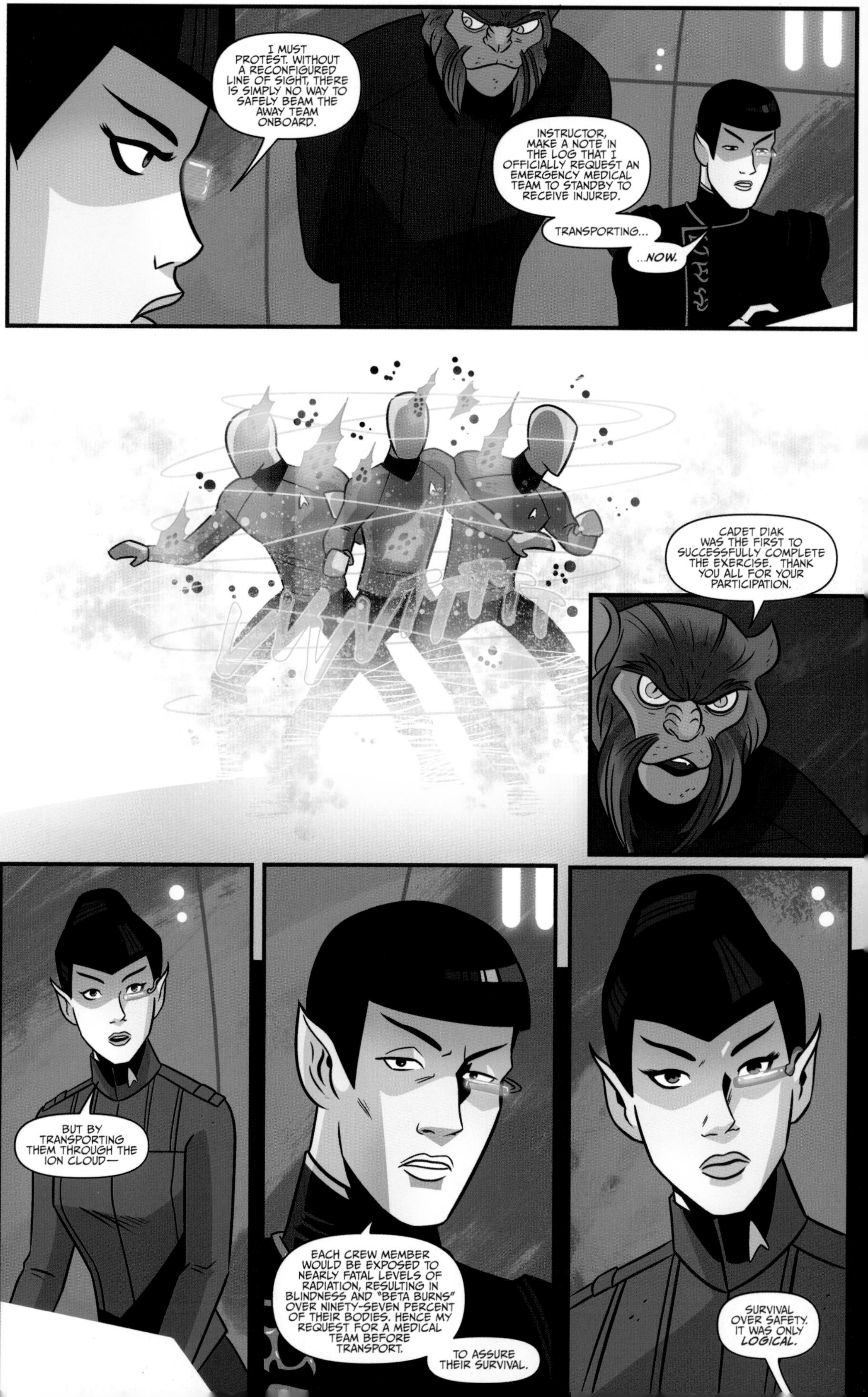
I MUST PROTEST. WITHOUT A RECONFIGURED LINE OF SIGHT, THERE IS SIMPLY NO WAY TO SAFELY BEAM THE AWAY TEAM ONBOARD.
INSTRUCTOR, MAKE A NOTE IN THE LOG THAT I OFFICIALLY REQUEST AN EMERGENCY MEDICAL TEAM TO STANDBY TO RECEIVE INJURED.
TRANSPORTING...
...NOW.
VVVVTTTT
CADET DIAK WAS THE FIRST TO SUCCESSFULLY COMPLETE THE EXERCISE. THANK YOU ALL FOR YOUR PARTICIPATION.
BUT BY TRANSPORTING THEM THROUGH THE ION CLOUD—
EACH CREW MEMBER WOULD BE EXPOSED TO NEARLY FATAL LEVELS OF RADIATION, RESULTING IN BLINDNESS AND "BETA BURNS" OVER NINETY-SEVEN PERCENT OF THEIR BODIES. HENCE MY REQUEST FOR A MEDICAL TEAM BEFORE TRANSPORT.
TO ASSURE THEIR SURVIVAL.
SURVIVAL OVER SAFETY. IT WAS ONLY *LOGICAL*.

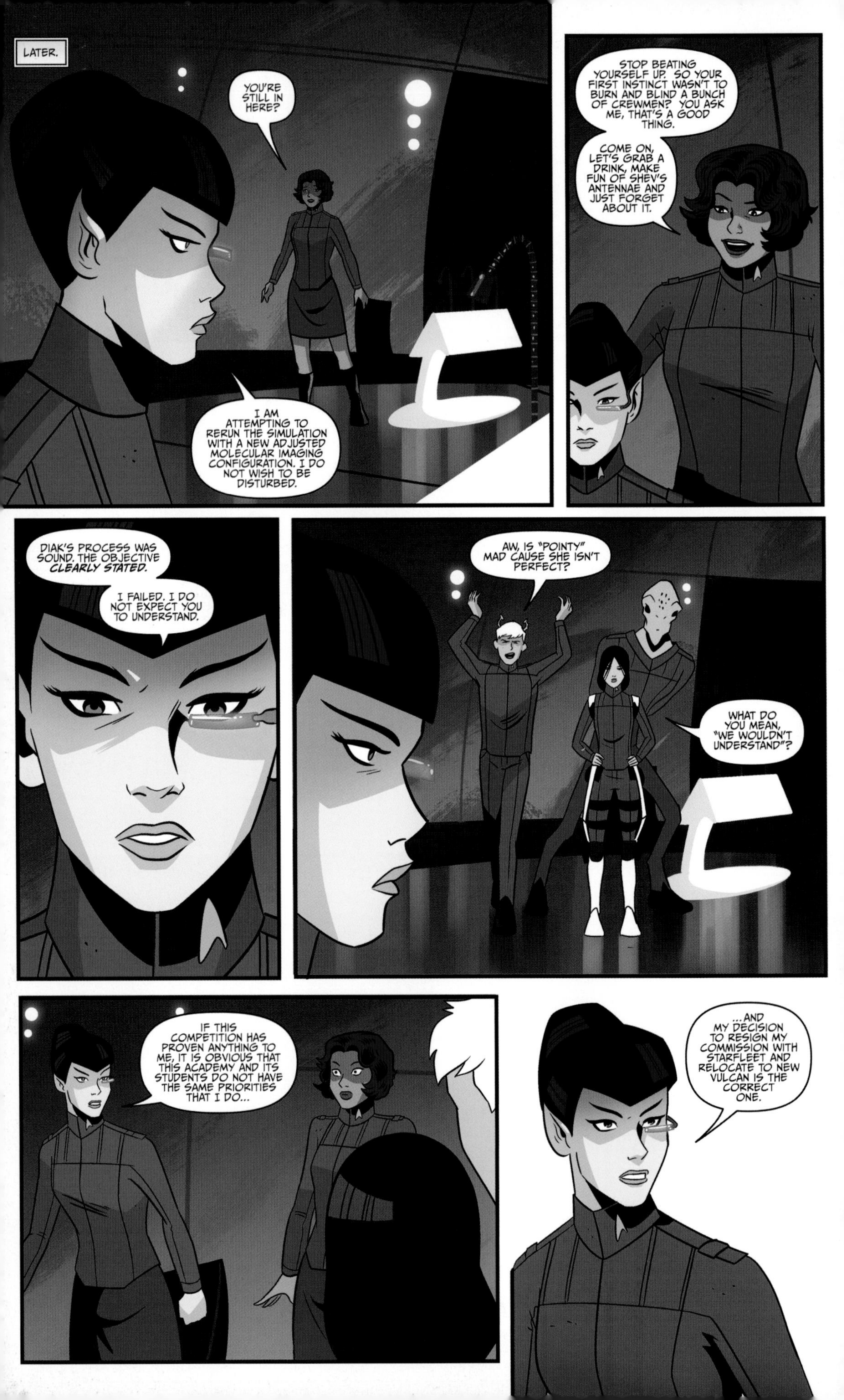
LATER.
YOU'RE STILL IN HERE?
I AM ATTEMPTING TO RERUN THE SIMULATION WITH A NEW ADJUSTED MOLECULAR IMAGING CONFIGURATION. I DO NOT WISH TO BE DISTURBED.
STOP BEATING YOURSELF UP. SO YOUR FIRST INSTINCT WASN'T TO BURN AND BLIND A BUNCH OF CREWMEN? YOU ASK ME, THAT'S A GOOD THING.
COME ON, LET'S GRAB A DRINK, MAKE FUN OF SHEV'S ANTENNAE AND JUST FORGET ABOUT IT.
DIAK'S PROCESS WAS SOUND. THE OBJECTIVE CLEARLY STATED.
I FAILED. I DO NOT EXPECT YOU TO UNDERSTAND.
AW, IS "POINTY" MAD CAUSE SHE ISN'T PERFECT?
WHAT DO YOU MEAN, "WE WOULDN'T UNDERSTAND"?
IF THIS COMPETITION HAS PROVEN ANYTHING TO ME, IT IS OBVIOUS THAT THIS ACADEMY AND ITS STUDENTS DO NOT HAVE THE SAME PRIORITIES THAT I DO...
...AND MY DECISION TO RESIGN MY COMMISSION WITH STARFLEET AND RELOCATE TO NEW VULCAN IS THE CORRECT ONE.

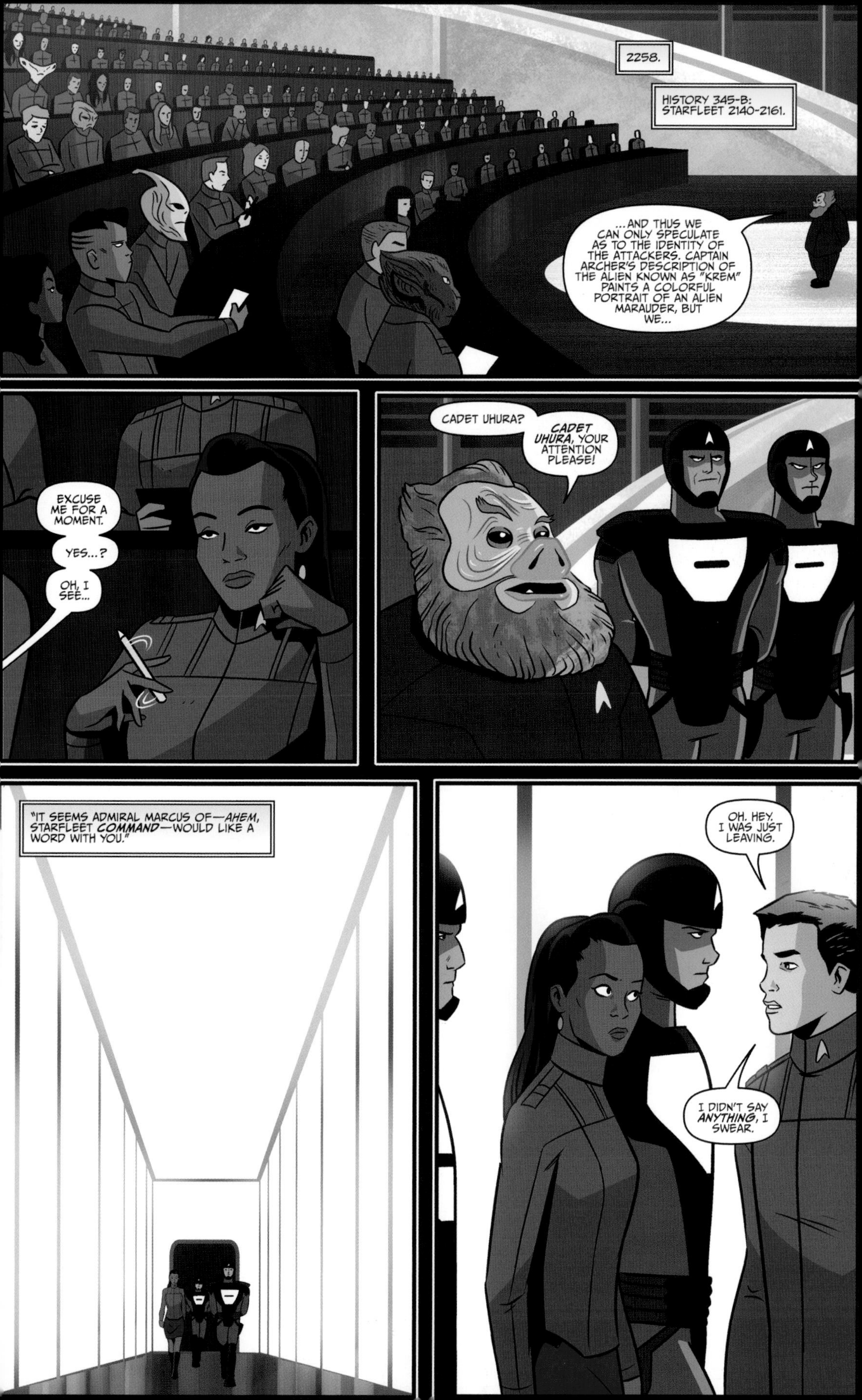
2258.
HISTORY 345-B: STARFLEET 2140-2161.
...AND THUS WE CAN ONLY SPECULATE AS TO THE IDENTITY OF THE ATTACKERS. CAPTAIN ARCHER'S DESCRIPTION OF THE ALIEN KNOWN AS "KREM" PAINTS A COLORFUL PORTRAIT OF AN ALIEN MARAUDER, BUT WE...
EXCUSE ME FOR A MOMENT.
YES...?
OH, I SEE...
CADET UHURA?
CADET UHURA, YOUR ATTENTION PLEASE!
"IT SEEMS ADMIRAL MARCUS OF—AHEM, STARFLEET COMMAND—WOULD LIKE A WORD WITH YOU."
OH. HEY. I WAS JUST LEAVING.
I DIDN'T SAY ANYTHING, I SWEAR.

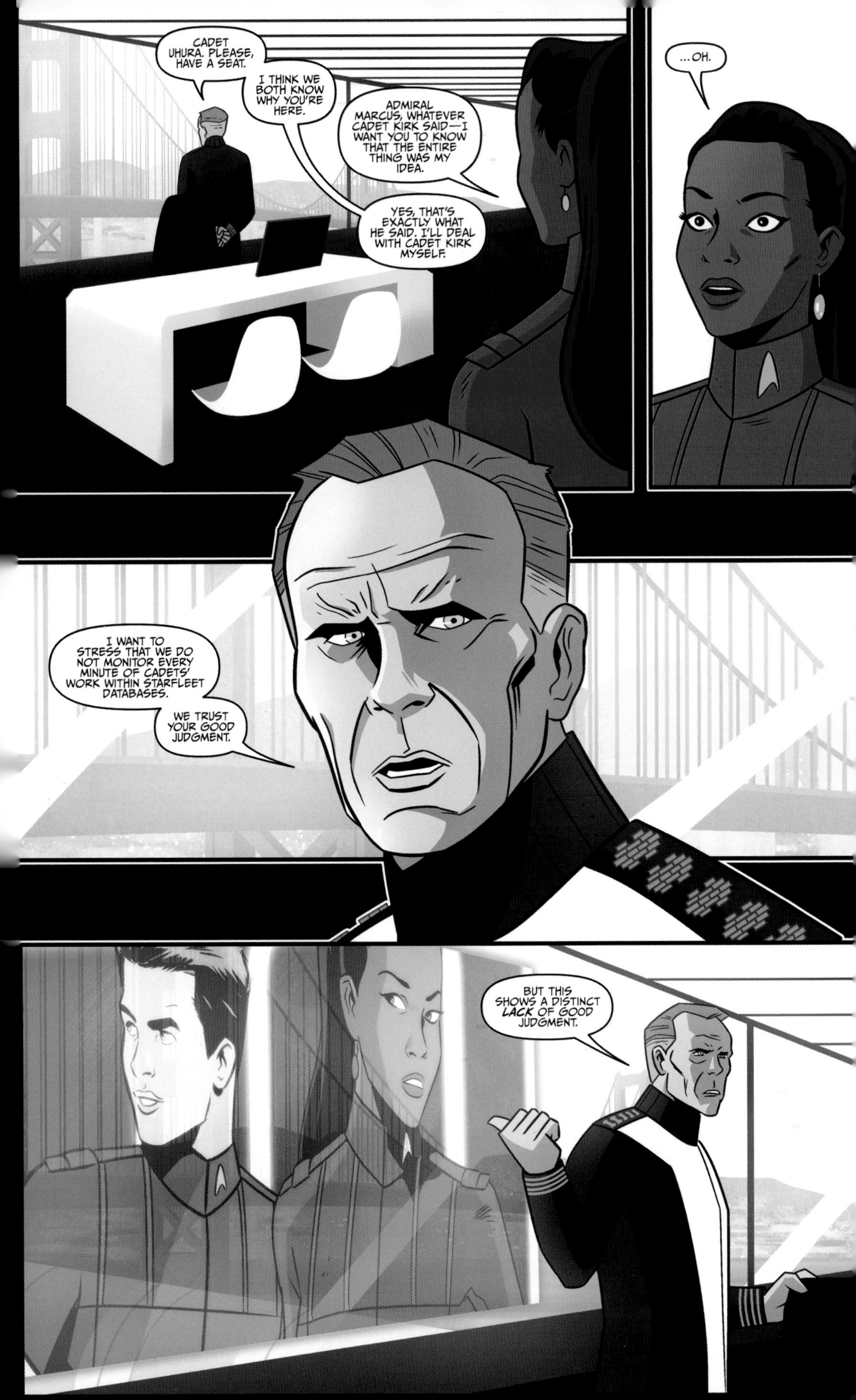
CADET UHURA. PLEASE, HAVE A SEAT.
I THINK WE BOTH KNOW WHY YOU'RE HERE.
ADMIRAL MARCUS, WHATEVER CADET KIRK SAID—I WANT YOU TO KNOW THAT THE ENTIRE THING WAS MY IDEA.
YES, THAT'S EXACTLY WHAT HE SAID. I'LL DEAL WITH CADET KIRK MYSELF.
...OH.
I WANT TO STRESS THAT WE DO NOT MONITOR EVERY MINUTE OF CADETS' WORK WITHIN STARFLEET DATABASES.
WE TRUST YOUR GOOD JUDGMENT.
BUT THIS SHOWS A DISTINCT LACK OF GOOD JUDGMENT.

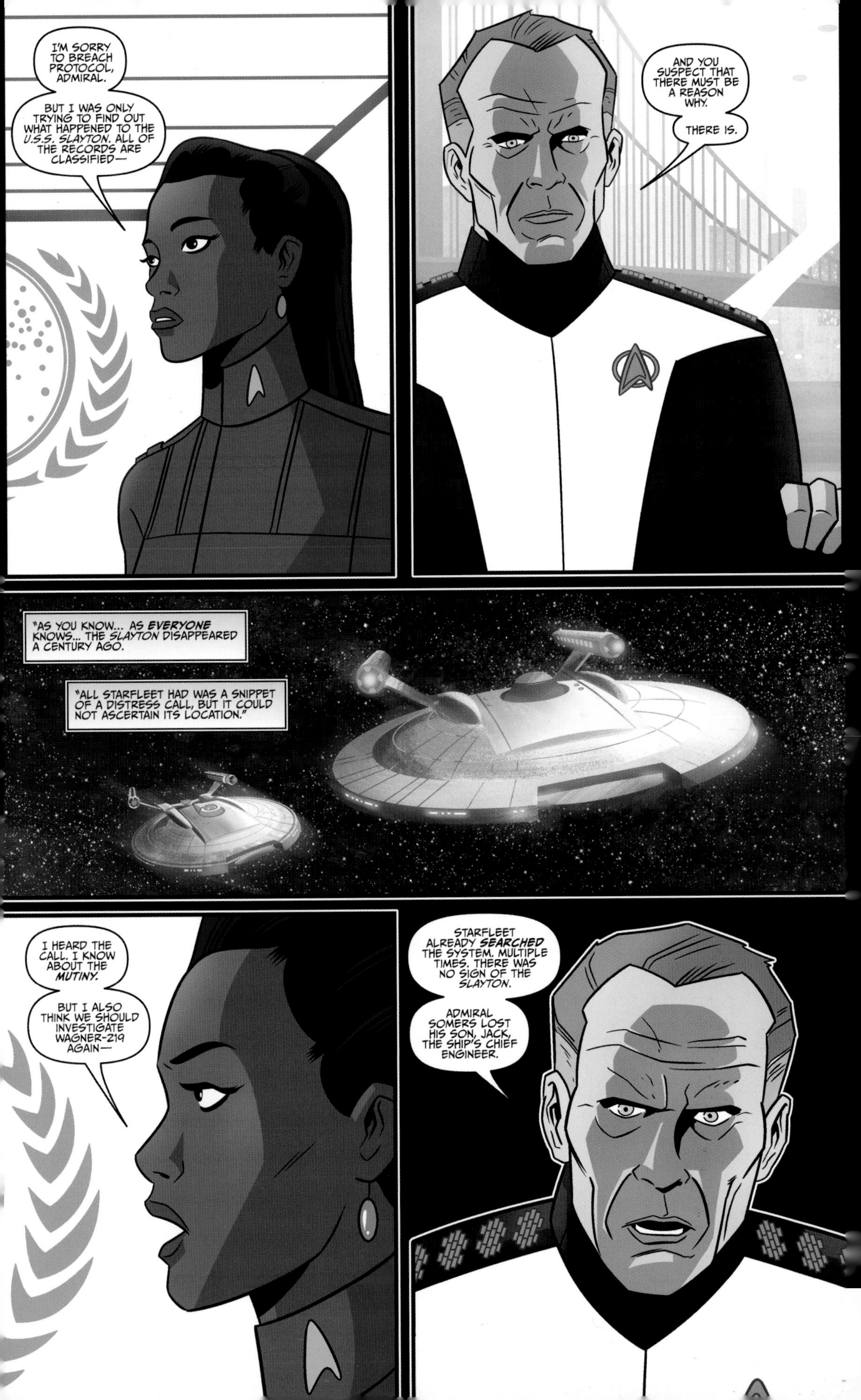
I'M SORRY TO BREACH PROTOCOL, ADMIRAL.
BUT I WAS ONLY TRYING TO FIND OUT WHAT HAPPENED TO THE *U.S.S. SLAYTON*. ALL OF THE RECORDS ARE CLASSIFIED—
AND YOU SUSPECT THAT THERE MUST BE A REASON WHY.
THERE IS.
"AS YOU KNOW... AS ***EVERYONE*** KNOWS... THE *SLAYTON* DISAPPEARED A CENTURY AGO.
"ALL STARFLEET HAD WAS A SNIPPET OF A DISTRESS CALL, BUT IT COULD NOT ASCERTAIN ITS LOCATION."
I HEARD THE CALL. I KNOW ABOUT THE ***MUTINY.***
BUT I ALSO THINK WE SHOULD INVESTIGATE WAGNER-219 AGAIN—
STARFLEET ALREADY ***SEARCHED*** THE SYSTEM. MULTIPLE TIMES. THERE WAS NO SIGN OF THE *SLAYTON*.
ADMIRAL SOMERS LOST HIS SON, JACK, THE SHIP'S CHIEF ENGINEER.

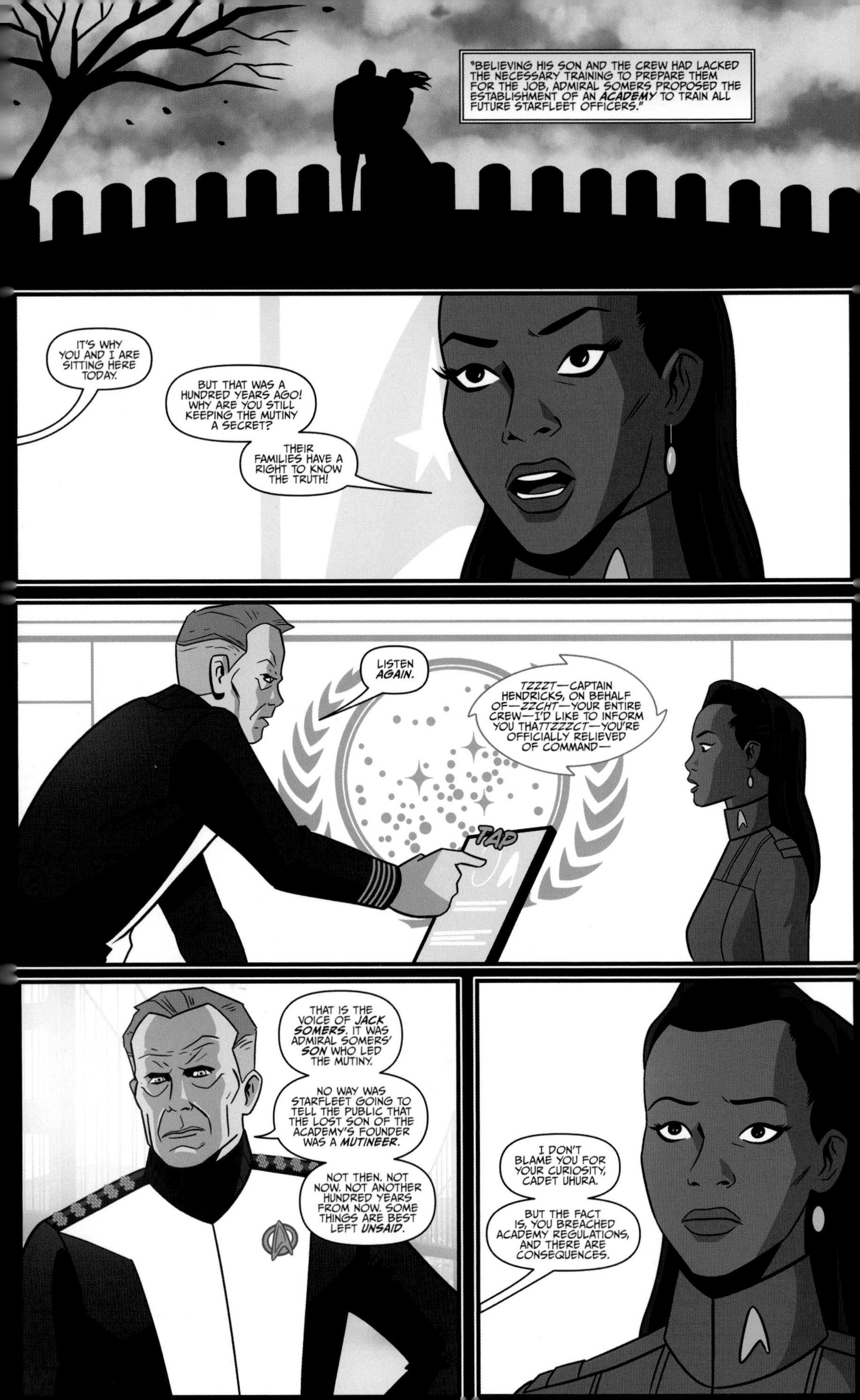
"BELIEVING HIS SON AND THE CREW HAD LACKED THE NECESSARY TRAINING TO PREPARE THEM FOR THE JOB, ADMIRAL SOMERS PROPOSED THE ESTABLISHMENT OF AN ACADEMY TO TRAIN ALL FUTURE STARFLEET OFFICERS."
IT'S WHY YOU AND I ARE SITTING HERE TODAY.
BUT THAT WAS A HUNDRED YEARS AGO! WHY ARE YOU STILL KEEPING THE MUTINY A SECRET?
THEIR FAMILIES HAVE A RIGHT TO KNOW THE TRUTH!
LISTEN AGAIN.
TZZZT—CAPTAIN HENDRICKS, ON BEHALF OF—ZZCHT—YOUR ENTIRE CREW—I'D LIKE TO INFORM YOU THATTZZZCT—YOU'RE OFFICIALLY RELIEVED OF COMMAND—
TAP
THAT IS THE VOICE OF JACK SOMERS. IT WAS ADMIRAL SOMERS' SON WHO LED THE MUTINY.
NO WAY WAS STARFLEET GOING TO TELL THE PUBLIC THAT THE LOST SON OF THE ACADEMY'S FOUNDER WAS A MUTINEER.
NOT THEN. NOT NOW. NOT ANOTHER HUNDRED YEARS FROM NOW. SOME THINGS ARE BEST LEFT UNSAID.
I DON'T BLAME YOU FOR YOUR CURIOSITY, CADET UHURA.
BUT THE FACT IS, YOU BREACHED ACADEMY REGULATIONS, AND THERE ARE CONSEQUENCES.

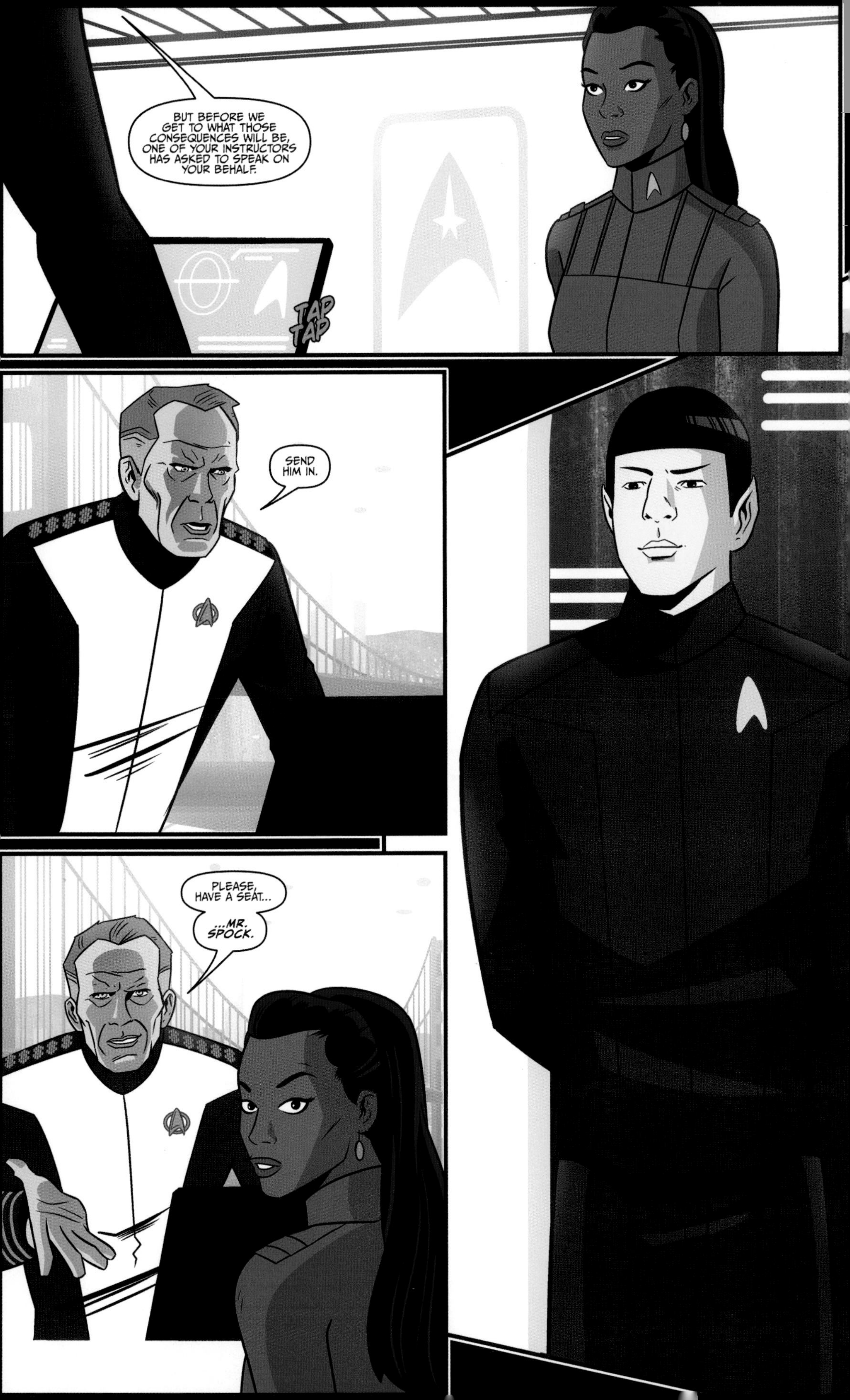
BUT BEFORE WE GET TO WHAT THOSE CONSEQUENCES WILL BE, ONE OF YOUR INSTRUCTORS HAS ASKED TO SPEAK ON YOUR BEHALF.
TAP TAP
SEND HIM IN.
PLEASE, HAVE A SEAT...
...MR. SPOCK.

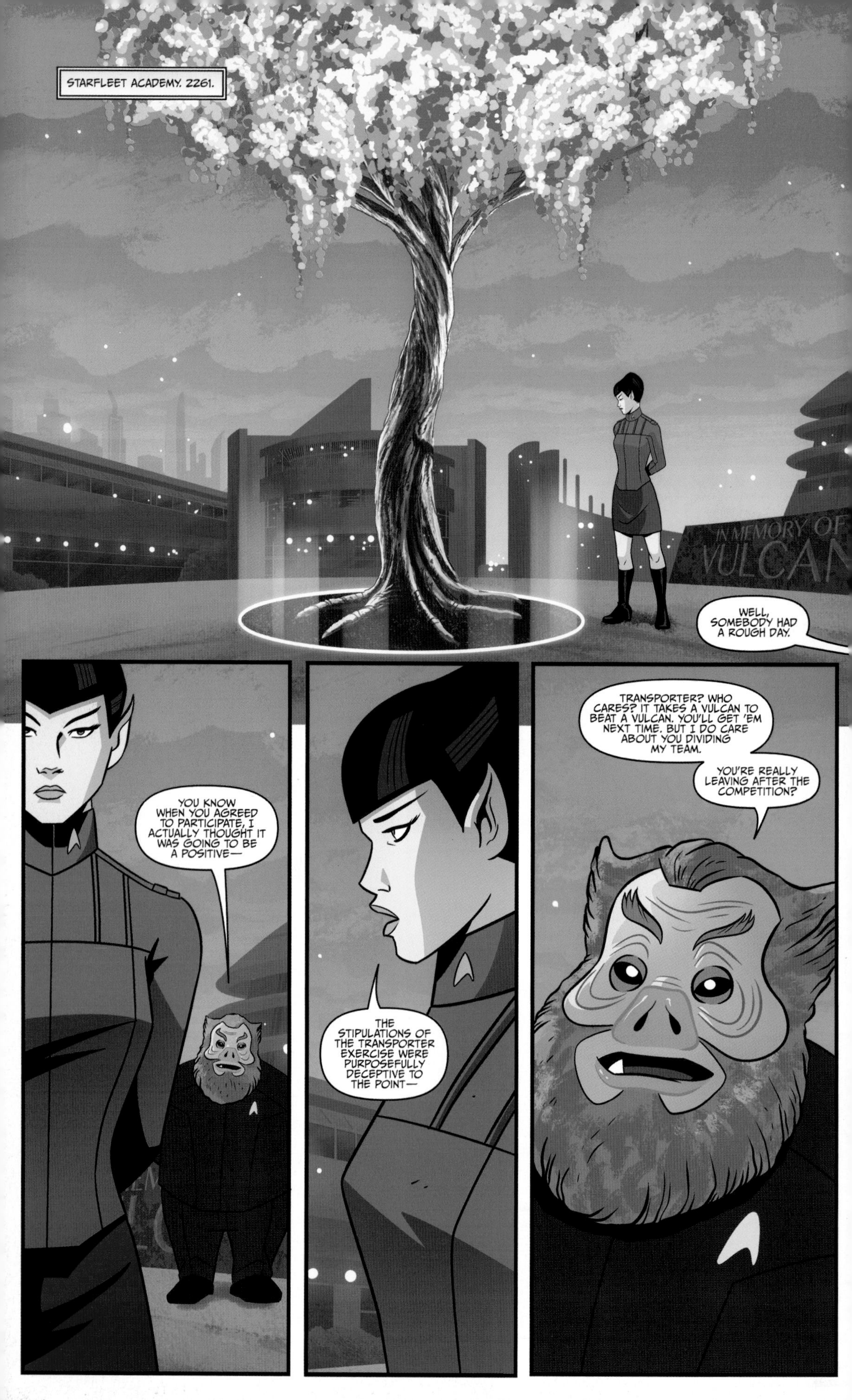

STARFLEET ACADEMY. 2261.
IN MEMORY OF VULCAN
WELL, SOMEBODY HAD A ROUGH DAY.
YOU KNOW WHEN YOU AGREED TO PARTICIPATE, I ACTUALLY THOUGHT IT WAS GOING TO BE A POSITIVE—
THE STIPULATIONS OF THE TRANSPORTER EXERCISE WERE PURPOSEFULLY DECEPTIVE TO THE POINT—
TRANSPORTER? WHO CARES? IT TAKES A VULCAN TO BEAT A VULCAN. YOU'LL GET 'EM NEXT TIME. BUT I DO CARE ABOUT YOU DIVIDING MY TEAM.
YOU'RE REALLY LEAVING AFTER THE COMPETITION?

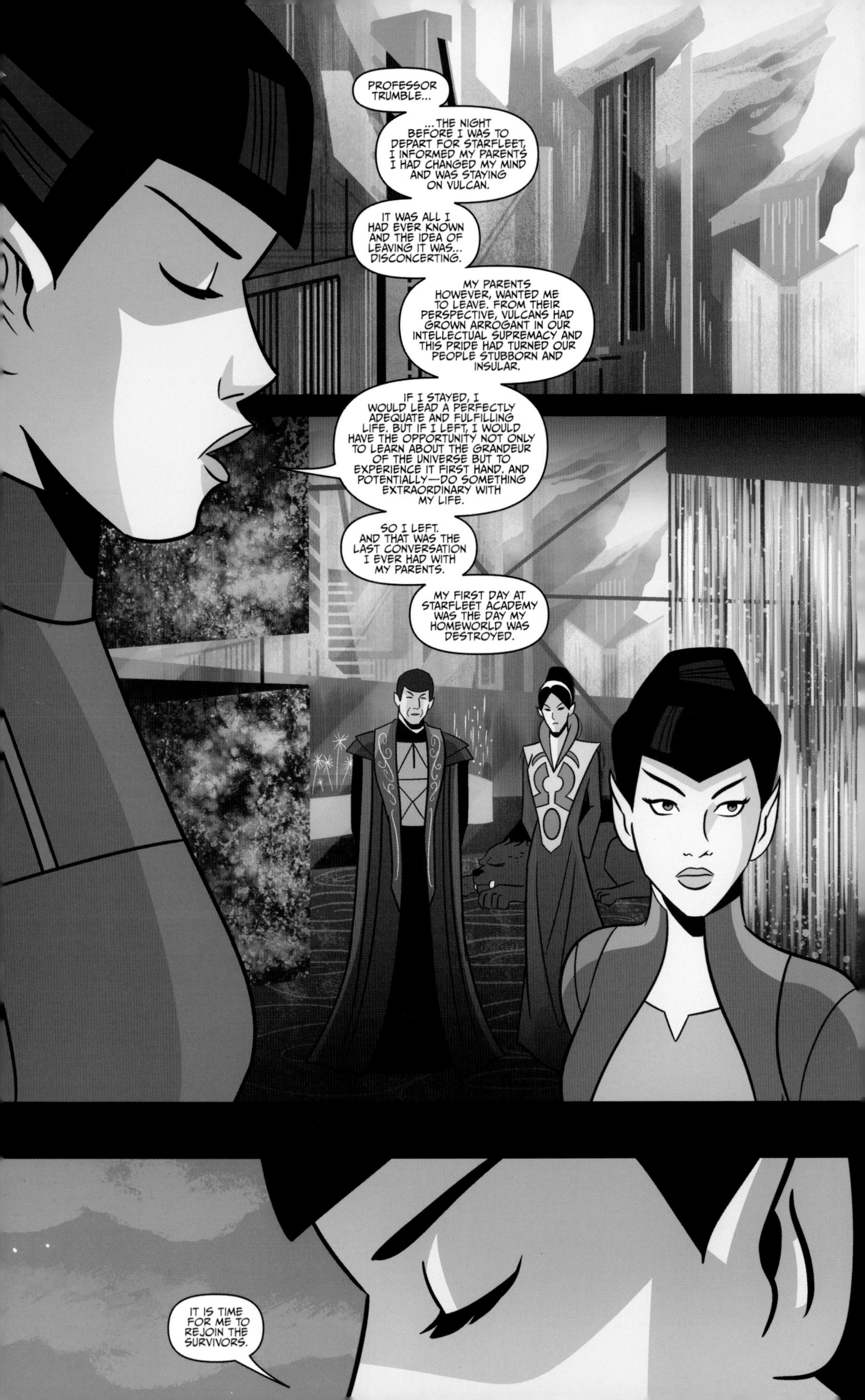
PROFESSOR TRUMBLE...
...THE NIGHT BEFORE I WAS TO DEPART FOR STARFLEET, I INFORMED MY PARENTS I HAD CHANGED MY MIND AND WAS STAYING ON VULCAN.
IT WAS ALL I HAD EVER KNOWN AND THE IDEA OF LEAVING IT WAS... DISCONCERTING.
MY PARENTS HOWEVER, WANTED ME TO LEAVE. FROM THEIR PERSPECTIVE, VULCANS HAD GROWN ARROGANT IN OUR INTELLECTUAL SUPREMACY AND THIS PRIDE HAD TURNED OUR PEOPLE STUBBORN AND INSULAR.
IF I STAYED, I WOULD LEAD A PERFECTLY ADEQUATE AND FULFILLING LIFE. BUT IF I LEFT, I WOULD HAVE THE OPPORTUNITY NOT ONLY TO LEARN ABOUT THE GRANDEUR OF THE UNIVERSE BUT TO EXPERIENCE IT FIRST HAND. AND POTENTIALLY—DO SOMETHING EXTRAORDINARY WITH MY LIFE.
SO I LEFT. AND THAT WAS THE LAST CONVERSATION I EVER HAD WITH MY PARENTS.
MY FIRST DAY AT STARFLEET ACADEMY WAS THE DAY MY HOMEWORLD WAS DESTROYED.
IT IS TIME FOR ME TO REJOIN THE SURVIVORS.

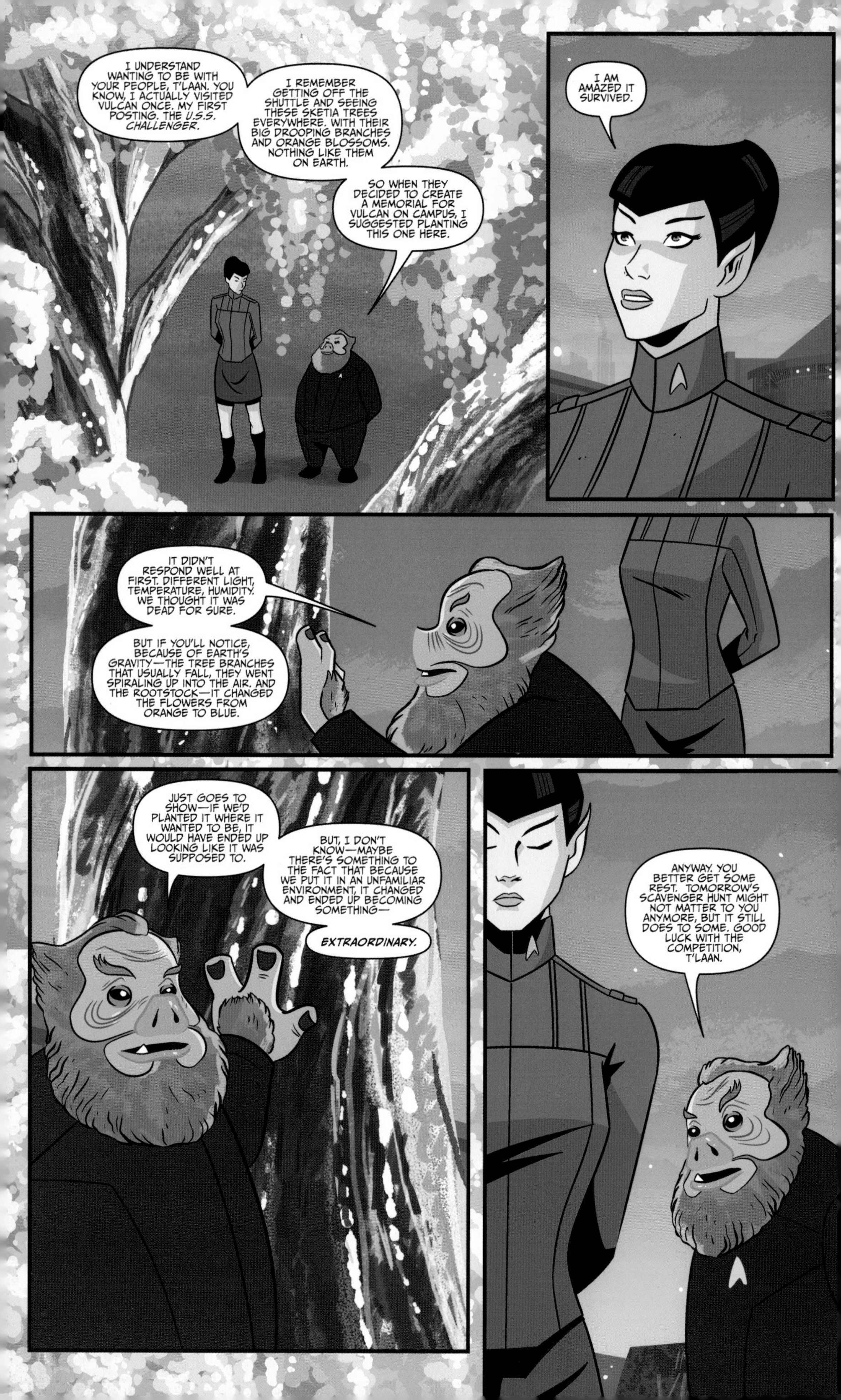

I UNDERSTAND WANTING TO BE WITH YOUR PEOPLE, T'LAAN. YOU KNOW, I ACTUALLY VISITED VULCAN ONCE. MY FIRST POSTING. THE *U.S.S. CHALLENGER*.
I REMEMBER GETTING OFF THE SHUTTLE AND SEEING THESE SKETIA TREES EVERYWHERE. WITH THEIR BIG DROOPING BRANCHES AND ORANGE BLOSSOMS. NOTHING LIKE THEM ON EARTH.
SO WHEN THEY DECIDED TO CREATE A MEMORIAL FOR VULCAN ON CAMPUS, I SUGGESTED PLANTING THIS ONE HERE.
I AM AMAZED IT SURVIVED.
IT DIDN'T RESPOND WELL AT FIRST. DIFFERENT LIGHT, TEMPERATURE, HUMIDITY. WE THOUGHT IT WAS DEAD FOR SURE.
BUT IF YOU'LL NOTICE, BECAUSE OF EARTH'S GRAVITY—THE TREE BRANCHES THAT USUALLY FALL, THEY WENT SPIRALING UP INTO THE AIR. AND THE ROOTSTOCK—IT CHANGED THE FLOWERS FROM ORANGE TO BLUE.
JUST GOES TO SHOW—IF WE'D PLANTED IT WHERE IT WANTED TO BE, IT WOULD HAVE ENDED UP LOOKING LIKE IT WAS SUPPOSED TO.
BUT, I DON'T KNOW—MAYBE THERE'S SOMETHING TO THE FACT THAT BECAUSE WE PUT IT IN AN UNFAMILIAR ENVIRONMENT, IT CHANGED AND ENDED UP BECOMING SOMETHING—
EXTRAORDINARY.
ANYWAY. YOU BETTER GET SOME REST. TOMORROW'S SCAVENGER HUNT MIGHT NOT MATTER TO YOU ANYMORE, BUT IT STILL DOES TO SOME. GOOD LUCK WITH THE COMPETITION, T'LAAN.

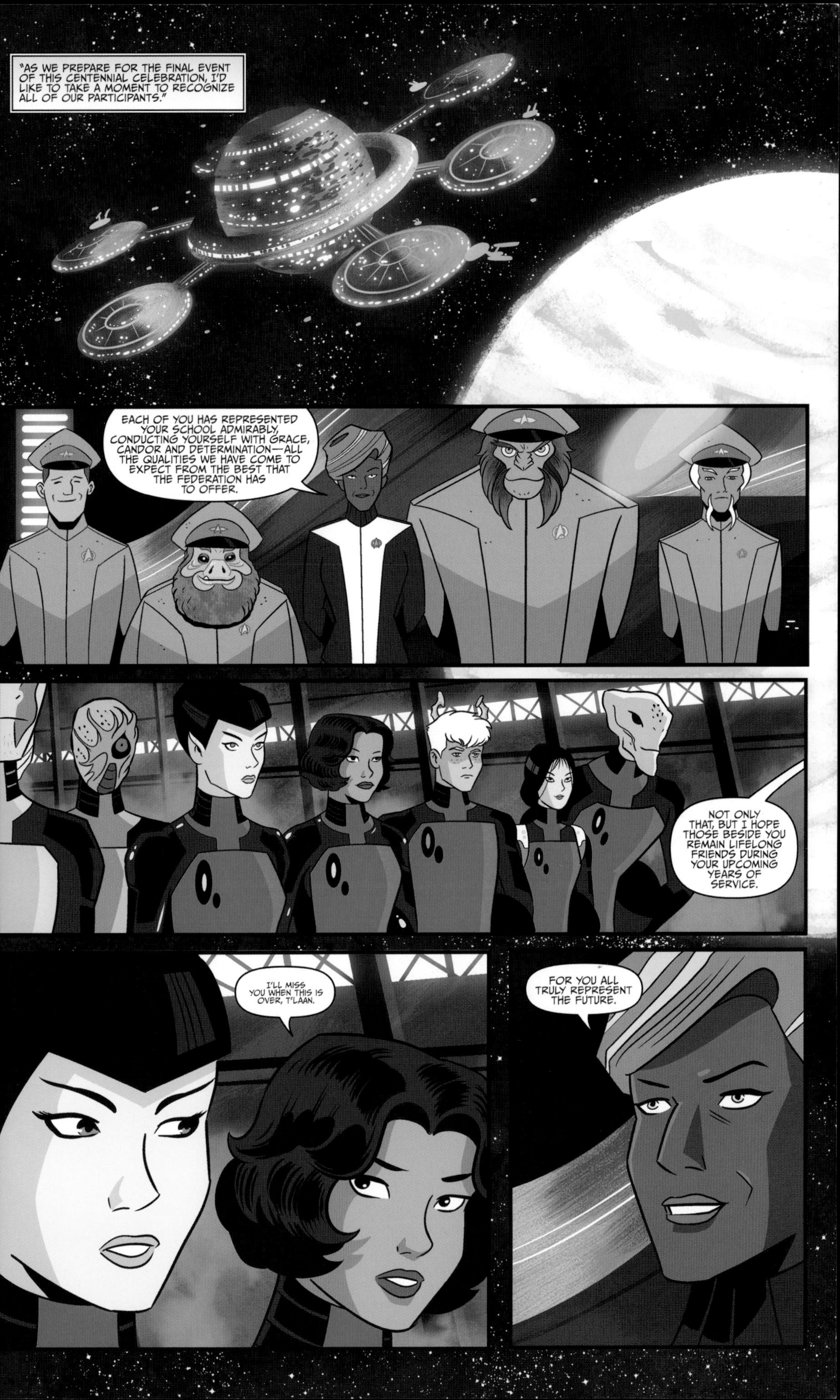
"AS WE PREPARE FOR THE FINAL EVENT OF THIS CENTENNIAL CELEBRATION, I'D LIKE TO TAKE A MOMENT TO RECOGNIZE ALL OF OUR PARTICIPANTS."
EACH OF YOU HAS REPRESENTED YOUR SCHOOL ADMIRABLY, CONDUCTING YOURSELF WITH GRACE, CANDOR AND DETERMINATION—ALL THE QUALITIES WE HAVE COME TO EXPECT FROM THE BEST THAT THE FEDERATION HAS TO OFFER.
NOT ONLY THAT, BUT I HOPE THOSE BESIDE YOU REMAIN LIFELONG FRIENDS DURING YOUR UPCOMING YEARS OF SERVICE.
I'LL MISS YOU WHEN THIS IS OVER, T'LAAN.
FOR YOU ALL TRULY REPRESENT THE FUTURE.

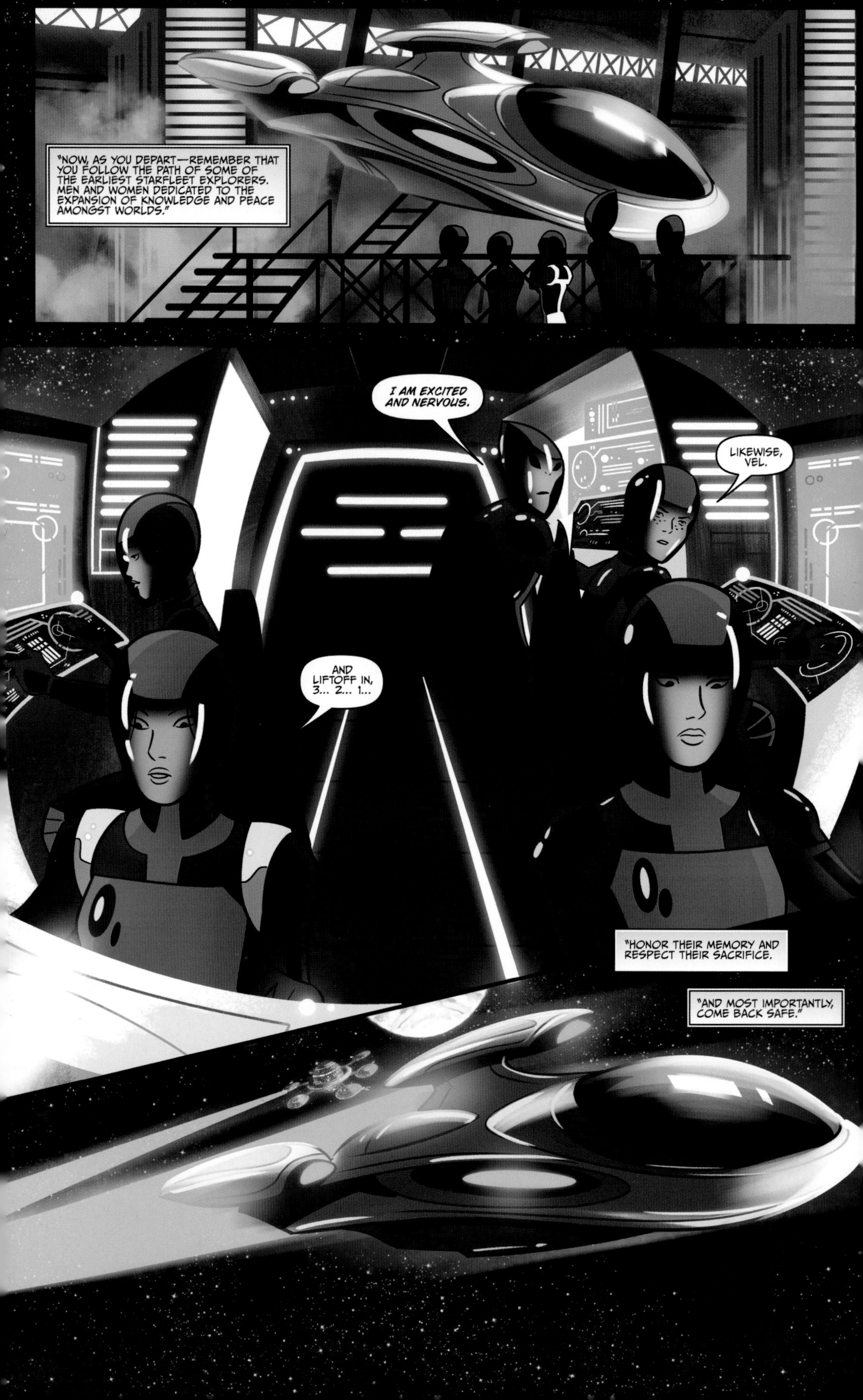
"NOW, AS YOU DEPART—REMEMBER THAT YOU FOLLOW THE PATH OF SOME OF THE EARLIEST STARFLEET EXPLORERS. MEN AND WOMEN DEDICATED TO THE EXPANSION OF KNOWLEDGE AND PEACE AMONGST WORLDS."
I AM EXCITED AND NERVOUS.
LIKEWISE, VEL.
AND LIFTOFF IN, 3... 2... 1...
"HONOR THEIR MEMORY AND RESPECT THEIR SACRIFICE.
"AND MOST IMPORTANTLY, COME BACK SAFE."

ART BY **PAULINA GANUCHEAU**

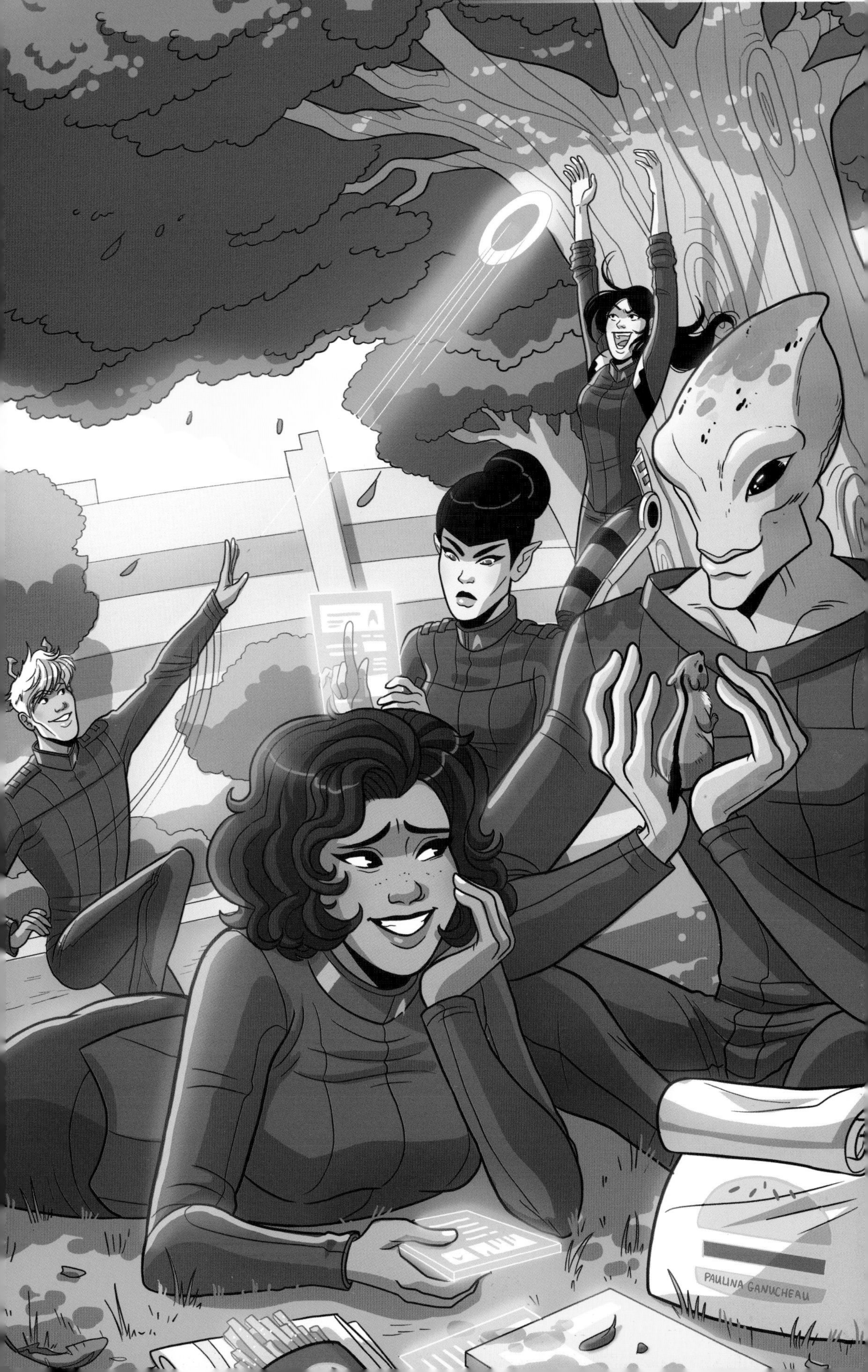
PAULINA GANUCHEAU

ART BY **DEREK CHARM**

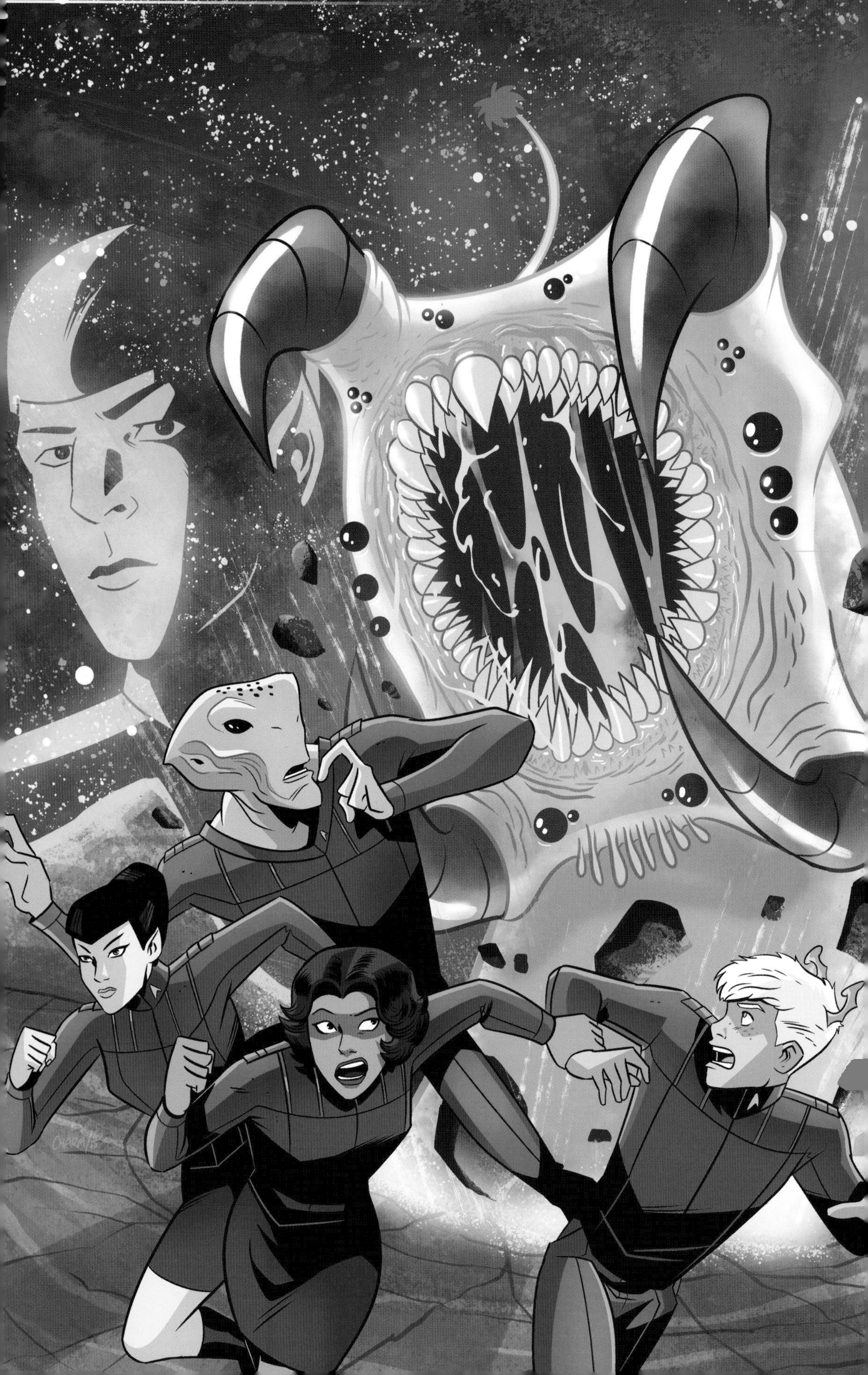

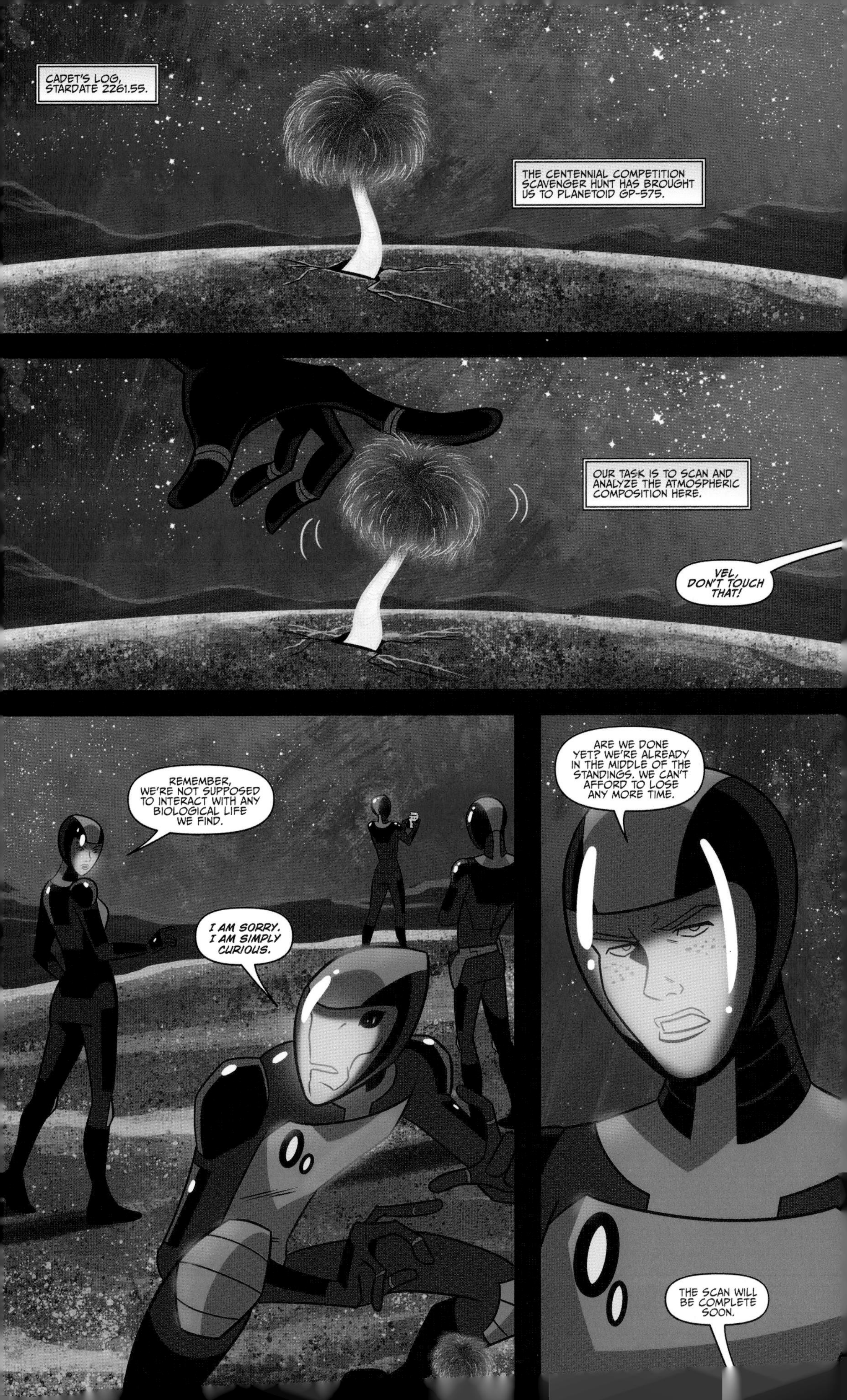
CADET'S LOG, STARDATE 2261.55.
THE CENTENNIAL COMPETITION SCAVENGER HUNT HAS BROUGHT US TO PLANETOID GP-575.
OUR TASK IS TO SCAN AND ANALYZE THE ATMOSPHERIC COMPOSITION HERE.
VEL, DON'T TOUCH THAT!
REMEMBER, WE'RE NOT SUPPOSED TO INTERACT WITH ANY BIOLOGICAL LIFE WE FIND.
I AM SORRY. I AM SIMPLY CURIOUS.
ARE WE DONE YET? WE'RE ALREADY IN THE MIDDLE OF THE STANDINGS. WE CAN'T AFFORD TO LOSE ANY MORE TIME.
THE SCAN WILL BE COMPLETE SOON.

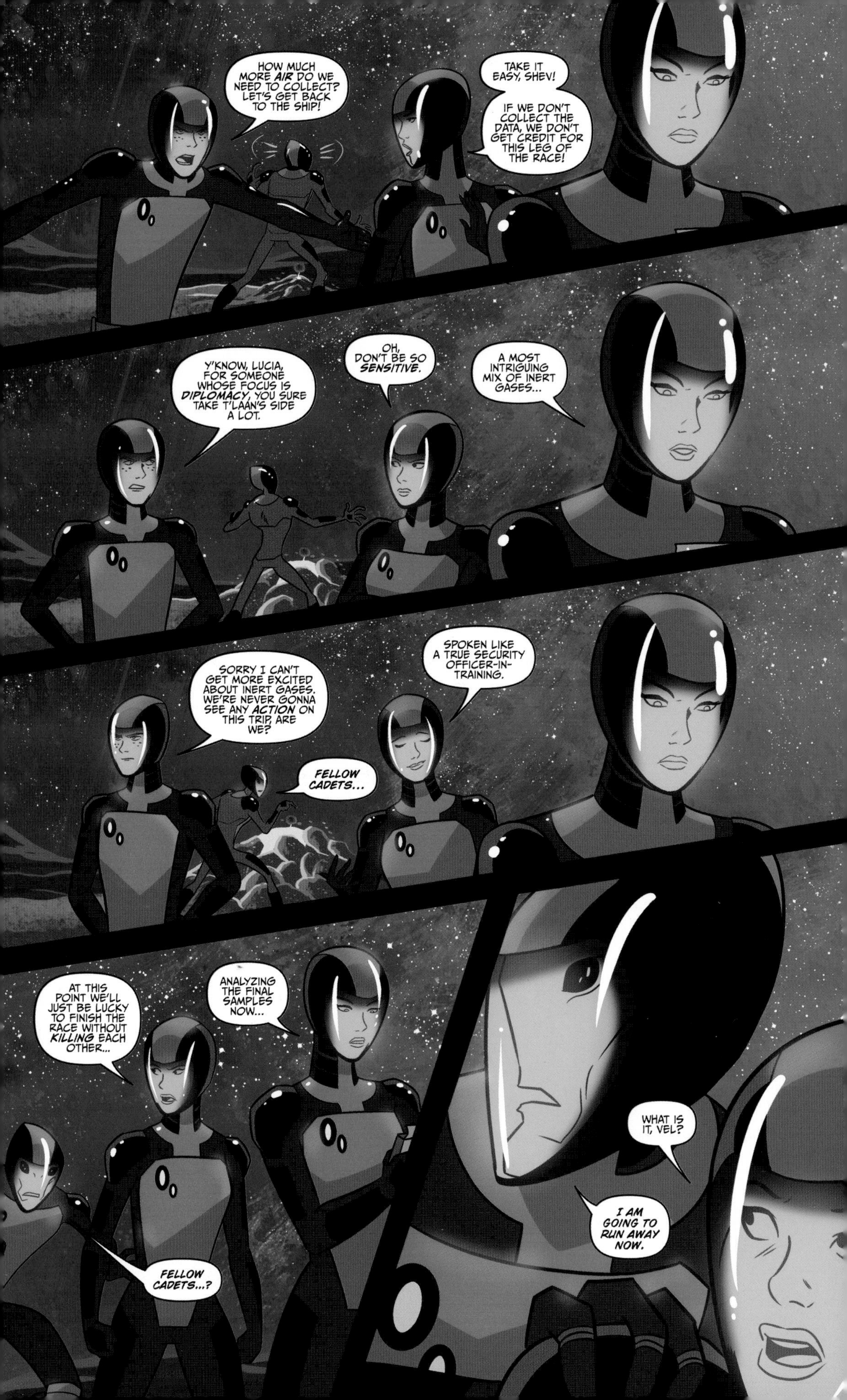
HOW MUCH MORE *AIR* DO WE NEED TO COLLECT? LET'S GET BACK TO THE SHIP!
TAKE IT EASY, SHEV!
IF WE DON'T COLLECT THE DATA, WE DON'T GET CREDIT FOR THIS LEG OF THE RACE!
Y'KNOW, LUCIA, FOR SOMEONE WHOSE FOCUS IS *DIPLOMACY*, YOU SURE TAKE T'LAAN'S SIDE A LOT.
OH, DON'T BE SO *SENSITIVE*.
A MOST INTRIGUING MIX OF INERT GASES...
SORRY I CAN'T GET MORE EXCITED ABOUT INERT GASES. WE'RE NEVER GONNA SEE ANY *ACTION* ON THIS TRIP, ARE WE?
SPOKEN LIKE A TRUE SECURITY OFFICER-IN-TRAINING.
FELLOW CADETS...
AT THIS POINT WE'LL JUST BE LUCKY TO FINISH THE RACE WITHOUT *KILLING* EACH OTHER...
ANALYZING THE FINAL SAMPLES NOW...
FELLOW CADETS...?
WHAT IS IT, VEL?
I AM GOING TO RUN AWAY NOW.

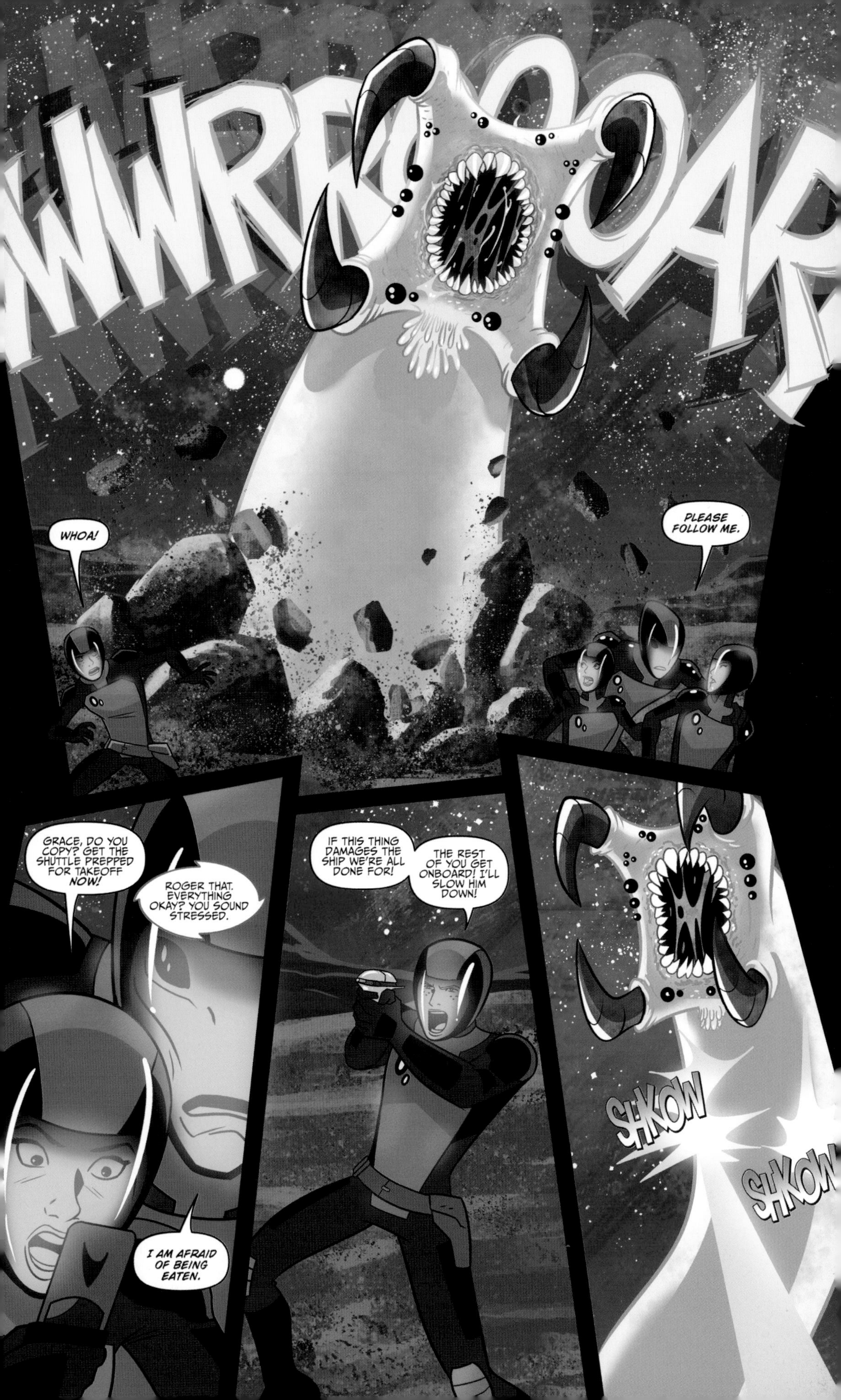
WWRROOOAR
WHOA!
PLEASE FOLLOW ME.
GRACE, DO YOU COPY? GET THE SHUTTLE PREPPED FOR TAKEOFF NOW!
ROGER THAT. EVERYTHING OKAY? YOU SOUND STRESSED.
I AM AFRAID OF BEING EATEN.
IF THIS THING DAMAGES THE SHIP WE'RE ALL DONE FOR!
THE REST OF YOU GET ONBOARD! I'LL SLOW HIM DOWN!
SHKOW
SHKOW

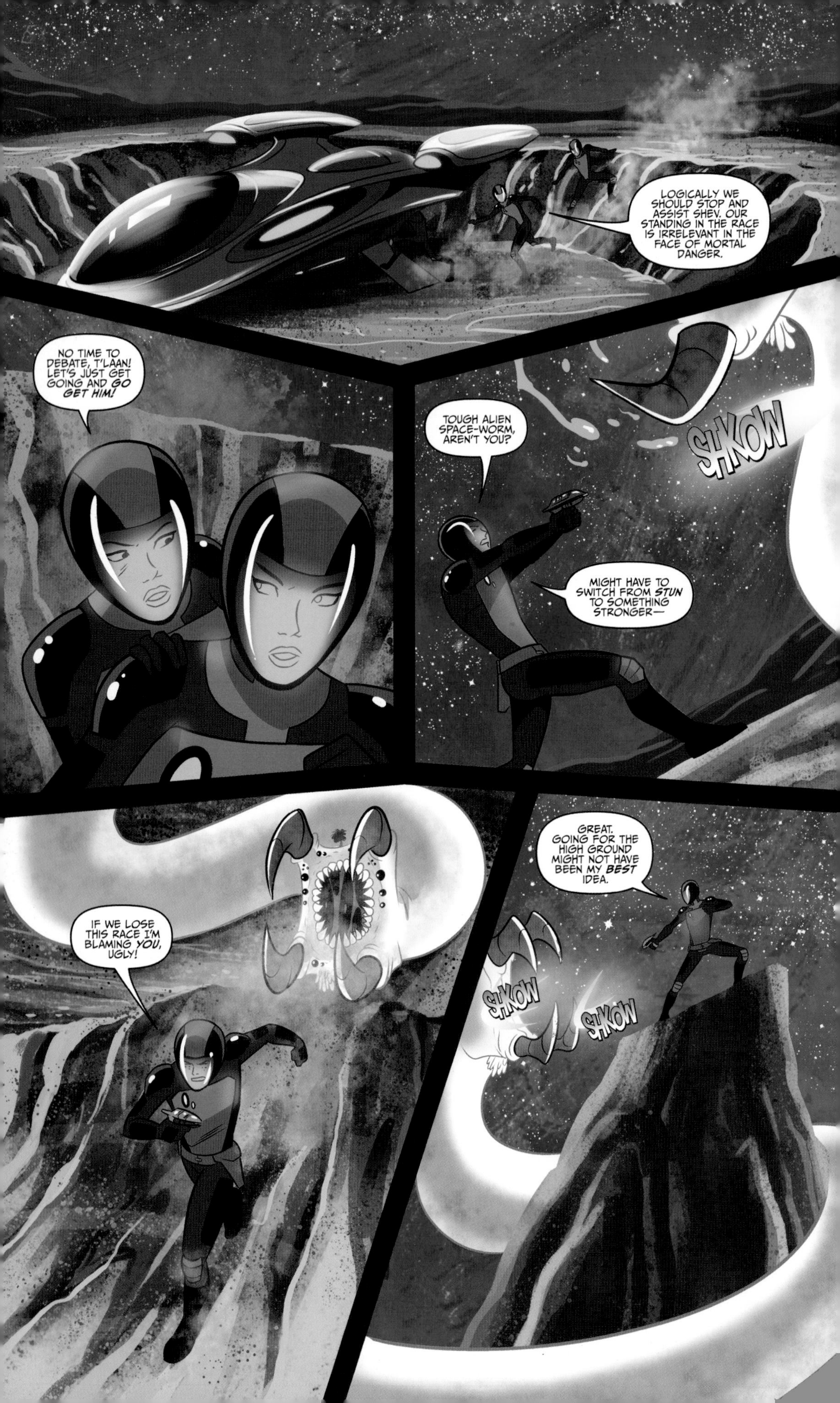
LOGICALLY WE SHOULD STOP AND ASSIST SHEV. OUR STANDING IN THE RACE IS IRRELEVANT IN THE FACE OF MORTAL DANGER.
NO TIME TO DEBATE, T'LAAN! LET'S JUST GET GOING AND GO GET HIM!
TOUGH ALIEN SPACE-WORM, AREN'T YOU?
SHKOW
MIGHT HAVE TO SWITCH FROM STUN TO SOMETHING STRONGER—
IF WE LOSE THIS RACE I'M BLAMING YOU, UGLY!
GREAT. GOING FOR THE HIGH GROUND MIGHT NOT HAVE BEEN MY BEST IDEA.
SHKOW
SHKOW

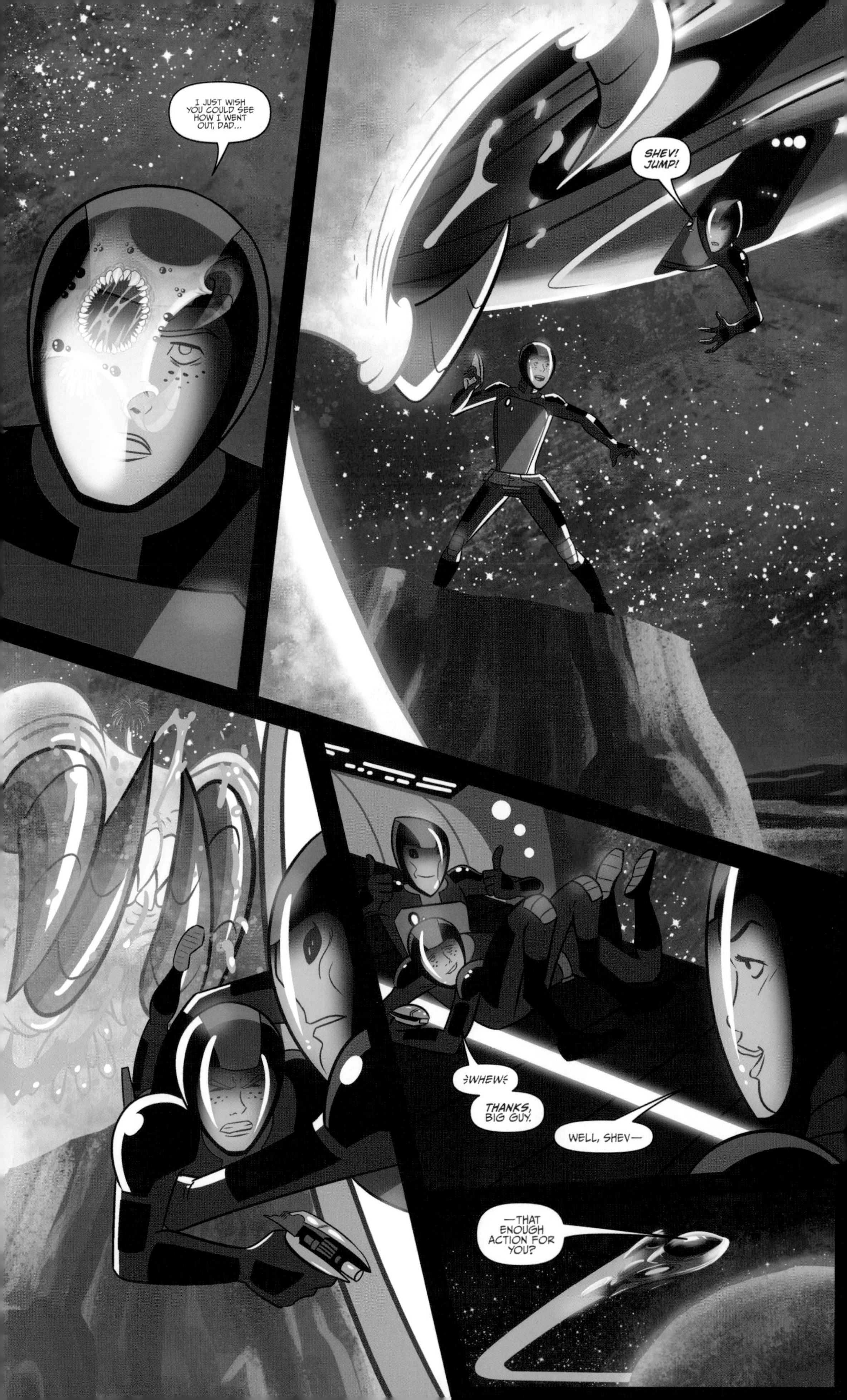
I JUST WISH YOU COULD SEE HOW I WENT OUT, DAD...
SHEV! JUMP!
WHEW
THANKS, BIG GUY.
WELL, SHEV—
—THAT ENOUGH ACTION FOR YOU?

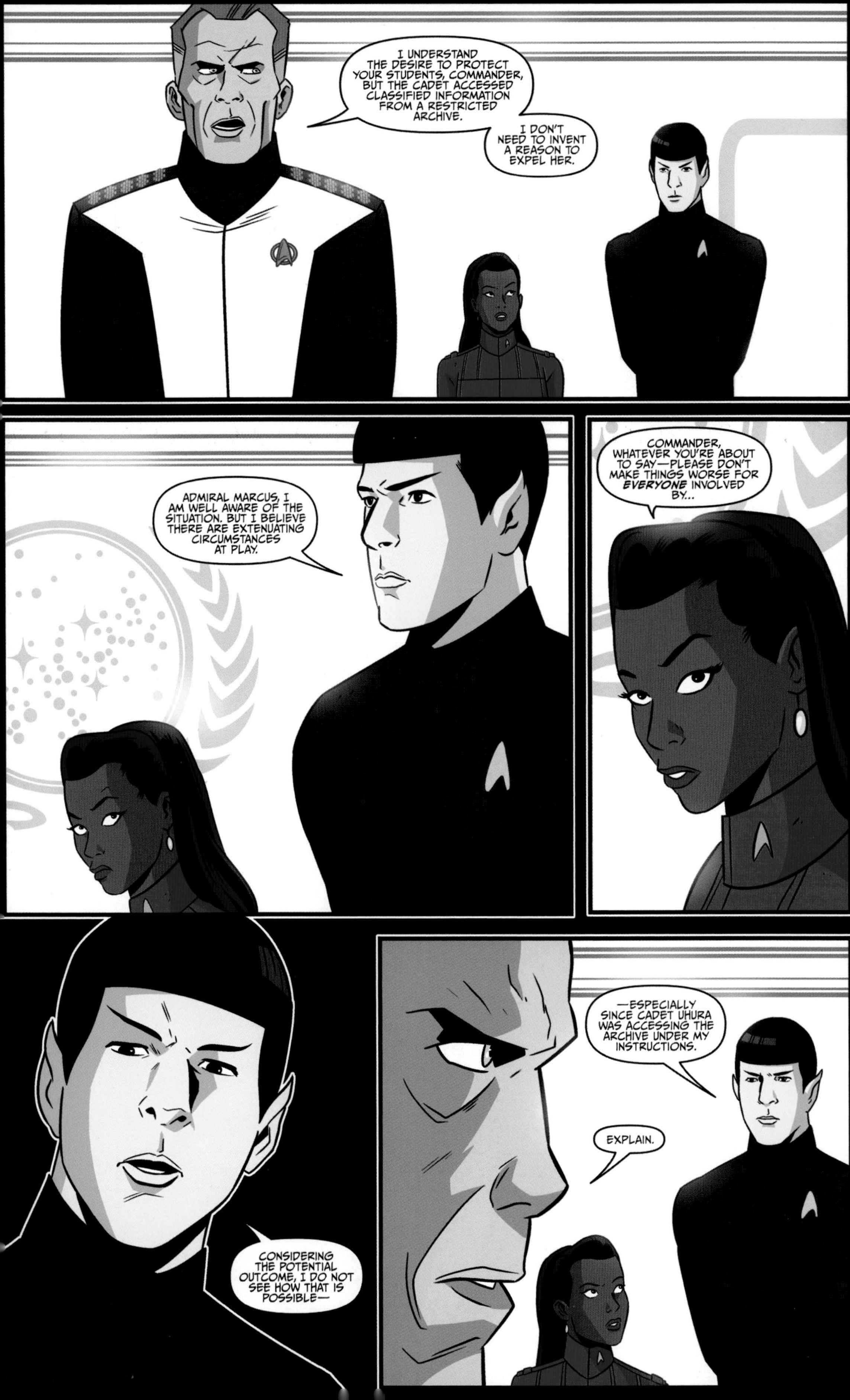
I UNDERSTAND THE DESIRE TO PROTECT YOUR STUDENTS, COMMANDER, BUT THE CADET ACCESSED CLASSIFIED INFORMATION FROM A RESTRICTED ARCHIVE.
I DON'T NEED TO INVENT A REASON TO EXPEL HER.
ADMIRAL MARCUS, I AM WELL AWARE OF THE SITUATION. BUT I BELIEVE THERE ARE EXTENUATING CIRCUMSTANCES AT PLAY.
COMMANDER, WHATEVER YOU'RE ABOUT TO SAY—PLEASE DON'T MAKE THINGS WORSE FOR *EVERYONE* INVOLVED BY...
CONSIDERING THE POTENTIAL OUTCOME, I DO NOT SEE HOW THAT IS POSSIBLE—
—ESPECIALLY SINCE CADET UHURA WAS ACCESSING THE ARCHIVE UNDER MY INSTRUCTIONS.
EXPLAIN.

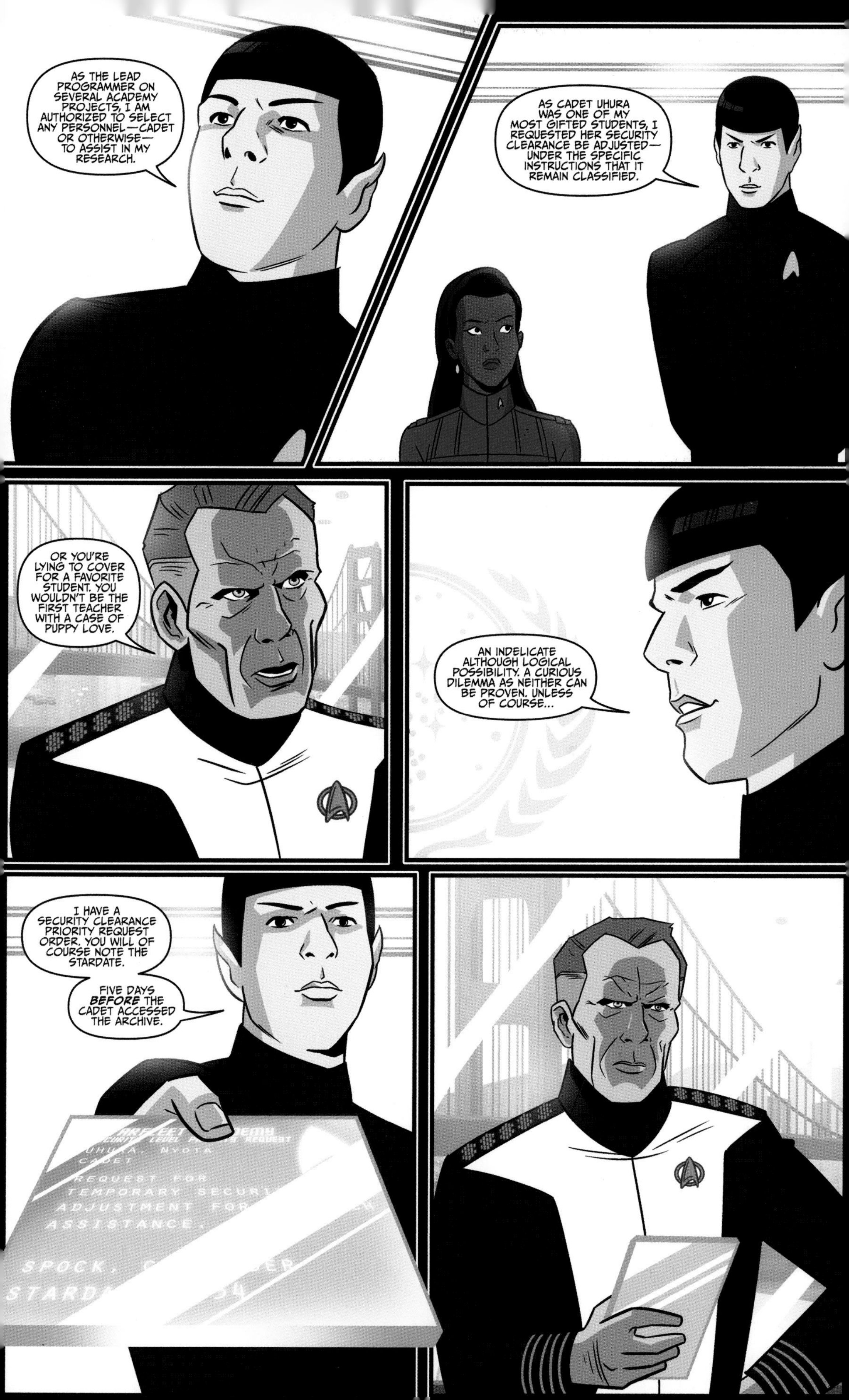
AS THE LEAD PROGRAMMER ON SEVERAL ACADEMY PROJECTS, I AM AUTHORIZED TO SELECT ANY PERSONNEL—CADET OR OTHERWISE—TO ASSIST IN MY RESEARCH.
AS CADET UHURA WAS ONE OF MY MOST GIFTED STUDENTS, I REQUESTED HER SECURITY CLEARANCE BE ADJUSTED—UNDER THE SPECIFIC INSTRUCTIONS THAT IT REMAIN CLASSIFIED.
OR YOU'RE LYING TO COVER FOR A FAVORITE STUDENT. YOU WOULDN'T BE THE FIRST TEACHER WITH A CASE OF PUPPY LOVE.
AN INDELICATE ALTHOUGH LOGICAL POSSIBILITY. A CURIOUS DILEMMA AS NEITHER CAN BE PROVEN. UNLESS OF COURSE...
I HAVE A SECURITY CLEARANCE PRIORITY REQUEST ORDER. YOU WILL OF COURSE NOTE THE STARDATE.
FIVE DAYS ***BEFORE*** THE CADET ACCESSED THE ARCHIVE.
UHURA, NYOTA
CADET
REQUEST FOR
ASSISTANCE.

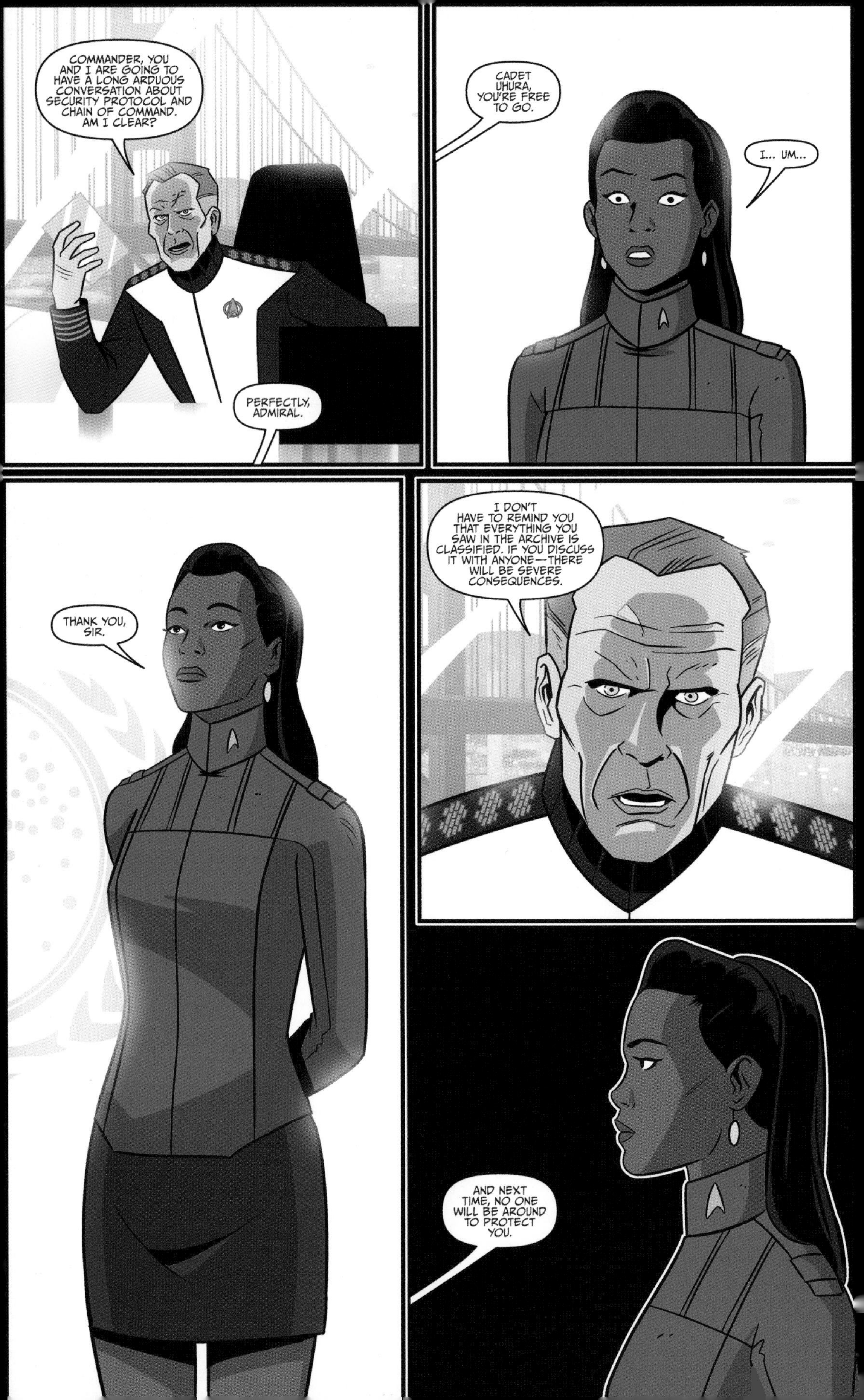
COMMANDER, YOU AND I ARE GOING TO HAVE A LONG ARDUOUS CONVERSATION ABOUT SECURITY PROTOCOL AND CHAIN OF COMMAND. AM I CLEAR?
PERFECTLY, ADMIRAL.
CADET UHURA, YOU'RE FREE TO GO.
I... UM...
THANK YOU, SIR.
I DON'T HAVE TO REMIND YOU THAT EVERYTHING YOU SAW IN THE ARCHIVE IS CLASSIFIED. IF YOU DISCUSS IT WITH ANYONE—THERE WILL BE SEVERE CONSEQUENCES.
AND NEXT TIME, NO ONE WILL BE AROUND TO PROTECT YOU.

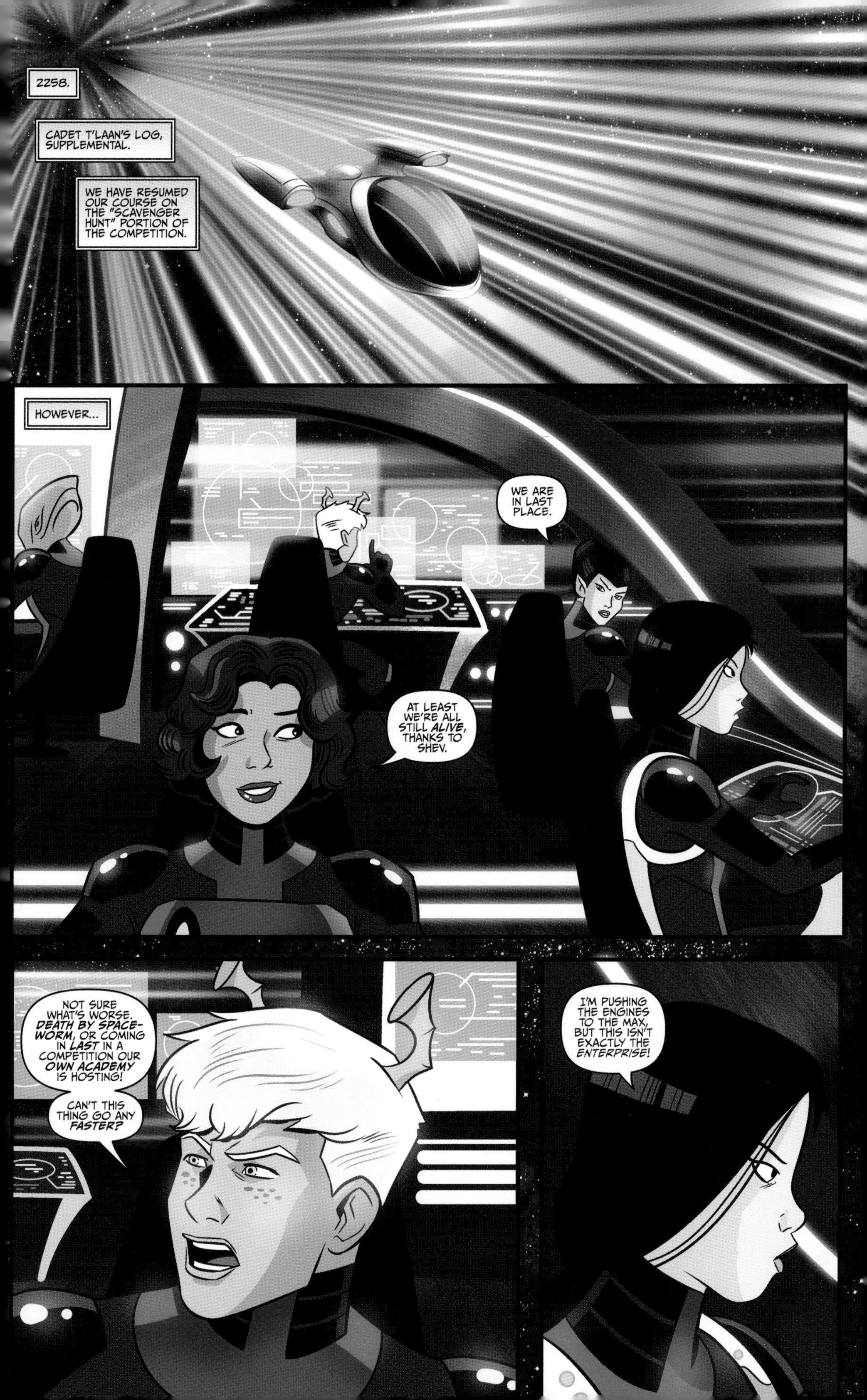
2258.
CADET T'LAAN'S LOG, SUPPLEMENTAL.
WE HAVE RESUMED OUR COURSE ON THE "SCAVENGER HUNT" PORTION OF THE COMPETITION.
HOWEVER...
WE ARE IN LAST PLACE.
AT LEAST WE'RE ALL STILL *ALIVE*, THANKS TO SHEV.
NOT SURE WHAT'S WORSE. ***DEATH BY SPACE-WORM***, OR COMING IN ***LAST*** IN A COMPETITION OUR ***OWN ACADEMY*** IS HOSTING!
CAN'T THIS THING GO ANY *FASTER?*
I'M PUSHING THE ENGINES TO THE MAX, BUT THIS ISN'T EXACTLY THE *ENTERPRISE!*

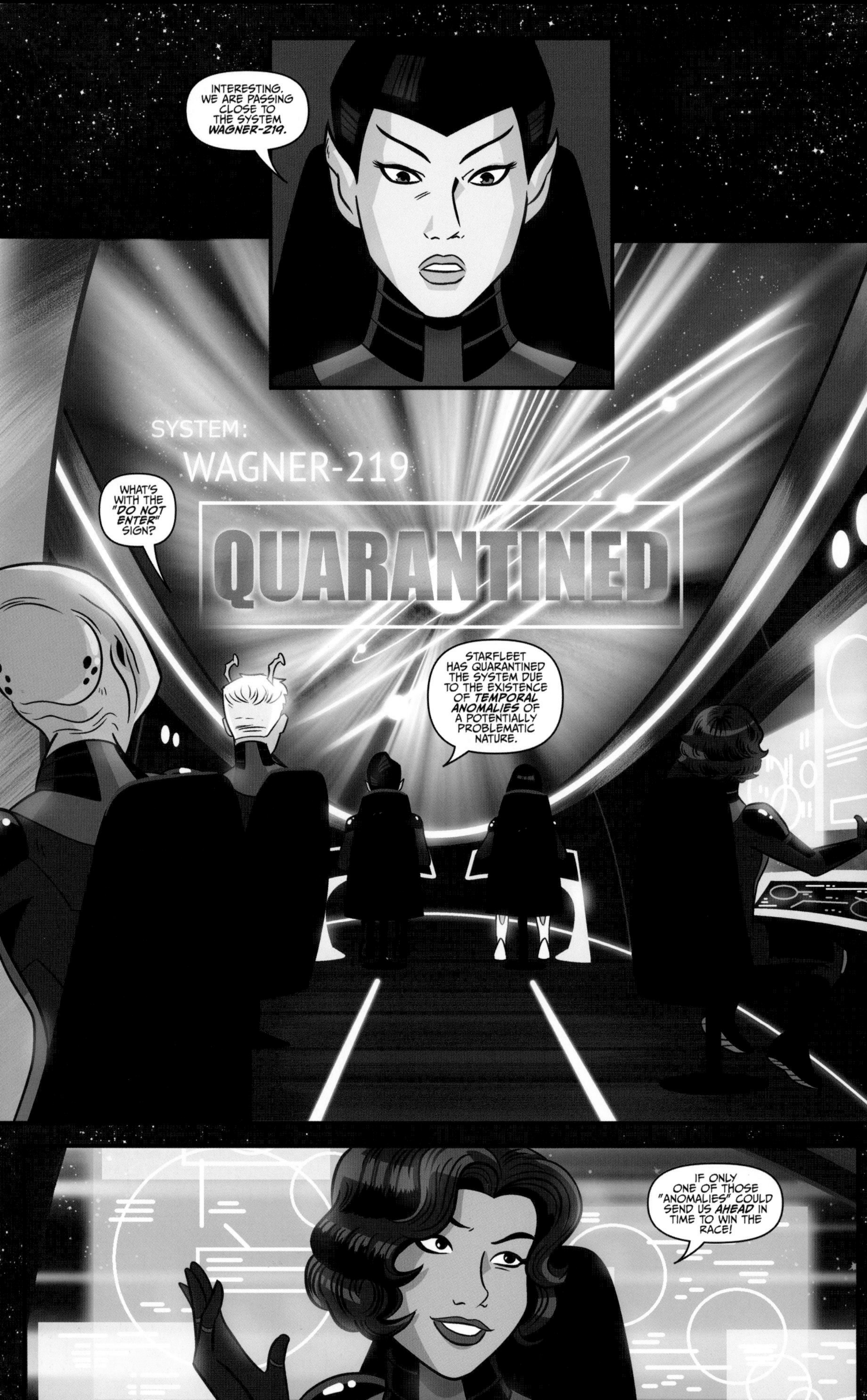
INTERESTING. WE ARE PASSING CLOSE TO THE SYSTEM *WAGNER-219.*
SYSTEM: WAGNER-219
QUARANTINED
WHAT'S WITH THE *"DO NOT ENTER"* SIGN?
STARFLEET HAS QUARANTINED THE SYSTEM DUE TO THE EXISTENCE OF *TEMPORAL ANOMALIES* OF A POTENTIALLY PROBLEMATIC NATURE.
IF ONLY ONE OF THOSE "ANOMALIES" COULD SEND US *AHEAD* IN TIME TO WIN THE RACE!

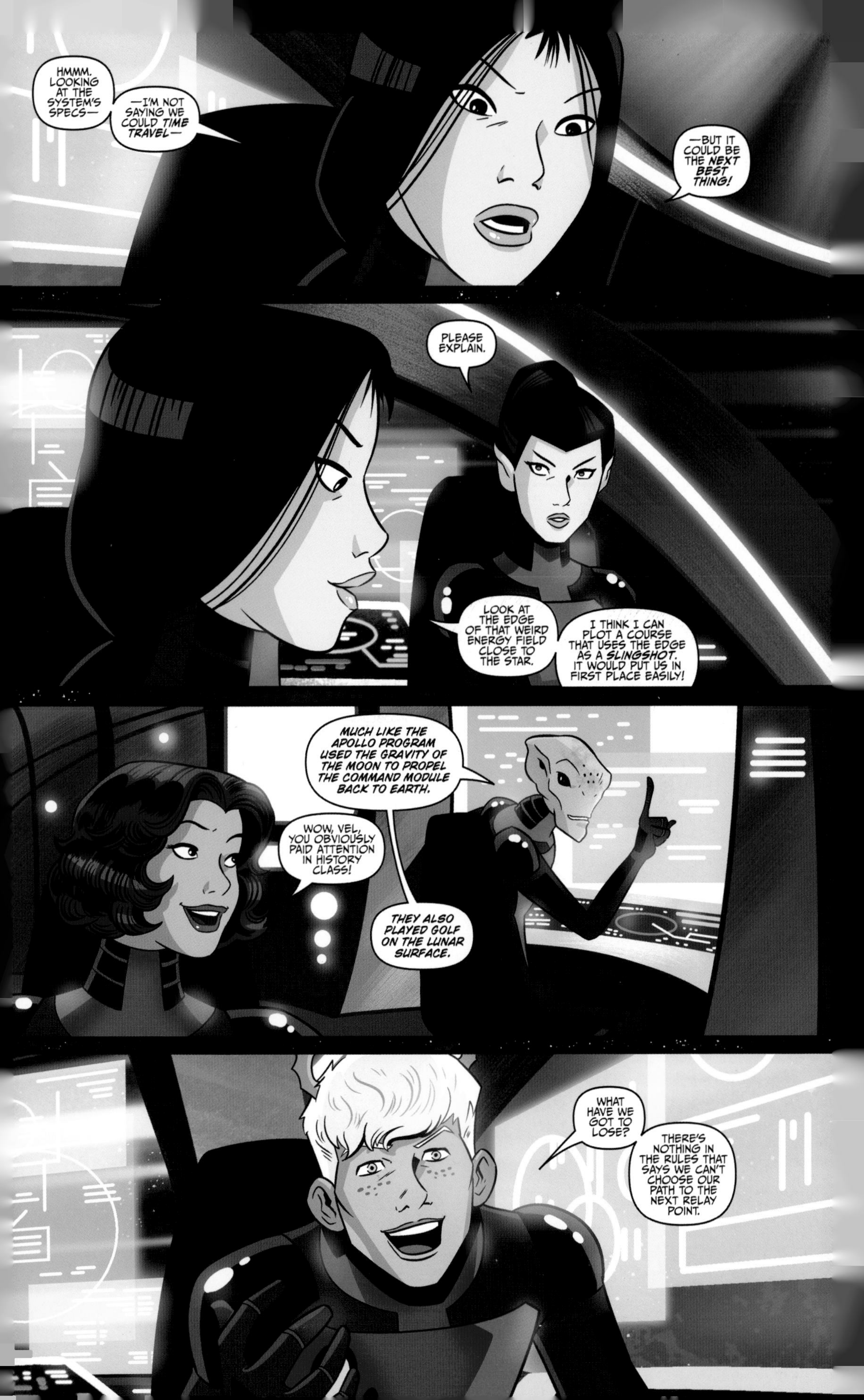
HMMM. LOOKING AT THE SYSTEM'S SPECS—
—I'M NOT SAYING WE COULD *TIME TRAVEL*—
—BUT IT COULD BE THE *NEXT BEST THING!*
PLEASE EXPLAIN.
LOOK AT THE EDGE OF THAT WEIRD ENERGY FIELD CLOSE TO THE STAR.
I THINK I CAN PLOT A COURSE THAT USES THE EDGE AS A *SLINGSHOT*. IT WOULD PUT US IN FIRST PLACE EASILY!
MUCH LIKE THE APOLLO PROGRAM USED THE GRAVITY OF THE MOON TO PROPEL THE COMMAND MODULE BACK TO EARTH.
WOW, VEL, YOU OBVIOUSLY PAID ATTENTION IN HISTORY CLASS!
THEY ALSO PLAYED GOLF ON THE LUNAR SURFACE.
WHAT HAVE WE GOT TO LOSE?
THERE'S NOTHING IN THE RULES THAT SAYS WE CAN'T CHOOSE OUR PATH TO THE NEXT RELAY POINT.

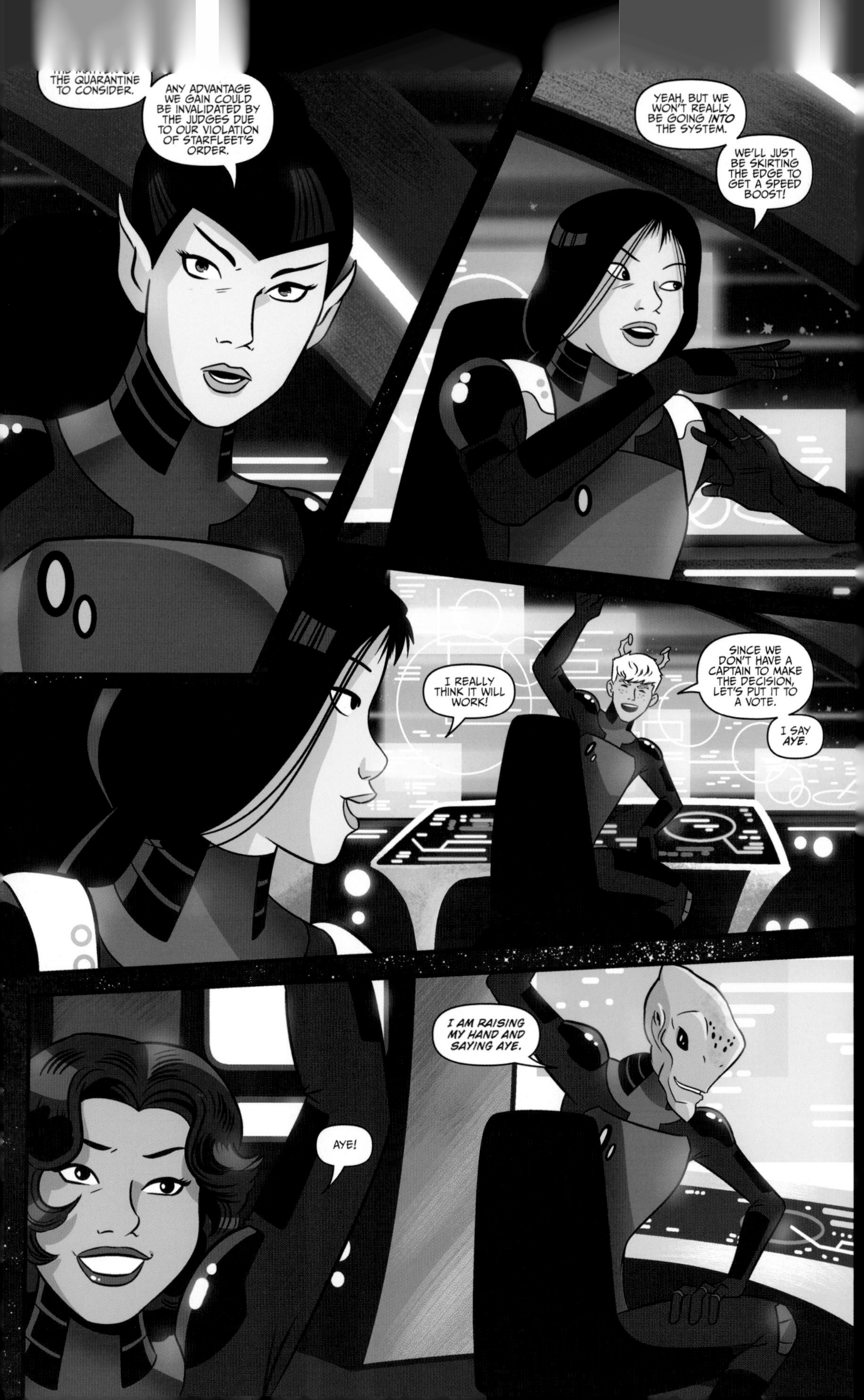
THE QUARANTINE TO CONSIDER.
ANY ADVANTAGE WE GAIN COULD BE INVALIDATED BY THE JUDGES DUE TO OUR VIOLATION OF STARFLEET'S ORDER.
YEAH, BUT WE WON'T REALLY BE GOING *INTO* THE SYSTEM.
WE'LL JUST BE SKIRTING THE EDGE TO GET A SPEED BOOST!
I REALLY THINK IT WILL WORK!
SINCE WE DON'T HAVE A CAPTAIN TO MAKE THE DECISION, LET'S PUT IT TO A VOTE.
I SAY **AYE**.
AYE!
I AM RAISING MY HAND AND SAYING AYE.

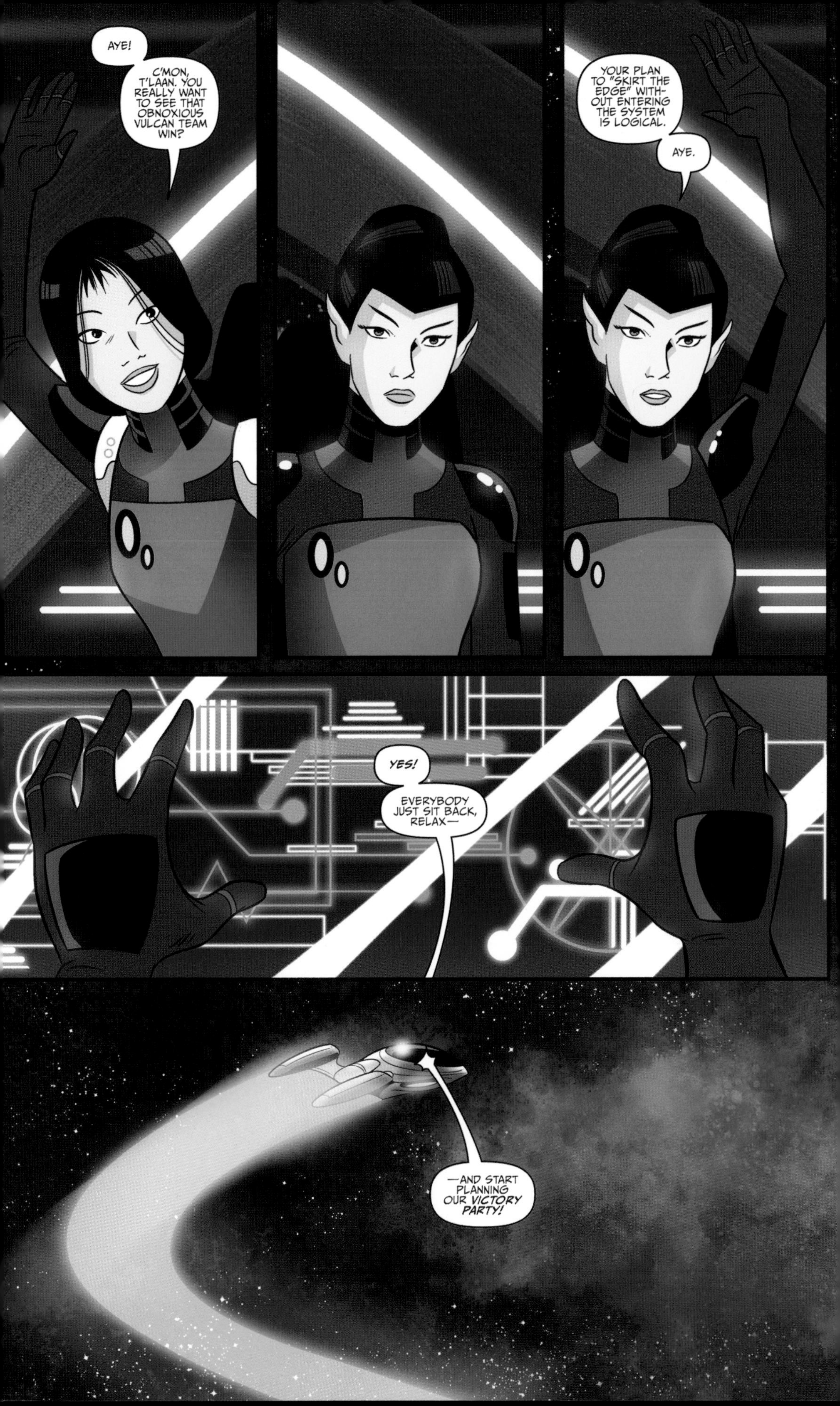
AYE!
C'MON, T'LAAN. YOU REALLY WANT TO SEE THAT OBNOXIOUS VULCAN TEAM WIN?
YOUR PLAN TO "SKIRT THE EDGE" WITHOUT ENTERING THE SYSTEM IS LOGICAL.
AYE.
YES!
EVERYBODY JUST SIT BACK, RELAX—
—AND START PLANNING OUR VICTORY PARTY!

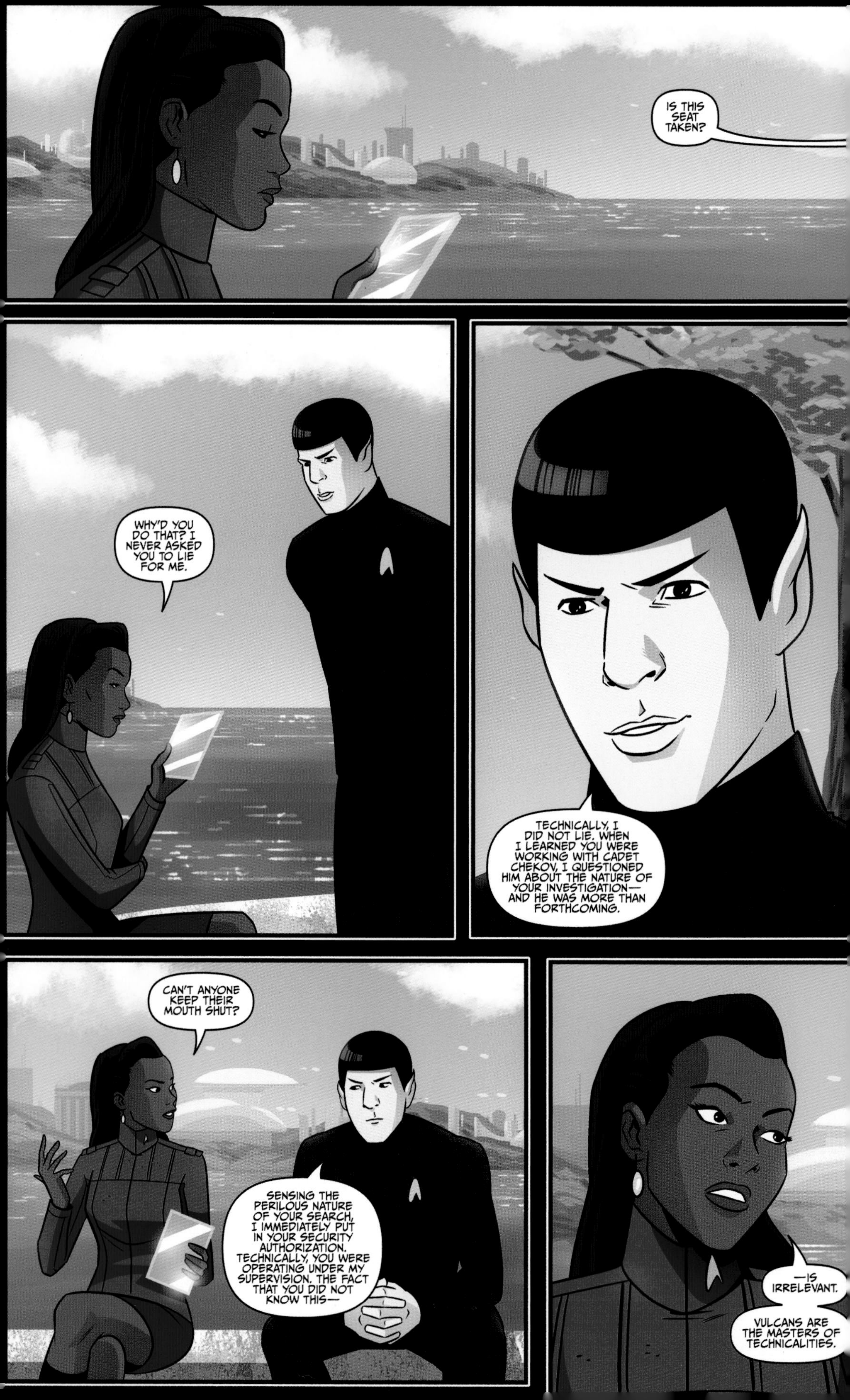
IS THIS SEAT TAKEN?
WHY'D YOU DO THAT? I NEVER ASKED YOU TO LIE FOR ME.
TECHNICALLY, I DID NOT LIE. WHEN I LEARNED YOU WERE WORKING WITH CADET CHEKOV, I QUESTIONED HIM ABOUT THE NATURE OF YOUR INVESTIGATION—AND HE WAS MORE THAN FORTHCOMING.
CAN'T ANYONE KEEP THEIR MOUTH SHUT?
SENSING THE PERILOUS NATURE OF YOUR SEARCH, I IMMEDIATELY PUT IN YOUR SECURITY AUTHORIZATION. TECHNICALLY, YOU WERE OPERATING UNDER MY SUPERVISION. THE FACT THAT YOU DID NOT KNOW THIS—
—IS IRRELEVANT.
VULCANS ARE THE MASTERS OF TECHNICALITIES.

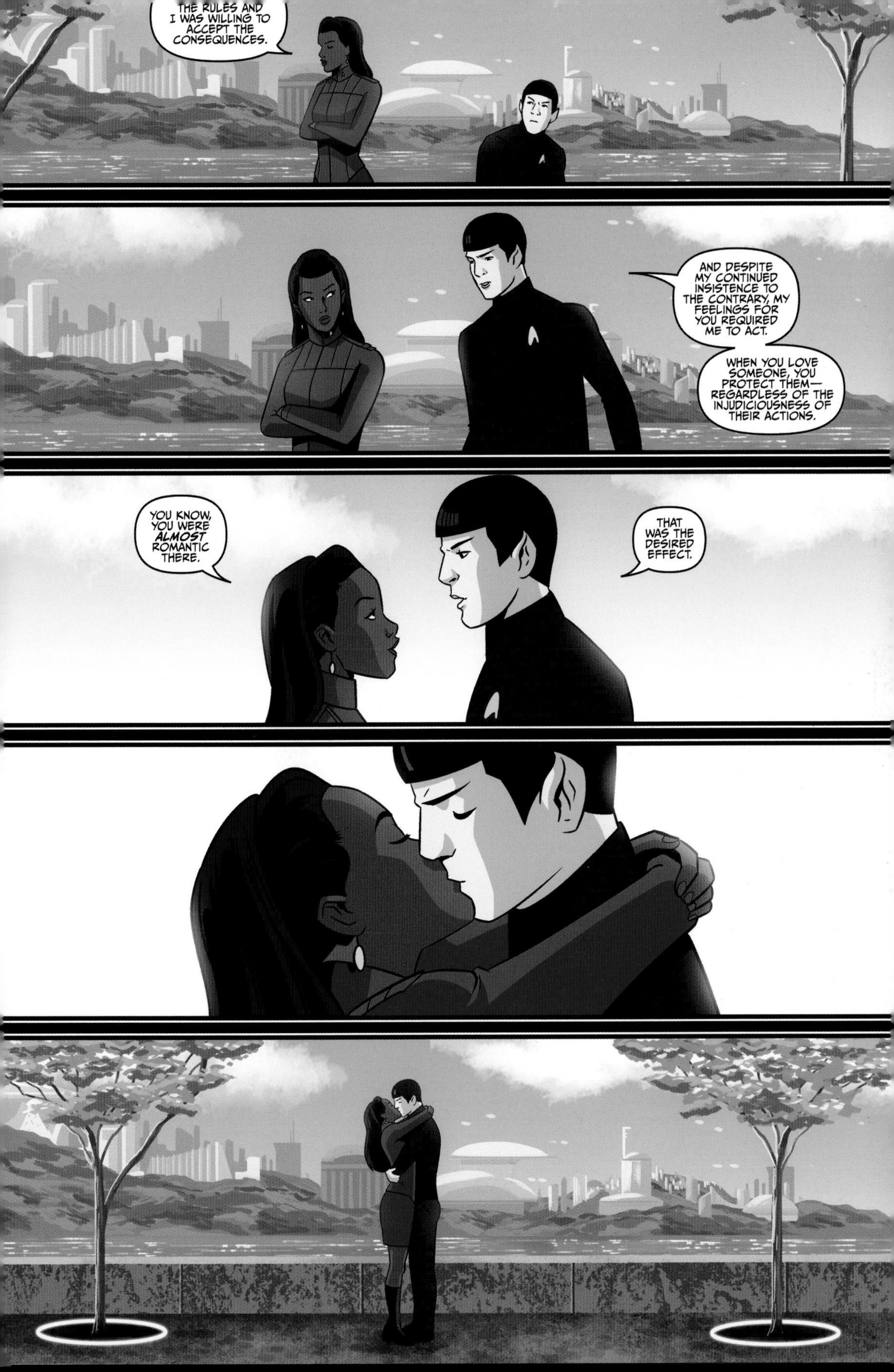
THE RULES AND I WAS WILLING TO ACCEPT THE CONSEQUENCES.
AND DESPITE MY CONTINUED INSISTENCE TO THE CONTRARY, MY FEELINGS FOR YOU REQUIRED ME TO ACT.
WHEN YOU LOVE SOMEONE, YOU PROTECT THEM— REGARDLESS OF THE INJUDICIOUSNESS OF THEIR ACTIONS.
YOU KNOW, YOU WERE *ALMOST* ROMANTIC THERE.
THAT WAS THE DESIRED EFFECT.

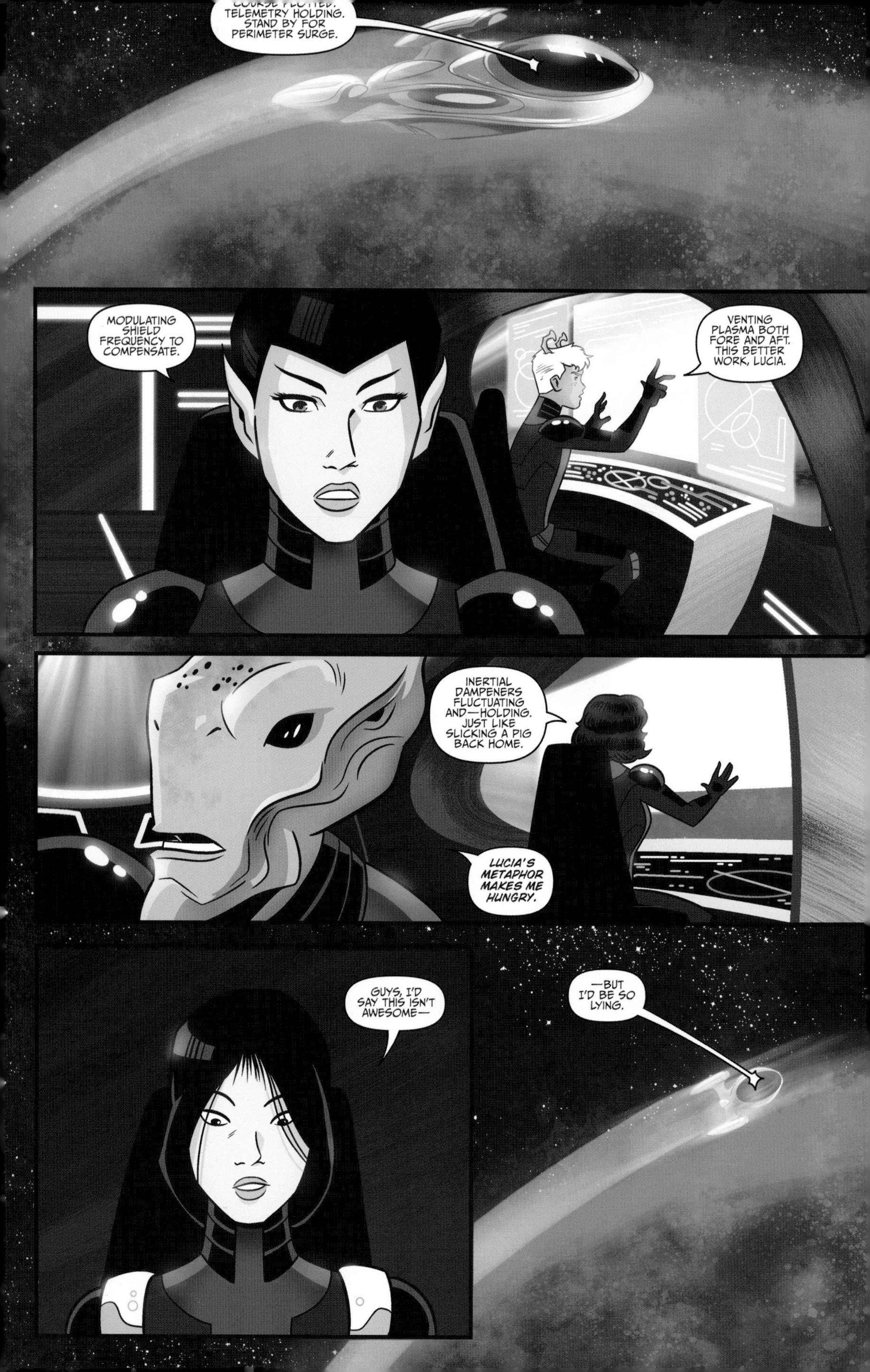
TELEMETRY HOLDING. STAND BY FOR PERIMETER SURGE.
MODULATING SHIELD FREQUENCY TO COMPENSATE.
VENTING PLASMA BOTH FORE AND AFT. THIS BETTER WORK, LUCIA.
INERTIAL DAMPENERS FLUCTUATING AND—HOLDING. JUST LIKE SLICKING A PIG BACK HOME.
LUCIA'S METAPHOR MAKES ME HUNGRY.
GUYS, I'D SAY THIS ISN'T AWESOME—
—BUT I'D BE SO LYING.

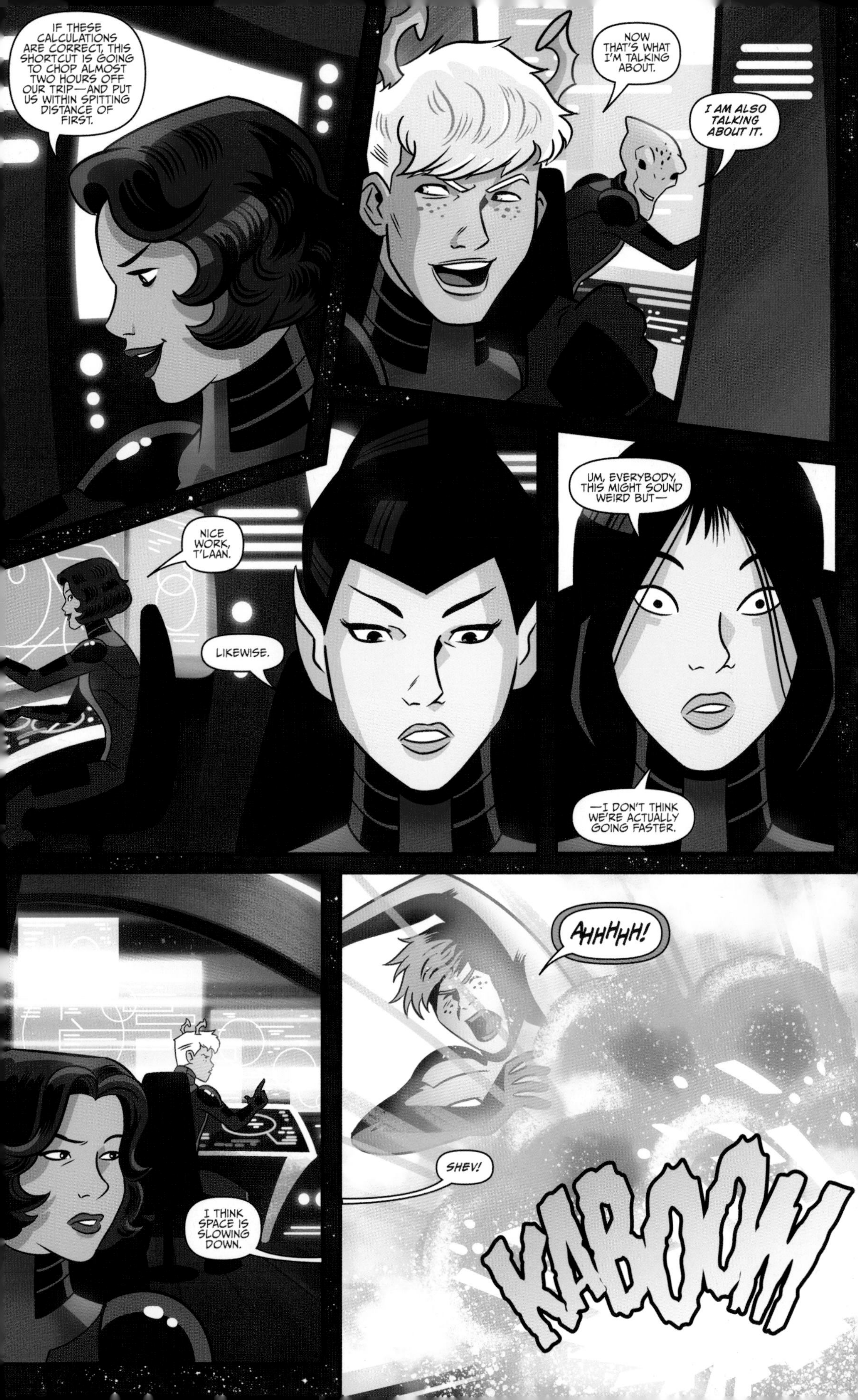
IF THESE CALCULATIONS ARE CORRECT, THIS SHORTCUT IS GOING TO CHOP ALMOST TWO HOURS OFF OUR TRIP—AND PUT US WITHIN SPITTING DISTANCE OF FIRST.
NOW THAT'S WHAT I'M TALKING ABOUT.
I AM ALSO TALKING ABOUT IT.
NICE WORK, T'LAAN.
LIKEWISE.
UM, EVERYBODY, THIS MIGHT SOUND WEIRD BUT—
—I DON'T THINK WE'RE ACTUALLY GOING FASTER.
I THINK SPACE IS SLOWING DOWN.
AHHHHH!
SHEV!
KABOOM

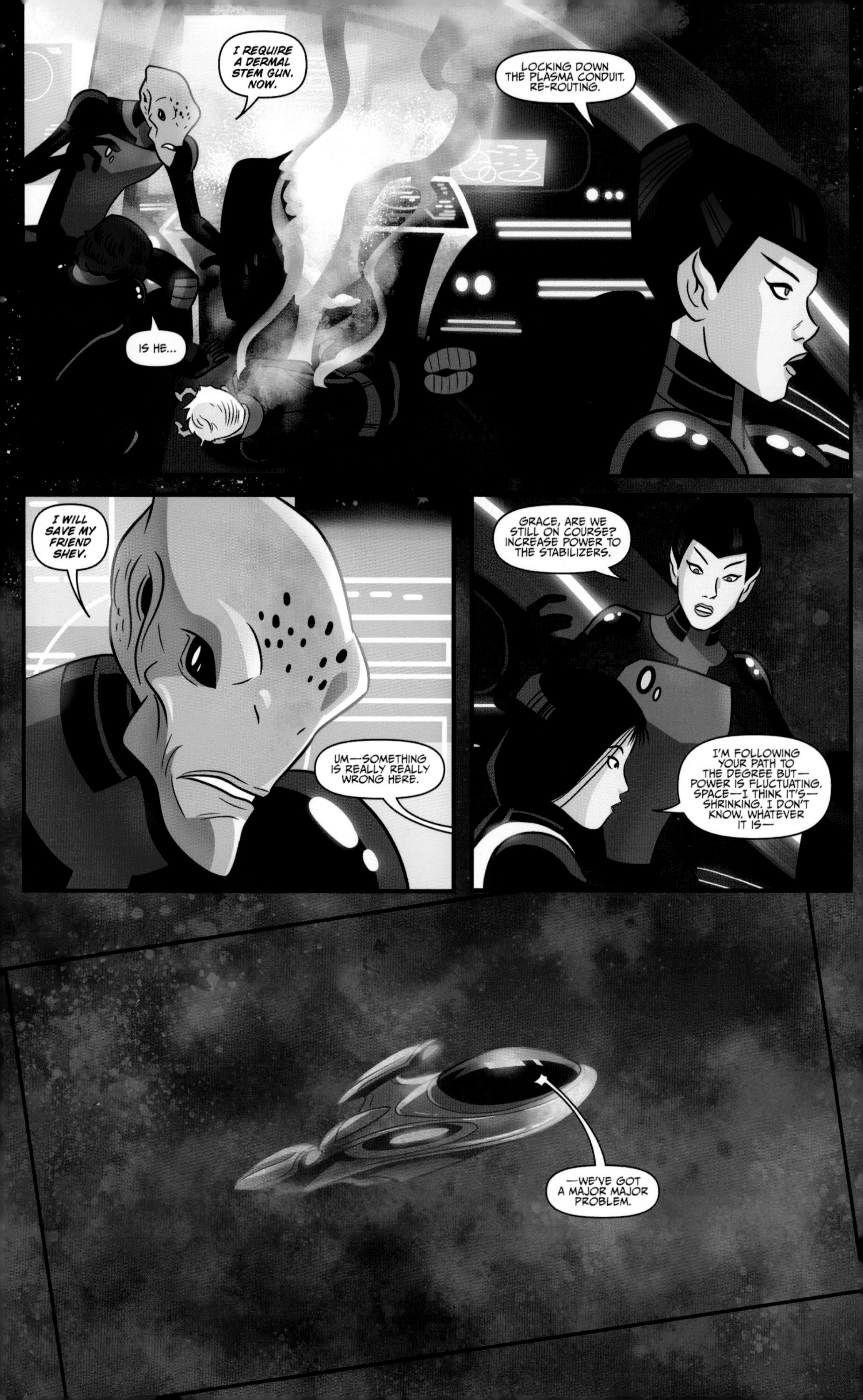

I REQUIRE A DERMAL STEM GUN. NOW.
LOCKING DOWN THE PLASMA CONDUIT. RE-ROUTING.
IS HE...
I WILL SAVE MY FRIEND SHEV.
UM—SOMETHING IS REALLY REALLY WRONG HERE.
GRACE, ARE WE STILL ON COURSE? INCREASE POWER TO THE STABILIZERS.
I'M FOLLOWING YOUR PATH TO THE DEGREE BUT—POWER IS FLUCTUATING. SPACE—I THINK IT'S—SHRINKING. I DON'T KNOW. WHATEVER IT IS—
—WE'VE GOT A MAJOR MAJOR PROBLEM.

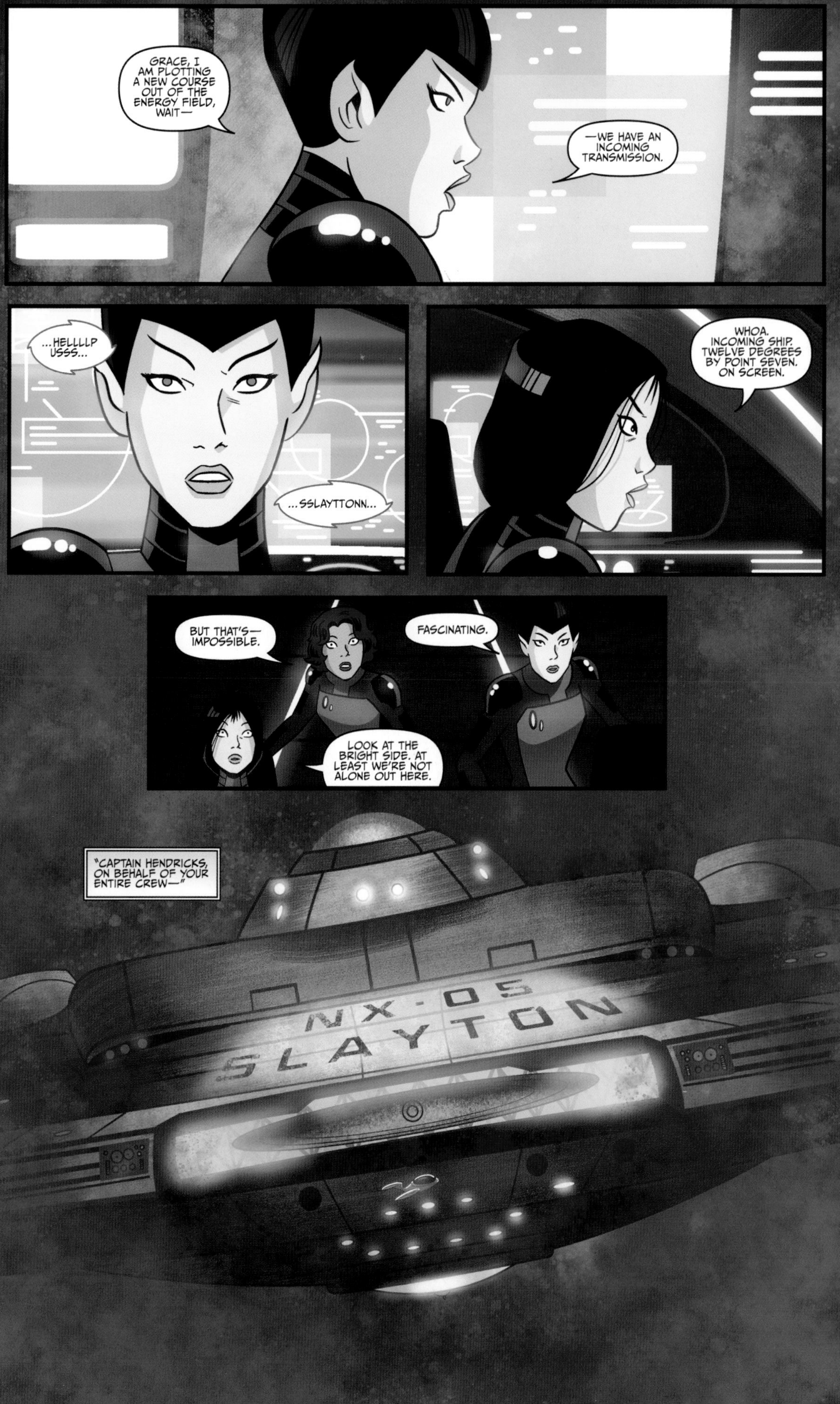

GRACE, I AM PLOTTING A NEW COURSE OUT OF THE ENERGY FIELD, WAIT—
—WE HAVE AN INCOMING TRANSMISSION.
...HELLLLP USSS...
...SSLAYTTONN...
WHOA. INCOMING SHIP. TWELVE DEGREES BY POINT SEVEN. ON SCREEN.
BUT THAT'S— IMPOSSIBLE.
FASCINATING.
LOOK AT THE BRIGHT SIDE. AT LEAST WE'RE NOT ALONE OUT HERE.
"CAPTAIN HENDRICKS, ON BEHALF OF YOUR ENTIRE CREW—"
NX-05
SLAYTON

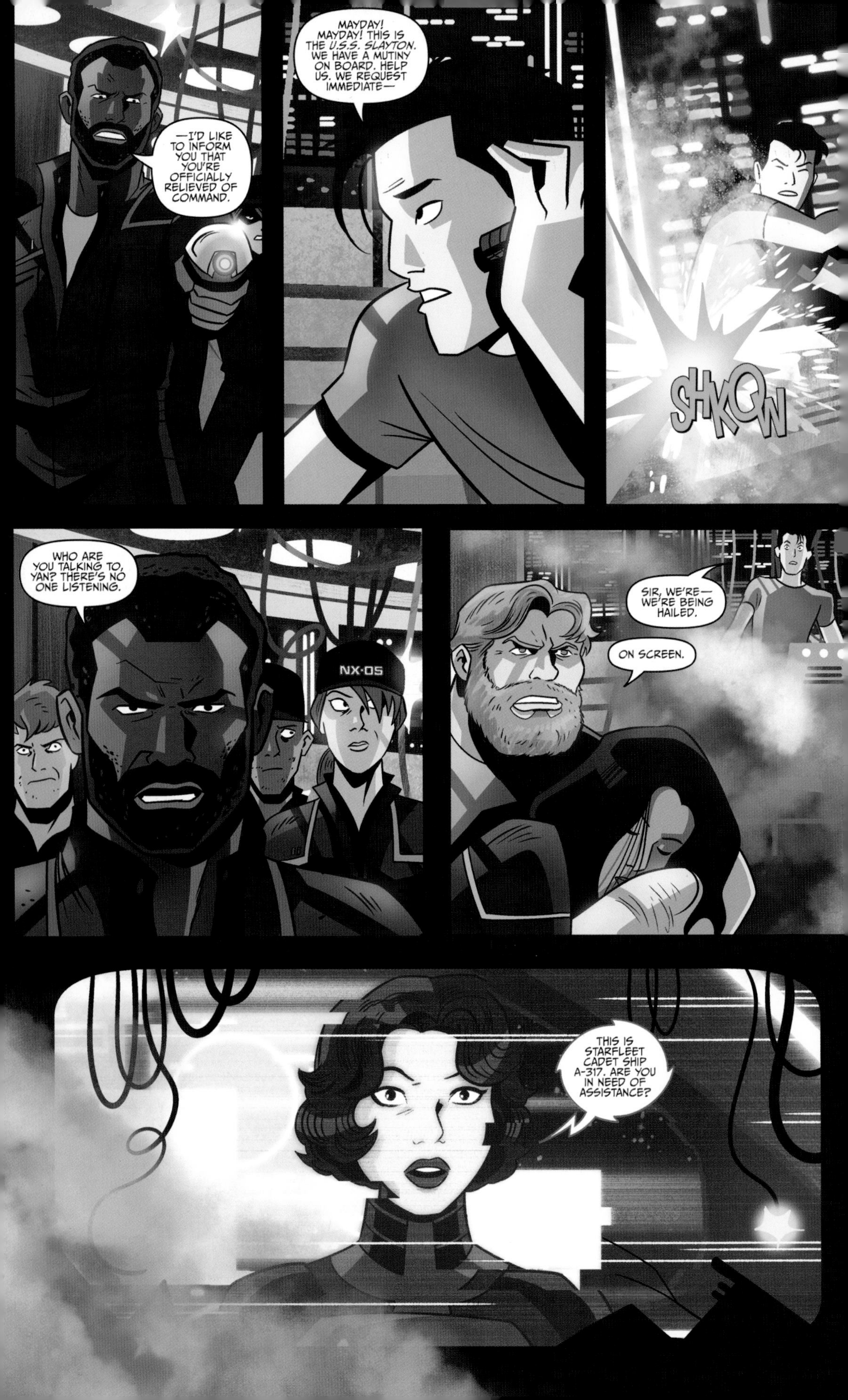
—I'D LIKE TO INFORM YOU THAT YOU'RE OFFICIALLY RELIEVED OF COMMAND.
MAYDAY! MAYDAY! THIS IS THE U.S.S. SLAYTON. WE HAVE A MUTINY ON BOARD. HELP US. WE REQUEST IMMEDIATE—
SHKOW
WHO ARE YOU TALKING TO, YAN? THERE'S NO ONE LISTENING.
NX-05
SIR, WE'RE— WE'RE BEING HAILED.
ON SCREEN.
THIS IS STARFLEET CADET SHIP A-317. ARE YOU IN NEED OF ASSISTANCE?

ART BY **ROBERT WILSON IV**

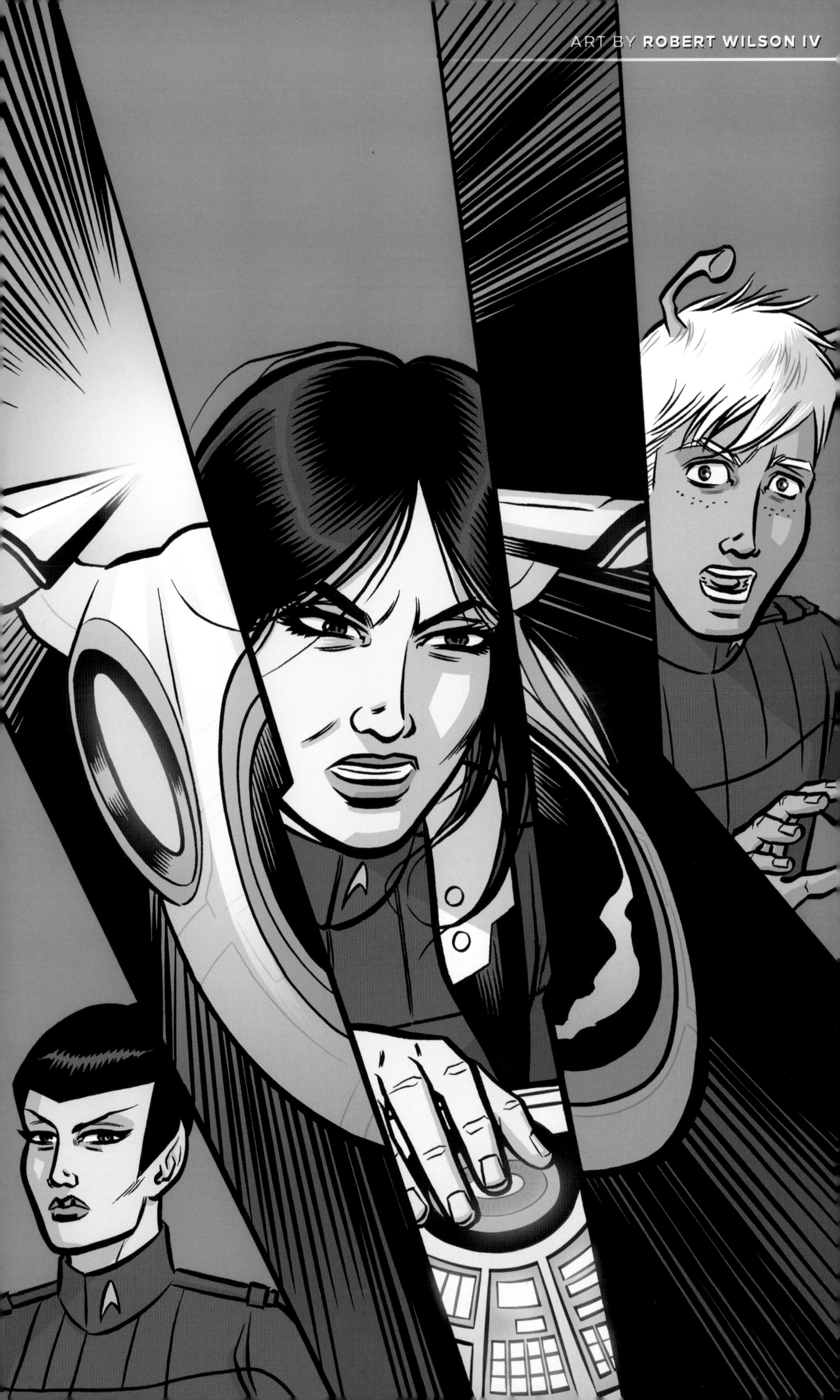

ART BY **DEREK CHARM**

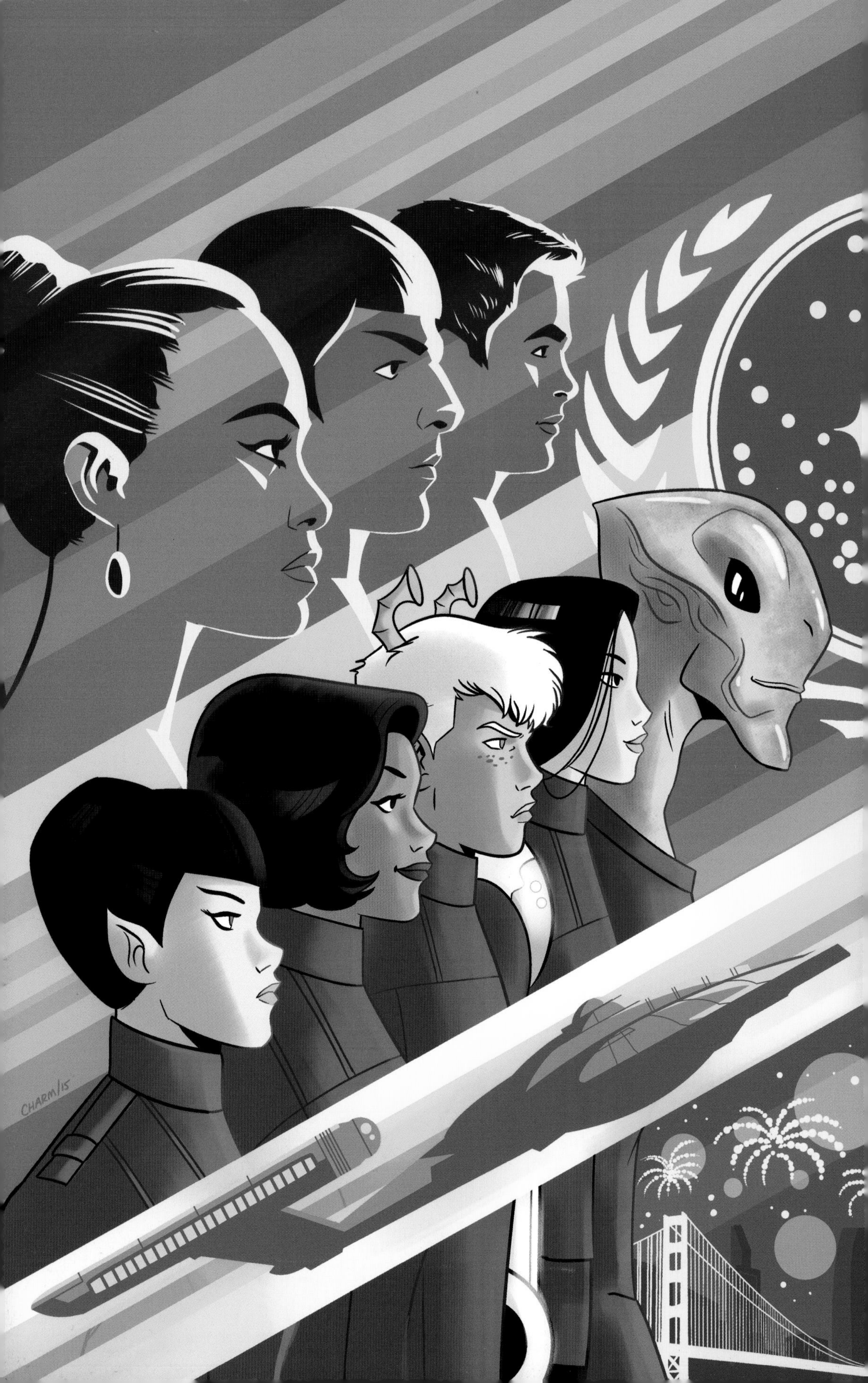
CHARM/15

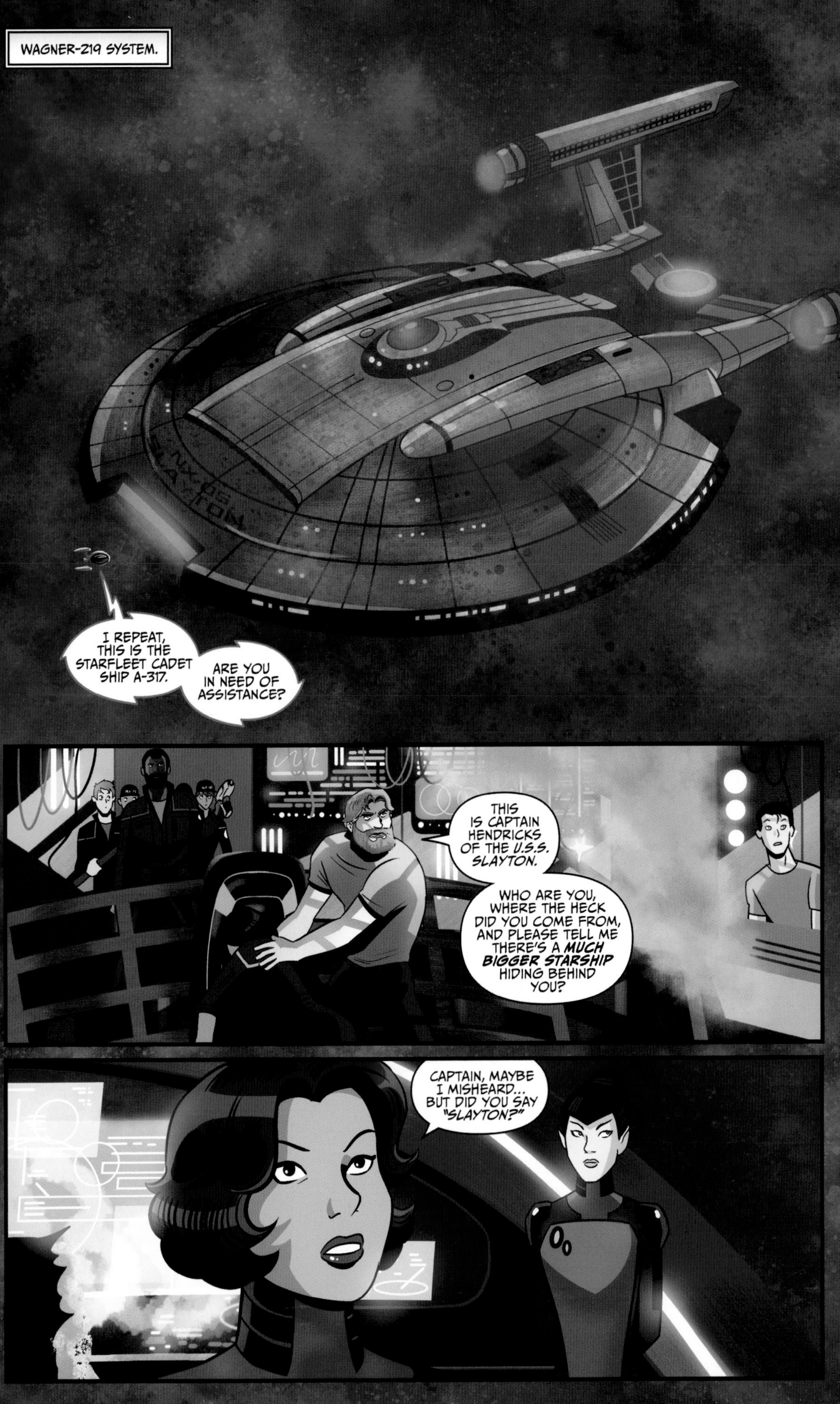
WAGNER-219 SYSTEM.
I REPEAT, THIS IS THE STARFLEET CADET SHIP A-317.
ARE YOU IN NEED OF ASSISTANCE?
THIS IS CAPTAIN HENDRICKS OF THE U.S.S. SLAYTON.
WHO ARE YOU, WHERE THE HECK DID YOU COME FROM, AND PLEASE TELL ME THERE'S A MUCH BIGGER STARSHIP HIDING BEHIND YOU?
CAPTAIN, MAYBE I MISHEARD... BUT DID YOU SAY "SLAYTON?"

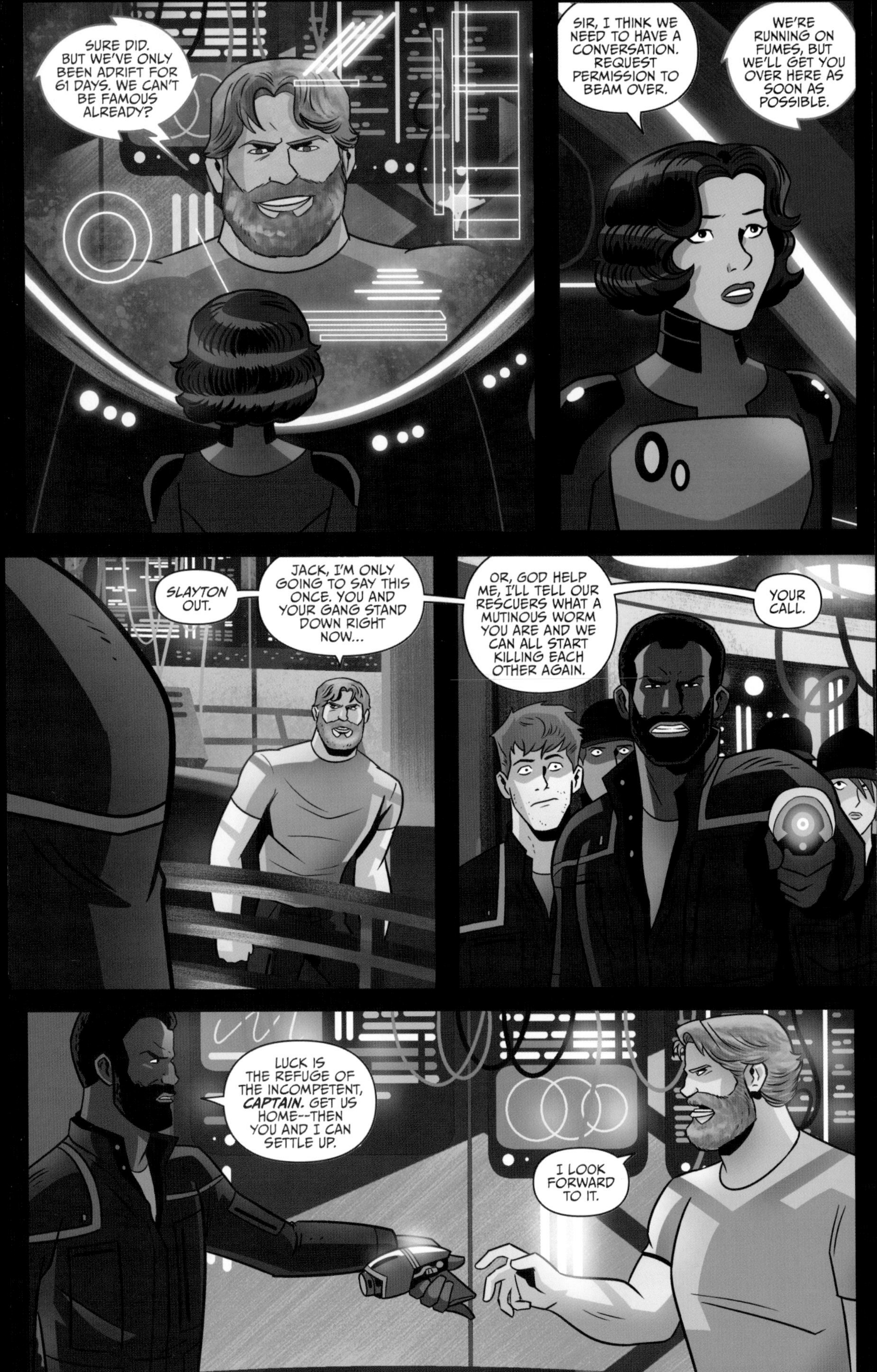

SURE DID. BUT WE'VE ONLY BEEN ADRIFT FOR 61 DAYS. WE CAN'T BE FAMOUS ALREADY?
SIR, I THINK WE NEED TO HAVE A CONVERSATION. REQUEST PERMISSION TO BEAM OVER.
WE'RE RUNNING ON FUMES, BUT WE'LL GET YOU OVER HERE AS SOON AS POSSIBLE.
SLAYTON OUT.
JACK, I'M ONLY GOING TO SAY THIS ONCE. YOU AND YOUR GANG STAND DOWN RIGHT NOW...
OR, GOD HELP ME, I'LL TELL OUR RESCUERS WHAT A MUTINOUS WORM YOU ARE AND WE CAN ALL START KILLING EACH OTHER AGAIN.
YOUR CALL.
LUCK IS THE REFUGE OF THE INCOMPETENT, *CAPTAIN.* GET US HOME--THEN YOU AND I CAN SETTLE UP.
I LOOK FORWARD TO IT.

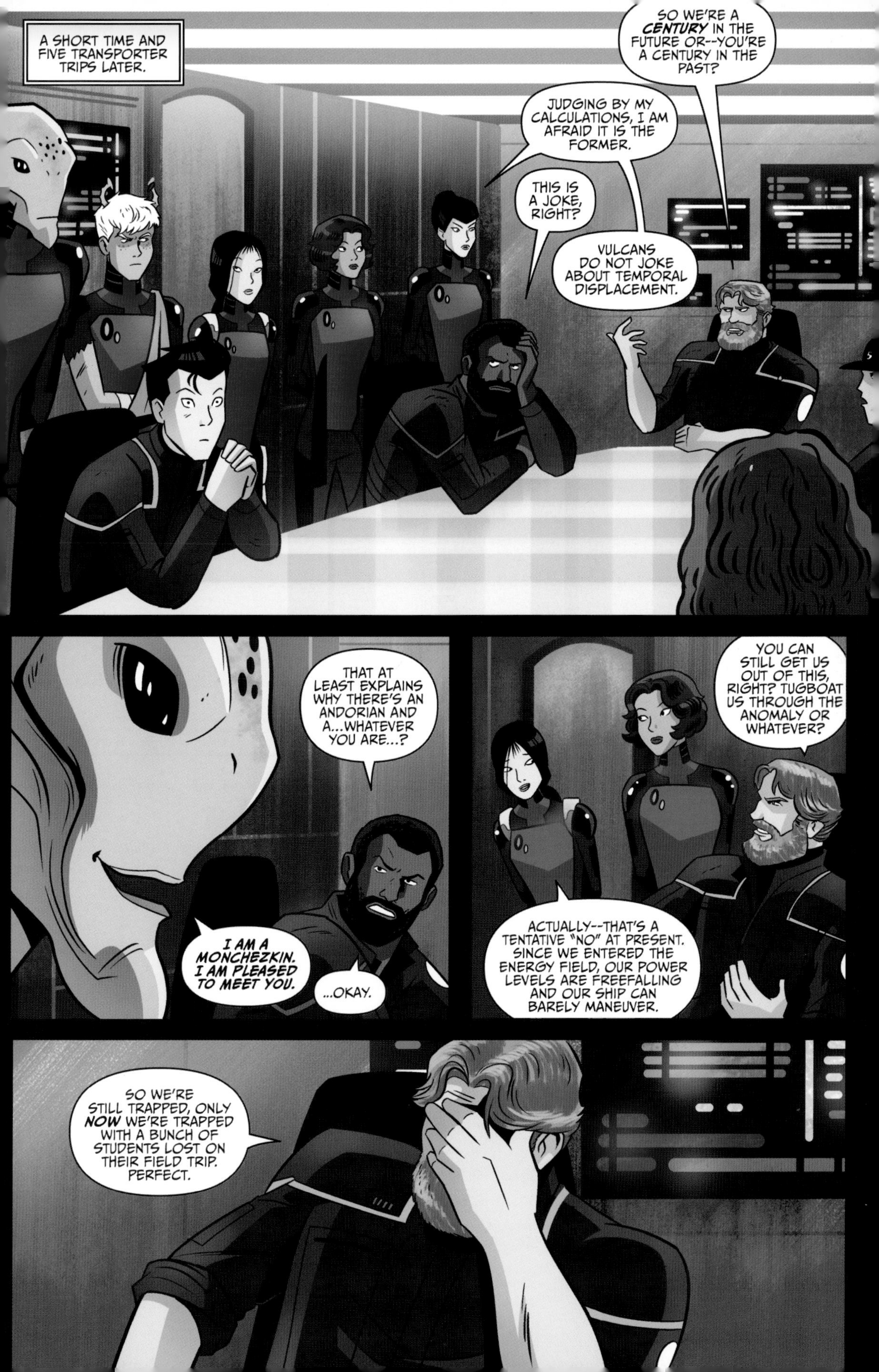
A SHORT TIME AND FIVE TRANSPORTER TRIPS LATER.
SO WE'RE A *CENTURY* IN THE FUTURE OR--YOU'RE A CENTURY IN THE PAST?
JUDGING BY MY CALCULATIONS, I AM AFRAID IT IS THE FORMER.
THIS IS A JOKE, RIGHT?
VULCANS DO NOT JOKE ABOUT TEMPORAL DISPLACEMENT.
THAT AT LEAST EXPLAINS WHY THERE'S AN ANDORIAN AND A...WHATEVER YOU ARE...?
I AM A MONCHEZKIN. I AM PLEASED TO MEET YOU.
...OKAY.
YOU CAN STILL GET US OUT OF THIS, RIGHT? TUGBOAT US THROUGH THE ANOMALY OR WHATEVER?
ACTUALLY--THAT'S A TENTATIVE "NO" AT PRESENT. SINCE WE ENTERED THE ENERGY FIELD, OUR POWER LEVELS ARE FREEFALLING AND OUR SHIP CAN BARELY MANEUVER.
SO WE'RE STILL TRAPPED, ONLY *NOW* WE'RE TRAPPED WITH A BUNCH OF STUDENTS LOST ON THEIR FIELD TRIP. PERFECT.

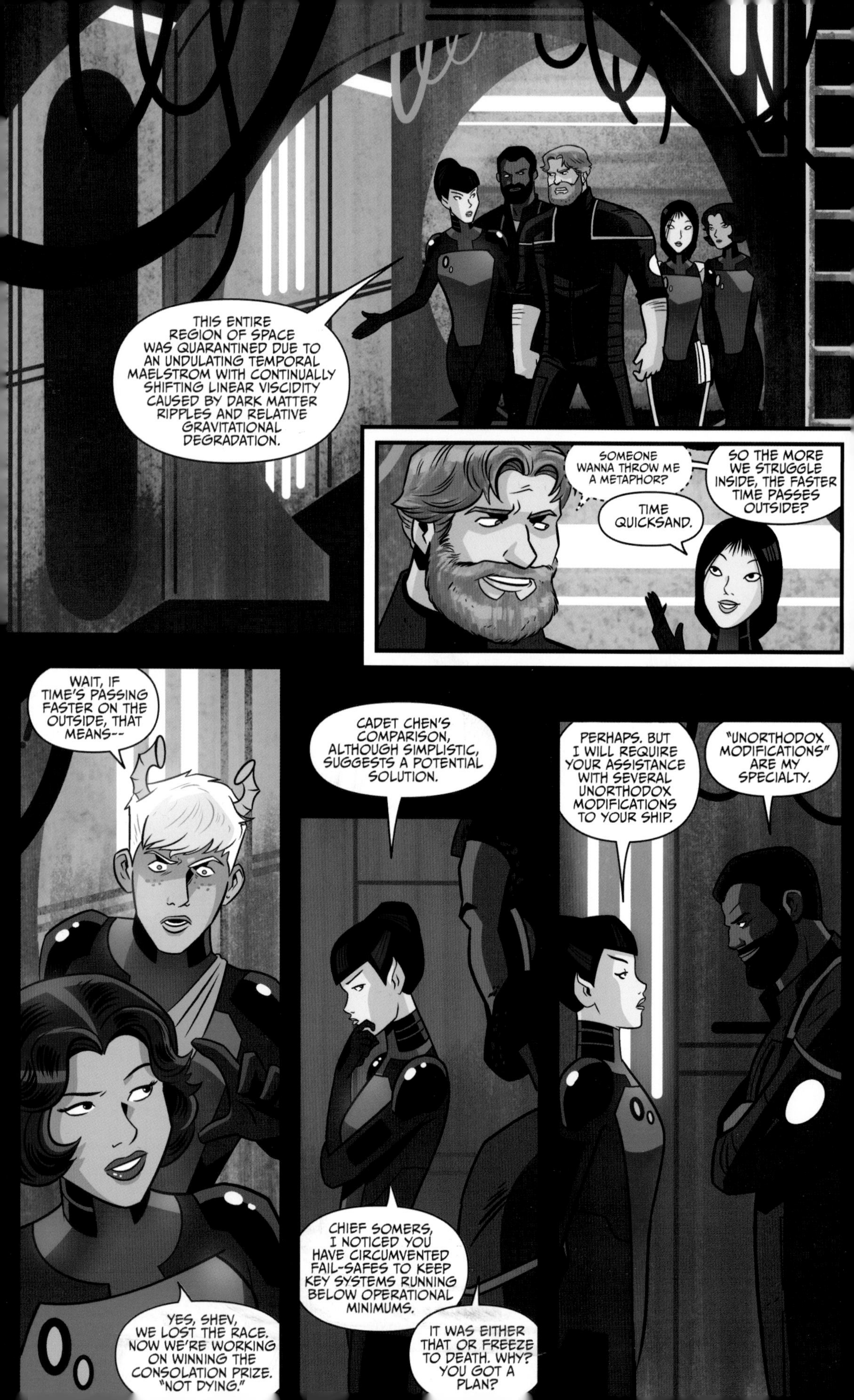
THIS ENTIRE REGION OF SPACE WAS QUARANTINED DUE TO AN UNDULATING TEMPORAL MAELSTROM WITH CONTINUALLY SHIFTING LINEAR VISCIDITY CAUSED BY DARK MATTER RIPPLES AND RELATIVE GRAVITATIONAL DEGRADATION.
SOMEONE WANNA THROW ME A METAPHOR?
TIME QUICKSAND.
SO THE MORE WE STRUGGLE INSIDE, THE FASTER TIME PASSES OUTSIDE?
WAIT, IF TIME'S PASSING FASTER ON THE OUTSIDE, THAT MEANS--
YES, SHEV, WE LOST THE RACE. NOW WE'RE WORKING ON WINNING THE CONSOLATION PRIZE. "NOT DYING."
CADET CHEN'S COMPARISON, ALTHOUGH SIMPLISTIC, SUGGESTS A POTENTIAL SOLUTION.
CHIEF SOMERS, I NOTICED YOU HAVE CIRCUMVENTED FAIL-SAFES TO KEEP KEY SYSTEMS RUNNING BELOW OPERATIONAL MINIMUMS.
IT WAS EITHER THAT OR FREEZE TO DEATH. WHY? YOU GOT A PLAN?
PERHAPS. BUT I WILL REQUIRE YOUR ASSISTANCE WITH SEVERAL UNORTHODOX MODIFICATIONS TO YOUR SHIP.
"UNORTHODOX MODIFICATIONS" ARE MY SPECIALTY.

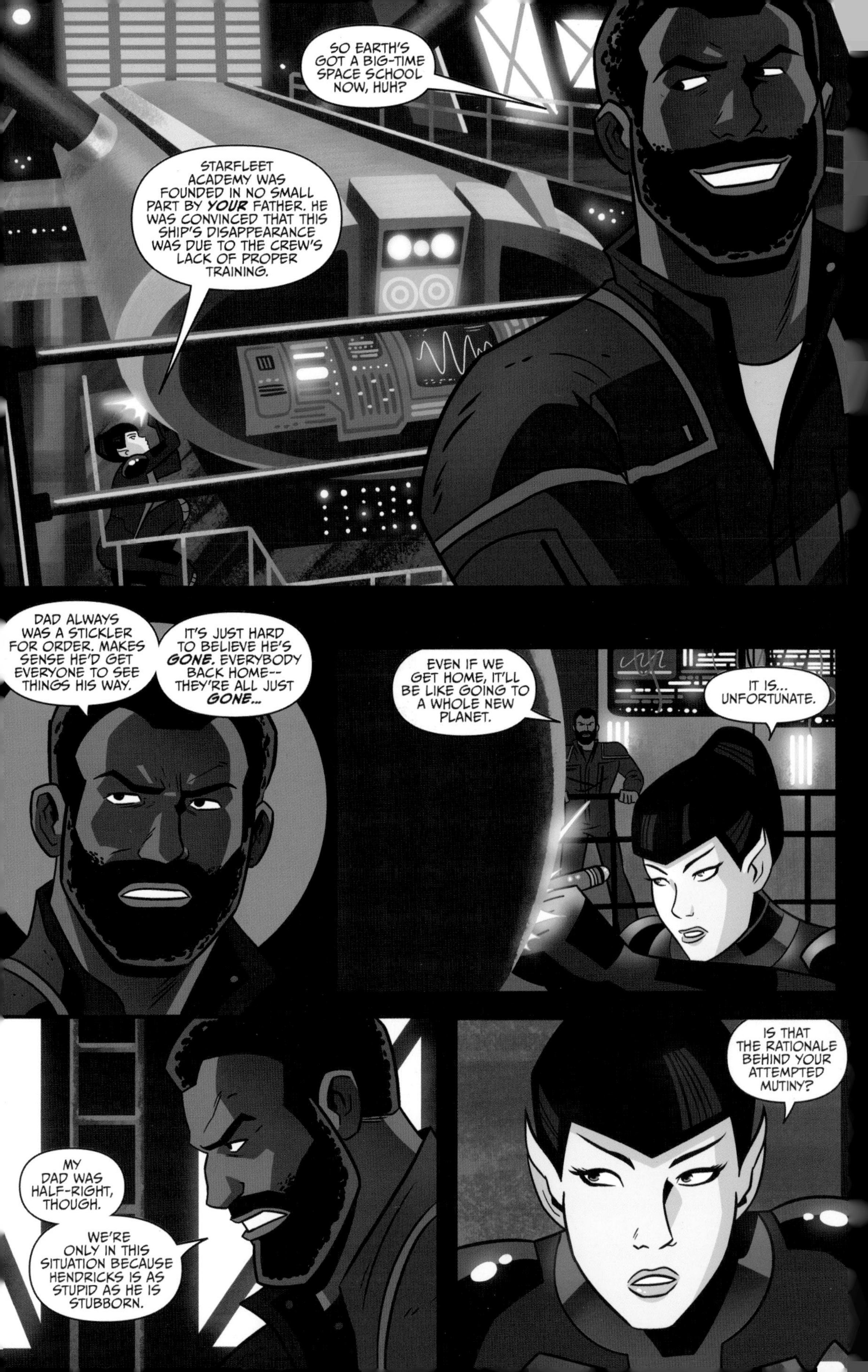
SO EARTH'S GOT A BIG-TIME SPACE SCHOOL NOW, HUH?
STARFLEET ACADEMY WAS FOUNDED IN NO SMALL PART BY YOUR FATHER. HE WAS CONVINCED THAT THIS SHIP'S DISAPPEARANCE WAS DUE TO THE CREW'S LACK OF PROPER TRAINING.
DAD ALWAYS WAS A STICKLER FOR ORDER. MAKES SENSE HE'D GET EVERYONE TO SEE THINGS HIS WAY.
IT'S JUST HARD TO BELIEVE HE'S GONE. EVERYBODY BACK HOME-- THEY'RE ALL JUST GONE...
EVEN IF WE GET HOME, IT'LL BE LIKE GOING TO A WHOLE NEW PLANET.
IT IS... UNFORTUNATE.
IS THAT THE RATIONALE BEHIND YOUR ATTEMPTED MUTINY?
MY DAD WAS HALF-RIGHT, THOUGH.
WE'RE ONLY IN THIS SITUATION BECAUSE HENDRICKS IS AS STUPID AS HE IS STUBBORN.

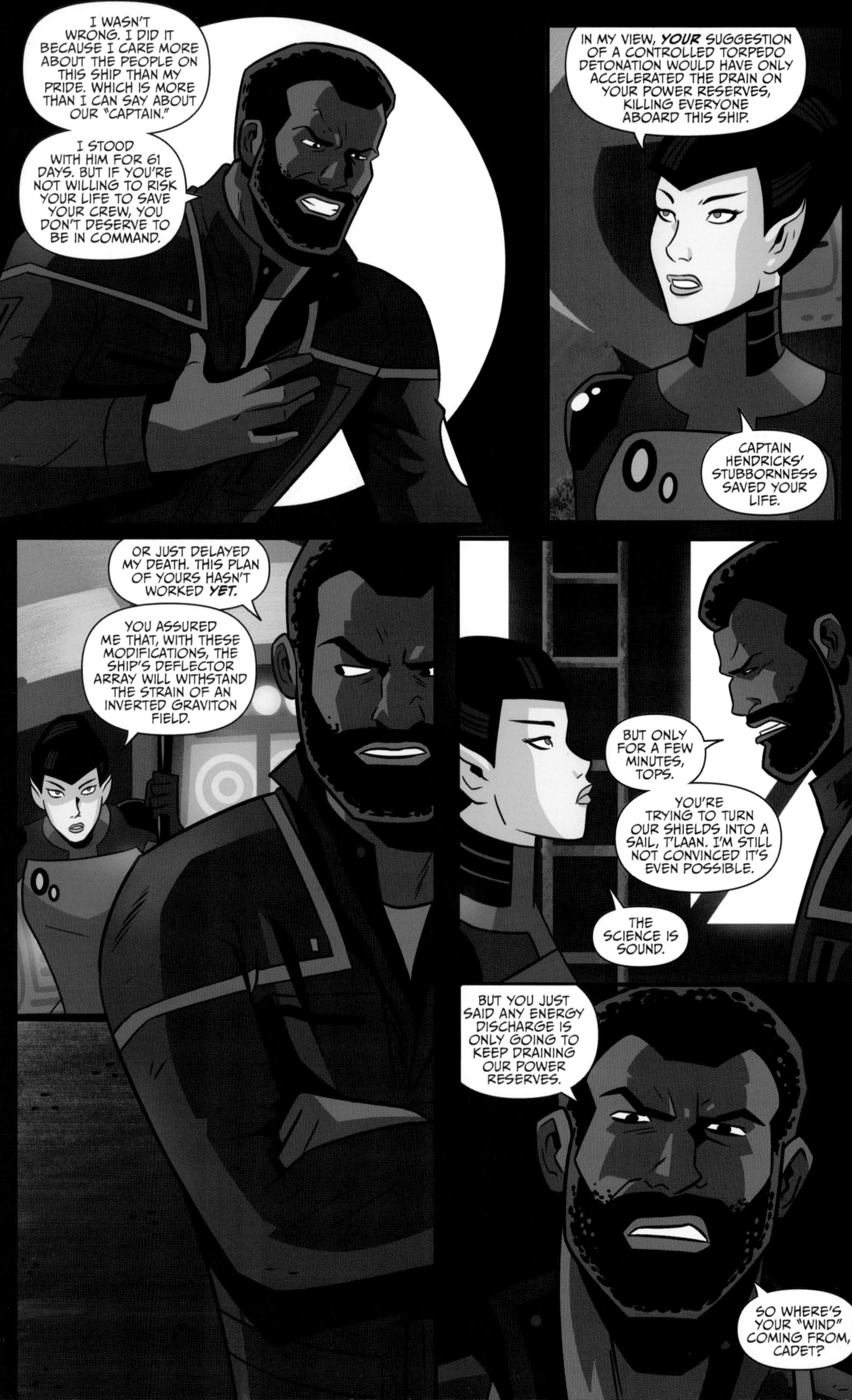
I WASN'T WRONG. I DID IT BECAUSE I CARE MORE ABOUT THE PEOPLE ON THIS SHIP THAN MY PRIDE. WHICH IS MORE THAN I CAN SAY ABOUT OUR "CAPTAIN."
I STOOD WITH HIM FOR 61 DAYS. BUT IF YOU'RE NOT WILLING TO RISK YOUR LIFE TO SAVE YOUR CREW, YOU DON'T DESERVE TO BE IN COMMAND.
IN MY VIEW, YOUR SUGGESTION OF A CONTROLLED TORPEDO DETONATION WOULD HAVE ONLY ACCELERATED THE DRAIN ON YOUR POWER RESERVES, KILLING EVERYONE ABOARD THIS SHIP.
CAPTAIN HENDRICKS' STUBBORNNESS SAVED YOUR LIFE.
OR JUST DELAYED MY DEATH. THIS PLAN OF YOURS HASN'T WORKED YET.
YOU ASSURED ME THAT, WITH THESE MODIFICATIONS, THE SHIP'S DEFLECTOR ARRAY WILL WITHSTAND THE STRAIN OF AN INVERTED GRAVITON FIELD.
BUT ONLY FOR A FEW MINUTES, TOPS.
YOU'RE TRYING TO TURN OUR SHIELDS INTO A SAIL, T'LAAN. I'M STILL NOT CONVINCED IT'S EVEN POSSIBLE.
THE SCIENCE IS SOUND.
BUT YOU JUST SAID ANY ENERGY DISCHARGE IS ONLY GOING TO KEEP DRAINING OUR POWER RESERVES.
SO WHERE'S YOUR "WIND" COMING FROM, CADET?

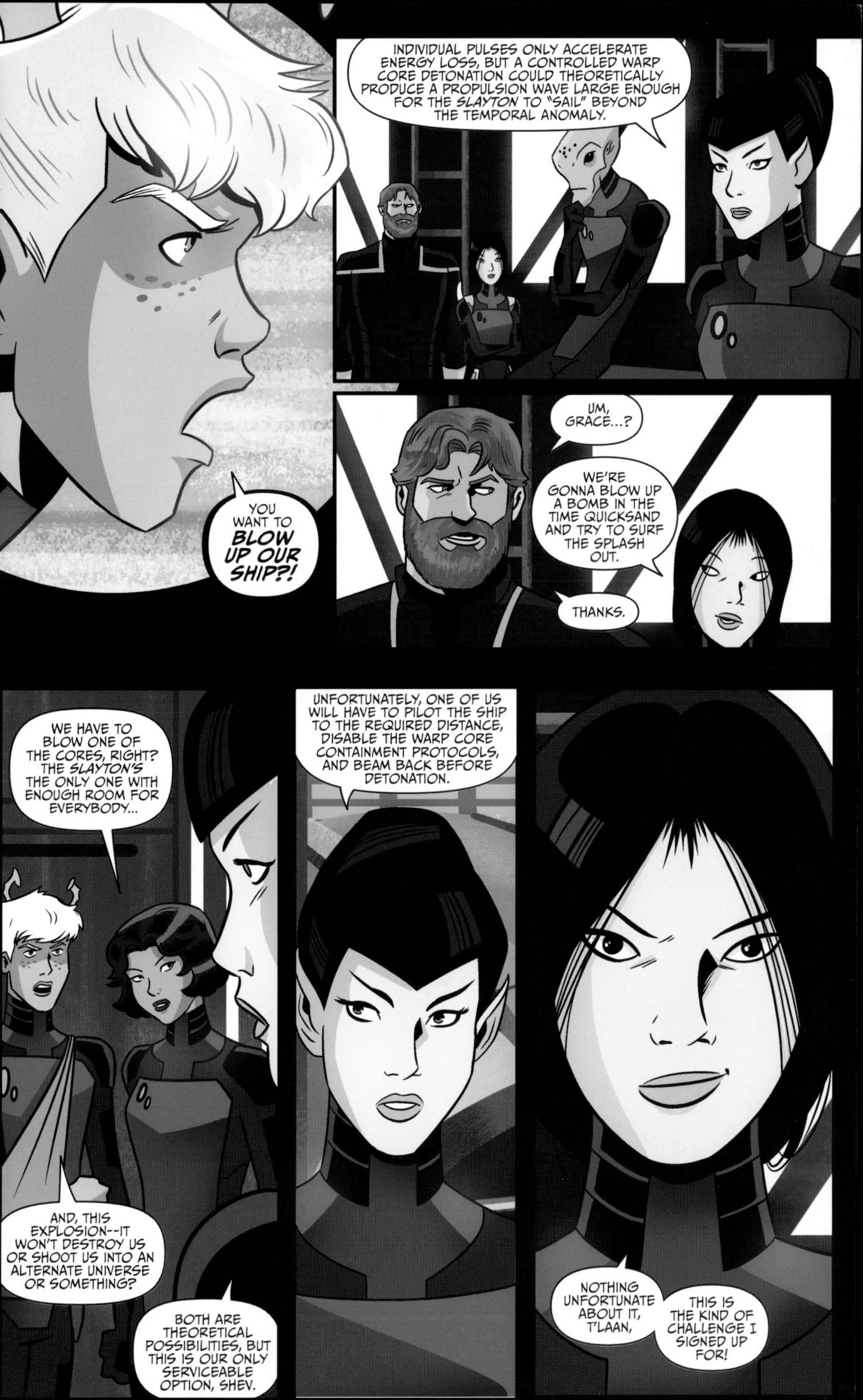
INDIVIDUAL PULSES ONLY ACCELERATE ENERGY LOSS, BUT A CONTROLLED WARP CORE DETONATION COULD THEORETICALLY PRODUCE A PROPULSION WAVE LARGE ENOUGH FOR THE *SLAYTON* TO "SAIL" BEYOND THE TEMPORAL ANOMALY.
YOU WANT TO **BLOW UP OUR SHIP?!**
UM, GRACE...?
WE'RE GONNA BLOW UP A BOMB IN THE TIME QUICKSAND AND TRY TO SURF THE SPLASH OUT.
THANKS.
WE HAVE TO BLOW ONE OF THE CORES, RIGHT? THE *SLAYTON'S* THE ONLY ONE WITH ENOUGH ROOM FOR EVERYBODY...
AND, THIS EXPLOSION--IT WON'T DESTROY US OR SHOOT US INTO AN ALTERNATE UNIVERSE OR SOMETHING?
BOTH ARE THEORETICAL POSSIBILITIES, BUT THIS IS OUR ONLY SERVICEABLE OPTION, SHEV.
UNFORTUNATELY, ONE OF US WILL HAVE TO PILOT THE SHIP TO THE REQUIRED DISTANCE, DISABLE THE WARP CORE CONTAINMENT PROTOCOLS, AND BEAM BACK BEFORE DETONATION.
NOTHING UNFORTUNATE ABOUT IT, T'LAAN,
THIS IS THE KIND OF CHALLENGE I SIGNED UP FOR!

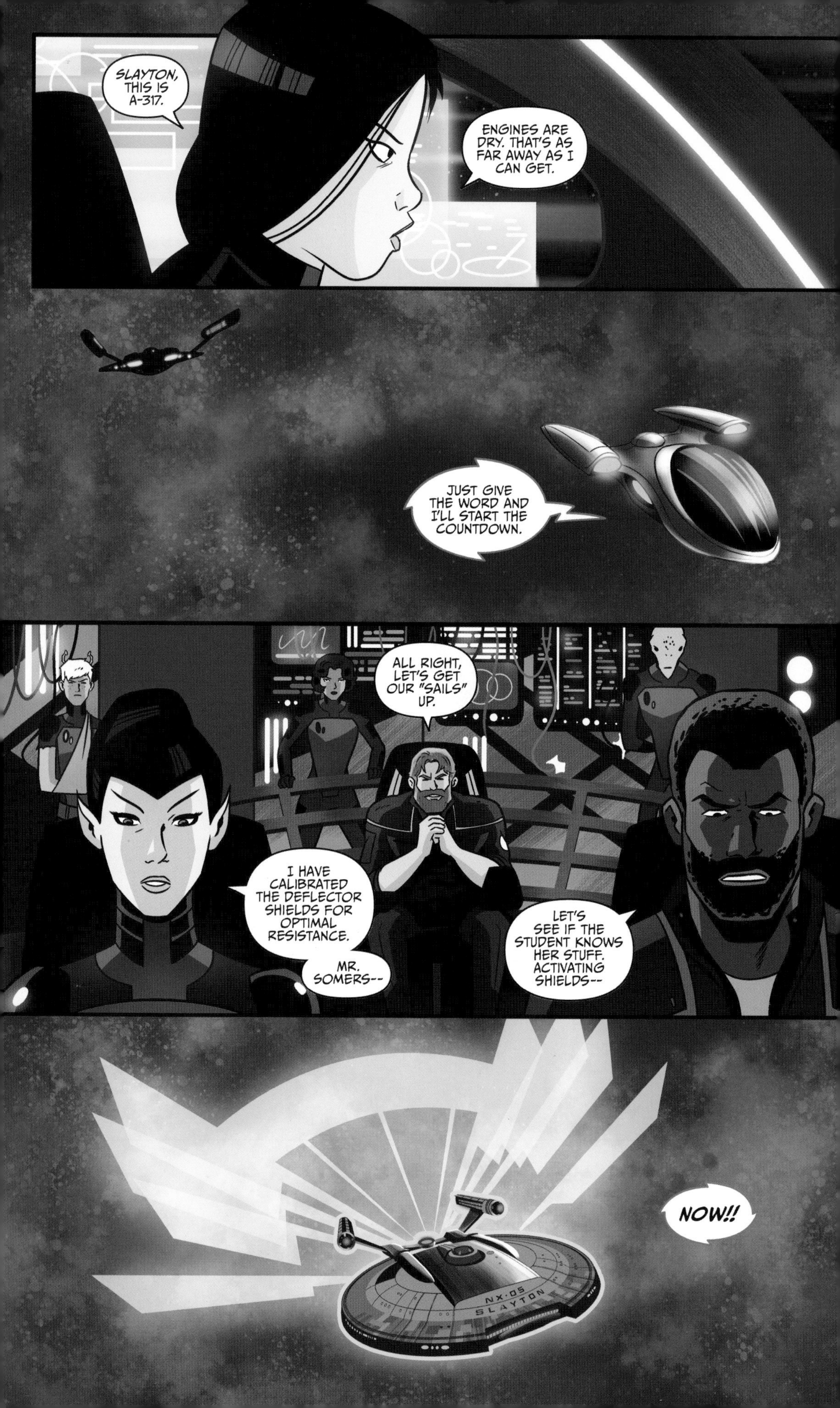
SLAYTON, THIS IS A-317.
ENGINES ARE DRY. THAT'S AS FAR AWAY AS I CAN GET.
JUST GIVE THE WORD AND I'LL START THE COUNTDOWN.
ALL RIGHT, LET'S GET OUR "SAILS" UP.
I HAVE CALIBRATED THE DEFLECTOR SHIELDS FOR OPTIMAL RESISTANCE.
MR. SOMERS--
LET'S SEE IF THE STUDENT KNOWS HER STUFF. ACTIVATING SHIELDS--
NOW!!
NX-05
SLAYTON

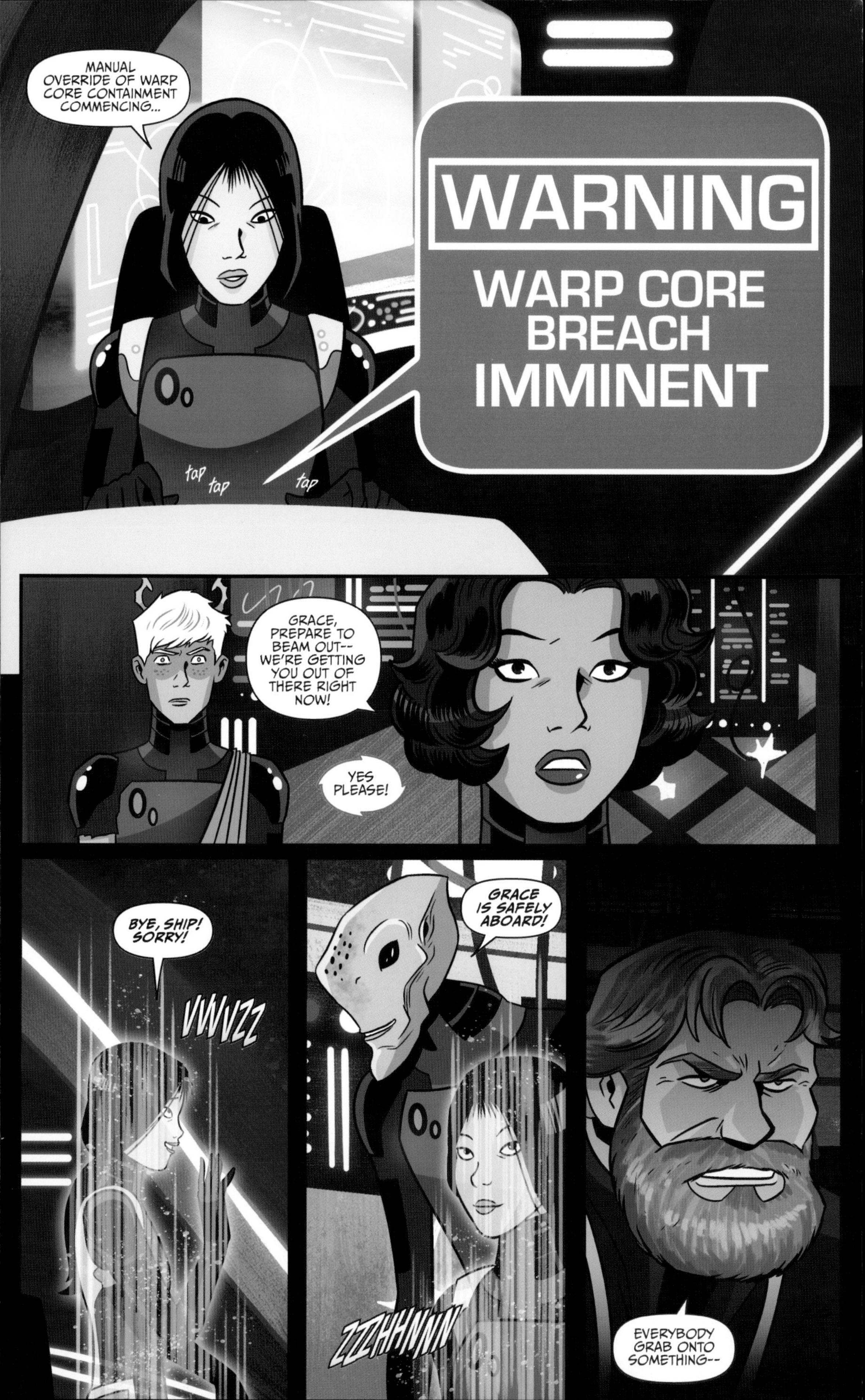
MANUAL OVERRIDE OF WARP CORE CONTAINMENT COMMENCING...
WARNING
WARP CORE BREACH IMMINENT
tap tap tap
GRACE, PREPARE TO BEAM OUT-- WE'RE GETTING YOU OUT OF THERE RIGHT NOW!
YES PLEASE!
BYE, SHIP! SORRY!
VVVVZZ
GRACE IS SAFELY ABOARD!
ZZZHHNNN
EVERYBODY GRAB ONTO SOMETHING--

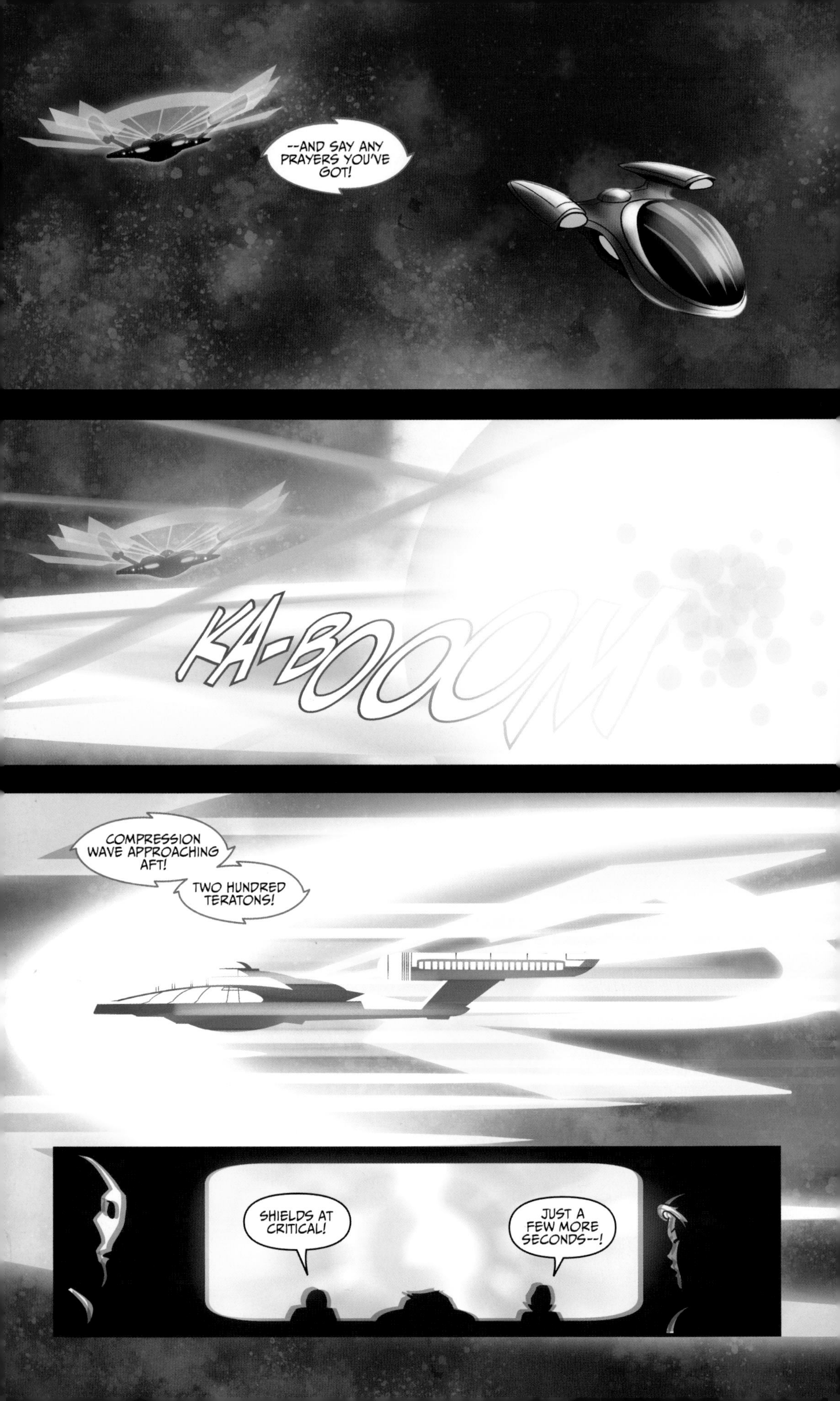
--AND SAY ANY PRAYERS YOU'VE GOT!
KA-BOOOOM
COMPRESSION WAVE APPROACHING AFT!
TWO HUNDRED TERATONS!
SHIELDS AT CRITICAL!
JUST A FEW MORE SECONDS--!

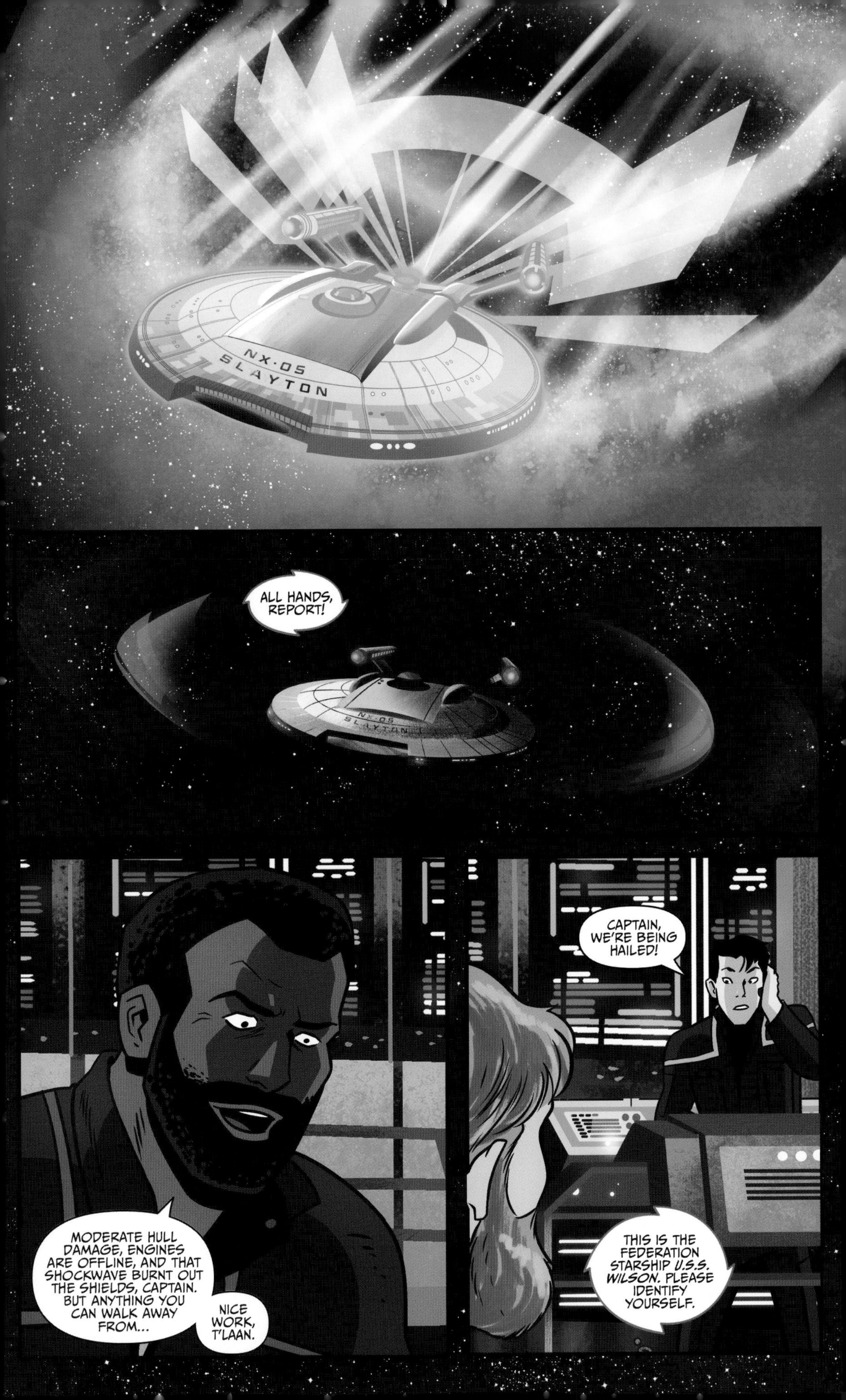
NX-05
SLAYTON
ALL HANDS, REPORT!
MODERATE HULL DAMAGE, ENGINES ARE OFFLINE, AND THAT SHOCKWAVE BURNT OUT THE SHIELDS, CAPTAIN. BUT ANYTHING YOU CAN WALK AWAY FROM...
NICE WORK, T'LAAN.
CAPTAIN, WE'RE BEING HAILED!
THIS IS THE FEDERATION STARSHIP *U.S.S. WILSON*. PLEASE IDENTIFY YOURSELF.

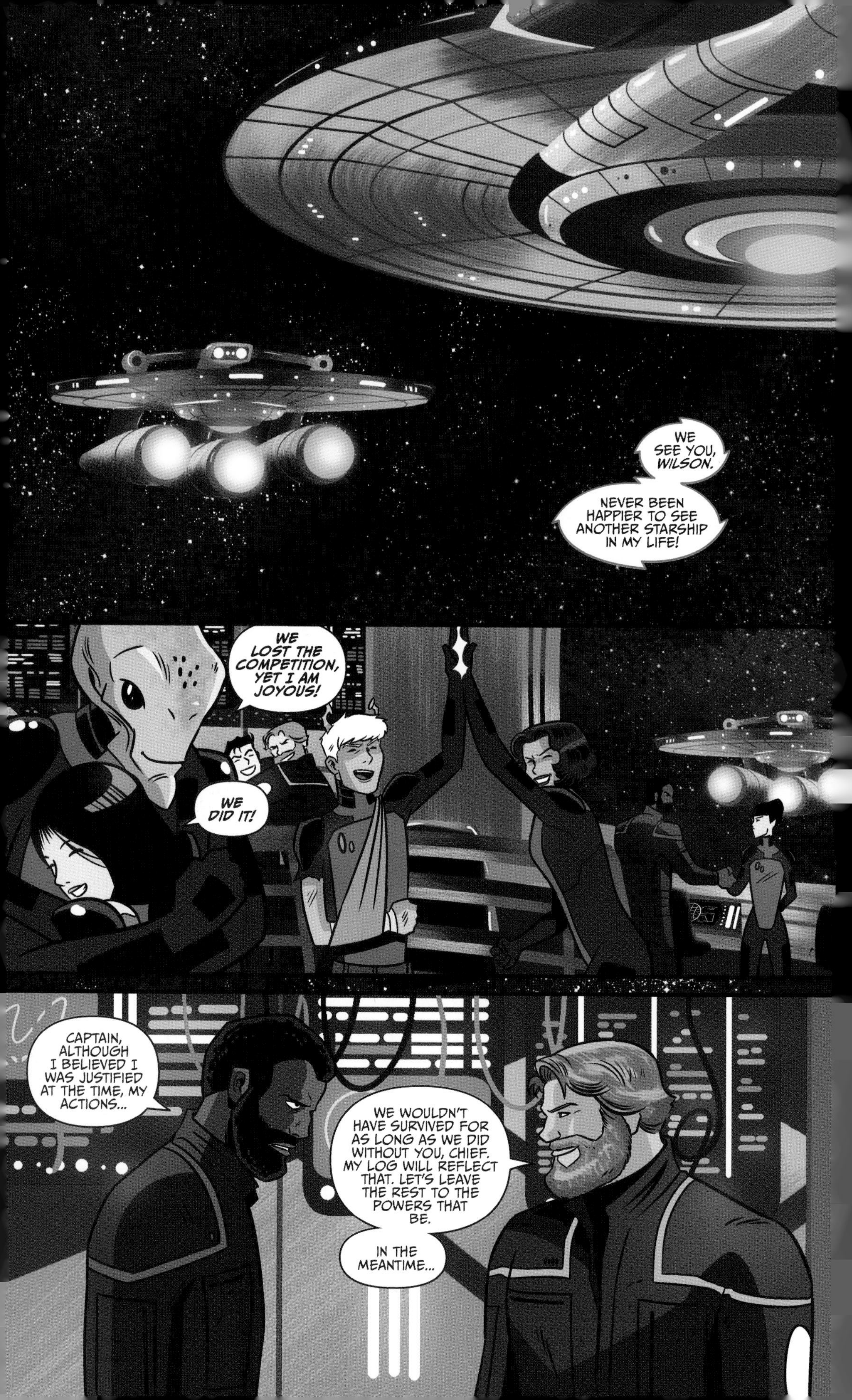
WE SEE YOU, WILSON.
NEVER BEEN HAPPIER TO SEE ANOTHER STARSHIP IN MY LIFE!
WE LOST THE COMPETITION, YET I AM JOYOUS!
WE DID IT!
CAPTAIN, ALTHOUGH I BELIEVED I WAS JUSTIFIED AT THE TIME, MY ACTIONS...
WE WOULDN'T HAVE SURVIVED FOR AS LONG AS WE DID WITHOUT YOU, CHIEF. MY LOG WILL REFLECT THAT. LET'S LEAVE THE REST TO THE POWERS THAT BE.
IN THE MEANTIME...

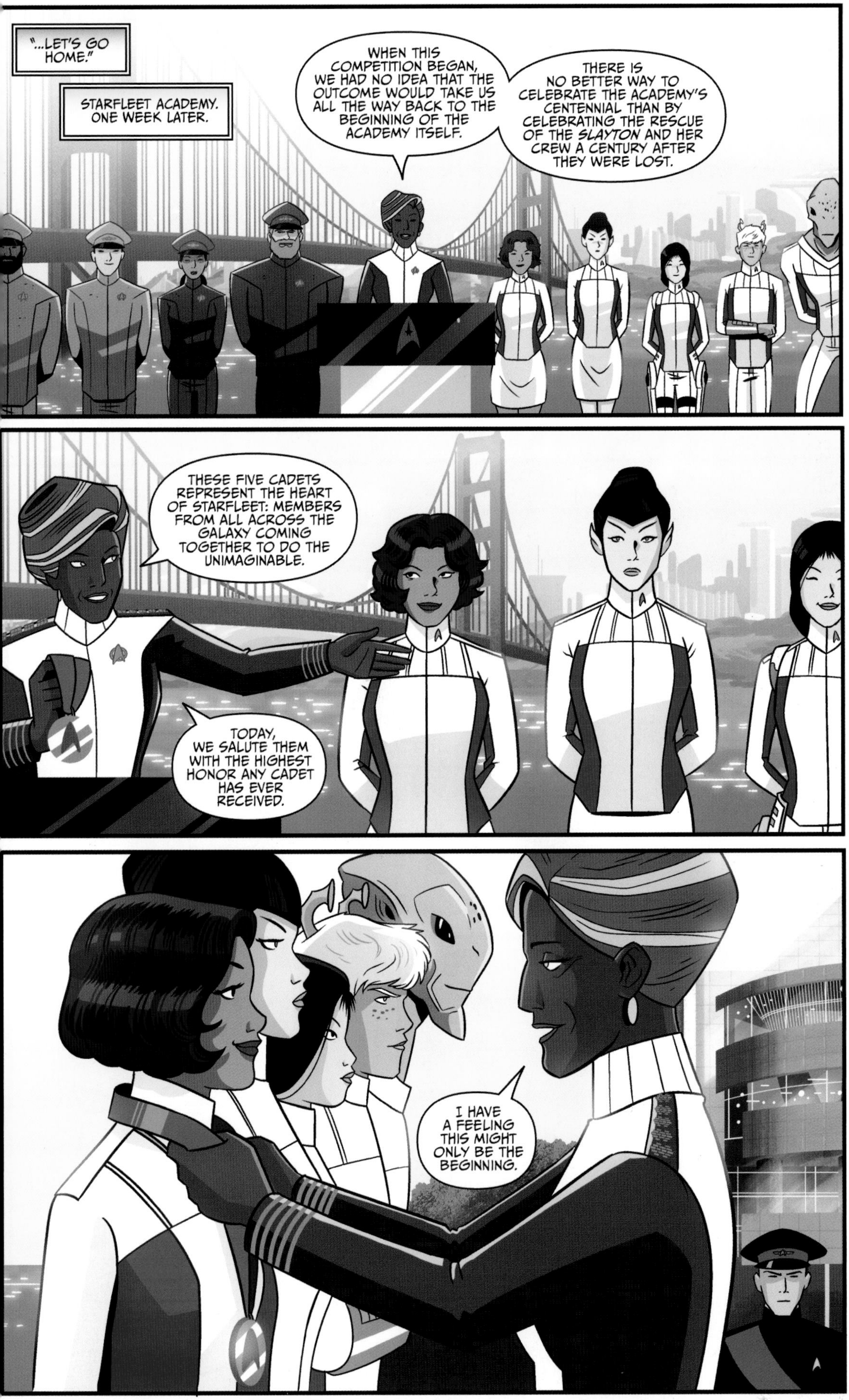
"...LET'S GO HOME."
STARFLEET ACADEMY. ONE WEEK LATER.
WHEN THIS COMPETITION BEGAN, WE HAD NO IDEA THAT THE OUTCOME WOULD TAKE US ALL THE WAY BACK TO THE BEGINNING OF THE ACADEMY ITSELF.
THERE IS NO BETTER WAY TO CELEBRATE THE ACADEMY'S CENTENNIAL THAN BY CELEBRATING THE RESCUE OF THE *SLAYTON* AND HER CREW A CENTURY AFTER THEY WERE LOST.
THESE FIVE CADETS REPRESENT THE HEART OF STARFLEET: MEMBERS FROM ALL ACROSS THE GALAXY COMING TOGETHER TO DO THE UNIMAGINABLE.
TODAY, WE SALUTE THEM WITH THE HIGHEST HONOR ANY CADET HAS EVER RECEIVED.
I HAVE A FEELING THIS MIGHT ONLY BE THE BEGINNING.

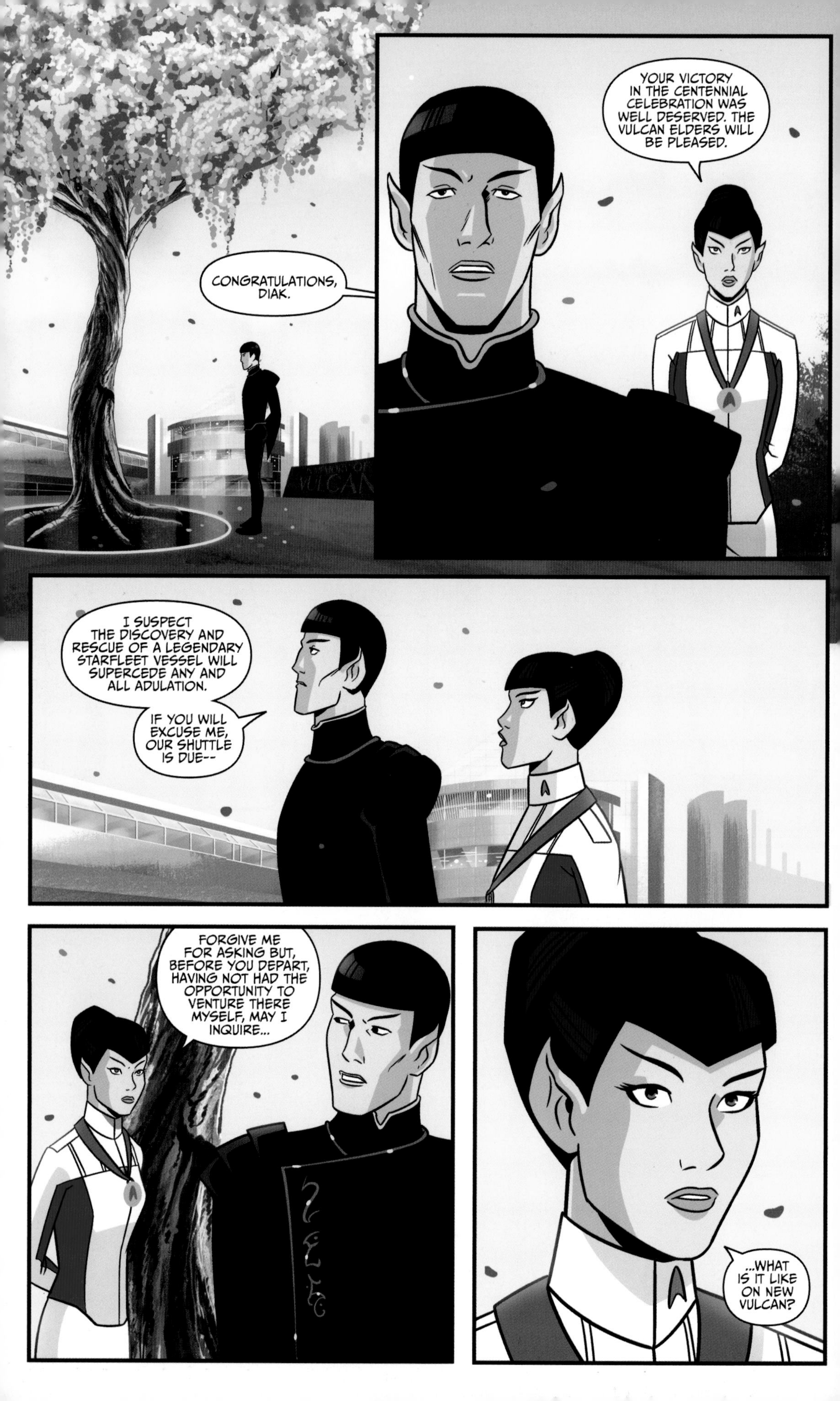
CONGRATULATIONS, DIAK.
YOUR VICTORY IN THE CENTENNIAL CELEBRATION WAS WELL DESERVED. THE VULCAN ELDERS WILL BE PLEASED.
I SUSPECT THE DISCOVERY AND RESCUE OF A LEGENDARY STARFLEET VESSEL WILL SUPERCEDE ANY AND ALL ADULATION.
IF YOU WILL EXCUSE ME, OUR SHUTTLE IS DUE--
FORGIVE ME FOR ASKING BUT, BEFORE YOU DEPART, HAVING NOT HAD THE OPPORTUNITY TO VENTURE THERE MYSELF, MAY I INQUIRE...
...WHAT IS IT LIKE ON NEW VULCAN?

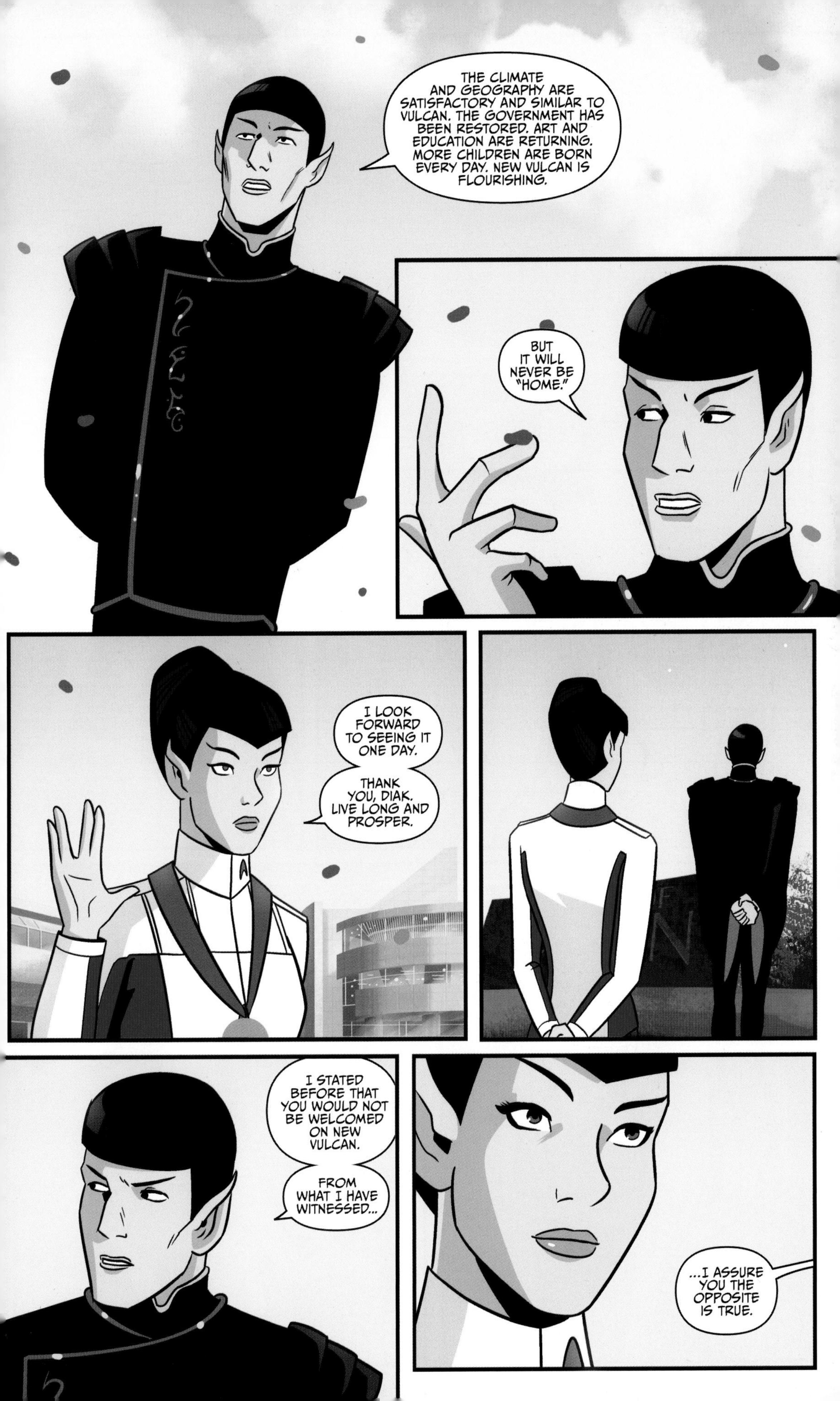
THE CLIMATE AND GEOGRAPHY ARE SATISFACTORY AND SIMILAR TO VULCAN. THE GOVERNMENT HAS BEEN RESTORED. ART AND EDUCATION ARE RETURNING. MORE CHILDREN ARE BORN EVERY DAY. NEW VULCAN IS FLOURISHING.
BUT IT WILL NEVER BE "HOME."
I LOOK FORWARD TO SEEING IT ONE DAY.
THANK YOU, DIAK. LIVE LONG AND PROSPER.
I STATED BEFORE THAT YOU WOULD NOT BE WELCOMED ON NEW VULCAN.
FROM WHAT I HAVE WITNESSED...
...I ASSURE YOU THE OPPOSITE IS TRUE.

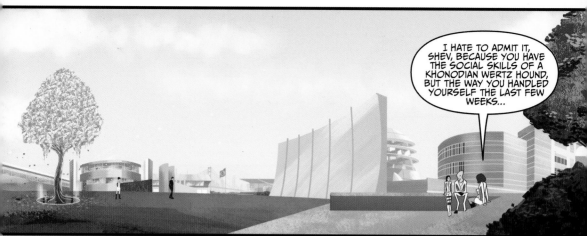

I HATE TO ADMIT IT, SHEV, BECAUSE YOU HAVE THE SOCIAL SKILLS OF A KHONODIAN WERTZ HOUND, BUT THE WAY YOU HANDLED YOURSELF THE LAST FEW WEEKS...

YOUR FATHER WOULD HAVE BEEN PROUD.

HE'D ONLY CARE THAT I *LOST.*

BUT THANKS.

THINK T'LAAN IS STILL GONNA GO HOME?

I THINK HOME IS NOT WHERE ALL IS EASY AND WORRY-FREE, BUT WHERE IT IS HARD AND WORTHWHILE.

VEL, I THINK THAT'S THE FIRST TIME YOU'VE VOCALIZED AN ABSTRACT THOUGHT!

THANK YOU, I--

--VEL SMELLS PIE!

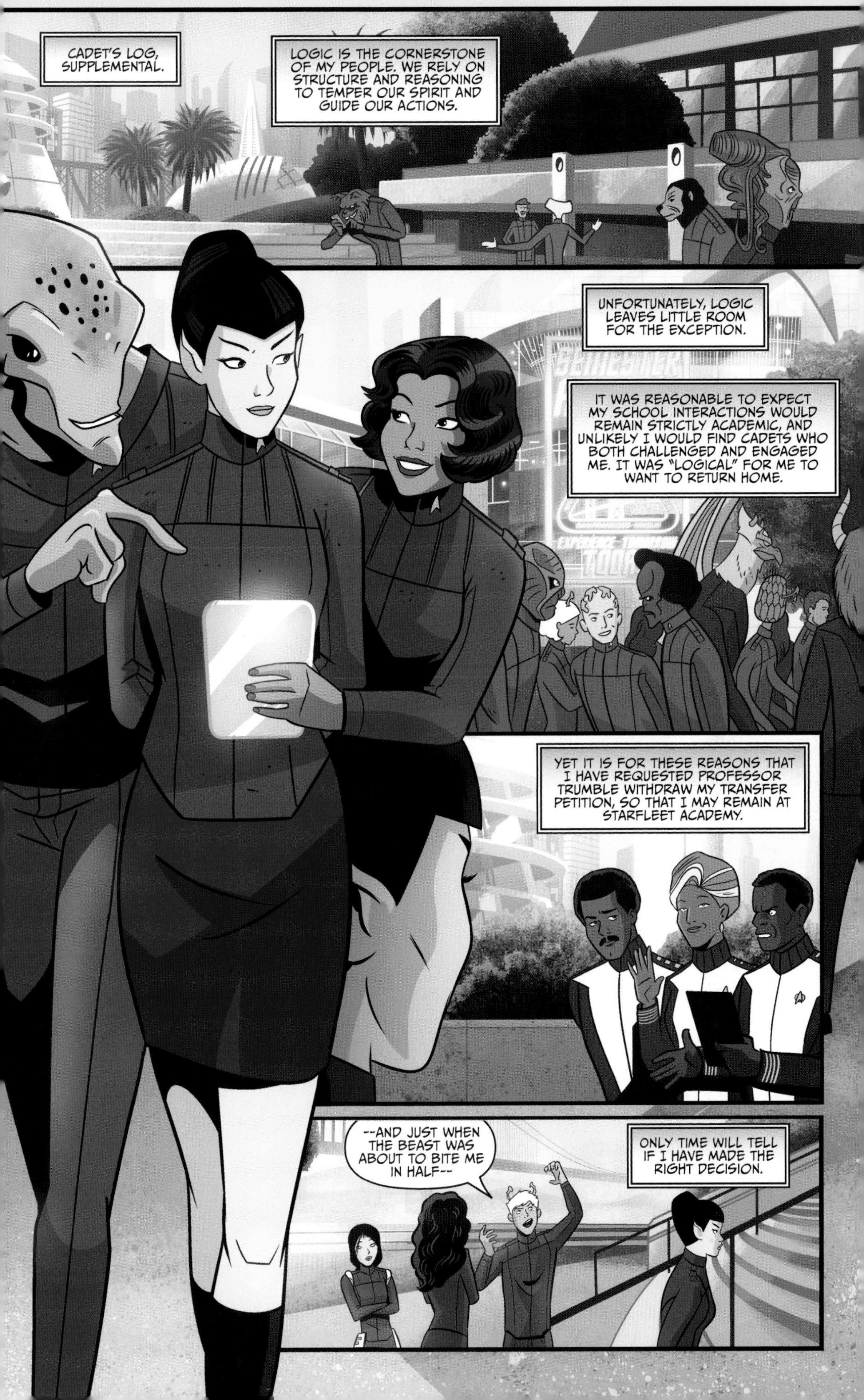
CADET'S LOG, SUPPLEMENTAL.
LOGIC IS THE CORNERSTONE OF MY PEOPLE. WE RELY ON STRUCTURE AND REASONING TO TEMPER OUR SPIRIT AND GUIDE OUR ACTIONS.
UNFORTUNATELY, LOGIC LEAVES LITTLE ROOM FOR THE EXCEPTION.
IT WAS REASONABLE TO EXPECT MY SCHOOL INTERACTIONS WOULD REMAIN STRICTLY ACADEMIC, AND UNLIKELY I WOULD FIND CADETS WHO BOTH CHALLENGED AND ENGAGED ME. IT WAS "LOGICAL" FOR ME TO WANT TO RETURN HOME.
YET IT IS FOR THESE REASONS THAT I HAVE REQUESTED PROFESSOR TRUMBLE WITHDRAW MY TRANSFER PETITION, SO THAT I MAY REMAIN AT STARFLEET ACADEMY.
--AND JUST WHEN THE BEAST WAS ABOUT TO BITE ME IN HALF--
ONLY TIME WILL TELL IF I HAVE MADE THE RIGHT DECISION.

T'LAAN, YOU'RE FIVE MINUTES LATE!

DON'T TELL ME YOU'VE BEGUN TO PICK UP HUMANS' PENCHANT FOR TARDINESS?

MY APOLOGIES, PROFESSOR TRUMBLE.

CADETS CORY AND SEARS WERE TEACHING ME THE RUDIMENTS OF AN ARCHAIC EARTH GAME CALLED "ULTIMATE... FRISBEE"?

YOU HAVE NO IDEA HOW PLEASED I AM TO HEAR IT.

AND EVEN MORE PLEASED TO TELL YOU THAT YOUR TRANSFER PETITION IS NULL AND VOID. WELCOME BACK TO THE ACADEMY.

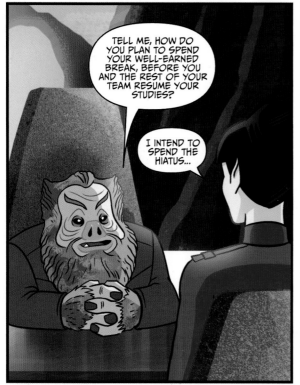

TELL ME, HOW DO YOU PLAN TO SPEND YOUR WELL-EARNED BREAK, BEFORE YOU AND THE REST OF YOUR TEAM RESUME YOUR STUDIES?

I INTEND TO SPEND THE HIATUS...

...STUDYING, OF COURSE.

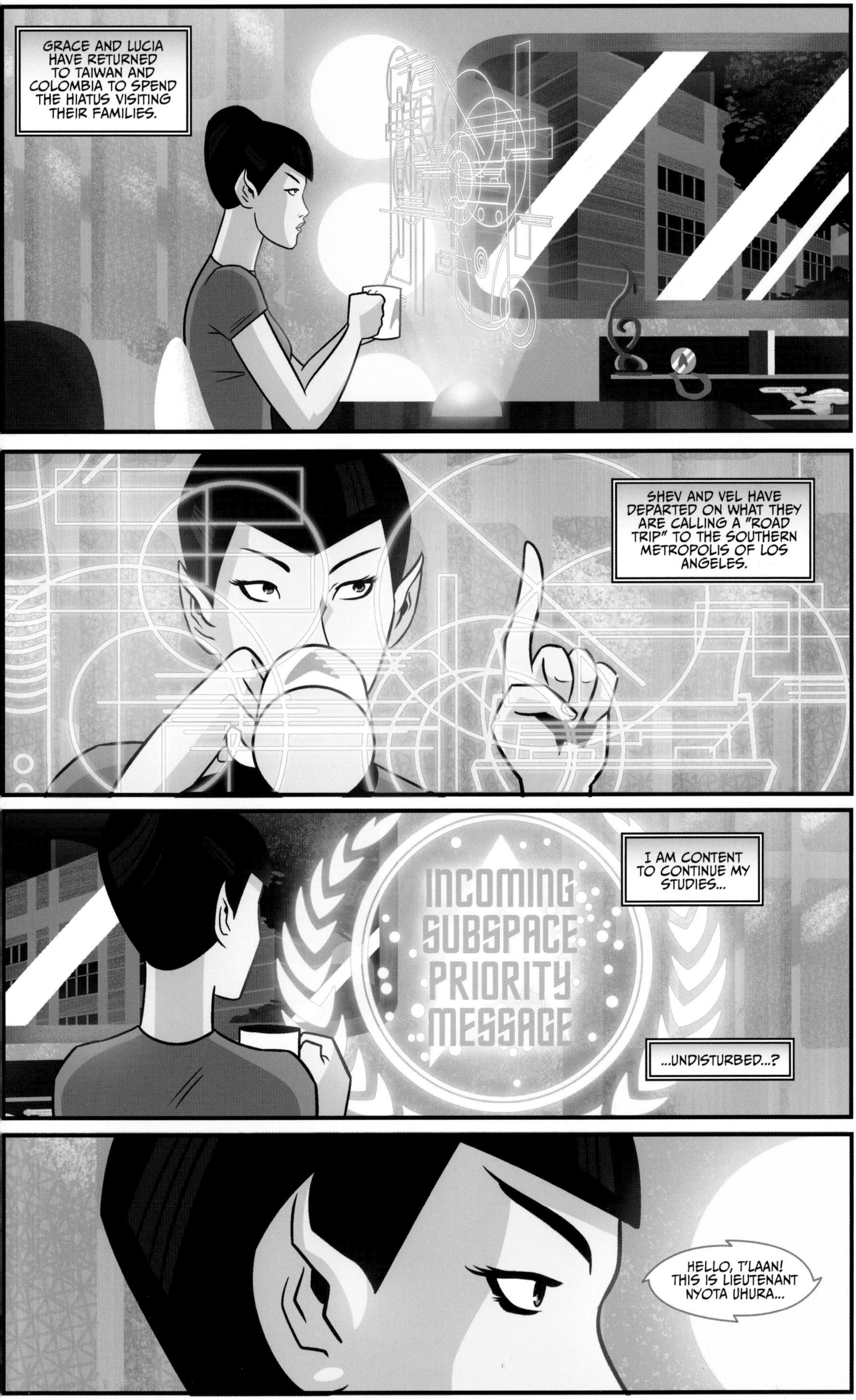
GRACE AND LUCIA HAVE RETURNED TO TAIWAN AND COLOMBIA TO SPEND THE HIATUS VISITING THEIR FAMILIES.
SHEV AND VEL HAVE DEPARTED ON WHAT THEY ARE CALLING A "ROAD TRIP" TO THE SOUTHERN METROPOLIS OF LOS ANGELES.
INCOMING SUBSPACE PRIORITY MESSAGE
I AM CONTENT TO CONTINUE MY STUDIES...
...UNDISTURBED...?
HELLO, T'LAAN! THIS IS LIEUTENANT NYOTA UHURA...

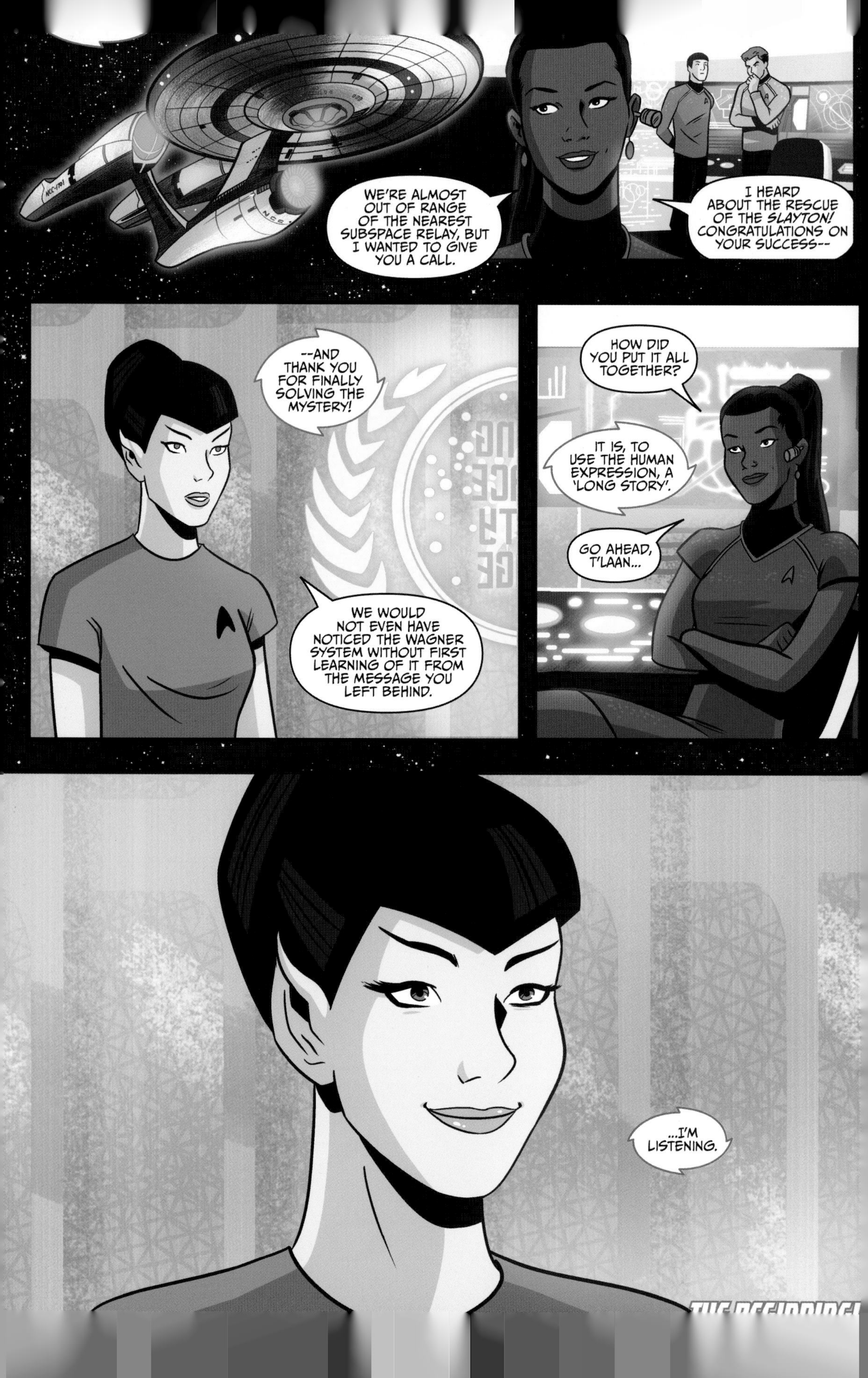

WE'RE ALMOST OUT OF RANGE OF THE NEAREST SUBSPACE RELAY, BUT I WANTED TO GIVE YOU A CALL.
I HEARD ABOUT THE RESCUE OF THE *SLAYTON!* CONGRATULATIONS ON YOUR SUCCESS--
--AND THANK YOU FOR FINALLY SOLVING THE MYSTERY!
WE WOULD NOT EVEN HAVE NOTICED THE WAGNER SYSTEM WITHOUT FIRST LEARNING OF IT FROM THE MESSAGE YOU LEFT BEHIND.
HOW DID YOU PUT IT ALL TOGETHER?
IT IS, TO USE THE HUMAN EXPRESSION, A 'LONG STORY'.
GO AHEAD, T'LAAN...
...I'M LISTENING.

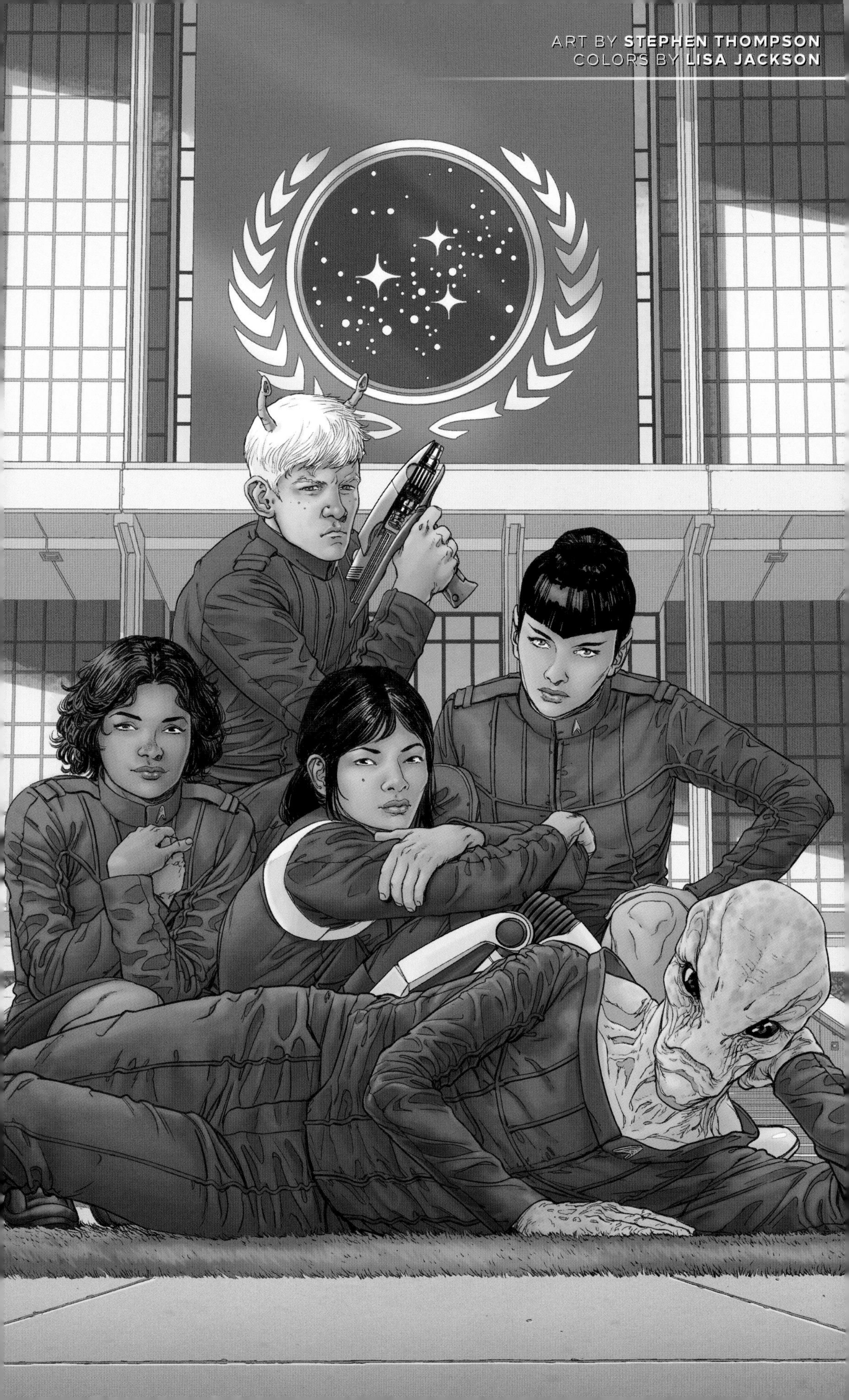
ART BY STEPHEN THOMPSON
COLORS BY LISA JACKSON

ART BY **ELSA CHARRETIER**

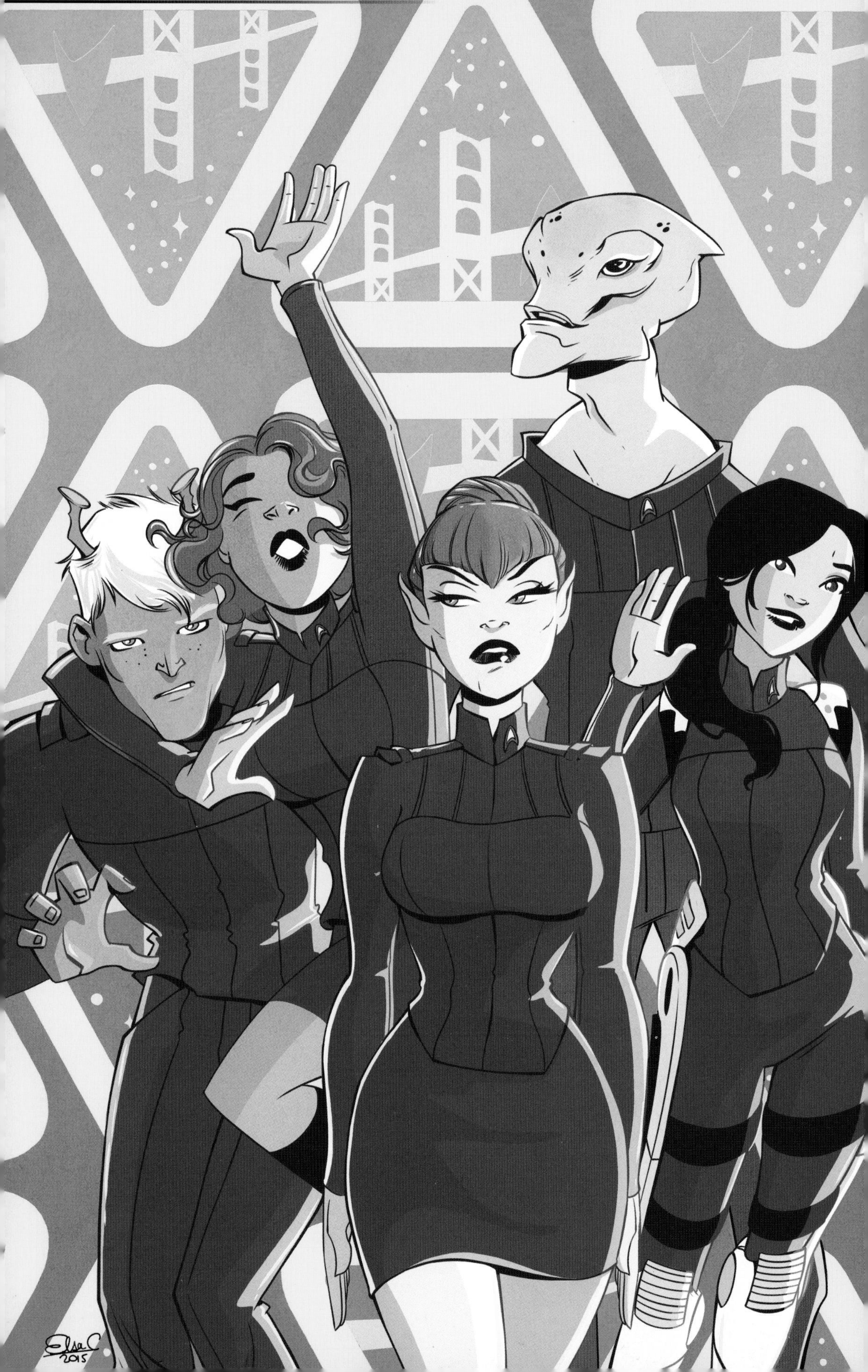
Elsa C
2015

ART BY **GEORGE CALTSOUDAS**

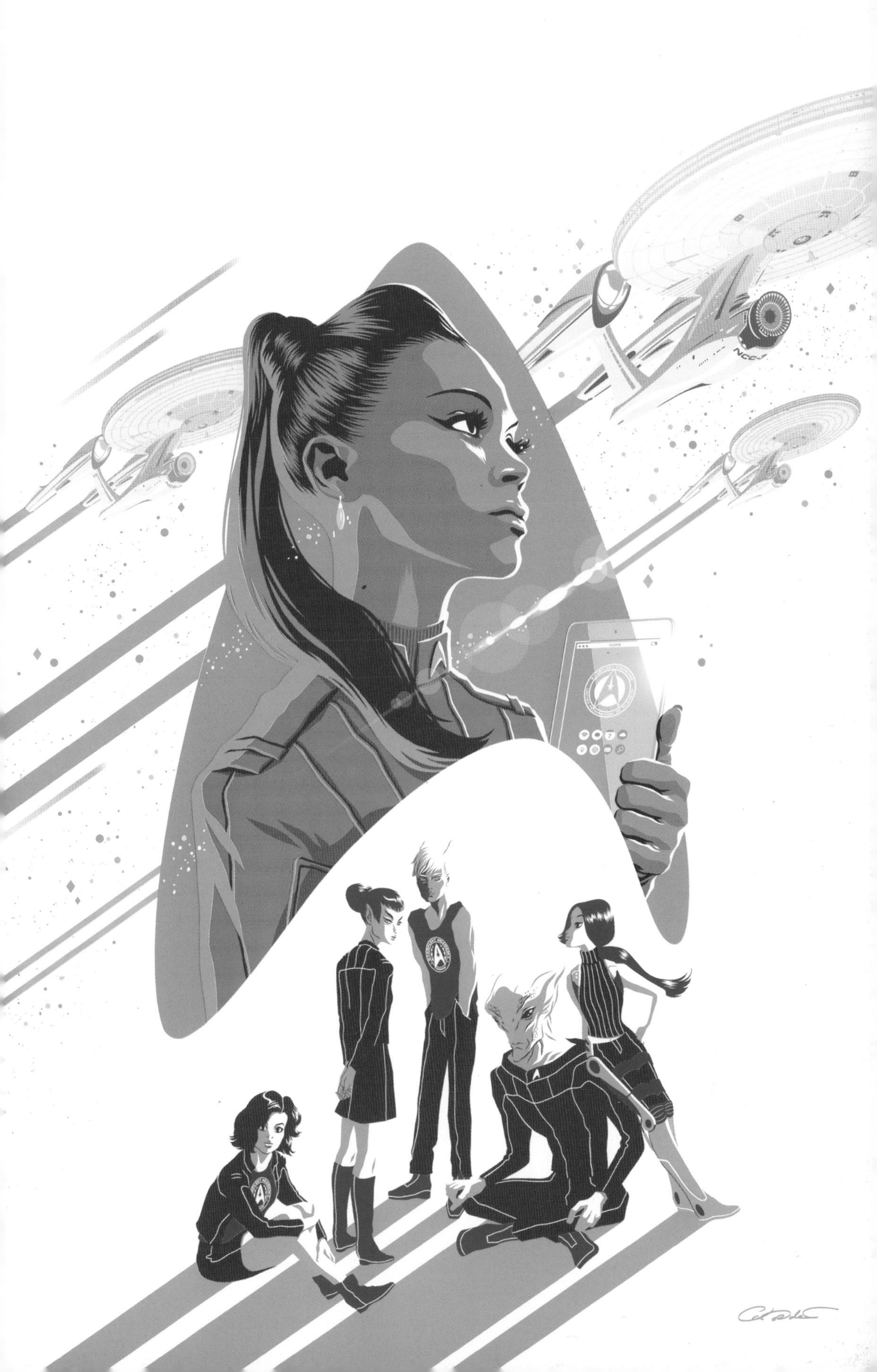

ART BY **ADAM ROSENLUND**

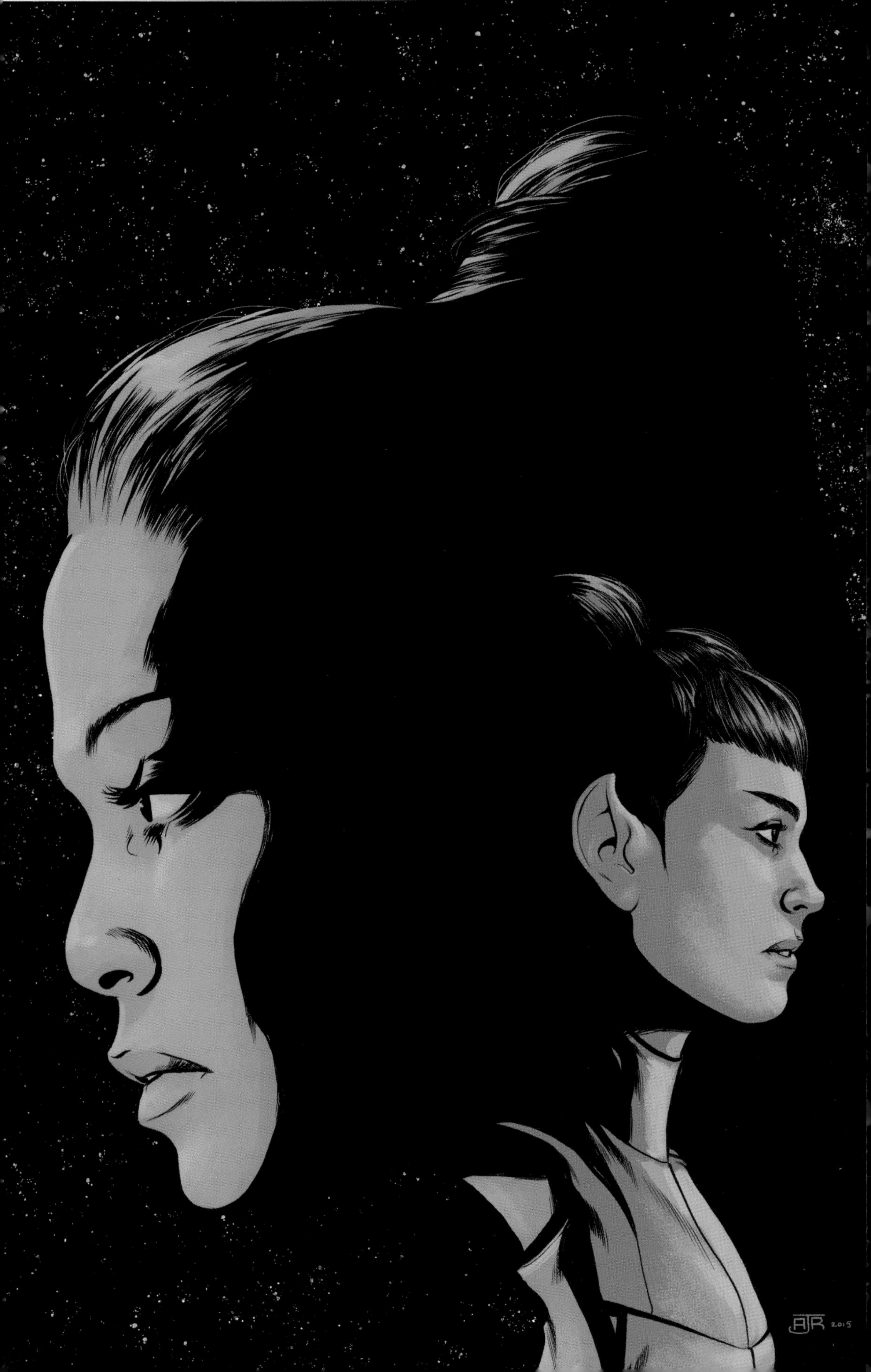

ART BY **DAVID MALAN**

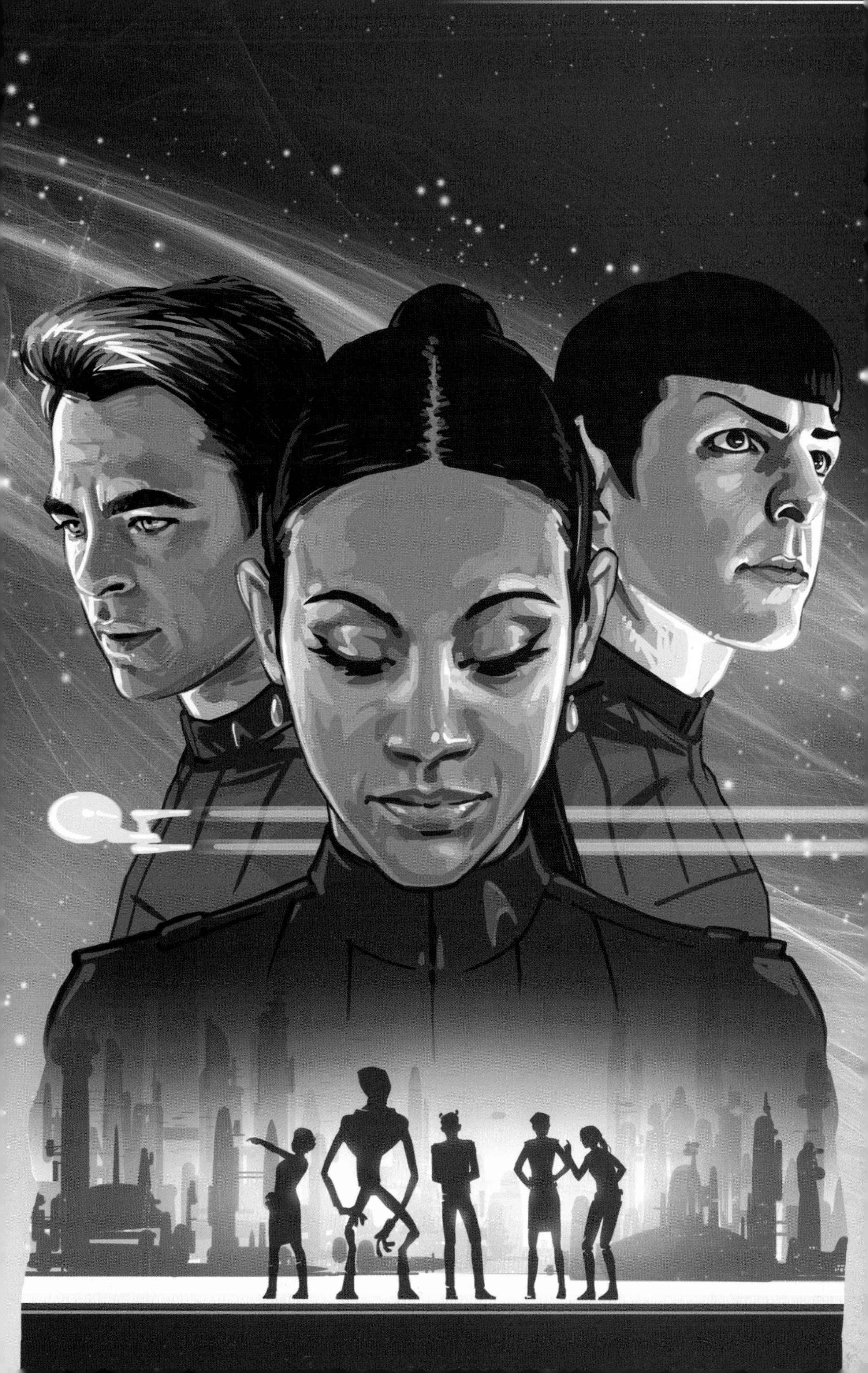

ART BY **MALACHI WARD**
AND **MATTHEW SHEEAN**

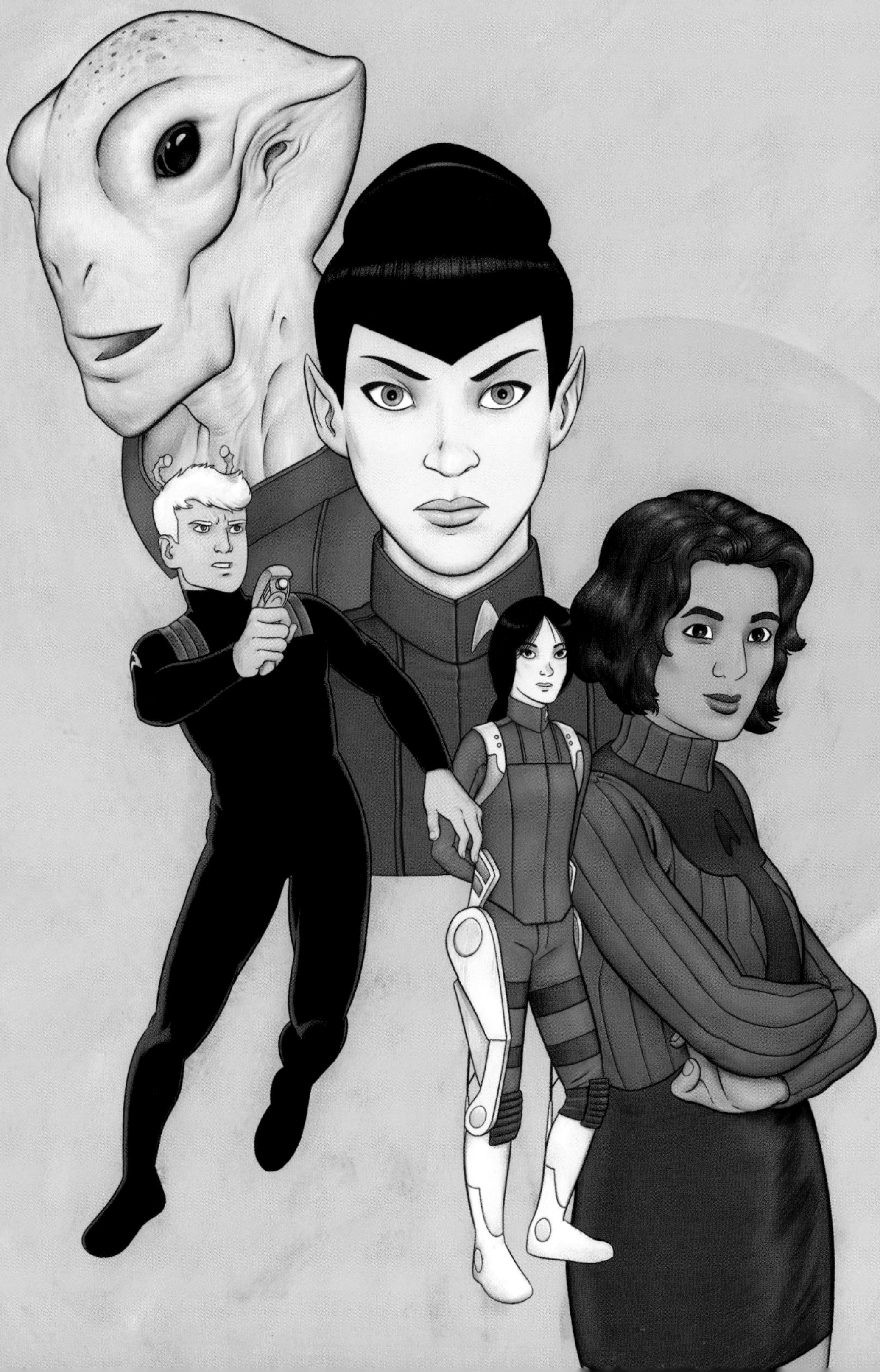

STARFLEET ACADEMY · EX ASTRIS, SCIENTIA

SAN FRANCISCO · MMCLXI

NAME:
GRACE CHEN

RACE: HUMAN
AGE: 19 YEARS OLD

ACADEMIC EMPHASIS:
ASTRONAUTICS

HOME CITY:
TAIPEI, EARTH

FAVORITE FOOD: TUBE
RICE PUDDING

LIKES: GOING FAST,
WARP CORES

DISLIKES: INERTIAL
DAMPENERS, BROCCOLI

FAVORITE QUOTE:
"SHIPS ARE SAFE IN
SPACEDOCK, BUT THAT'S NOT
WHAT SHIPS ARE FOR."

STARFLEET ACADEMY
CADET

STARFLEET ACADEMY · EX ASTRIS, SCIENTIA

SAN FRANCISCO · MMCLXI

NAME:
T'LAAN

RACE: VULCAN
AGE: 21 YEARS OLD

ACADEMIC EMPHASIS:
 ENGINEERING

HOME CITY:
SHIKAHR, VULCAN
(DESTROYED)

FAVORITE FOOD:
HESTIGAPT NOODLES

LIKES:
PROBLEM-SOLVING,
ROCK-CLIMBING

DISLIKES: OVERT
DISPLAYS OF EMOTION,
RAINFALL

QUOTE:
"I WOULD PREFER TO FIND THE
SOLUTION WITHOUT
ASSISTANCE."

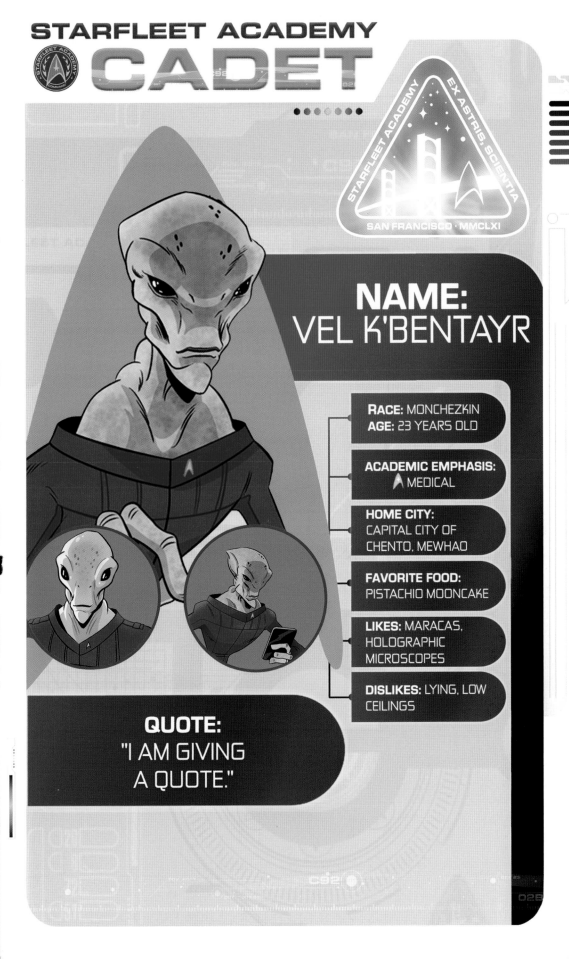

STARFLEET ACADEMY
CADET

STARFLEET ACADEMY · EX ASTRIS, SCIENTIA
SAN FRANCISCO · MMCLXI

NAME:
VEL K'BENTAYR

RACE: MONCHEZKIN
AGE: 23 YEARS OLD

ACADEMIC EMPHASIS:
MEDICAL

HOME CITY:
CAPITAL CITY OF
CHENTO, MEWHAO

FAVORITE FOOD:
PISTACHIO MOONCAKE

LIKES: MARACAS,
HOLOGRAPHIC
MICROSCOPES

DISLIKES: LYING, LOW
CEILINGS

QUOTE:
"I AM GIVING
A QUOTE."

STARFLEET ACADEMY CADET

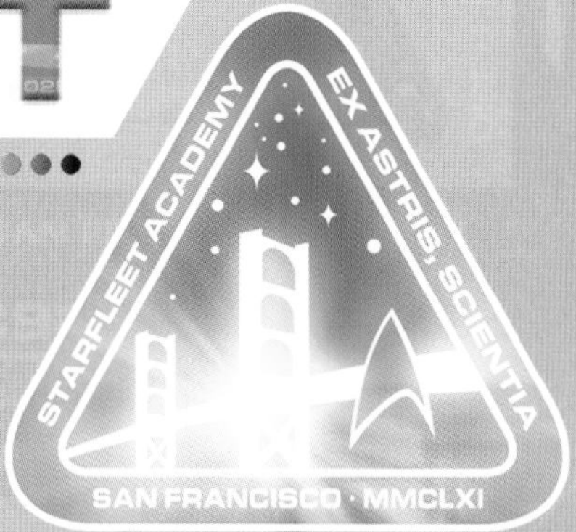
STARFLEET ACADEMY
EX ASTRIS, SCIENTIA
SAN FRANCISCO · MMCLXI

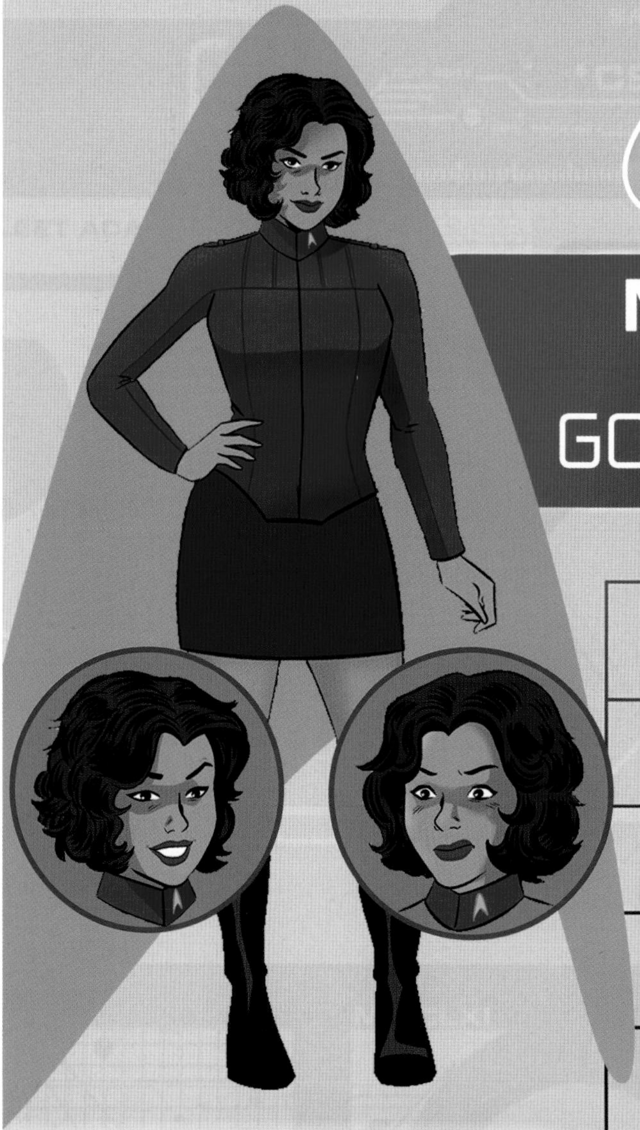

NAME:
LUCIA GONZALES

RACE: HUMAN
AGE: 20 YEARS OLD

ACADEMIC EMPHASIS: DIPLOMACY

HOME CITY: BARCELONA, EARTH

FAVORITE FOOD: CREMA CATALANA

LIKES: FEDERATION HISTORY, ZERO-G FUTBOL

DISLIKES: SILENT ROOMS

QUOTE:
"ANY PROBLEM CAN BE SOLVED WITH ENOUGH IMAGINATION."

STARFLEET ACADEMY · EX ASTRIS, SCIENTIA
SAN FRANCISCO · MMCLXI

NAME:
SHEV AKRIA

RACE: ANDORIAN
AGE: 21 YEARS OLD

ACADEMIC EMPHASIS:
SECURITY

HOME CITY:
CITY OF TH'RHOLT,
MOON OF ANDORIA

FAVORITE FOOD: GHOST
PEPPER NACHOS

LIKES: ICE KAYAKING

DISLIKES: SLOTHS,
WHINING

QUOTE:
"ANYONE CAN GET ANGRY,
BUT NOT EVERYONE CAN USE IT
TO THEIR ADVANTAGE."

C92

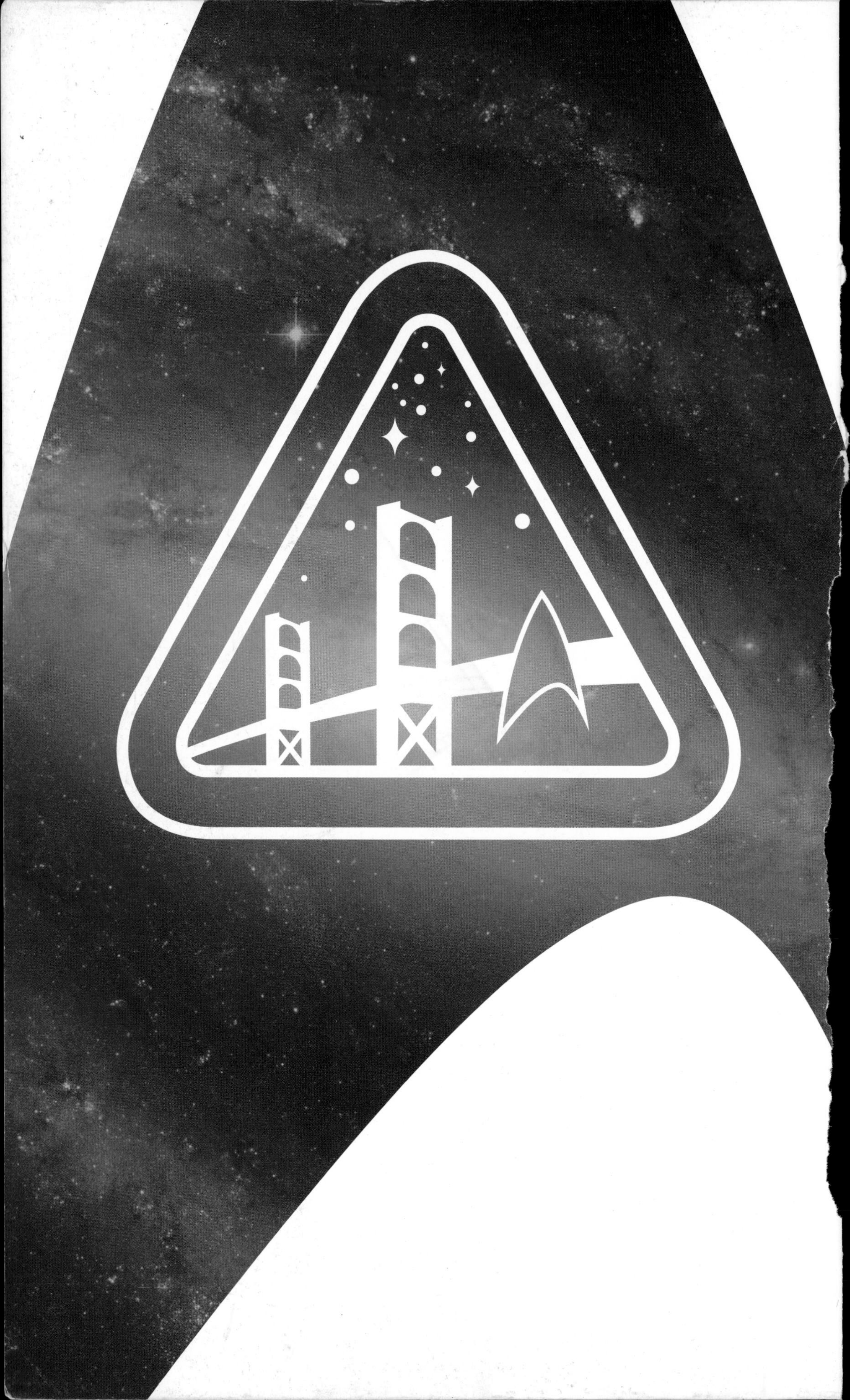